KEEPER OF SHADOWS

SCARLETT KOL

The characters in this book are fictitious. Any similarity to real persons, living or dead, places, or events is coincidental and not intended by author.

KEEPER OF SHADOWS
Copyright © 2020 by Scarlett Kol
All rights reserved.

ISBN: (ebook) 978-1-7752260-3-1
Print: 978-1-7752260-2-4
Second Edition: 2021

Edited by Amy McNulty

Cover Art by Jessica Allain

No part of this book may be reproduced in any form or by any electronic or mechanical means, including information storage and retrieval systems, without written permission from the author, except for the use of brief quotations in a book review.

Published by Vicious Pixie Press

To the ones who have faced their own darkness and the ones who light the paths of others.

"Alas, that love, so gentle in his view,
Should be so tyrannous and rough in proof!"

- William Shakespeare,
Romeo and Juliet

CHAPTER ONE

KELLAN

"Kellan Casey, can you please answer the question?" The words drifted in and out, garbled, as if I'd fallen asleep under water. I forced my eyes open. A haze of staring faces and uniform desks spread out in front of me. English class. *Damn it. Not today.*

Mrs. Pringle's heels clacked my direction, each strike pulsing louder and louder in my foggy brain. She pressed the tips of her fingers on the top of my desk and leaned toward me—like a cat, but more feral. I choked as the stench of burnt coffee and old lady perfume attacked my personal space.

She glared at me over the top of her wire-rimmed glasses. "Kellan, are you high again?"

I shook my head and sat up straight to meet her irritated gaze, staying as stone-faced as I could. "Maybe. Why? Are you looking for a hit?"

Muffled laughter erupted around us. Mrs. Pringle curled up her lip, as if to snarl, then flexed her hands and launched herself back to standing. "Get out of my class."

She didn't need to point toward the hall. She didn't even need to tell me to go to the principal's office. We'd run this drill more times than either of us cared to count. Another day. Another detention.

Being sentenced to detention didn't bother me anymore. I couldn't remember what class I was in for half the time; it had just become part of my daily routine. And no matter how many hours I wasted away, they wouldn't even expel me. Apparently, you needed to cause physical harm to someone before they took you seriously enough for that. Right now, I was just a pain in their asses. A dirty, pus-filled blemish tainting the face of the senior class. They only had to put up with me until graduation, and then I was no longer their problem. If I managed to live that long.

I grabbed my books and slid them off the desk with a slow scrape and took my time marching out of the room. The whole class expected a show, so why not give it to them? They'd seen us do this dance before, and I doubted it had become any less entertaining. Pringle's pursed lips held the hint of a smirk as she watched me leave. She'd probably been waiting a whole half hour to find some reason to get me gone. I'd bet she kind of enjoyed it. With a dramatic slam of the door that made the glass inserts ripple, I walked out.

Two heavy, defiant steps until I disappeared from view, then I let myself collapse against the wall. My head swam, cloudy with fog, and I shook it to try to get the last bit of dizzy out. The pain in my chest and arms burned like my muscles coursed with turpentine and might melt off my bones. Pringle had pounced on me too quickly this time. I'd barely had the chance to get myself straight before she started staring me down. I pulled out my phone with shaky hands. Already 10:57. The bell had just rung when I'd started to slip out of this world and into the Keeper's hell, and now it was halfway through second period already. I stared at the ceiling and counted the minutes

I'd lost in my head. Yep, this had been the most drawn-out bout yet. Next time, I might not snap out of it at all.

Every time the Keeper called seemed worse than the last. Longer. Tougher. More painful. And no one knew. No one had any idea. Everyone in this stupid town saw some waste of skin stoner, not the scared-ass idiot fighting for his life. Fighting for one more day as a human. But that was the thing about keeping secrets. If you didn't tell anyone, no one knew anything. Besides, everyone just needed to keep their distance. It would be safer in the long run. At least for them.

One last deep breath that stung all the way down my esophagus, and I peeled myself away from the wall before anyone could walk by and catch me struggling. I had a reputation to uphold. It wasn't a good one, but it kept people from asking questions. Questions I wasn't going to answer anyway.

In the office, Mrs. Carter sat behind the reception desk, all cheerful and bubbly and annoying, until I walked in and her unnatural pink lips sunk into a frown to match the death glare in her eyes. She hated me. I knew it. She knew it. I meant more paperwork for her. An interruption to her coffee break when she flirted with the overweight and balding gym teacher, Mr. Donaghue.

"Again, Kellan?" she said with a heavy sigh. It wasn't really a question, more like a way of reminding me how big of an inconvenience I was to her. "Mr. Joffrey's in meetings. It might be a while."

"Then I guess I get to spend some quality time with you." I bent across the counter and winked.

She rolled her eyes and I thought I saw her gag. "Outside, Mr. Casey."

I gave her my best devious smile and made sure to close the door just hard enough to make her twitch. If I timed it right, she might even spill her coffee down that hideous mustard yellow sweater vest.

The line of chairs against the office wall sat empty. The rest of the student body must have been trying to hang on to their freedom and actually behaving themselves, or the entire faculty had given up on trying to maintain order this close to the end of the year. Except for maybe Pringle. She seemed to revel in her authority a little too much.

I dropped into the first seat and chucked my books into the open chair beside me. Stretching out my feet and crossing my arms, I took my place as the Middleton High office gargoyle— perfectly still and a little scary. People stared as they walked by. I could hear their thoughts on their disgusted faces. *Kellan's in trouble again, what did he do this time?* Not that I cared. There wasn't one of them out of the entire lot who actually had any idea what it felt like to be me.

Everyone wanted me to be some simple dumbass trouble-maker. People were easier to deal with when they fit in a box— especially one they could close the lid on and forget about—but I didn't. I wasn't failing, and that pissed everyone off. I could see it in their eyes—that disappointed drop of each administrator's jaw when they checked my GPA. I wasn't supposed to do well. I wasn't that guy. It didn't matter anyway; it wasn't like I could go to college. Maybe one day I'd pay them back for their judgments by taking their souls. At least I could look forward to *that* during my afterlife of torment.

I stretched out my forearm and twisted it in front of me. No unusual marks. No gaping, bleeding wounds. Nothing. Just pain. I ran my fingers over the skin. Even the lightest pressure ripped through my nerves and stung in my brain. Maybe if I stopped fighting back, the pain would go away.

Some girl slowed down as she watched me feel up my own arm, her big, blue eyes biting my skin like hungry, blood-sucking mosquitoes. Abby Marino. Beautiful, poised, and perfect, Abby Marino. A shining star to my space junk reputation. Hell, not even junk, I wasn't even in the same orbit as this girl. She lived in the house next door, but after I eventually disappeared, I doubted she would even remember me. Another hazy memory in her senior class yearbook when she moved on to the glamorous life that lay ahead for her. For me, this was it. The penultimate ending to a pathetic existence.

I glared back at her through narrow, slatted eyelids, my forehead down, and the start of a scowl on my face. Sure, I probably looked like a weirdo, but didn't she know it wasn't polite to stare, especially not at me? She pulled her books closer to her chest as her nose wrinkled and she walked away with the effortless strut of high school royalty. *Yeah, that's right. Keep walking. I wasn't worth it.*

She flipped her golden hair over her shoulder and pushed out the main door, letting a sliver of sunlight in. A warm breeze blew across my face, winding the fresh smell of spring through the stuffy school hallway. I sat there watching the light cut across the dingy linoleum tiles, wondering how many minutes I'd wasted sitting in this chair waiting on someone who wasn't going to change anything. No one could save me now. I was beyond saving.

Stretching and twisting my back, I glanced through the office window. Mrs. Carter sat chirping on the phone and examining her hideous claw-like fingernails. They had people like her running administration, and *I* was the problem? Forget this.

I pushed myself out of the chair and followed the sun outside. I never bothered looking back.

CHAPTER TWO

Abby

Kellan Casey. He stalked across the grounds with heavy determined steps trying to intimidate anyone who dared to come within a mile radius of him. As if anyone would bother with the perma-glower he expertly wielded as his weapon of choice. He had the potential to fit in with those muscular arms and piercing stare, except he was just so utterly toxic. And of course, even with a heatwave in May, he still dressed in all black, from his T-shirt to his combat boots. Just like yesterday. Just like every other day since junior year.

He walked into the parking lot and jumped into a beat-up hatchback, slamming the door loud enough that it echoed in the open air. Peeling out of the lot, he sped down the street like he'd just robbed a bank. Not even lunchtime and he'd already visited the principal's office, to which they must have sent him home. Shocker. Maybe they finally expelled him this time? For a boy who used to be scared of frogs, he sure promoted quickly to his reputation as one of the most notorious stoners in all of Middleton High. I'd bet that didn't do him any favors with the white-fence, polo-shirt crowd in this town.

"Earth to Abby."

A hand waved in front of my face. I scrunched up my nose and shook my head, only then realizing that I'd been staring. Marcus straddled the picnic table bench and flashed a mischievous smile—charmingly crooked with a glint of perfectly white teeth. He leaned in to kiss my cheek and I turned just in time to catch the corner of his lips. The slow, caramelly flavor of toffee soothed my troubled mind.

"You went on a latte run without me?" I teased as I ran my tongue over my bottom lip.

"Couldn't find you. Besides, how would I be able to surprise you if I told you I was going?" Marcus winked and set a paper coffee cup on the weathered wooden tabletop. "No one questions the student council president when he leaves campus, even if it's just for coffee."

I lunged forward and wrapped my arms around his neck. "Thank you."

"No problem. What's got you staring off into space? Everything okay?" His brow furrowed as he disentangled himself from my embrace.

I took a quick sip of my latte, letting the smooth caramel slide down my throat before answering. It might have been scorching outside, but I would never pass up a Starbucks. "I'm fine. I just noticed Kellan Casey walking by."

"Your neighbor Kellan? What was he torturing stray dogs today or something?"

I scoffed. "No, he was just walking by and I couldn't help thinking about how we both ended up on two completely different paths."

"People change, you know."

"I know that. It's just ... He's a lot different than what I would've pictured he'd be like now."

Marcus laughed. A light easy laugh that made my deep thoughts seem like candy daydreams.

I crossed my arms. "What's so funny?"

"You." He jerked forward and sat even closer to me. His hands wrapped around my biceps and rubbed my arms, coaxing goosebumps to form across my bare skin even in the late spring heat. "I know your life has been planned out since you were a kid, but I didn't know that you had scripted the lives of everyone around you too. Do you have a vision for the old cat lady who lives at the end of your street?"

"Ha ha." I swatted him playfully, and he caught my wrist in his hand, lacing his fingers in mine and squeezing before resting it back in my lap. "And you know what I mean. Kellan never used to be ... well ... like he is. He used to have friends. He played sports. He wore colors. Then, out of nowhere, he just changes. It's kind of weird."

"What's the big deal? So he changed. It happens."

"I sometimes wonder if there's something else going on with him."

"Of course there is." He took two of his fingers and tapped the inside of his elbow like he was searching for a fresh vein.

"Not funny, Marcus. Maybe it has something to do with what happened to his dad."

He sighed and leaned back to rest on his hands. "But how is that your problem?"

"It's not. I would just hate to see someone I know hurting or whatever."

"You are too nice of a person, Abby." He tilted his head back and closed his eyes. Rays of sunlight illuminated the bronze tones in his dark hair, elevating him from handsome to flat-out gorgeous. And the way he smirked; he knew exactly what he was doing. "People make their own choices and sometimes, it gets them into bad stuff. And that guy is definitely bad news."

"Maybe you're right." I took another sip of my latte and blinked, trying to get myself out of this weird funky trance that staring had put me in. First Kellan, now Marcus. Since when had I lost my ability to think clearly? Maybe it was from sitting under the direct sun or something. "So, what inspired you to abuse your political power today?"

"No real reason. Parker felt like taking his new car for a drive, so we went on a coffee run for you and Rachel. Getting this close to graduation has made this place start to feel like a prison. Sometimes you've just got to escape, you know?"

"And sometimes you just have to study for calculus." I tapped the cover of my textbook with the end of my pen.

"I wouldn't worry about it. You're a bonafide genius. A little math isn't going to stop you."

Genius? Yeah, right. Just hearing the word prompted an ache deep in my stomach. "Thanks, but I'd rather not take my chances. They can still take my college acceptance away if I flunk out in my last semester."

He sat up straight and brushed his hand through the air dismissively. "That's never going to happen. You worry too much."

"And that's a bad thing?" I bit my lip, instantly regretting the venom in my tone. I didn't want to start a fight, but sometimes he just didn't get that everything didn't come as easily to everyone else as it did to him.

"No." He dragged the word out, low and careful, his dark eyes trying to read my reaction before I gave it. A born politician. "I'm only trying to make you feel better."

I forced a smile. "Sorry. I guess I'm a little stressed about this test."

"Forget about it. Besides, I have a very serious question for you." His eyes narrowed to slits as a sly grin snuck across his face. He wrapped an arm around my waist and pulled me close, then pressed his forehead against mine as his soft breath fell on my cheeks. "What color is your dress for prom?"

"That *is* serious." The tension building in my shoulders melted away as I watched him fight the full-blown smile trying to force itself onto his lips. "But why do you need to know?"

"No girl of mine is going to have a mismatched date. Especially one who's going to be voted prom queen. That would be a travesty."

"Yes, President Diaz, it would." I slid my head to the side and nuzzled my nose against his neck, making a small trail of light kisses on his sun-warmed skin. He smelled like fresh ground coffee beans and expensive cologne. Tasty and decadent all at once. "Whatever will we do?"

He sighed, unable to compete with my attempt to derail the conversation. Placing his hand along my jaw, he gave me the deep, slow kiss I longed for.

"You're trouble," he said playfully, short of breath. "You know that, right?"

I nodded. "But I'm the best kind."

CHAPTER THREE

KELLAN

I pushed open the door at quarter after five. Ancient Mrs. Krull actually made me change the trash cans in every classroom in the entire school. Apparently, regular detention wasn't good enough for me anymore. They needed to find worse, more menial tasks to make sure I learned my lesson. Good luck with that. I considered not even bothering to show, but if I didn't, they'd call home and I couldn't handle that right now.

"You're late again." Mom bent over the kitchen counter, shuffling through the mail like a deck of cards. She'd pulled her dark hair up into a bun on the top of her head and had already changed into her uniform. The shapeless blue apron hung oversized on her small frame and the faint greasy smell of the diner still lingered around her no matter how many times she washed it. But she made it work. "I almost didn't think I would see you before I headed out."

I leaned against the fridge and watched the addresses fly through her hands. She glanced up at me and cast the letters aside.

"I know," I said. "Just working on a school project. A report on the state of sanitation practices in third world countries."

"Sounds like a very important topic." She smiled as she pulled a stray hair back and pinned it into place. "I am so impressed with you, Kell. There's barely a month left of school and you're still working so hard. Any college will be happy to have someone as smart as you."

"Thanks, but you're my mom. You have to say things like that."

She rubbed her hand down my arm and my shoulders eased under her touch. "No, actually, I don't. But I'm serious. I'm very proud of you."

Glancing away, I pushed myself upright again and out of her grip, then trudged across the kitchen. *If she only knew.*

"I'm sure your father would be too," she continued.

I dropped my bag beside a chair and plunked down at the table. Why did she have to bring him up again? With a heavy sigh, I studied the faint lines of the lacquered woodgrain. Lines darting every which way without any reason or pattern. Just like life.

"He wouldn't want to see you this gloomy, though." She rested her hand on the back of a chair and it made a clicking noise. She was wearing her wedding ring again. Somedays she took it off, but days when she missed him, I guess like today, she would slide it back on, hoping I wouldn't notice. "Something the matter?"

"No, Mom, I'm fine. Just have a lot of things on my mind lately." I forced a smile and nodded. Her tired gaze bobbed along with my head until her concern finally gave way to a sympathetic grin.

"Well, make sure you try to relax a little bit, though. You're still young, honey. Make sure you have some fun before life gets too serious on you."

I chuckled to myself. A little too late for that. "Sure. I'll try."

"Speaking of serious, have you finally decided which college you're going to? It's starting to get a little late to let them know if you still want those scholarships."

"Too many decisions. I'll sort it out, though. Don't worry." I turned my head away as heat started to rise up my neck at the tops of my ears.

"Good." She nodded sharply. "Now, there are leftovers in the fridge and please remember to take out the trash before you go to bed. I'll probably be home late tonight, but maybe I'll see you when I get home if you're still up."

Great, more trash cans to empty. "No problem. I just plan on working in the garage tonight anyway."

"I peeked in the other day. It's really coming along," she said as she hurried to the front door and pulled on a pair of worn sneakers.

I followed and rested against the kitchen doorjamb with crossed arms, watching her scramble out the door. "Thanks. Still a lot left to do, though."

"It'll get there. There's no hurry." She gave me a wink and headed out the door with a slam.

Between the pulled-back curtains, I watched Mom slide into her car and leave. A dark heaviness weighed down on my chest, and my breath struggled against the pressure. Lying to her killed a part of me every single time. Trying to fake that everything would be okay when I knew it wouldn't. That one day I would let her down if I didn't break her all together. She'd already lost too much. It wasn't fair.

At least work would keep her busy. Or maybe she'd move away after I was gone. Start a new life somewhere. Meet someone new who might make her as happy as Dad had. She deserved that. She deserved a lot of things in life that she was never going to get. She definitely didn't deserve to see her son die, though. No one did, especially not someone as good as her.

I rubbed my hands over my face and hung my head, watching the dust motes float around in the evening light. I'd made the mistake. Why did she have to be the one to suffer?

I flopped into the faded brown chair in the corner. Mom had sat in this chair when I'd come home that day. The day he'd died. Every day, I'd come home from school and she would wait to take me back to the hospital with her. Barely a half hour away from him to shower, maybe eat, then take me back to sit with him until I couldn't keep my eyes open anymore. Then one day I'd walked through the door and she hadn't moved. She'd just stared at the door like she'd been the real corpse and Dad had been somewhere else, still alive. The blank, vacant look on her face. The empty shell he'd left behind to pick up the pieces. I'd crawled across the floor and held her hand while her thumb traced circles along my knuckles. I'd cried. She'd stared. And then the sun faded away.

The uncomfortable, heavy feeling pushed stronger behind my sternum, each breath weighing one hundred pounds as I shook my head, trying to make the image go away. I stumbled back to the kitchen and tried to push all the bad thoughts from my head. No point in dwelling. What was done was done. Now all I could do was wait.

I flipped through the mail on the counter but didn't find the package I wanted. That water pump should have been here by now. I'd ordered it almost a month ago. Of course, when I really needed to throw myself into something distracting, I couldn't even do that right. *Damn it.* I cradled the back of my neck and stared at the ceiling. I'd never finish the Nova at this rate. If only I knew how long I had left.

CHAPTER FOUR

Abby

Decadence and deliciousness rushed at me as I opened the front door. The whole house smelled sweet and thick like chocolate fudge, and my mouth watered immediately like a Pavlov dog. I followed my nose to the kitchen. Mom puttered around, sashaying to some tune in her head, her suit jacket tossed on the table and replaced by a frilly pink gingham apron over her suit skirt and impeccably pressed collared shirt. She looked like a poster for some sort of feminist movement.

"What are you doing home so early?" I asked as I took a seat at the breakfast bar and tossed my schoolbag to the floor.

"Your father and I have dinner reservations with the Lupinskis tonight, and it's our turn for dessert and a nightcap." She opened the oven and pulled out an aluminum foil dish of the most sinful brownies I had ever seen in this kitchen.

"Wow. You went all out. I can't believe you baked."

"Of course not." Mom wrinkled her face like I'd insulted her. "I picked these up at a bakery by my office. I asked them to leave them slightly undercooked so I could get the right home-baked scent."

"That sounds like a lot of work to *not* have to bake something." I laughed and reached for the brownies. Mom swatted my hand away and placed the pan on the far counter out of my reach.

"Don't judge me, missy. Last time we were over, Juliet served these ridiculous mini crème brûlées. How am I supposed to compete with that?"

"By faking an equally delicious dessert?"

"Exactly." She winked at me, brushed a pinch of flour across her apron, then placed it strategically on the pantry doorknob. "So, how was school?"

I swiveled on my stool and shrugged. "Same as yesterday."

She rolled her eyes and ran a dishcloth across the counter, scooping up unseen crumbs on the impeccably clean surface, then shook it out in the trash. "Try to contain your excitement. At least it's one day closer to graduation."

"That is true."

She slid a thick legal envelope across the island. "This came for you today."

I clutched the manila corner and ripped it open. The Cornell crest stared at me from the cover letter page. I flipped through the stack of attached pamphlets and guidebooks, looking at lush green lawns, old buildings, and artificially smiling students. My stomach churned as I slid the pages back into the envelope, hoping Mom wouldn't see my hands quivering. I couldn't deal with this today. Especially not in front of her. "It's the rest of my admissions documents."

"Then I guess you're really going, aren't you?" Her stare drifted away from the envelope as she placed a knuckle under her lash line.

"You won't even know I'm gone. I'm sure you and Dad will be off having the time of your lives with me out of the way."

"I doubt that." She laughed and glanced back, a watery look

still in her dark cappuccino gaze but under control. "But I still don't understand why you didn't just apply to Yale or even Harvard. Cornell, honey? I don't get it."

"It's a good school, Mom."

"But it's not the *best* school. And you, my dear, should only accept the best. It's not even in the top ten."

"It's still an Ivy, and besides, I have to get my undergraduate first before I can even apply to law school. I can apply to Yale then, or Cornell can be my safety school. It has a great law program."

She leaned across the island and gently sandwiched my cheeks in her palms. "I know you, Abby. You don't need a safety school. If it were up to me, you wouldn't be wasting your time in Ithaca."

I twisted my face out of her grip and focused on the jagged veins in the marble counter. I couldn't have this argument again. It was too exhausting. "But it's not up to you."

"It might not be, but don't forget who's paying for your four years of distraction." Her perfectly made-up lips narrowed into a tight garnet line, but at least she seemed to have held her tongue.

I hung my head. She gathered up her jacket and headed for the stairs. I loved my mom but getting out of here wasn't going to come quick enough. It would be harder to be a disappointment with thousands of miles between us. At least I hoped so anyway. Except the thought of college didn't seem like a comfort either.

Mom sauntered halfway up the staircase before she turned around. "Oh, and Abby, the mailman left a package for the neighbor on our doorstep. Would you mind walking it over to Mrs. Casey?"

"Sure." I slid off the stool and hid the Cornell envelope in my bag.

THE PACKAGE LOOKED the right size for a shoebox, but unless someone had ordered lead stilettos, they definitely weren't shoes. I looked at the return address. Some company I'd never heard of. Oh, well, guess I'd never know.

I cut across the side yard and up the front walk to the Caseys' porch. Old paint curled and peeled in places as a few loose railings leaned crookedly to the right. A little bit of the shine of pride wearing off. Nothing too awful, but not how it used to be. Maybe Mrs. Casey didn't have time to keep up with the maintenance over the past few years? Sadly, not even for her precious garden.

The flowerbed under the window sat empty. Most of the houses on the street already sported beautiful crops of tulips and roses, but here, nothing grew, except for a pathetic-looking little shrub screaming for hydration. Mrs. Casey used to have the nicest flowers on the block. She spent hours on her knees, weeding and watering her little garden in a floppy straw hat and a ratty pair of overalls. I would watch her from my driveway, carefully tending to each bloom like they'd been an extension of her family. Her *flower children*, I'd called them. But her flower children didn't live here anymore, and I hadn't seen Mrs. Casey much at all, especially not in her straw hat.

I rang the doorbell and the chime echoed through the house. No one answered. I rang again, just in case, but still, no footsteps pounded down the stairs and across the living room floor. No sound at all. I propped the box up against the screen door and walked away, peeking through the small opening in the living room curtains as I passed. No lights.

Kellan's car sat glistening clean in the driveway, yet no one seemed to be home. Maybe he was inside and just ignoring me? Whatever. I'd done my job.

"Screw off!"

The voice echoed from inside the garage, along with the sound of metal clanging on concrete. I leaned against the garage door and heard the scuffling and shuffling of feet. I knocked. The door shuddered to life and began to rise. I straightened myself out, trying not to look like I'd been listening.

When the door finally opened, Kellan appeared with a scowl less than inches away from where I stood. I jumped, not expecting him to be so close, then backed up a step to give him, and me, some space. I couldn't remember the last time we'd actually talked, even if only about inept postal service. For someone I'd known so well, it felt like running into a stranger.

He loomed over me in his black-on-black uniform, a streak of mud or grease or something smeared across his cheek and his hands covered in the same dark substance. A triangle of sweat stained the front of his shirt, making it cling to his skin, and up close, I could see the muscular definition in his arms beneath the thick lines of tattooed black ink that peeked out from underneath the edge of his sleeve.

"Can I help you?" The lift at the end seemed like a question, but it sounded like a death sentence. The irritated tone of his voice made me wish I'd kept walking. Apparently, not just his appearance had changed.

"A package got delivered to our house by mistake. I left it on the doorstep." I started to point, then dropped my hand. *Stupid. He already knew where his front door was. He lived here.*

"Sure. Thanks," he said, rubbing his dirty hands with an equally grimy hand towel. He nodded once and walked back into the garage, leaving me alone on the driveway.

I waited for a minute, maybe two, as the late afternoon sun bore down on the top of my head, but he didn't come back. Talk about a lack of social skills. Or maybe since he hadn't slammed the garage door down in front of me, I needed to take it as a backhanded invitation. Or maybe not, but I invited myself in, anyway.

Every tool imaginable probably lived in this garage. Dad had most of the common ones, wrenches and hammers in a toolbox under the stairs, but this collection beat any I'd ever seen. Workbenches and red toolboxes with hundreds of tiny little drawers, which probably housed more tools and gadgets, lined every wall except for one dedicated to an old-fashioned Coke fridge. A sharp smell of gasoline and a heavy oily odor filled the air, and I guessed that whatever stained Kellan's hands must have been the source.

"What are you working on?" I asked, following him farther into the depths of the dimly lit garage.

He looked back at me, his brow furrowed in what might have been confusion or irritation. "Nothing."

I tried to peek under a black tarp that shrouded a large object in the middle of the space, but he stepped in front of me before I had the chance.

He crossed his thick arms over his chest and scanned me over with a hooded stare. "Is there something else you needed?"

"No. I ... Never mind." The plaguing feeling in my stomach from earlier today crept in again. Maybe Marcus was right. People change. There didn't always need to be a reason, but in this case, I wasn't so sure.

I matched his stance, arms crossed and standing tall. That attitude might work on everyone else, but if he thought he'd get away with giving it to me, he was mistaken. "How are things going with you? I haven't talked to you in a really long time."

He leaned forward and screwed up his face to appear more menacing, but I glared right back, refusing to relent.

Kellan chuckled, then stomped past me as if flicking away a pesky fly. "Is this the part where I say *fine* and you tell me all about whatever super important 'it' girl business you have going on?"

"Um, no. I really wanted to know how you've been doing."

He picked up a ratchet off the counter and rubbed it down with the rag he had been carrying then carefully placed it in a large red toolbox on the other side of the room. He didn't bother looking back, but his head dropped to his chest. "I'm great. Really great. Thanks for asking."

The words rolled flat off his tongue, either a dry attempt at sarcasm or potentially him just telling me what I wanted to hear. Either way, he didn't sound 'great'.

But I couldn't exactly *make* him tell me more than that. "Well, I'm glad. Are you planning on going anywhere next year or are you going to stick around home for a while?"

He finally turned around, a nasty sneer across his lips. "Is that your way of asking if I'm actually going to graduate?"

Maybe.

I fought the burn in my cheeks and stuck my hands on my hips with a loud scoff. "No, of course not."

"I haven't made a plan yet, but I know it's going to be as far away from here as I can get." He paused with his hand resting on the top of the toolbox. His shoulders bowed forward for the briefest of seconds and I swore his body shuddered, but he straightened up before I could tell for sure. "I definitely won't be coming back."

"Yeah, I'm getting out of here too. Can't wait."

I walked around the garage, trying not to touch anything for the risk of getting some sort of grease on my hands. In the corner stood a tall red bar stool. I brushed it off with my hand and checked to see if something had come off. Looked clean enough. I jumped up and tucked the toes of my sandals behind the support bar around the bottom.

Kellan shot me a weird look. A raised eyebrow and a

scrunched-up nose that asked what I was doing without saying a word. I'd seen it a hundred times and could read it like my favorite book. Funny, his facial expressions hadn't really changed much. He'd aged, of course, but the ticks and stares had stayed the same. I wondered if he smiled the way I remembered, but I doubted he would demonstrate for me.

"You still spend a lot of time in here, huh?" I asked.

He nodded. "Looks like it."

I settled into my seat on the stool and stretched my legs out in front of me, taking a closer look around. Oil stains and car parts. Less than thrilling stuff. But what had I really expected for a garage? Especially this one. "Whenever I used to look for you, I could always find you in here, playing assistant for your dad on his projects. Passing him tools, getting him—"

"Oh no." Kellan gripped the tool counter, his knuckles red, then blanching bone white. His head tipped forward as his knees bent, almost buckling, beneath him.

My stomach twisted as my skin flushed. Stupid. He was probably still sensitive about his dad. He hadn't been gone that long. Should've kept my mouth shut. "Kellan, are you—"

"You can't be here." He launched across the garage floor and yanked my arm, ripping me off the stool.

"I'm sorry." I tried to wriggle out of his grip, and he let go with a slight push toward the open door. I hesitated by the entrance, rubbing my bicep. "No reason to be such a jerk."

"You need to go." He put a hand on his forehead. His chest puffed in and out far too fast to be normal. Tripping backward, he doubled over, jabbing his elbows into his knees. His haggard breaths echoed in the cavernous space.

"Are you okay?" I stepped forward, but he thrust out his arm to keep me away. "Kellan?"

"Go now!" he shouted.

Too late.

CHAPTER FIVE

KELLAN

Why did every bloody girl in my life go out of their way to make me miserable? I told her to go, but would she listen to me? No. Of course not. Now I had an audience.

I grabbed my knees. If I didn't, I'd throw up. I'd learned that much. The world spun like it always did, closing in on itself and taking me with it. Color and light swirled until they became nothingness. Black. Dark. Nothing.

First came the feeling of falling. Like I'd been plucked out of my world and flicked into another. Someone's snot-riddled Kleenex or cigarette butt that they wanted nothing to do with anymore. Next, the slam landing followed. I'd been trying to prepare myself for it, brace my body or tuck in my feet or something, but no matter what I did, it always came as a shock. Another steel-toed kick while I was already down. Last came the dread. The nauseating feeling that something bad was definitely going to happen—because it always did.

I jumped to my feet. No time for thinking about the uneasy feeling building in my stomach and the overwhelming dread bubbling through my veins. I needed to be alert in The Meeting

Room—at least that was what I called it—the dark cavern between dimensions that I'd visited more times than I wanted to count. Sometimes there would be a table or something, but most of the time, like today, it was just an empty hole. A void that filled the purpose of screwing with me then dumping me back into my own world scarred and broken.

I quickly scanned the room, and seeing nothing, grabbed the sides of my head and rubbed my face. My heart pounded like a fist against the inside of my chest. Fear. Anxiety. Adrenaline. Like it sensed what was coming and was trying to bust through my ribcage and run off.

A rustle of footsteps crept behind me, and I gasped as the looming darkness pushed down on my shoulders. It was here, and ready to party. It slammed its staff on the floor. The rumble vibrated through my body, mixing with the already present quaking in my knees. The Shadow Keeper. I turned to see it standing there, watching me with its fiery stare boring through my skull, making it ache and burn. Its eyes glowed red from beneath the hood pulled down over its face, and its dark purple robes floated above the floor. A sickening smell of smoke or sulfur hung in the air, making sure that even if I closed my eyes, I would still sense him. Tall, thin, and absolutely terrifying.

It stretched out its arm. One slim finger made of only bone stuck out from the thick, purple sleeve and pointed at me. I stared back at it and breathed deeply. Twice in one day. Maybe the ghostly jackass missed me or something.

"Are you ready to join us?" the Shadow Keeper asked, its low, hoarse voice echoing from everywhere and nowhere at the same time.

"No," I said in my most defiant tone, but I immediately hung my head. Refusing meant another test. Another punishment. I tried not to guess what might come anymore as my imagination couldn't create the horrific things I'd seen in this room. Maybe dying would be easier.

"Very well." The Shadow Keeper waved his staff and a door in the non-existent wall opened to unleash the next of my trials.

It snorted and growled. A griffin? Maybe a bear? Then a foot appeared. A paw bigger than my head with claws large enough to slice me into strips. It walked forward, reared back its head, and howled. A beast from hell like no other I'd seen—the head of a rabid dog, the body of a lion, and the tail of a dragon. I steadied my feet and clenched my hands into fists at my side. No weapons, just me and it.

The thing pulled its head down and a growl erupted from somewhere deep in its belly. Black, hollow eyes locked on me. I held my breath. Whether it was hungry or just vicious, it was not going to back down from a fight.

It lunged. The Shadow Keeper laughed its deep, raspy cackle. The weight of the thing slammed into my body, knocking me down and crushing me to the floor. Tucking my feet in, I kicked forward, pushing the beast back, giving me room to breathe. It yelped. Everything started to spin. I grabbed my head as the thing charged again. What was happening to me? I pushed forward with balled fists. I couldn't see anything. I couldn't feel anything. Warm spit built up in the back of my throat as the vertigo intensified. The Meeting Room fell away. A bright light far away started to come into focus.

Bam!

I hit the concrete with a thud that jarred through the back of my brain. The heavy burn of gas and oil flooded my nostrils, but I welcomed the relief of returning home so fast. Rays of evening sun carved shadows across the familiar garage floor as I stretched out and tried to process what happened. Back so soon? Something wasn't right. A guttural howl sounded to my left, and I whipped my pounding head toward it. Black, hungry eyes stared back. *No. This couldn't be happening.* Beasts stayed in The Meeting Room. They had to. Right? So how did this hell dog follow me home?

I struggled to a crouch, aimed and ready to strike. The beast pinned me against the back wall with no options for escape. I swung an arm at its head, making contact near its eye socket. Pain exploded in my knuckles as they bounced off the rock-solid skull. I shook my fist and tried to block out the agony. It lowered its head and a sliver of blue tank top flashed behind the creature. Abby. Still here and leaning against the tool bench, not knowing what was about to go down. Her face paled bright as a cue ball, and her jaw had practically dropped to her knees. Great. Now not only did I have to save myself, but I had to save her too. Girls.

The beast snarled and snapped its jaws at me. Rows of pointed teeth appeared ready to tear me into bite-sized pieces. I grabbed a stray screwdriver from the floor. Eyes closed, I stabbed at it. The thing moved back, snarling louder and angrier than before. Its back feet flexed, and it launched through the air toward me. I held the screwdriver, ready to strike again, the handle slipping from the mix of blood and oil soaking my hands.

The beast came in low and caught my flesh in its teeth. Lines of piercing knives ripped through my abdomen. It let go, blood dripping from its mouth. My blood. I pushed at its snout and it recoiled. Its muscular tail swung at the toolbox, knocking it over, the metal corner slicing down my shoulder blade. I screamed.

It wasn't real. It couldn't be. So many times, I'd fought these things in The Meeting Room or in some other distant realm and been laid waste, then suddenly reappear back in my own dimension with nothing but a cloudy head, pointed stares, and pain. Worlds of pain. But here it was, this thing in my garage ripping away at me like a chew toy. But if this was the end, I'd go out swinging.

I wound up and crashed my fist against its throat. It stumbled back. Abby appeared in my periphery again—motionless and completely defenseless. Didn't she get it? If this thing, whatever it was, turned around, she'd be next. Another death coming way too soon.

"Run!" I shouted as I pushed at the monster again.

Abby turned, and I hoped that she'd finally listen for a change, but instead, she grabbed a wrench from my worktable and chucked it at the beast. Wind whistled as it whipped through the air and nailed the monster in the back of the head. It made a sound, like a combination of yelp and growl, reared its head back, and bared its jagged fangs. Another whistle. A hammer hit the thing again and clanked to the floor. The beast stepped forward, forcing me back against the fallen toolbox. Abby wound up with a crowbar. The thing spread its claws and swung at my face. I wailed. The crowbar slammed its head. A cloud of purple smoke erupted around me. The beast vanished. I fell backward on my ass, the jolt of the hard ground stabbing through my spine.

Through a haze of pain, the glow of the sun lit around a golden head staring down at me—the pathetic pile of raw meat on the ground. I blinked and Abby's glassy, wide-eyed face came into focus, sporting a familiar look of terror. The one I'd sought after when I'd told her ghost stories or chased her with a dead bug when we'd been eight. The look that meant she was too scared to think. Except now that look punched me in the gut. Hard.

I rolled forward to my knees and tried to stand, but my shaking legs wouldn't let me get past a crouch. Abby leaned toward me and took my arm, but I pushed her away. This wasn't her fight. This wasn't her problem.

"I told you to get out of here," I snarled as I held my ribs and tried to put pressure on the pain ripping through my side.

She backed away with those big, baseball-sized eyes. A pang of guilt surged through my chest. I reached out to apologize, but she turned and bolted. Why couldn't she have just listened to me and done that in the first place?

CHAPTER SIX

Abby

I did what I do when things don't make sense: I ran. Not like running away, more like pumping my brain with enough endorphins to process the things that it couldn't seem to do so without the boost. I didn't count the miles; I just ran until I reached clarity, but it still seemed too far out of reach. No matter how much distance my legs carried me, I was still just as confused as I'd been the moment that Kellan shouted at me to leave.

I stood outside Marcus's house a few times. Bent in half and hiding behind his father's squad car, trying to catch my breath and debating whether or not to ring the doorbell. He'd texted. A lot. My phone vibrated like an earthquake in my pocket, but I couldn't figure out how to respond.

Marcus: *How's it going?*

I don't know.

Marcus: *Whatcha doin'?*

I have no idea.

Marcus: *Where r you?*

Depends.

Marcus: *R U Okay?*

Nope. Definitely not okay.

But how to explain that without setting off alarm bells? That thing. That monster. Whatever it was, it had rattled me more than I wanted to admit, and if I told Marcus, he'd try to shush it away. He'd hold me close and bury his face in my hair and whisper that everything would be all right. That there must have been some reasonable explanation for what I saw. A stray dog, or at best, a wolf who'd strayed too far from the woods outside of town. But I knew what I'd seen, and I didn't want anyone to dismiss the memory. At least not yet. That thing hadn't appeared out of thin air, but it wasn't from this world, either. It couldn't have been. A scaly crocodile tail, but with fur and paws like a jungle animal—it wasn't natural. Then to just disappear in a puff of smoke? It didn't make sense.

The streetlights radiated rings along the sidewalk and a low, hazy moon hung at the end of the street like a destination I could actually run to. Except even if I could have reached it, there wouldn't be any answers there to find. Time to give up and go home. I jogged the last few blocks, letting the night air wash through me as I breathed deeply through my nose. The damp, fresh smell of spring still lingered under the stars, but it didn't help me relax. The nighttime magic was muted for me tonight. Painted over with dark and confusing thoughts.

Our front porch light shone across the lawn and all the main floor windows glowed in the dark. Silhouettes of my parents and their friends danced in the front glass like happy marionettes. So much for sneaking in unnoticed. It must have been later than I'd thought. I glanced over at Kellan's. The empty driveway lurked under the shadow of the lightless house. Even with the garage door shut tight, I pictured the horrors inside and shuddered.

I stayed close to the side of the house and slid off my sneakers on the back step before slowly opening the door. My sweaty tank top glued itself to my flesh as the slight evening breeze died in the calm of my kitchen.

"Abby, is that you?" Dad called from the living room.

I let the door slam closed behind me. No sense in creeping now. "Yeah."

"Come on in here for a second."

Laughing and giggling floated from the other room. Music from a decade before I'd been born drifted through the air, and three empty wine bottles already lined the kitchen island. I shook my head.

"There you are," Mom said as she rose from the couch with a large glass of red wine sloshing in her hand. "Arthur. Juliet. You remember Abby, don't you?"

"Of course," Juliet said, waving her hand dismissively through the air with a flair that only years of etiquette lessons or old money could develop. "She looks so grown-up now, Meredith. Such a young lady."

I looked down at my stinky gym clothes and tried not to smirk as the men rumbled in agreement.

"Abigail is going to be attending Cornell this fall," Dad said, rolling a scotch glass in his hand.

"That's wonderful. Isn't it wonderful, Arthur?" Juliet said.

"Yes, wonderful," Arthur added as instructed, studying the bottom of his tumbler as he spun it in hypnotic circles and tried to avoid eye contact with any of the women in the room.

"Abigail." Mom's lips twitched, her beaming smile fighting the pending frown. "Why don't you sit down and tell us all about why you *chose* Cornell out of all the Northeastern schools."

"Yes. Sit. Sit." Juliet tapped the couch cushion between her and Mom.

No thanks. I'd had enough of talking about school for one day. For one lifetime even. My parents wouldn't dare say anything discourteous in front of company, but even kind words about college would twist my insides into knots. I plastered on my best smile and pointed toward the stairs. "I'd love to, but there is a paper that needs my full attention. Gotta keep my grades up for those scholarships."

Dad stood and attempted to wrap an arm over my shoulder, but as he approached, his nose scrunched at my pungent sweaty scent and he shrugged it off, choosing to ruffle my messy hair instead. "Don't work too hard, princess. You're still young, you know."

"Noted." I tried to back out of the room.

"Wait, Abby. You must have one of your mother's brownies before you go. They're divine," Juliet said before taking a large bite of store-bought fudge.

I snickered, garnering a glare from my mother. "I'm good. Thanks."

KELLAN

I bit down on a face cloth as I climbed into the shower. The hot water blasted on the bite marks and the pain rippled through the rest of my body, more painful than the bite itself. I grunted a scream against the cloth, hoping that Mom wouldn't hear me. The last thing I needed was her pounding on the door, thinking I was being murdered in here. Or worse, see the bloody crescents lining my stomach.

Finally, the pain stopped, and I looked at the lines of holes. Clean and deep. Those teeth must have been sharper than razors to cause this type of damage without ripping chunks of skin off. At least it hadn't gotten its jaws anywhere near my head. But it still didn't make sense. How could that thing just show up here? Had it been my fault? Had I done something differently, or was this some new form of Shadow Keeper torture?

I opened the shower door and sucked air through my teeth as the coolness hit my cuts. These would be a problem. Hopefully, they'd heal quickly.

As I rubbed a towel through my hair, I glanced in the mirror. I didn't look any different. Just me. The same reflection I'd always seen staring back. Except maybe a little more tired. More worn down. Part of me dreaded that one day I'd look and I wouldn't see myself anymore. My skin peeling away from my face revealing the white bones beneath. My murky eyes morphing from human to blood red. I looked closer, pulling back my eyelids. Nope, still okay.

But what about Abby? That look on her face. The sheer panic. I'd have freaked out, if I were her. It was so much easier when people didn't know about this stupid curse, but now she did and I did not handle it well. I banged my head against the mirror. *Why did I yell at her?* I needed damage control.

I dressed and ran downstairs, wincing on every step. Mom sat at the kitchen table scratching items onto a shopping list.

"You're still up? I thought I heard the shower." Her eyes drooped and the obvious bad day lines creased along her forehead, but she simply smiled as I walked toward her.

"Yeah. I was working in the garage. Didn't want to go to bed smelling like gas."

"A wise choice. I hated when your dad used to do that."

I sat down in the chair across from her and leaned forward, hooking my fingers together and unhooking them again. The cuts burned, but I forced myself to sit up straighter. Maybe I should just go back upstairs. It wasn't like Mom could really help. Besides, where did I even start? I already felt like an idiot for considering talking to her about this, but the whole situation had really gotten inside my head.

I swallowed the last of my doubts and cleared my throat. "Can I talk to you about something?"

"Anything. What's up?" She put down her pen and rested her chin in her hands, her elbows on the table. "It's not serious, is it?"

"No." Yes.

She let out a short, relieved breath.

"I was rude to someone today and I want to apologize, but I'm not sure if I should, or just drop it."

"Well, do you think you need to apologize?"

"I don't know. It's really their fault, but I feel bad. Plus, I'm worried that they might take it out on me publicly."

Her brows furrowed and she leaned in closer. "That's pretty heavy, Kell. What did you do?"

"It's complicated. Never mind. I'm sure she's over it." I lunged up out of the chair to escape, but Mom placed a hand on my arm.

Her face perked up. "She? So, it's about a girl."

"Not like that, Mom. It's just Abby Marino from next door. We got into an argument this afternoon, that's all."

She released my arm and chuckled, settling back into the wooden chair. "Abby's always been a sweet girl. I wouldn't worry about it too much."

"Thanks." I rushed to my feet and started for the stairs.

"It's nice to know that you two are getting to be friends again," she called after me.

That wasn't exactly what I would call it. We weren't friends. We hadn't even been on speaking terms until today, and after I'd screamed at her and she outed me to the entire school, I'd probably have to move or something. All I wanted was for her to keep her mouth shut. I rubbed my hand through the back of my still-damp hair. "Sure, Mom."

Something flashed outside the window. A quick flutter of motion.

"Huh?" I crossed the kitchen in two painful strides and bent over the sink, opening the blinds wider to see out into the dark backyard. Nothing but moonlight and patio furniture.

"What is it?" Mom swiveled in her chair, then rushed over to join me.

I shook my head and blinked. "Nothing. Just thought I saw something."

She pushed onto her tiptoes and inched closer to the glass.

"I don't see anything. You do leave the garage door open when you're working around all those chemicals, right?

"You're so funny." I nudged her with my elbow, and she let out a giggle belonging to someone at least ten years younger than her. The ominous cloud over my thoughts drifted for a second, and I couldn't stop myself from laughing with her.

"Just had to check." She yawned and stretched her arms over her head. "I should probably go shower myself. I'm sure gas is pleasant compared to bacon grease."

I gripped the edge of the countertop and smiled. "But I love bacon."

"You would." She rolled her tired eyes and patted me on the arm.

Once she'd gone, I scanned the backyard again. Seeing nothing, I slammed the blinds shut. Hopefully, the Shadow Keeper hadn't let something else out of its cage.

CHAPTER EIGHT

Abby

After I'd washed my hair, I propped against the wall of the shower and let the warm water flow over me. Something didn't feel right with me anymore. Like walking around in someone else's life and not knowing where to start. Kellan's oily thumbprint was still smeared across my forearm. I grabbed the soap and scrubbed until the dark mark faded away and my skin glowed bright pink. Now my arm matched my brain—raw and sore.

I tiptoed back into my room, my parents' guests' drunken laughter echoing from downstairs. They would probably be at it for most of the night. Fine by me, as they didn't bother checking in. I curled up in sweatpants and a hoodie, pulling my hands into the cuffs, but I couldn't stop shivering. A chill ran down my back and through my bones. Sort of like that achy feeling before getting full-blown sick. Maybe I'd overdone it with my run? I'd gone way too long for it to have been healthy. My hamstrings already quivered as they tried to repair themselves since I'd finally sat down and given them a reprieve. Or maybe I'd caught a chill being out so late in the dark. Doubtful. The hot breeze outside didn't even resemble nighttime. There was likely a simpler explanation, one I dreaded—I was scared.

I'd never seen anything like that thing before, whatever it was. Random stuff like that didn't happen here, especially not to me. My life followed a straight line, drawn by my parents, my teachers, or anyone else with an opinion, and I simply walked along like Dorothy on the yellow brick road. But even Dorothy found a flying monkey or two. Except that thing was definitely not a monkey.

Kellan hadn't seemed frightened, though. Surprised, maybe, but not scared. Like he'd somehow known something like that could and would appear out of nowhere and try to eat him. It didn't make any sense.

I rubbed my forehead, but it didn't help. I needed answers and only one person would be able to give them to me. I walked over to the window and peeked out. A square of yellow shone on the neighbor's first-story roof right in front of Kellan's window.

After sliding my sneakers back on, I snuck out the back door, dashed across the yard, and stood just outside the Caseys' deck. Before today, I hadn't even thought of coming here in forever, but now I needed answers. I could have gone to the front door, but I didn't want to wake Mrs. Casey, and with Kellan's toxic attitude, he'd probably slam the door in my face anyway. It would be much harder to get rid of me this way. At least I hoped so.

I stared at the trellis and took a deep breath, letting it out as slowly as I could. I'd done this a hundred times before, but even thinking about it now made my palms sweat. The roof extended over the deck, only a few feet up, five at the most, but high enough. Maybe I should go back home and come back in the morning?

No. I had to do this.

I closed my eyes for a second. Nothing was going to happen. I'd be fine. I charged at the trellis before I could change my mind and climbed. The long, dead roses weaved between very alive, very pointy thorns. They pulled at my clothes, and I lost my grip from the pain of one digging into my palm, but I kept going. Up seemed easier than down.

Staying low, I moved across the first-floor roof like a clumsy cat. Gravel from the shingles ran down the side of the peak and clinked in the gutters like rain. Nothing like letting someone know you were coming. I tilted slightly forward. I couldn't see the drop down to the deck, so I pretended it wasn't actually there. The blood pulsing in my head started to slow.

Pressing my body against the side of the house, I peeked in the window. Kellan's room hadn't changed much. Same blue walls. Same desk. Same dresser. Only a different comforter and a few new posters on the walls. Oh, and the piles of black clothes tossed all over the floor seemed new. Except no Kellan. I leaned forward on the balls of my feet and tried to peer around the corner to see if maybe he stood just out of view. Nothing. Then suddenly, the bedroom door swung open. I wavered on my toes but managed to settle back against the house without being seen, hard stucco scratching at my back.

His dark hair looked damp and hung limp around the sides of his face. He'd changed into a navy-blue T-shirt and a pair of navy plaid flannel pajama pants—the most color I'd seen on him in months. I reached out a fist to knock but stopped as he stepped closer to the window. He didn't look up, but he clicked the desk lamp off, leaving only the overhead on. Maybe he was already going to bed. It must have been later than I'd thought.

I attempted to knock again, but before I could, he slid his T-shirt over his head. An arced line of red dots traced the side of his abdomen, probably from where the monster had bitten him. As much as I told myself that maybe I'd imagined things, seeing those bloody marks changed my mind again. He walked closer to the window, and I noticed that he'd been hiding not only bites under his clothes. A crimson-and-black tattoo stained the top of his chest and laced its way over his shoulder to wind down his bicep. From what I could see during the day, the tattoo looked like just an armband, but this was art and lots of it. I squinted, trying to decode the picture in the tattoo, but my line of vision kept straying to the other, more impressive sights.

I'd only ever seen athletes with that kind of body. Parker and his jock football friends mostly, but Kellan wasn't an organized sports kind of guy. However, he had a taut chest and flat stomach that looked like he'd trained along with an elite varsity squad. Maybe he'd been cranking out push-ups those late nights his garage lights glowed in between our houses? My stare followed the outline of the muscles on his abdomen, criss-crossing back and forth across the faint ladder-like pattern rippling through his skin. The chill in my bones faded as I angled closer to the window, the red glow in my cheeks reflecting in the glass. He stretched his arms over his head and his body tightened, highlighting the V-shaped ridge of muscle that ran along the side of his hips down into ...

My foot slid on the unstable shingles. I grabbed the window ledge and pulled myself forward, banging my head against the glass with a thud. So much for being inconspicuous.

I regained my footing and squatted in front of the window, smoothing out my hair and forcing a smile to hide that I hadn't just been staring at him getting undressed.

The curtains whipped to the side as Kellan crushed his nose against the glass, staring wide-eyed into the night. His gaze caught mine and I waved, as he hung his head and pushed open the window. I backed up, giving him some room, as clean smells of soap and shampoo wafted out into the night.

He glared at me with a stare so sharp that I twitched. "What the hell are you doing up here? You scared the crap out of me."

"Sorry. I needed to talk to you." I pulled my left foot forward and tried to force myself over the frame.

Kellan stood in front of me and started to close the window. "There is no way I'm letting you in here."

I thrust my foot through the small space left between the window and the wall before he could close it further. "Well, then you need to come out."

"Fine." He sighed. The muscles in his chest heaved with his deep intake of breath. I turned away, but not before all my blood rushed to my cheeks again.

"And I suggest putting on a shirt," I added. "It's getting cold."

CHAPTER NINE

KELLAN

I climbed out the window and sat down beside Abby. She didn't acknowledge me, just sat with her knees pulled up to her chest and her head tilted straight up, looking at the sky. I glanced up to see what was so fascinating, but only the moon stared back down. Maybe she had her eyes closed.

Abby had always liked coming up here to look at the stars. She'd said there were fewer tree branches in our yard, so they didn't obstruct her view as much. Honestly, I just thought she didn't like to be alone in the dark.

"So," she began without moving her head or bothering to look at me, "what exactly was that thing?"

"I'm not sure." I never knew what they were called. I didn't care, either. Just one more reason on the long list of why I hated myself.

"But that wasn't the first time you'd ever seen something like that, was it?"

I shook my head. She may not have been able to see the movement, but I'd have bet my silence gave her the answer she fished for.

"How long has this been happening?"

"About eight months. It's the first time one has ever attacked me in this world, though."

"'In *this* world'?" She finally broke her concentration and turned toward me. I couldn't read the expression in her questioning eyes. They seemed a deeper blue than I'd remembered. But from the dark night shadows or fear? I'd already said too much.

"It's complicated. Besides, if you'd just left when I'd told you to, you wouldn't have seen anything."

"And this is my fault? If I had left, that demon puppy would have ripped you in two. Or"—she lowered her voice—"was that what you were aiming for?"

"No. Do you think I actually *wanted* that to happen?"

"I have no idea. I don't know anything about you anymore, Kellan. How am I supposed to know what's going through your head?"

It was true. She didn't know me anymore. Except for the occasional nod of recognition if we happened to leave the house at the same time, we barely spoke. But I liked things that way. The fewer people who knew about all this, the less I had to explain. The less I had to leave behind.

"You're not supposed to know. Besides, it's better for both of us if you stop trying."

A warm breeze drifted across the roof, and she pulled her hands in her sleeves then drew her knees closer to her body. It wasn't even remotely cold out here, but as she shivered, I considered getting her another sweater. She looked different out here than she had earlier in the garage. Smaller somehow, like when we'd been younger. A messy ponytail and a wary smile, not all the makeup and pretense she wore during the day. She dropped the popular girl act she gave to the Middleton High elite. Out here, she was just Abby.

She sighed and rolled her head down until her chin touched

her chest, then turned, quickly analyzing my face. "If you're in some kind of trouble, maybe I can help."

She looked sincere. That reserved, almost innocent gaze pierced through my skin and tangled itself in my despair. Offered me hope. But I'd fallen for that one too many times from too many others for it to work on me now.

"I doubt it." I pushed my hands down onto the rough shingles and shifted away from her.

"How do you know if you won't tell me?"

Persistent. I hated that. Besides, what could she really do? Just put her perfect nose where it didn't belong and give me a liability to deal with. Not going to happen. Keeping people safe meant keeping them at a distance. A far one. "I guess I never will, then, because this is none of your business and you need to just get off my roof and leave me the hell alone."

I got up to leave, but she just kept sitting there, staring at me like I'd slapped her in the face or something ridiculous.

"What?" I said. "Just go."

"You are the most stubborn person I've ever met, you know that?" She pushed herself to her feet and glared at me like I wasn't a foot taller than her. "Since when did you turn into such a callous asshole?"

I stepped forward and narrowed my eyes, her anger pulsing hot against my skin. "Since when did you turn into such a know-it-all bitch?"

Too much. Maybe. But hopefully a means to an end of this conversation.

She scoffed and crossed her arms, her hip jutting to the side like I should yield to whatever she wanted. That trick probably worked wonders on that rich boyfriend of hers. Too bad for her, I wasn't him.

I pulled out the most menacing snarl I owned and flashed it back at her. "You should leave."

"No. Not until I get some answers about what happened in your garage."

"Then I guess you're going to be out here for a long time." I crawled back in my window and slammed it shut hard enough to blow back the curtain and a stack of papers off my desk. I flipped the latch and yanked the curtains closed so she couldn't keep prying into my life.

Standing perfectly still, I tensed as regret started to creep into my chest. But how was this my fault? She shouldn't have been there. I'd told her to go. Now she'd probably go run and tell everyone about the freak who lived next door. I wouldn't blame her, but I didn't want anyone to know. I shouldn't even bother going to school tomorrow. It would be all over. And I'd thought the stares cut deep before—just wait until everyone heard about me battling hell beasts in my garage.

Eventually, the gravelly sound of her walking across the roof faded and a quiet banging echoed into the distance as she climbed back down the trellis. I exhaled. At least she'd given up quickly. Maybe I should apologize? It might keep her mouth closed. At least I had a chance that way. I leaned out the window and scanned the back lawn looking for her, but she disappeared through her back door before I could call out. Man, she ran fast.

I closed the window again and picked up the sheets of paper spread across the floor. The bite marks on my side stung as I bent over. I lifted my shirt and ran my fingertips over the cuts. Dark scabs had already started to cover the wounds, but until tonight, nothing had ever left a mark. Usually, all my battles and my bloodstains stayed in The Meeting Room. I would be beaten to a pulp, then come back to Earth in a shitload of pain but not one mark on me. Tonight, the game had changed. Something had shifted, but considering I'd never really known the rules, I didn't know what.

And now someone else was being dragged into all of my crap. It wasn't fair. I'd worked so hard to push everyone away so they would never find out the truth. But now she knew. For the briefest second, I considered telling her. Telling her all the things I'd been going through and finally having someone I could talk to who wouldn't think I was completely batshit crazy. Except that she probably still did, even after seeing a beast with her own eyes. Besides, I definitely didn't need her hanging around. It was dangerous for both of us. I didn't have time to protect her too. Hopefully, she would get the hint and stay away.

I fell back on my bed and put my hands under my head, gripping tightly on my hair. The small jolt of pain as I pulled, relaxed the sore, tight muscles in my shoulders. Comforted me. Like I deserved to hurt. Like I wasn't okay unless I was suffering —in a constant state of pain. And I could tell that tonight was only the beginning. My suffering was about to get a hell of a lot worse.

CHAPTER TEN

Abby

The sun dangled high in the sky, and the effortless glow of it somehow eased my lousy mood. I'd been in a bad funk all day. Mad at Kellan for being a jerk. Mad at myself for caring.

Instead of coping, I doodled. I let my pen trace out all the things my brain hadn't managed to connect the dots to. Before lunch, my entire notebook was filled with line drawings of the thing—whatever it was—that had attacked Kellan. I couldn't get it out of my head. It haunted my dreams, both when I slept and as I struggled to stay awake.

"What do you think, Abby?" Rachel sat across the table from me, her perky little smile starting to melt down in the corners when she realized that I hadn't listened to a word she'd said.

I shook my head and sat up straighter. "Sorry, what?"

She jerked back from the table, her curly cinnamon ponytail swaying in perfect rhythm like a metronome. "Someone didn't bring her A game today. What's up?"

My body drooped. *Nope. I sure didn't.* But hopefully, I didn't look too bad. Rachel would notice, of course. But besides my best friend, I had kept my distance from everyone else this morning. Every voice suddenly so much louder than yesterday.

"I'm really tired. I went to bed super late last night," I said.

"Really?" Rachel turned her smile up again and leaned across the table on her elbows. "Did Marcus come by?"

"Very funny. No. I didn't even see him last night."

"Oh. Then what were you doing?"

"Not much." Just hanging out on my neighbor's roof discussing the scary demon thing that had inexplicably appeared out of thin air. But I wasn't ready to have that conversation with anyone yet. They'd think I'd lost my mind. "Had some stuff to deal with at home. I just didn't sleep well."

"Yeah. You do look pretty rough."

"Thanks, Rachel." I scoffed and rubbed my hands over my face. Not that I hadn't expected it.

"Oh, come on. You'd tell me if I looked like you do right now. I honestly thought you were going to pass out in English class this morning. If I didn't see you scratching in that book of yours, I would have thought you had since your eyes were closed. It was kind of creepy."

"Sorry. I'll try to do better next class. Promise." I yawned again and tried to fight my mouth closed but failed. "Besides, I don't want to be creepy."

"What are you even writing in there anyway?" She reached for the notebook in my hands, but I slammed the cover closed and tucked it away in my backpack.

"Nothing. Just a few notes for ... biology class."

She glared across the table, slowly scanning me over. "As I was saying, before you completely ignored me, you and Marcus are definitely going to win prom king and queen this year."

Prom queen. I'd almost forgotten. Nominations had come out this morning during history class and I'd been so in my own head that I hadn't even noticed when they'd announced my name. Last week Rachel had even come over to pick out an outfit to wear today so that I looked the part if and when the announcement came, but then the whole world had turned upside down and I'd missed the entire thing, with that perfect ensemble still sitting on a hanger in my closet. No one would vote for a prom queen who rocked faded sweatpants for her announcement to prom court. I glanced down at my lap. At least they were cute sweatpants, though.

"I don't know, Rachel. There are way better contenders for queen. Ashley is gorgeous, head cheerleader, and captain of the girls' soccer team, which based on every stereotype available makes her the perfect choice. If not, there's Lyla Evans, who's head of debate, yearbook, and both prom and grad committees."

"But Lyla isn't half as smart as you, and not even close to as pretty. Besides, you're on a few committees too. You planned homecoming practically by yourself." She took my hand and squeezed. Her perfect pink manicured nails shone glossy and pristine next to my ragged, chipped polish. "With my gracious help, of course."

"Thanks, Rachel, but I'm not sure." I tugged my hand away from her and hid my fingers underneath the table.

"Oh, come on. You also have the one thing that neither of those girls have."

"Really? What's that? A basket full of hundred-dollar bills in my locker to bribe everyone with?"

She rolled her eyes. "No, silly. You have Marcus."

"And that makes sense how?"

"Because Marcus has this prom king vote locked down. He's popular, he plays both baseball and basketball, he's president of the student council, and he's a front-runner for valedictorian. He'll have support from every single group here in school, except maybe the freaky people who hang out in the boiler room, but they never vote anyway. And besides, don't hate me, but Marcus is hot, Abby. Don't tell me you don't know that."

I smiled. Sure, I knew all these things already, but as Rachel listed them off, I actually felt lucky. And she wasn't wrong, Marcus was pretty smoking. A smoldering stare any girl could get lost in for days coupled with his movie star smile made for a lethal combination. My pulse raced as I pictured him, analyzing him piece by sexy piece. He didn't quite have the physique Kellan did though, but ... wait ... *get out, get out, get out.* I shook my head trying to erase the image of Kellan and his abs that popped into my brain. I shouldn't have been thinking about him. Especially not in that context. Not ever again.

Letting out a shaky breath, I gripped the picnic table seat until my head cleared.

"Are you sure you're okay, Abby?" Rachel stood and bent over the table, putting her cool palm against my forehead. "Do you need to go home or something?"

I shook her off. "No, I'm not sick." Just twisted. "So, what were you saying? How would Marcus affect the prom queen vote?"

"Because you're his girlfriend, and you are perfect together, so no one is going to come in the middle of that. You're like the reality TV version of Barbie and Ken."

Ugh. Another image I'd never live up to. Was that really what people thought of us? My stomach knotted. "But maybe we really aren't all that perfect. No one really is, Rach. I mean, no one can be all things to all people. It's impossible."

Rachel ran her eyes over me like I wore last season's shade of pink. "Whoa. Melodramatic much? Whatever's gotten into you needs to go. Maybe you *should* tell the office you're sick and go take a nap or something."

"I'll think about it." I rolled my eyes. "But what about Parker? You don't think your own boyfriend stands a chance?"

"He doesn't really care about all that stuff. I'd like him to win, but if he doesn't, it's just more time to spend with me." Clouds moved across Rachel's sky-blue eyes and the table seemed to double in width.

"Omigod." I leaned forward to close the sudden gap between us. "I'm sure a horrible friend. Honestly, I just assumed you were going to make the court. I'm so sorry."

"It's okay." She looked down and let her hair fall forward, then with one deep, sharp breath, she pulled her head back up and grinned like nothing had happened. "Less pressure for me to worry about."

"Well ... you can help me if you want. I'm probably going to need it." I forced a smile, but it didn't help the lump growing in my throat.

"Obviously. What happened to the outfit we picked out?" She feigned disappointment, but it didn't match against the sparkle in her eyes. One thing Rachel couldn't fight was her innate positivity. Like she'd been born on a sugar high that just wouldn't fade. "You couldn't have at least tried to dress up today, or are you going for some 'I'm calm and relaxed and I don't even have to try' vibe?"

"Uh, no?"

"Well, you might want to pick a strategy, then. I don't want to be campaigning for votes for someone who's trying to lose." She shot me a sympathetic smile.

"I'll see what I can do."

She pushed herself away from the table. "I've got to stop by the yearbook office before class. Have fun doing whatever it is you're doing." She twirled her hand in a circle to emphasize the hot mess she clearly saw me as today.

"Bye, Rach." I waved and watched her walk away in an almost too-perfect cobalt skirt and tank top. She'd make a better candidate for prom queen than me, and on top of that, she wanted it way more than I did. So much. Even if she wouldn't say it out loud. I just wished everyone else could see that. And she was probably right about getting myself together for the campaign, but I just couldn't right now. Maybe tomorrow, but not today.

I tipped my head back and stared into the sun. Little orange and yellow dots appeared across my peripheral vision, but the warmth on my skin made it worth it. The chill from last night had faded, but a small bit lingered in my core and sent shivers through my limbs every so often. I closed my eyes and let the heat wash over me. I was already attracting the wrong kind of attention today. Might as well go full-out sociopath for the next few hours.

Then, suddenly, the sun disappeared, taking its glorious heat with it. I snapped my eyes open as Kellan loomed over me from the other side of the table. I straightened myself out and reflexively covered my bookbag with my arm like he could see through the canvas to my crude artwork.

"So, you still willing to help me?" He dropped down in Rachel's vacant seat and the entire table shook.

I turned my eyes up at him. "No *hello* first? *How's it going,* maybe?"

"Fine. Hello." He gave me an overdramatic little wave, his raised eyebrows killing any sentiment that there may have been. "Now are you going to help me or what?"

"How am I supposed to help you? You haven't told me anything about what's going on."

"I know, but that's an easy fix. I can tell you what you need to know, and you can help me get out of this stupid mess that I got into. Deal?"

I shook my head and blinked a few times. "I'm sorry, but I think you might have the wrong person. I'm the one you yelled at repeatedly and then left out on your roof in the dark—or did you forget about that?"

A slight red tinge spread across his cheeks, but it was probably just the sun. "Look. I was pissed that you didn't listen to me because"—he sloped across the table and dropped his voice—"you wouldn't have seen what you saw. But you did and I can't change that now." He sat back and stretched out, taking up as much space as possible. "Besides, you've never listened to me before. I shouldn't have been surprised that you wouldn't listen to me now."

I grabbed my bag and swung my feet around to the other side of the table. "I think we're done here."

"What?" he said, his brows knitting together.

"Do you seriously think I'm going to jump at the chance to help you after that?" I started to walk away.

"Abby, wait."

I turned around with a scowl on my face so deep, it strained my face muscles.

"I'm sorry." He dropped his head down and wouldn't look at me while he'd said it, but at least it sounded sincere. Not with his usual edge. "I shouldn't have yelled at you, and I should have told you what was going on when you asked."

"That's a bit better." I dropped my bag back onto the bench seat but remained standing. "And what exactly do you think I'll be able to do for you?"

He shrugged. "You're the one who offered. I thought you might have an idea."

I sighed. Like I had any idea what was going on? "What made you change your mind? Last night, you practically threw me off your roof for trying to help."

"Don't be so dramatic. Or are you just not used to people not agreeing with you?"

"Seriously?" I turned again. "Find someone else to deal with you and your weird baggage."

"You didn't tell," he shouted, then continued in a whisper. "I expected you to tell everyone, but you didn't."

"Why would I? I can keep a secret, Kellan, or have you forgotten?"

"But I never told you it was a secret."

"You didn't have to. I figured you wouldn't want anyone prying into your business. Besides, it's not like anyone would have believed me anyway."

"Thanks for that. It's been a while since someone hasn't sold me out the first chance they got. I'm not used to it." His shoulders dropped and for the briefest moment, so did his armor.

I sighed and sat back down. "If you want my help, you're going to have to stop this angry bad boy garbage with me. Got it?"

"Bad boy?" His lips curled into a delighted smile.

"You know what I mean. Drop the act."

"Who said it was an act?"

"Whatever. So, what's your story?"

He glanced around. "Not here. Can we talk outside school? I don't want anyone hearing."

"Sure. If I come over later, can I use a door this time?"

He laughed. I crossed my arms and posed as tough as possible, but I lost the fight against myself and laughed too. Then nothing but silence. Awkward silence.

"So ..." I started trying to make some sort of noise, but I wasn't sure what else to say.

"And I'm sorry I called you a know-it-all bitch. I don't really think that. I was just mad that you ambushed me." He laced his hands together on the table, like a kid in a confessional.

"Thanks." I sighed and flipped my hand through the air dismissively. "And maybe you're not a callous asshole."

"Oh, I am." He smirked and tilted his head to the left.

I laughed again.

"Hey, Abby." Marcus appeared behind me and gave me a kiss on the cheek, his eyes locked on Kellan across the table. "Is it okay if I sit?"

"Sure." I glanced quickly between the two of them. "Kellan was just looking for a tutor and thought I might be able to help."

Marcus sat down beside me. So close that he almost landed on my lap. "What subject?"

I glanced quickly over at Kellan. I might have been good at keeping a secret, but outright lying was a whole other skill that I hadn't mastered. Besides, I didn't lie to Marcus. I never needed to. Except how could I simply turn Kellan over five seconds after he'd asked for help? As if Marcus would believe the truth anyway.

Kellan shrugged. "All of them."

Marcus laughed, assuming it was a joke, but I had a strange feeling it wasn't. Kellan spent more time in the office than in class. If he actually planned on graduating, he must have been doing all sorts of extra credit work. Or maybe he was blackmailing a teacher? A definite possibility.

"I'll come by around 6:30 and we can get started," I said to Kellan, hoping he would take the hint and leave.

"Sounds good." He pushed himself away from the table and gave us a rough salute. "Later."

I watched him swagger off. Suddenly, a weight bore down on my shoulders. Sure, I wanted to help him, but I had no idea what I was doing.

"I guess there's no point in seeing if you wanted to go to a movie tonight, then?" Marcus said, interrupting my thoughts with a dark scowl.

"Sorry." I gave him a halfhearted smile, but it did little to change his mood. "He really needs my help. Maybe this weekend?"

"It won't be playing anymore." He dropped his bottom lip into a pout.

"Why don't you take Parker with you? Rachel was just telling me that she had a late cheerleading practice tonight."

"Parker?" He snapped his head back. "He's competition for prom king now."

I raised an eyebrow and stared at him, expecting him to chuckle, but he stayed completely stone-faced.

"I'm kidding," he said after a beat. "I'll see what he's up to. Give me a call when you're done with your charity project and maybe I can come by."

"Yeah. Sure."

He wrapped his arm around my shoulders and landed a soft kiss on my cheek. "And call me if that guy gives you any trouble. I'm not sure I like him being around you."

He slid on a pair of sunglasses, then flashed me a wide smile and launched up from the table.

I watched him walk away and a slow, nagging pain grew in my gut. I wasn't sure how, but I knew, trouble had already come for me, and things were never going to be the same.

CHAPTER ELEVEN

KELLAN

At 6:29, a knock pounded on the front door. Right on time. No surprise. Abby Marino was the most punctual person I had ever met in my life. I supposed that was one thing that had stayed the same after all these years.

"You showed up," I said as I pulled the door open. "C'mon in."

She arched her eyebrow and glared at me. "Are you surprised? *You* were the one who asked *me* to help *you,* remember?"

"Yeah, but I thought you might've decided not to."

"I'm here, aren't I?" She stepped in and kicked off her strappy little sandals. How she didn't twist an ankle putting them on made zero sense.

She looked around as I led the way into the kitchen, staring and swiveling her head as if I lived in a museum instead of a suburban two-story. I supposed it had been a while since she'd been here. Maybe things had changed from what she remembered, or worse, hadn't changed at all. Her questioning eyes crept along my skin like tiny insects, testing my nerves and keeping me on edge. I clenched my hands into fists to hide the clamminess of my palms, then let them go so I didn't come off too aggressive. After all, I'd promised her I would try to be nice.

"Want anything to drink or something?" I asked as she settled herself down at the table. I hadn't really brought friends home since junior high, let alone a girl. The foreign fruity scent of her wafted through our quaint kitchen and put me off my game. I disappeared into the cool of the fridge and let out a deep breath.

Stop being so weird, you idiot.

"No, I'm okay. We should really get going on this."

"Yeah. Right." I grabbed a bottle of water and leaned against the counter, screwing and unscrewing the lid. No surprise she already wanted out. But why wouldn't she? I hadn't exactly made the best impression. Maybe I shouldn't have bothered.

She pulled out a notebook with a sparkly purple pen and wrote the words KELLAN'S STORY across the top with a double underline. My story. Like it was some sort of stupid fairy tale. I opened the bottle again and pounded back several mouthfuls. The cold water stung my throat and woke up my brain. This was dumb. She should leave.

Abby narrowed her eyes and watched me. I was being weird again. I caught her gaze, and she looked down. A stray hair fell in front of her face and she smoothed it back over her ear as she stared at her almost completely blank page. Maybe she didn't know where to start, either. I sure didn't. I'd never actually told anyone about this before, just kept it all locked up in my brain. The thought of letting it out made my stomach queasy.

"So," she said, finally breaking the silence, "how long has all this been going on?"

I swung a kitchen chair around and straddled it, resting my forearms across the back. "About eight months ago. There was this girl. Rhiann."

Abby wrote Rhiann's name across the page. I cringed as her

loopy scrawl misspelled the one name burned into my memory for the rest of my miserable life.

I pointed at the page. "It's Rhiann Glenn. R.H.I.A.N.N. Not Ryan. And double 'N' on Glenn too."

She sighed and scribbled it out, writing the correct name beside the messy blob of ink. Her shoulders tensed.

Way to go, Kellan. Already irritating her.

"I met her just over a year ago. She used to hang out with some guys who threw drag parties down by Miller Creek."

"Drag parties?"

"Yeah, drag racing. Cars. How do you honestly live in this nothing little town and not know that?"

She rolled her eyes and ignored my question. "So, what kind of person is she? What is she into?"

I shrugged. I hadn't really thought about it much. She'd been into me and that was all that had mattered. Maybe if I'd paid more attention, I wouldn't be in this mess. "I don't know. She liked trippy house music, take-out Chinese food, and horror movies. Plus, I guess, like other girl stuff."

"Wow, *girl stuff*. You're so enlightened. Anything else that might actually be useful?"

I paused, downed the rest of the bottle, then chucked it toward the recycle bin from my chair. It bounced off the lip and tumbled across the tile floor. I looked back to meet Abby's glare. "Well, she's a witch."

Her eyes popped and her mouth fell open. An ominous glug echoed through the kitchen as she swallowed. "A witch. You're kidding me, right? You actually expect me to believe that?"

I shook my head. "Not kidding. And after seeing that thing in my garage the other night, you doubt that witches could be real?"

"You're saying for the last year, you've been dating a witch?" She chewed the back of her pen, mulling over the concept, a flash of something burning in her eyes. The same something that had darkened her stare when she'd tossed hand tools at the demon dog in my garage. "Like a real witch?"

"I didn't know she was a witch when we got together." I pushed down on the back of the chair and launched myself up to standing. I picked up the bottle and tossed it in the bin, watching it settle against the empty soup cans and last week's flyers. "She didn't even tell me until it was too late."

"After she'd already cursed you?"

"That's a way to put it."

I closed my eyes. Just for a second. Rhiann's red hair all a mess and that sexy, lazy, half-smile on her face. The flames of her candles shooting up through the dark as she levitated in the air. Crazy and scary and hot as hell all at once.

"How did this all work?"

I snapped out of my own head. "What?"

"Were you some sort of sacrifice or something? Did she have to like bleed you or make you drink some potion or whatever?"

"I said she was a witch, not a Satan worshiper."

"Well ..." Her pen tapped against her notebook. The thumping sound dug into the back of my skull.

"She'd been acting off for a while and I actually thought she was seeing someone else. Then one night she called crying and told me she owed a debt that she couldn't pay. I took out every dollar I had and drove to her place, but when I got there, she was fine. Like nothing had happened. I tried to talk to her about it, but she didn't want to talk. She ..." Heat rose up my face and I refused to turn, much happier that the wall see my reaction than Abby. I clenched my fists to break the memory of Rhiann in my hands. My skin burned remembering her lips on my neck. "Later, she told me she was a witch and then she fell to the floor screaming."

"Later? What happened when you showed up?"

Abby's high-pitched voice cut through the buzzing in my brain. Memories spliced into pieces and fused together on an unending loop. Haggard breaths. The sharp hit of incense. Shadows moving in candlelight. "Not important."

"It might be. You never know."

"I'm not talking about this with you." I smacked my hand against the wall and she stopped tapping.

"Oh." Her eyes widened to match her rounded lips. Thankfully, the answer came to her without me having to spill all the private details.

"She started to scream and then this cloaked skeleton-looking thing showed up. The Shadow Keeper."

"Shadow Keeper." Abby dragged the words out as she scribbled them across her list of messed-up words. "I've never heard one of those before."

"It's this thing. A ghost or whatever. It travels dimensions collecting souls." I exhaled sharply then made my way back to the chair and sat down. Her notebook pages overflowed with curly handwriting. I guessed she found my story interesting enough. "It came to collect Rhi's soul, and she begged me to help her. I said yes because I didn't know what to do, but I couldn't stand to see her in pain."

I closed my eyes again. Just for a second. Her earsplitting screams echoed through my head. I gasped, the air thick and hard to breathe. Almost smoky. Like that night. The burn of it still in my nostrils after all these months. "And then it was over, and the Shadow Keeper disappeared."

Abby stared, the end of her pen crushed in her teeth as she slid to the edge of her chair. I expected her to erupt into laughter. Revel in my idiocy. I would. What kind of loser gets played this bad?

"And that's it?" Her head jerked back as she freed the mangled pen cap from her mouth. "It just showed up, then disappeared. Is this Rhiann girl a Shadow thingy too? Did she collect you?"

"No. She traded me for her. But instead of just becoming a collected soul, I'll turn into one of those things. A Shadow Keeper. Rhiann lives and I'll die." The word hurt. Dug under my skin and burned. I tried not to say it out loud, but I couldn't avoid it much longer. *Die.* I was going to die.

Abby winced as her pouty red lips squeezed into a tight line. "Seriously? How could she just do that?"

"Because I let her." Because I was a love-drunk moron. Because I hadn't read the fine print. Because I'd thought I'd been invincible. Because I'd screwed up. "I agreed to take her place, except I didn't know that was what I was agreeing to. Didn't know I'd really die."

"Can't you just change your mind? Ask her to break the deal?" Her eyes pooled for a second, but she pushed her tears down as her neck and cheeks pulsed an angry crimson.

"She won't. The night all this happened was the last time I saw her."

"And where is this ... *witch* now?" She tripped on the words like she wanted to say something meaner, but she exercised better self-restraint than me.

"I don't know. She disappeared. No forwarding address. No note. No nothing. She just vanished."

"Nice." There was no way to miss her sarcasm as she jotted something else down in her book. I leaned forward, trying to see what she wrote, but she conveniently positioned her arm in the exact right spot so I couldn't see.

"I know it sounds bad, but she wasn't like that. Not all the time. She was really good to me until—"

"She totally hustled you?"

"Hey. It wasn't like that."

"Whatever. See it how you want to." She kept writing. "So how does this curse thing work?"

"Apparently, there are these challenges until you either forfeit your life or die trying, then you rise as this wraith thing. Rhiann knew all about it. They talked about them when she was growing up, like some kind of creepy kids' book or something."

"No wonder that girl's got issues."

I bit my tongue, fighting hard not to rip her for the comment. She knew nothing about Rhiann, but if I wanted her help, I should try to play nice. And besides, it looked bad. I knew it did, but some screwed-up, broken part of me still cared about her.

Abby shook her head as she scanned over her notes. "All right, so what does this Keeper thing do with them? The souls it collects?"

"I don't know."

"And how does it flip dimensions and stuff?"

"I don't know."

"Okay. Let me get this straight." She raised her hand and let out an exasperated sigh, her righteous popular girl head snap in full effect. "You were cursed by a girl—and you don't know where she is—to turn into this thing that I've never heard of before, and then bounce around space and time for the rest of eternity collecting souls."

My stomach twisted. Put in plain English, it sounded stupid. Beyond stupid. Colossally, epically, brainless. I nodded.

"O-kay." She flipped the cover of her book closed. "I think I better get going."

"Are you still going to help me?"

"I don't know." She tilted her head toward the ceiling, letting out a heavy breath. Her hair rippled in waves as her entire body trembled under the weight of all this insanity.

"What would you want me to do? What could I do? This isn't really something I know how to deal with."

I pushed off the chair and paced the kitchen floor. Of course. What did I really expect? Digging the heels of my hands into my eye sockets, I sighed. "I don't really know either. I just ... I don't know. You're the only one who knows about all this, and I've tried to find a way out of this stupid curse, but nothing ever worked."

I dropped my hands to my sides and looked at Abby. She'd lowered her head back down and crossed her arms, but not in an angry way, more protective. Like my words could hurt her.

She relaxed a bit as I backed up against the counter and gripped the edge.

"I gave up looking for a way out a while ago. This whole mess got so big, I just didn't know what to do anymore, and the beasts kept coming. Bigger. Stronger. It's getting harder and harder for me to keep fighting." My chest tightened, and I struggled against the pressure to breathe. "But then you showed up at the wrong place and the wrong time and insisted on getting me to talk about things I didn't want to talk about. And since the second I left you outside on my roof, I haven't been able to think straight."

"Kellan, I didn't mean—"

I held my open palm up in the air as my chin fell to my chest. "I know. I was dumb to ask you to help. But you offered, and I thought maybe you'd be able to find something I overlooked. Except I get it. I'm the one who screwed up. It's my problem to deal with, not yours. Forget I even said anything."

The chair legs screeched across the linoleum floor as Abby pushed away from the table and swung her bag over her shoulder. Then silence ... one second ... two seconds ... until her deep sigh filled the space between us.

"I'll think about it. I doubt I can do anything, but give me some time to just process all this. Okay?"

I glanced up at her staring at me. Her blue eyes locked on mine, cloudy like a storm raging across the sky, but it lifted some of the weight around my ribs. "Okay."

She nodded and beelined through the living room to the front hall. I chased after her but tried to keep my distance. Give her space. She focused on her strappy sandals, her fingers shaking as she tried to close the clasps, until she eventually gave up and reached for the door.

Damn it, Kellan. Say something.

"Thank you."

She froze. Her hand gripping the doorknob. "What?"

"Thanks for not telling anyone. And thanks for listening to all this. I know it's hard to believe—"

"Yeah," she scoffed.

"But out of anyone who could have found out, I'm glad it's you."

She pushed open the screen door and paused for a minute. She glanced back and opened her mouth as if she wanted to say something, but she didn't. Wiping the back of her hand over her eye, she sighed again and then she bolted. I watched her through the front window, sprinting across the lawn with her notebook held tightly to her chest. Telling Abby might have been a major mistake, but last night she'd activated a strange feeling in my chest that I hadn't felt for a long, long time, and I couldn't make it go away now. It felt a lot like hope.

CHAPTER TWELVE

Abby

Smoke rose in the distance as we pulled into the worn-down field that served as a parking lot. I stretched my feet out in the front seat and took a deep, deliberate breath hoping to push out the tension in my chest and replace it with something that might resemble calm. The past week blurred with prom stuff, school stuff, and just so much stuff that I couldn't even remember all of it if someone had asked me to. And Marcus seemed even busier than me—basketball finals, council meetings, more stuff. I'd barely seen him except for when we'd posed for the mandatory prom court photo that sprawled across the front of the school paper, so when he called, the last thing I wanted was to go to a bonfire party. What I really wanted was to do something—just me and him—but anything to get me out of the house seemed better than nothing. Mom went off on me at dinner about Cornell again, and even though Dad tried to back me up, she wasn't listening to either of us. My daily reminder that I wasn't making the decisions she wanted me to make. Almost, but never quite good enough.

The sun hadn't finished fading behind the hills, but more cars than half our high school student body and the one in the next county already formed crooked lines across the empty field. Getting out of here later would be disastrous, but leaving early never factored into a bonfire party plan anyway.

Marcus shut off the ignition and looked over at me, squeezing my hand and giving me a hopeful smile. "Ready?"

I nodded and kept my mouth closed, as I probably would've blurted out *no* if I moved my lips. I pulled my cardigan tight around my chest and opened the door. A horn blasted and I slammed it again, shutting myself inside as Parker's shiny silver car sped into the space beside us. Inside, Parker laughed and pointed at me held up in the passenger's seat. I frowned, but I doubted he cared. Instead, he jumped out of the car and opened my door.

He swept an arm in front of me as I stepped out. "Lighten up, Abby. It's a party, remember?"

I scowled, but his idiotic crooked smile turned into a smirk, ignoring my hostility. I let out a deep breath and accepted his hand as he yanked me from my seat onto the grass in one swoop.

"This is a crap place to park, Marcus," Parker said as he shut my door. He rubbed a speck of dirt off his door handle with his thumb. "She's not even a month old yet."

"Might as well get her dirty quick before some soccer mom smashes her minivan door into the side of it."

He pointed an angry finger gun at Marcus and narrowed his eyes to a glare, his close-shaven head making him look like a passable wannabe gangster. "Watch your mouth, man. I love her more than I love you right now. Don't make me choose."

"That's the most romantic thing I've ever heard you say, Parker. I'd be jealous if I didn't already know you were talking about a car." Rachel shut the passenger door and shook her head as she slid over beside me.

"Hey," she said, brushing her long curls back and securing

them with an elastic. "What's with the grouchy face? You look like they just canceled your favorite show or something."

I forced a smile and started walking through the lines of cars toward the well-worn path to the beach. "I'm good. Rough week."

I kept my voice low, trying to keep Marcus from overhearing, but he seemed too deep into football stats with Parker to notice anyway.

"Well, then we'll just have to make sure you have a great time tonight, then." She wrapped her arm over my shoulders and gave me a squeeze tight enough that her flowery perfume lingered on me when she let go. "Oh, and I have to tell you—"

A horn honked behind us. We both jumped, Rachel with a yelp.

"Back off, jerk!" Parker shouted at the noisy car that had nearly clipped the back of his legs.

I looked back. Kellan's Civic. I hadn't expected to see him here. Didn't seem like his kind of thing, but honestly, what did I really know about him anymore? Besides, if the rumors were true, a crowded party would be the perfect place to score some weed or other contraband candy.

Kellan flashed the high beams. Parker shielded his eyes from the lights until Kellan screeched off.

"What a jackass," Parker said, watching the car disappear into the dusk and flipping the driver off.

Rachel wrapped her arm around his back and pat him on the chest. "You better not get in a fight tonight. I don't want to have to show my parents your graduation photo with a black eye in it."

"You have so little faith in me." He linked his arms around her waist and pulled her back against his chest, her chin resting on her collarbone. "When I fight, I don't lose."

Rachel rolled her eyes and pushed him away, but he simply held her tighter. She laughed, melting into his muscular arms.

I stared after Kellan's car and a slow, dull pain clamped tight around my chest. Guilt leeched deep into my skin like a sunburn. I hadn't given an answer about helping him. In fact, I'd basically been avoiding him at all costs. I'd done a bit of research on Shadow Keepers, but hardly anything existed. Like he'd made it all up. The facts didn't add properly and everything seemed far too unreal. School. My family. My friends. These things made sense, but that thing in Kellan's garage didn't. No matter how hard I tried to find a logical explanation, it wouldn't come. It couldn't be real. I shivered. But how could it not be? Maybe I'd been too scared to actually find anything useful? Either way, I couldn't handle a confrontation. He probably wouldn't call me out here with all these people around, but who knew what he'd do? Staying away from him needed to be a priority tonight.

We hit the edge of the parking lot. A beat-up, half-broken sign that read, *Brigade Beach* led the way to a wide path down the hill to the water. It wasn't a real beach, just a survival drill training ground for the defunct army base outside of town, but the thick woods surrounding the place kept the noise from attracting cops. Besides, it was way too rocky to be a proper beach anyway.

Everyone rushed down the hill as if the keg would run dry before they got there, while I straggled behind, still rattled from seeing Kellan here and wishing I didn't care. Marcus dropped back beside me and maneuvered us over to the side next to the tree line and out of the way. As the crowd around us thinned, we walked slower and slower, side by side, silent.

"So, are you going to tell me why you're mad or did you want me to guess?" Marcus asked, eventually breaking the awkward stillness.

I sighed. "Sorry, I'm just off today. My mom's been on my case lately and I've had all this stuff going on, and there was this wicked calculus test this afternoon and I'm not sure how it went."

He pulled me close and kissed my forehead. "You worry too much. I'll bet you did fine."

"Doubt it," I grumbled. "And ..." I didn't know how to put this without sounding like a spoiled five-year-old. "I was kind of hoping we could have stayed in tonight. You know, me and you and not a hundred of our closest friends."

His eyes widened, the deep brown irises blending with his pupils in the dark, intensifying his already fiery stare. He placed a crooked finger under my chin. "I told some people I'd show, but if you're not having fun in an hour, we'll go. I promise."

"Thanks." I pulled my arm down and entwined my fingers in his. Relief washed over me and my sour mood lifted the slightest bit. One hour. I could get through anything for an hour.

We continued walking toward the crowd below, our arms swinging between us as the ball of firelight grew brighter and brighter ahead of us.

Marcus stopped and tugged on my hand. "You still haven't told me what color your dress is."

My shoulders sank. "Still not sure. Why does it matter?"

He lowered his forehead and looked through me.

"Fine," I said. "Blue. I found a blue one that I don't hate. I'll go pick it up tomorrow."

"Thank you." He leaned over and kissed the hair on the top of my head. "Besides, I look hot in blue, and you"—he stretched our arms back and swung them hard, twirling me in front of him so we met face to face in the fading twilight—"look beautiful in everything. But you might want to tone down the hotness. I don't want people to be more jealous of me than they already are."

He leaned forward to kiss me, but instead, I laughed and pushed my hand into his chest, maintaining some distance between us. "And you are terrible, you know that?"

He gave me a lopsided smirk, his white teeth distracting me as he lunged forward, his lips pressing against the ticklish skin between my neck and shoulder and starting a slow but familiar path toward my face.

"Easy, Diaz," I said, grabbing onto his biceps and stepping backward, even as his hot breath on my skin started a twinge in my blood that rippled all the way down to my toes. "Too many people."

He backed off, but not without a disappointed scowl that he wore the rest of the way down to the fire.

"Here." Rachel popped up beside me with two red cups in her hands. She gave one to each of us, Parker trailing slowly behind with their drinks.

"Thanks." I raised the cup and took a sip. Honestly, I kind of hated beer. The rank smell of fermented barley never appealed to me, and I could live without the nasty bloated feeling in my gut. But as with most parties, it was beer or nothing. I'd bet there wasn't so much as a glass of water around here, let alone something with a fruity taste. I clenched my jaw and took another drink, letting the foam run over my lips to inevitably hang out in my stomach later. At least it was cold. "So, what were you going to tell me before?"

"Right, right." Rachel's face beamed like her parents had bought her not one, but two new Gucci bags, then with a squeal, she said, "We're going to Europe."

"We? Like you and Parker?" I asked, a little surprised.

She gave me three quick nods and glanced over at Parker like he'd suddenly turned into a boy band god or something.

"I'm so pumped, Abs. All the art and museums and fashion. I've hardly been able to breathe since my parents told me we could go," Rachel said, her hands telling as much of the story as her racing lips.

"Museums and fashion, that's exactly your kind of vacation, eh, Parker?" Marcus said with a chuckle.

Parker smirked back at him, but his narrowed stare looked more dangerous than friendly. "Laugh all you want, but while she's off shopping, I'll be drinking legally at the pub checking out the Euro hotties."

The two guys pounded fists while Rachel put her hands on her hips and gave them a death stare.

"Oh, relax, Rach. As if you won't be drooling after any guy with an accent who talks to you," Marcus added in Parker's defense.

Her face cracked, unable to lie. "Maybe, but I wouldn't brag about it."

Parker slid a hand into the waist of her shorts and yanked her close. "And that's why I'm lucky to have you."

She giggled. Parker moved in, but Rachel turned her head.

"Hey, Jessie. Guess what?" She waved into the crowd and busted away from Parker, pulling him behind her by his well-defined bicep. Parker shook his head and rolled his eyes at Marcus as he followed her farther into the party.

"Man, is that guy ever whipped." Marcus took a huge sip from his cup as he watched them walk away.

I hit him on the shoulder. He coughed and sputtered as he choked on his beer.

He glared at me. "What was that for? You can't tell me you don't see it too."

"How does wanting to go to Europe with his girlfriend make him whipped?"

"It doesn't. It's not wanting to go to Europe but doing it because she said so that makes him whipped. He's never been more than a hundred miles from here. He's small town like that. He'd never want to fly across an ocean if it weren't for her."

"You wouldn't want to go to Europe with me?" I'd never really thought about it before, but Rachel's announcement had me kind of yearning to see some landmarks and eat some great food.

"This isn't about us. Parker's just drifting. He has no idea what he wants, so he'll go along with anything she says." He shrugged. "He's not like you or me."

What? Words built on the end of my tongue but stuck there, stinging the inside of my mouth. In silence, I tilted my head to the side and stared as I tried to find Marcus's point.

He huffed a loud sigh. "We have drive, Abby. Ambition. A future plan. We're not waiting for something to randomly happen. We're waiting for something better to start."

"That sounds awful."

Marcus's head jerked back as if I'd slapped him.

"And besides, Parker is your friend. Your best friend. You don't seriously think he can't make up his own mind?"

"He hasn't even applied to any colleges, he doesn't have a job, and his dad is going to cut him off when he finds out that he blew off the interview with a football scout last week. He is my friend; that's why I know he's being a complete idiot."

I paused for a second. I hadn't known these things about Parker, but did it really matter? Wasn't he allowed to be happy, even if Marcus didn't agree with him?

"So what?" I blurted out, unable to fight the unknown feeling rising in my chest. "There's more than just one way to do things, Marcus. What if we did that? Just said, 'screw the plan' and ran off somewhere for a few months? What's wrong with that?"

He chuckled until he realized that I wasn't joking around. "Wait. Is that what you want?"

"I don't know." I hung my head, unable to meet his eyes. In this moment, right now, running away sounded like a relief. "Maybe. Sometimes I think—"

"Shh." He held his finger to my lips. I cringed at the tang of salt and beer foam. "It'll be fine. You're probably scared with everything changing and graduation coming so fast."

I turned my head to free my mouth. "Maybe I'm not."

"Of course you are. You've always been focused. That's one of the things I love about you."

"But what if I'm really not?"

"You are so frustrating." He let out a low growl as he ripped his free hand through his hair. "Do you seriously have to disagree with everything I say to you tonight? Stop being such a buzzkill."

"Just because I'm trying to have a real conversation with you?"

"Exactly. Buzzkill. Look around, Abby. You're the only one here not having a good time. You and I guess me too because you've caught me up in this nowhere mood you've gotten yourself into. Can you just let it go and relax for a few hours?"

The world blurred into a haze. The fire rose into a pyre as my eyes narrowed to slits. "Well ... maybe I should've stayed home."

"Yeah." He tossed a hand through the air, dismissing me. "Maybe you should have."

"Fine then. Take me home. I'm not having fun."

"We just got here." He growled again. "I said an hour and I haven't even talked to anyone other than you yet."

"Do whatever you want, Marcus. I don't care." I threw my hands up and headed toward the fire. I thought I heard him call after me, but I didn't bother to look. At least he was smart enough not to follow.

Marcus made me so mad sometimes. He always tried to

contain me, like I was some situation to handle. It used to comfort me, having someone to reassure me that everything would be okay, but at some point, it had stopped being endearing and become a pain in the ass. If I needed to know my opinion didn't matter, I'd just go home and talk to my mother.

I breathed in and let my thoughts follow my breath through my body, letting some of my fury out of my mouth with a sharp exhale. *Okay. Maybe I am being crazy.* It wasn't like I'd actually run off and disappear. I didn't even have enough imagination to consider it. My life had been mapped out for me for as long as I could remember, and at some point, I'd bought in so hard, I couldn't go back. I wouldn't know what to do if I could.

My stomach gurgled. I turned my half-drunk beer around the edges of my cup before giving up and tossing the whole thing in the flames. The leftover liquid hissed and the red plastic melted, dripping into the growing pile of ash like drops of lava.

I grabbed a seat in the sand and watched the flames dance against the black night sky. Tiny sparks snapped and floated up until they fizzled out and disappeared. Everything else sat cloaked in darkness. Even the moon hid behind a thick pouf of clouds, so only our fire lit up the night.

After I'd finally calmed down, drowsy from the hypnosis of the flames, I dared to look back over my shoulder. Marcus had moved on. He laughed and smiled and just continued being him. The center of attention. The life of the party. He did it so well, it didn't seem real anymore, more like what people expected of him. I definitely knew how that dance went.

I turned away and scanned through the rest of the bodies. Marcus was right; the only miserable one here was me. Even caustic Kellan Casey appeared to be having fun. He stood on the edge of the party talking to a few people I didn't really know. One of the guys had graduated last year—Chad Warner or something like that—and the rest were just faces I'd seen around but didn't really know. A bouncy, pixie-looking girl with long, white blonde hair bobbed in the middle of the group. She kind of looked like a cheerleading squad reject, with her all-black low-slung yoga pants and crop top, coordinated with an armful of leather bracelets and thick, black army boots. All she needed was a big cheer bow with a skull in the middle. Pixie said something and poked Kellan in the chest while everyone laughed. He took the drink out of her hand and tipped it back, chugging what looked like every last drop. He wiped his face with his arm and gave her back an empty cup, beaming with his annoying perfect smile.

He didn't smile much, at least not that I'd seen, but when he did, you didn't forget it. As I'd walked away from his house last week, he'd flashed that same smile in the window. A delighted, goofy grin that had put me on edge. He was messing with me about this curse nonsense. He had to be. I couldn't really buy into demons and witches and all that other fairy tale stuff he tried to sell me, could I? The whole thing seemed too impossible to be true. Some kind of cruel joke. Feed me some stupid line about all this nonsense, just to laugh in my face if I actually bought in. I wondered how he managed to get that demon thing in front of me. Robot? Hologram or something? Kellan had issues, but I never thought he'd end up being so callous, but proof kept piling up as I watched him poke at the Pixie girl. What was his problem?

She scowled, evident even from here, then she stomped off in her too-big boots, her empty cup in hand. One of the other guys in a backward trucker hat gave Kellan a high-five with some sort of handshake grip that I couldn't follow. Apparently, whatever had happened amused the rest of the group. Were Kellan and Pixie Girl a thing? She'd definitely looked interested, or at least she did before he embarrassed her. Maybe he hadn't been lying about having a girlfriend, and under all that sarcasm and swear words, she'd actually broken his heart. Or maybe he was just a big jerk—end of story.

Kellan looked back the way Pixie had left, probably still relishing in her rage. Then he headed off into the woods with the jerks he'd been standing with. Whatever.

The skin on my face itched from the burn of sitting too close to the fire. I liked the lick of the heat, but now it stung. I got up and walked down the beach. The wind brushed light against my flesh as a few lazy rolling waves lapped upon the shore. The roaring sound of the water crashing against the rocky ground drowned out the clamor of voices near the fire. Everything fell away. An alternate reality, but this one I understood. Darkness shrouded the inky, black water. Not even a star reflected off the surface. Like a huge empty hole swallowing up the stones beneath my feet. An odd sensation crept up the back of my spine and I trembled in the cool breeze coming off the water. Maybe I shouldn't be lurking out here alone?

A scream pulled me out of my own head. A deep-toned shriek. Definitely male. Sharp and pained with an edge of terror that must have ripped his vocal cords as it had come hurtling out. What the hell? I spun around and ran back toward the fire. Ahead of me, everyone scrambled, their heads swiveling for the source. Another scream.

From the left, a figure staggered across the beach toward the crowd. People backed away as he approached. Bright red blood stained his face and trailed behind him in the sand.

"You need to get out of here. Run!" he shouted.

All conversation stopped. Music still pumped loudly, but no one said a word, making everything all the more unsettling. Blood pooled at the guy's feet. I couldn't see his face. Suddenly, the screaming started again, but not from the bleeding guy, from everyone else. People ran. Shoulders, elbows, and knees pushed and shoved their way up the hill. I doubt anyone knew what had happened, but no one seemed interested in finding out.

From the beach, I'd never be able to claw through everyone to get to the top of the hill. At least not fast enough. I might even get trampled. I looked back and forth. The thick stands of trees left few options: fight the panicked hoard, double back through the bushes and race my way up through the woods, or stay behind and wait. I glanced back over the dark water and shuddered, then ran toward the trees.

The farther I ran from the firelight, the more I struggled to see the paths weaving through the brush. Only small slivers cutting through the treetops remained to light my way as I headed deeper and deeper into the woods. Engines roared ahead of me. Above me. Getting louder with every step. I must have been close. I pushed myself to run faster and faster until, suddenly, I lost control of my feet. My stomach slammed into my chest as weightlessness took hold. Falling. Almost sliding. The ground beneath me kicked up dirt and leaves as I landed on my butt and careened down a small hill. My breath heaved hard and fast. My pulse pounded in my head, lights sparking in my vision. So much for escape.

I scrambled to my feet. The ripped skin on my palms prickled from unsuccessfully trying to slow my descent, but otherwise, I seemed okay. Lost, but okay. The darkness thickened here. Farther down and hidden away from the rest of the world. I pulled out my phone. No bars. *Shoot.* I listened for a second, straining for the engine noise to figure out the right way to go. Hearing voices to the west, I pushed on. Marcus better not have left me here. If we hadn't fought, maybe we'd be in his car driving out of this mess instead of me blindly fumbling through the trees like a lost deer. Guilt rushed through me like the dark waves had pounded on the beach.

Another scream. Louder. Close. My heart pounded in my

head as I forced my leaden feet to drag me forward. I looked back. Nothing but black, ominous, night. My foot slammed into an exposed root, but I caught my balance and stumbled on.

The brush thinned as I entered a small clearing. On the far side, a pathway led up a steep climb. Up and hopefully out. I grit my teeth and ran, the shadows burrowing deeper and deeper under my skin.

Almost there. I pictured myself running into Marcus's arms and apologizing for being so cranky with him. Hopefully, he'd be so happy that I'd survived that our fight wouldn't matter. That the whole thing wasn't even a big ...

I tripped and spiraled into the ground. *Ow!* My knee smashed on something hard and tore the skin. Footsteps crashed through the bushes behind me, hard and fast. Someone was coming.

"Hello? Who's out there?" I called.

No answer. I struggled to my feet. A stare bore down between my shoulders. Heavy. Paralyzing. I whirled around. The piercing eyes glared, but not from a human head. Not a bear, or a wolf, or anything I'd ever seen before. Paws bigger than my torso, with talons the length of swords. Fur all over its body with a pair of twisted antlers coming out of its massive head and fangs, those fangs, dripping with something dark, and black, with a smell like pennies left out in the rain. Something born straight from the gates of hell, with its eyes glowing like twin October moons in the night sky. And the worst part—it stared right at me.

CHAPTER THIRTEEN

KELLAN

I ran. Tripping over twigs and branches in the dark, wishing my feet could move faster. The dizziness in my head didn't help. Everything blurred and moved, drifting in and out of a hazy focus. My thoughts jumbled up and I struggled to get my brain to tell my limbs what to do. Whoever the hell had done this to me was going to pay. Either by my hand or from the thing I'd accidentally let loose. The super-quick thing, too quick for me to catch, especially in this state. But I had to.

I'd tried to get out of here when the haze started. I'd known this wasn't going to end well and I needed to get as far away as I could, but in the dark of the woods and with my lack of motor control, I couldn't find my way out. So many times, I'd come here. I'd laughed and drank in front of that fire, made out with Rhiann against one of these trees, the pieces of bark still sticking in her hair for hours after, but now this place had turned dangerous and deadly, and it was all my fault. If I didn't stop the thing soon, people were going to die—violently.

Chad was supposed to pay me. Otherwise, I wouldn't have followed his dumb ass into the woods. He'd wanted to toke up, which didn't bother me as long as he gave me my money. I'd fixed his beater car for him nearly three months ago, and I needed my cash in hand. That was when it hit. The drifting feeling. Out of control, my hands wavy and fat like sausages. When the spinning started, I'd tried to escape, to not let the others see. Jackasses let me stumble off in the woods alone. Not like I'd wanted them to follow, but I never would've let someone else do that. Then it happened, the same as before. The Shadow Keeper's twisted smile, his question, my refusal, then the punishment. But this time, it got worse. This time, the beast roamed free and only yards from a human buffet.

The first guy had gotten away. The thing thrashed at him with its antlers, scraping the skin off his arm, but I'd managed to distract it enough for the guy to escape. The thing had run off farther into the woods and the guy had run toward the fire. Nothing sent a message like a guy bleeding out in a crowd full of people. After that came the screaming. The voices blurred, loud and sharp in my brain. Hopefully, people would escape before it came after them. If they didn't, it would be a total massacre. And that bastard Chad never gave me my money.

I wasn't even sure where to look. I tried to track the thing through the broken path of brush, but between the darkness and the haze, it kept getting harder. Suddenly, I felt a presence. Weighing down heavy on my back. I wasn't alone out here anymore, and whoever, or whatever it was, was close.

Leaning against a tree to keep myself from falling, I stared out into the dark. The shadows of the treetops smeared against the light of the stars then cleared and smeared again. I shook my head. Movement. Feet rustling in the bushes. I stumbled forward into a clearing. Down the hill from where I stood, loomed the beast. Large and savage and ten feet away.

The thing's ragged breath hung in the air, deep and menacing. It didn't turn, even though I thumped around as quiet as an air horn in a library. But it wasn't interested in me—it was stalking something. A figure moved in front of the thing. It blurred in my haze, but it looked like a girl, all pink and sparkly like candy.

The girl didn't scream. She didn't run. Which was probably the smartest thing she could have done, as the beast only needed one long jump and she would be a late-night treat. Maybe she was on something too and didn't realize what was happening, but unfortunately, if she didn't figure it out, she wouldn't come down from this trip.

At least I had the advantage of attacking from behind if the bubblegum-coated chick didn't make any stupid moves. I might be able to get in a few swings before it knew I was coming. Slow. Stealthy. Surprise.

Good plan. I stepped forward, fired up on good intentions, but my foot never hit the ground.

I fell. Branches poked and ripped at my skin as I slid down the hill, straight at it. So much for stealth. I stumbled to my feet.

The thing whipped around and barked loud from the pit of its stomach. Somewhere deep and dark inside. Somewhere a bit hungry and a whole mess of angry. Before I could strike, it rammed its head into me, knocking me on my back. I scrambled backward on my hands and tried to get to standing, but the low brush kept getting in my way. My head shook back and forth as I tried to make a plan, but I kept getting clouded, my brain overwhelmed or checking out and leaving me to fight this battle alone. As fast as I retreated, it kept coming toward me in slow, fluid movements that were more terrifying in their lack of urgency than if it had run at me full speed. It didn't need to. It already knew I was done for.

Soon my hands started sliding. I'd been backed up against the hill and unless I was half-ninja, half-spider, there was no way out. At least not backward. My only options were to fight or die—and dying didn't seem so bad as long as it was quick. But that was the point, wasn't it? Eventually, one of these things would kill me, and that was how the Shadow Keeper would take me. A renewed source of fury burst through me. The only thing I hated more than myself was that rack of bones who thought I was his plaything. He might win in the end, but I was going to make him wait for me as long as possible.

It lunged. I rolled. Its razor-sharp horns ripped across my back, slicing a set of racing strips that stung all the way through to my chest.

I grabbed a stick from the ground and took a swing. Little League baseball failed me as I missed its head, but its jaws snapped through my club like a toothpick.

Its eyes focused on me. I knew that look. Going in for the kill. So, this is how it would end. Torn to pieces at the bottom of a ditch, scattered among the leaves like a dead squirrel. Would they even be able to identify my body? Would anyone want to?

"Hey!" A voice broke through the thing's snarling.

"I said *hey*, you dumb beast. Over here."

It was the girl. I thought she would have been a million miles away by now.

"Over here, hell freak!" she yelled again.

Something flew by and landed with a thud near my foot. Another sailed past me and rolled back down the hill, hitting my arm. Rocks. She was throwing rocks at the stupid thing. This girl was going to be snack food in a matter of minutes. The beast cocked its head to the side again. A rock thudded against its skull and bounced off into the bushes beside me.

It snarled and headed back to the girl. I grabbed the rock from the ground and pushed myself up. Only one chance to get this right. I leapt forward, my body landing on its back, my fist full of gritty fur. I gagged at the wet dead dog smell but held tight. It bucked. I slammed the rock against its head. Again, and again, thrashing out at it, even though I wasn't sure if I was even close. It howled. A pained, mournful howl as it reared its head back toward the sky. One last try. I thrust the rock down into its fleshy throat. It jerked forward, teeth snapping and body twisting like a bull beneath my grip. Then the second I lost my hold, it disappeared. Evaporated into the air and dropped me face-first to the ground.

Air rushed out of my lungs. I'd made it. I'd won. My arms shook as I pushed myself up. If I could just get out of here. I tried to walk forward, but my legs gave way and I fell to my knees on the rocks. Pain shot through my thighs and mingled with the other pain shooting through my head and my arms. My head bobbed and nodded, the weight of it suddenly more than my neck could bear. Maybe if I just went to sleep, it would be over already. I felt myself falling down, down, down into a black abyss that might just be my end, but before I crashed to the bottom, my shoulder jerked upward, bringing me back into the woods.

"Kellan." Someone had grabbed my arm and was trying to hold me up. Rock girl. I tried to shrug her off, but my body wouldn't do what I told it to. I couldn't understand what was happening. The world had moved completely out of focus now. I kept my eyes closed because when I opened them all I could see was the hazy far-off light of the bonfire. At least I hoped it was the bonfire and not the burning flames of hell coming my way. If it was, maybe I deserved it.

We stumbled together out of the trees, me trying to get my legs to move but more of her dragging me along. People were still running for their cars, but it was impossible to get out. I recognized the smell of her shampoo as I rested my head on her shoulder, the soft cadence of her voice. I knew this girl from somewhere. What the hell was she doing in the middle of those woods? She could have been killed.

"Abby, where the hell have you been?" A male voice came toward us with heavy footsteps and even heavier mouth breathing.

"Help me," she said with an exasperated gasp.

Abby. The smells and sounds solidified in my brain as I heard that guy call her name.

"Whoa, what happened to him?" A taller figure wrapped my arm around their shoulder and hoisted me higher.

"We need to get him home, Marcus."

"No, we need to get him to the hospital."

"No hospital," I mumbled through lips that felt fake and foreign. I leaned into Abby. "Can't go to hospital. Take me home. Please."

"He's not getting in my car all covered in blood," the guy on my right said.

Blood. That must have been the tingling feeling running down the side of my face, clouding my left eye. I forced my head to turn, a much harder task than I'd expected. I couldn't see his face, but from his shadow, he looked like a dickhead. A dickhead with zero compassion.

"Then take his car." A hand dug in my pockets. At least if I could feel a hand against my thigh, I still had to be alive.

"But what about my car?"

"I'll drive it."

"Why don't you drive him home?"

"It's a standard and I can't drive a stick. Can you just do this for me, please?"

Abby slid away from my side. I tried to call out, but my vocal cords wouldn't cooperate. My body slumped as she let go, my limbs numb and completely giving up on me.

My new handler pushed me into the car, and I fell across

the back seat. The seatbelt buckle under my face pressed at my temples. The car door jarred my knees as it slammed, my foot throbbing as it thunked against the window. *Please don't take me to the hospital.* I couldn't say the words, though. My voice wasn't responding to me. Neither was anything else. I fought my eyes closing until I couldn't anymore. Pain. Heavy. Dark.

CHAPTER FOURTEEN

Abby

I woke up half-drowned in a pool of my own saliva. My pasty mouth tasted like rotten vegetables, or maybe worse, but I couldn't quite place the exact type of disgusting. Sun blasted through the window and I covered my eyes to keep the pounding in my head from making me nauseous. This felt like the worst hangover ever, except that two mouthfuls of beer weren't nearly enough alcohol for this torment.

I stretched my arm out to grab my phone from the floor. Already after one and fifty-six text messages from Marcus. I hadn't even heard it buzz. I scrolled through his levels of anxiety, anger, a bit of begging, and then finally concern. The last one, *R U still mad?*, had come in about fifteen minutes ago. My finger hovered over the screen for a few seconds, but instead, I flipped the phone off and laid my head back down. Was I still mad? I wasn't even sure. There were so many other things going on in my brain that last night's argument didn't even matter anymore. I'd almost died last night. Him being a jerk was not even a blip on my radar.

I'd almost died last night. Even though I'd known it had been true from the second I'd stared into that thing's evil yellow eyes, this was the first time I had actually let myself think about it. I'd almost died. Any doubts I'd had about Kellan telling me the truth had fallen away. There was no denying what I saw this time. Something bad was happening to him.

I dragged myself off my bed, still dressed in last night's clothes, and wandered to the window at the end of the hall. The house lay quiet and goosebumps rippled across the back of my neck at the eerie silence, but the sunlight helped keep me from jumping out of my skin. Kellan's car sat in the driveway, which probably meant he hadn't woken up yet. Or maybe he had just rolled out of bed and eaten breakfast like nothing had happened. But there was no way I'd ever forget.

Marcus had helped me drag Kellan to his room, then took off mumbling something about not being caught, but I couldn't just leave him there. He'd looked like he'd gone through some hideous ancient form of torture, and I owed him one for saving my life. I'd washed off all the visible blood and tucked him underneath his sheets to cover his bloody clothes. I'd considered peeling off his shirt, but as soon as I'd touched the hem, it had felt awkward and a little violating. When I'd heard his mom come home later, I'd curled up on the floor next to his bed, hidden from view. There would be too many questions I didn't know how to answer if I'd been caught.

He hadn't woken up, but he'd rolled over a few times and I'd checked to make sure he kept breathing. His heart rate had slowed substantially, and it looked like whatever he'd been on was starting to wear off. I made sure he didn't swallow his tongue or something stupid, or maybe I just hung around to avoid being alone, or worse, walk across my dark lawn by myself. The fear of what I'd seen had kept me wide awake, and the image of the beast when I'd closed my eyes was enough to bring me back if I'd wavered. When the first rays of sunlight crept across his floor, I'd quietly tiptoed out the front door and into my own house. I'd sat on the bed holding my knees to my chest until I must've passed out.

My stomach roared and snapped me out of my nightmarish memories. I'd barely eaten at dinner last night and all the running and panicking had made a giant-size hole in my stomach, not to mention the shredded skin on my palms and sore spots on my calves.

Downstairs, there was still no sign of life. Small plates and used cocktail napkins sprawled across the tables in the living room and a collection of wine bottles lined the kitchen counter. No wonder no one had heard me sneak in this morning. I grabbed some Cheerios in the pantry, as well as some milk and orange juice from the fridge, then popped myself up on a stool at the island. It was already the afternoon, but I still craved cereal. Plus, I desperately needed something to drink. The Advil I'd grabbed upstairs and swallowed dry still stuck to my throat and kept making me gag, but at least it seemed to be taking the edge off the headache.

I dug into my bowl, devouring my food like I hadn't been fed in weeks, enjoying the scrape of the cereal down my throat more than was normal. Then I stopped. A sound. A scratching. I gripped the counter and looked around. Nothing. I eyed up the shadows on the staircase, then forced my lungs to breathe. *I must be going crazy.* There was nothing here.

I grabbed the newspaper and flipped through the pages, trying to find something to distract me. The pictures and the words blurred together as I turned page after page, not really committing to reading anything. I had to calm down. How was I supposed to function if I couldn't even eat breakfast in my own kitchen?

Sliding the paper away, I finished my cereal and cleared my dishes to the sink. As I plunked my bowl against the stainless steel, I heard a noise again. Louder. Closer. I whirled around, my hand reaching for the steak knife in the sink.

The back door opened. I balled my hands into fists, clutching the knife and preparing to fight, my breath hitching in my throat.

Sunlight and the smell of cut grass poured in the doorway, followed by my father in a ballcap and a teal golf shirt. I exhaled and relaxed my hands, the pain of tension still spring loaded in my knuckles.

"Hey, Dad," I said, my voice a mere squeak as I started to calm. *It's just Dad,* I repeated over and over in my head, the thought making me feel safe again.

"You're alive. I thought you were going to sleep all weekend," Dad said with a smile as he choked up on the driver shaft in his hand. He walked past me and grabbed a dishcloth, rubbing out a grass stain on the head of the driver. I watched him work, letting the familiarity of him push out the bad thoughts that had been flying around my head. He looked younger today. Maybe because the ballcap covered the gray that had started creeping in around his ears, or maybe because there was a mischievous twinkle in his ice-blue eyes. I was sure that was what must've sold Mom back then. When he was happy, he looked like he was about to start some sort of wonderful trouble. "Did you have a good time last night?"

I leaned against the counter. *Heck no. I'm actually surprised to see the light of day.* "It was all right. Mom going golfing with you?"

"No. Spa day with the girls." He fluttered his fingers in the air and batted his eyelashes in an unmanly kind of way that actually made me snicker. "What are you up to today?"

"Not sure yet. Might just hang around the house." Even though the thought of being alone in here was almost as terrifying as being outside in the open.

"Suit yourself, but it's a beautiful day out there. You should make sure that you get out there and enjoy it." He turned around and pumped his fist in the air like he'd forgotten something. "Oh. Marcus called the house for you. He said you weren't answering your phone, so I told him that you'd probably slept in and to let my princess have her beauty sleep."

I made a face. "Please tell me you didn't actually say that."

"No. But next time, I will now that I know how much you hate it." He turned his face to the side while keeping his gaze locked on me. "He seemed kind of rattled, though. Is everything okay with you two?"

Nope. "Yeah, Dad. He just worries. That's all." I walked past him and sat back down at the island, sandwiching my half-empty glass of orange juice in my hands, the coolness soothing the raw skin on my palms.

"Okay. Just checking." He grabbed an apple from the dish on the counter and flipped it in the air, caught it in his opposite hand, then gave me a smile. "I know you can handle yourself, but I feel better knowing that he's looking out for you."

My cheeks flushed.

"And speaking of looking out," he said, "you weren't at Brigade Beach last night, were you?"

I choked on my juice. "What? No."

He stared at me closely. I forced a smile, hoping that it would push down the red crawling up my neck.

"Well, do me a favor and stay away from there. Heard there was a bear attack there last night, so the police are warning people to be careful in the woods outside town."

I stared at the pulp floating in my juice and swallowed. A bear attack. A lot better story than a crazy other-dimensional hell beast.

"Don't look so worried. Department of Fish and Wildlife guys are heading down there to remove it. It'll be okay."

I nodded. But I'd bet they weren't going to find anything. "Thanks for the warning."

"Hey, what's that?" Dad pointed at the wall just past my left ear.

I swiveled in my chair and looked around. "What?"

"Right here." He leaned across the counter and ran his finger near my temple. I touched the side of my face and a few flakes of dried blood fell to the white countertop. "Looks like mud or something."

"Yeah, Dad. That must be it. Mud." I swallowed hard.

"What were you doing in the mud?"

Think, Abby. Think. "Marcus got his car stuck last night and I helped him push it out. But everything's fine now."

"That's my girl. Tough as steel."

"Thanks."

"But don't tell me he's out driving around like an idiot with you in the car. I won't be too happy with him if that's the case."

"No, Dad. No big deal. I swear."

He narrowed his eyes and stared at me like he had some lie detector installed in his brain.

"And don't tell me you didn't drive like an idiot when you were young," I said. "Mom told me all about it."

"Did she now?"

I nodded.

"Well, I'm sure she didn't tell you everything because there are things that even she doesn't know."

I slid to the front of my chair. "Like what?"

"Like this conversation is over, but I can tell you that there isn't one of your little guy friends around here that could have taken on me and Suzanne."

I laughed. Who called a Mustang "Suzanne"? Must've been real macho.

Dad tugged on the brim of his hat and nodded. "Well, I'm off. Have fun hanging around the house like a hermit."

The lightness I felt attached itself to my dad and followed him out the door, dread creeping back in as soon as it shut behind him. Just me and the empty house again. I picked up the phone and dialed while checking myself over in the hall mirror. Only a few spots of blood. Thank goodness. At least I didn't look like a murder victim or something. That would have been much harder to cover up.

The other end of the line picked up. "Hello?"

"Hey, Rachel. Wanna do something? I really need to get out of here."

⁂

"ONE SCOOP CHOCOLATE and one scoop bubblegum in a waffle cone, as promised."

Rachel reached out a hand without removing her face from the sky, a pair of massive sunglasses and a wide smile covering her petite face. "You remembered the sprinkles, right?"

"Of course," I said as I stretched out in the cool grass beside her.

People scurried around the park like ants, but not too quickly in this heat. A couple jogged by and I cringed thinking how disgusting they must feel. Holding up my ice cream was enough to make me sweat. Maybe it would've been a better idea to stay indoors today, or at least somewhere with shade, but the sun seemed to be able to burn away the bad memories from last night. Plus, there weren't any bushes for something to lurk in and throw me on edge.

"So, what's the matter?" Rachel said after a few minutes of silence mixed with the crunching of waffle cone.

"Huh?" I mumbled, my mouth full of pralines and cream.

"Don't give me that dumb look, Abby, it's ugly."

I scrunched up my face in protest, but then forced it off, wondering how awful I must have looked.

"Randomly wanting to hang out in the park on a Saturday. You don't do things without a plan unless something's bugging you."

Tension spread across my shoulders. Well played. Rachel probably knew me a little too well. Or at least better than I wanted right now.

"Besides, Marcus called me looking for you this morning and said you weren't answering your phone. So spill."

I sighed. "Did he file a missing person's report too?"

"Harsh."

"Sorry. We had a fight last night, then he left me a crazy ton of messages this morning."

"Is everything okay?" She pulled off the glasses to give me her serious face, but she was squinting so hard, it didn't really work.

"Oh, yeah. All good. I texted him back before we left." I forced a smile, hoping she'd drop the topic. And I wasn't lying. I *had* texted Marcus back telling him that I was fine, but she didn't need to know that he'd been blowing up my phone the entire time we'd been sitting here.

"Then what's going on? You look like you're thinking way too hard for the level of slacking we're rocking now."

"Have you ever thought about what it would feel like if you had a whole secret life? One that no one really knew about?"

She laid her warm hand on my forehead. "Are you really *that* hungover?"

I jerked away, drops of ice cream landing in my lap. "Never mind. Forget I said anything."

"Wait, are you cheating on Marcus? Is it that Casey guy whose house you were creeping away from when I pulled up?"

My face flushed. "No." There wasn't anything going on, but I didn't think Rachel had seen me go over to his house. Not like it mattered. His mom had said he was in bed sick. But I guessed sick was a better excuse than half-dead and high.

She eyed me closely, then shook her head, hopefully, convinced. "Good, because the whole bad-boy, biceps-the-size-of-my-head thing looks hot on paper, but boy's got some serious issues. I mean like possible expulsion, possible criminal record type stuff."

"And you know that for sure?"

"Oh, it's no secret. Everyone knows all about that guy. I heard he might even be in a gang."

I laughed. "Since when have you ever heard of a gang around here?"

She shrugged. "Just something I heard."

I shook my head. "Hey, did you see anything odd at the bonfire last night?"

"Hmm." She scrunched up her nose and rolled her gaze toward the sky. "Becky Farmer was making out with the skeezy Tyler guy from our math class. Is that what you mean?"

"Not quite. Besides, you kind of disappeared. What happened to you guys?"

"We left early. Parker almost got in the middle of a scrap, but I managed to talk him down. Then he was focused on other things." A delicious smirk slid across her face. "Then we took off. I looked for you, but you weren't around."

"How do you put up with him fighting all the time?"

"It's not that bad. He's more talk than anything. Besides, the guy who got his ass kicked totally deserved it. He was slipping roofies into girl's drinks until Max Duncan caught him red-handed and jumped him."

I jumped forward. "Who was it?"

"Remember that guy from last year, Chad Werther or something?"

"Warner?"

She clicked her tongue and pointed at me. "Yeah, that's the guy. I mean, how desperate do you have to be to do something like that? I could have given him a list of girls at that party who would've given it up stone-cold sober."

Someone drugging people? The thought turned over and over in my brain like it meant something, but I wasn't really sure what.

Rachel popped me out of my thoughts. "Well, if you're not having a crisis, can we please go somewhere that doesn't feel like the center of the sun?"

We walked across the park toward Main Street and the few little air-conditioned shops with large shady awnings. As we passed the fountain, the light droplets of water misted my skin. I turned my face toward the fountain, hoping for some more euphoric spray, when a curtain of unnaturally white blonde hair fluttered in the distance. I stopped in my tracks.

"Hold on a second, Rachel," I said. She grumbled something about melting into the pavement, but I'd already closed the gap between me and the blonde girl sitting on the far side of the fountain.

"Hey, were you at the bonfire last night?" I asked, not sure where to start and clearly not having enough tact to bother figuring it out first.

Pixie snorted, making her nose ring jiggle. In the daylight, she looked even more unnatural. Spidery black lashes, ashen skin, and chipped black nail polish, but with clear green eyes bright and wide like a porcelain doll. Her parents must have been so proud, but I bet they didn't tell her where to go to college, either.

She glared up at me. "Uh, who are you?"

"Abby Marino." I extended my hand, but she simply looked at it like I hadn't washed it in a week and scowled. "I wanted to ask you about someone—Kellan Casey."

"Who?" She managed to make her irritated frown more irritated and added a scoff in case I didn't get the point.

"Kellan Casey. I saw you talking to him last night at the bonfire."

She flipped her hand up and picked at her fingernail polish. "I talk to a lot of people."

"Well, it looked like you two were arguing. You gave him your drink and then stormed off."

"Oh, yeah. That stupid jerk." She jumped to her feet and widened her stance. "And I didn't give him anything. He just took it. Slammed the whole thing, right in front of my face."

I took a step back, at least out of arm's reach. "I'm sorry that happened, but would you mind telling me what you were arguing about?"

"Wow, stalker. Are you like his girlfriend or something?" She lurched toward me and jabbed her finger in my face. "Because I'm not interested in your pathetic loser. I have a boyfriend and he could kick that guy's ass. If you don't watch yourself, he still might."

I took a few more steps back. This was probably a huge mistake, but I suddenly needed to know everything that happened last night. "No, I'm not his girlfriend ... or his stalker. I'm just a friend, and I wanted to make sure he didn't cause you any trouble. If he did, I'll make sure I tell him about it."

"Well, good. He deserves some wrath. No one tells me what to do and gets away with it."

"Absolutely." I nodded, hoping she'd warm up to me. If warm was even a temperature she did. "What did he tell you to do?"

"To stop being so mean and stop whining because life is short or some crap."

Interesting. At least it wasn't something disgusting that I actually would have to call him out for. Except what happened from him being a do-gooder to when he'd practically passed out in the woods?

"Did he say anything else? What was everyone doing before your fight? Did you see him any time later on?"

"Enough." She backed away, hands up. "Get the hell away from me. You're freaking me out."

"Just a few more questions." I stepped toward her, but she turned and bolted.

"Leave me alone," she yelled as she leapt over a low retaining wall and disappeared down the street, refusing to turn around.

Ugh. Too eager. I should've toned it down. I shook my head, exhaustion and confusion still clouding my better judgment. But did she know what had happened when those guys walked off into the bush? Except there was no way she was going to talk to me now.

Rachel came up beside me as I stared after Pixie. "You sure spooked Sasha. What was that about?"

"You know her?"

She shrugged. "Yeah. Sasha Dupre. Used to cheat off me in tenth grade chem. Why?"

"I saw her at the party last night and I wanted to ask her a few questions."

"What's with you and this party? Did something happen that you aren't telling me?"

"Nothing, Rach." I hung my head.

She placed her hands on my shoulders and maneuvered herself to stare me in the eyes. "I will find out if you're lying, you know."

I sighed. She'd better not find out.

When I didn't answer, she tugged me into an awkward hug, then pulled out her phone. "Want to hit a movie later? Parker just texted and told me to ask. Double date thing."

"Can't," I mumbled against her shoulder. "I have something I've been putting off that needs to get done."

CHAPTER FIFTEEN

KELLAN

I didn't know how long I'd been asleep, but way too long was probably a good guess. Everything in my room glowed red, the sun either rising or setting or maybe signaling the start of the apocalypse. The way things had been going, any of these were possible. A quick check of clenching fists and flexing toes gave me some relief that all of my parts were still intact, at least the majors anyway. I sat up and swallowed back the nausea from even trying to lift my head, my brain banging against the inside of my skull as punishment.

Faded pink streaks of smeared blood ran down my arms like someone had tried to scrub me clean but had given up halfway through the job. Two Tylenol and a glass of water sat on my nightstand. What the hell? Panic grabbed my chest and squeezed. Mom. If she had seen me this way, there were going to be questions. There should be questions. But how was I supposed to answer? I pushed through the pain and tried to remember what had happened. How I'd gotten home. How I'd gotten up the stairs. How I wasn't lying in a morgue somewhere. Fragments of images and garbled words meshed together into either memories or fevered dreams, my head still trying to figure out what was real and what wasn't. All that was left were flashes —the eerie shadow of the trees above me, the sound of screaming, and the wet sensation of the beast's blood on my hands.

I crept to the door, each step a delicate game of balance until my equilibrium started to even out. The lights glowed in the kitchen and a whistle from the kettle on the stove drifted up the stairs. I slid down the hall and into the bathroom. I pulled my T-shirt over my head, the fabric sticking to the splatters of dried blood still on my torso. Under my clothes, dark red splashed across my skin, like I'd been painting the devil's bedroom—naked. I showered quickly, the water helping the smoky, dirty smell of the other night slide off my body and down the drain on red-tinged soap bubbles. Best not to remind Mom how much of a disaster I was while she interrogated me about my screwed-up life.

Clean and prepared for the worst, I pounded down the stairs. My left foot ached, but the starving hunger pangs in my stomach hurt much worse. Maybe she would grant me a last meal. Otherwise, I might pass out again. I stopped short in the middle of the staircase. Voices. Happy voices. I scrunched up my face. But we never had company.

I checked myself over again then stepped into the kitchen all chill and casual. This might be the break I needed. Play nice then get out of the house before Mom had a chance to kill me.

"Morning, sleepyhead," Mom said as she picked up her teacup and put it to her lips. "Feeling any better?"

But I couldn't respond. All my words caught in my throat as I stared at Abby sitting across the table, running her manicured fingers over the handle of my late grandmother's ugly floral china.

"Your mom said you were sick, or at least that's what you told her yesterday when I came by to see you." Her lips curled into a smile, but her eyes shot sharp, icy daggers.

I rubbed the back of my head and squeezed my eyes tight. Yesterday? Was it possible that it was already Sunday? Vague blurs of my bedroom door shutting flashed through my mind. Did I talk to my mom yesterday? Must have. Mom would be super pissed right now if I hadn't.

"Yeah. I think I'm through the worst of it now," I said.

Mom grabbed the two teacups from the table and brought them to the sink.

"What are you doing here?" I mouthed to Abby, not letting any sound escape.

"I stopped by to see how you were doing and you were still asleep, but your mom was nice enough to invite me in. We were having a great chat before you came in." Abby lit up and gave Mom a wink. Her face flushed at the compliment, and she looked at the floor. Weird. Mom never had friends over and the phone hardly ever rang. Maybe she needed to get out more.

"It's no problem. It's nice to see you come around again. It's been a while," she looked at Abby but grinned at me.

No, Mom. Not what you think.

"Anytime, Mrs. Casey," Abby replied.

Mom walked over and ruffled my wet hair like I was eight. "Hopefully, you aren't contagious. I can't really sleep away a weekend like you anymore. Must be nice."

Abby chuckled, and I looked away. "Trust me, that wasn't the plan."

Mom slid past me. "I'm going to get some laundry done. I'll grab your sheets, but is there anything else you need washed? Get rid of all those germs."

My room. I spun around and put my hand on her arm. "No, Mom, you're busy enough without doing my laundry. Besides, I wouldn't want you to get sick too. I can toss them in later. Promise."

The lines around her eyes relaxed as she patted my hand with hers. "Love you, Kell."

I blushed.

"Okay, I won't bother you in front of your friend anymore." She started up the stairs while I stared at the wall, trying to force the embarrassment to drain out of my face.

"Nice talking to you, Mrs. Casey," Abby called after her, then she turned to look at me with a mischievous smirk. "Isn't that sweet?"

I shrugged. "So, my mom loves me. Big deal. You jealous?"

She cringed for a second, then looked away, straightening her skirt that already sat perfectly across her thighs.

I pulled out a chair and straddled it, putting my arms across the back. I was still far too dizzy to be standing for long periods of time. "What are you doing here?"

"Already told you, I came to check on you and your mom invited me in. Plus"—she lowered her voice—"I've been doing some digging and I have some information on your ... condition."

"Really?" Maybe I really was still drowsy. Or did she just say she'd help? "I figured you'd changed your mind?"

She shook her head and reached into her bag, pulling out a handful of printed pages.

"Not here. Too many ears." I whispered as I pointed at the ceiling. "Head up to my room. I'm going to grab something to eat, and I'll be right up."

Abby nodded and pulled her bookbag off the back of her chair. She marched toward the stairs, and I followed her long legs until they disappeared around the corner. I grabbed my head in my hands and let out a huge sigh. She actually wanted to help, and maybe she could piece together what happened since Friday night, as I had no idea where to start. A warm sting shot through my limbs as I thought about the possibility of ending this curse, but I pushed it down. I'd been disappointed too many times before to start getting optimistic now.

I pulled open the fridge. Oh, thank you, universe. Leftover pizza. I'd never been more excited to see those sauced pieces of cardboard in my life. If Mom had ordered it, it was probably some veggie, low-calorie, whole-grain crust or some crap, but right now I didn't even care. I piled a bunch of slices on a plate, popped them in the microwave, and grabbed a couple of bottles of water.

Leaning against the counter, I watched out the window as the last strip of sun slipped away behind the back fence. Two days. I'd lost two days to that beast. Two days I hadn't had to lose. I had no interest in seeing that thing again, but if I did, I swore I would rip it apart with my hands for what it had done to me. The microwave beeped and I balanced my feast, plus a bag of cookies I'd found hidden in the back of the pantry, as I walked up the stairs and backed into my room.

Abby had already made herself comfortable on the floor, or as comfortable as she could be on my scratchy gray carpet. Books spread out in haphazard piles around her as she lay on her stomach with her feet folded up and crossed in the air. I tore my stare away from the hem of her skirt that inched up the back of her thighs, nearly dropping the bag of cookies. She was the only girl who had ever been in my room before, but now it seemed different. She was different. No more skinned knees and pigtails. The way her tight, curvy body stretched out under her thin sundress would make every guy in the state drool. Except most guys wouldn't be facing a death sentence without her help.

I glanced over at the bed. A pile of red-stained towels sat in the middle of my blood-splattered sheets. I looked back at Abby on the floor. She stared back at me but said nothing. Did she clean me up last night? I shook my head and tossed the comforter over the mess, then sat down at the end of the mattress.

"Want a slice?" I asked.

She pushed up on her elbows. "No, I'm good. I'm sure you're starving."

"You're right. I am." I barely got the words out before shoving the slice in my mouth. So good. I could actually feel the food go down in my esophagus and land in my stomach. It almost hurt but in an enjoyable way.

"So ..." she said, dragging out the word as long and awkwardly as possible. "How are you doing? Really."

The pizza crust suddenly stuck to the sides of my throat. I swallowed. No better. She was giving me that look. A little sad. A little curious, but most of all, pitying. That was the last thing I wanted from her. From anyone. "Tired. Hungry. But otherwise, fine."

She raised an eyebrow and stared. "That's good. Because the last time I saw you, you were all passed out and bloody. You looked like a murder victim."

Every ache in my body twitched at her words, calling me out for lying. "Is that why you came here then? Come to see if I lived through the night?"

"Um, no. What I meant was—"

"Doesn't matter." I looked away and concentrated on the chipped paint where the ceiling met the edge of the wall. My leg began to tap, but I grabbed my thigh and dug in my fingers until it stopped. So, she was the one who had taken me home and put me to bed. The real reason Mom wasn't ripping my head off or calling the cops. She'd cared. Seen the worst I'd ever been and still came back. But people who cared only got hurt in my world. "Doesn't change anything."

"Then what am I even doing here?" she demanded.

My mouth wouldn't stop. I'd already let this go too far. It wasn't fair. "Not sure. Maybe you should just go."

She pulled up to her knees and slammed her books into a messy stack. "*Just go?* Seriously? This is how you're going to play it?" She shoved the books in her bag and rose to her feet. "No wonder I didn't believe all this. I tried to tell myself that you weren't that much of a sociopath to do something that evil, but maybe you are?"

I snapped my head from the paint and met her pouty glare. She'd crossed her arms over her chest and jutted her hip out at me, warning me to keep my distance. So, this was what it felt like to have a queen bee turn on you. Look out, unattractive and socially awkward freshmen. "Wait. You thought I made all this up? After everything I told you?" I lowered my voice. "Even after one of those things tried to rip you open like a microwave popcorn bag in my garage?"

Fear flashed in her eyes, but her stance didn't give an inch. "Obviously, I have to believe you now, but before Friday I convinced myself it was all a sick prank. You seem to have some rage-type issues, maybe you're sadistic too. Like a twisted gang initiation or something?"

"I'm in a gang now?"

She growled in a very un-girl-like way and stormed past me toward the door. Before I could stop myself, I grabbed her forearm. Her soft skin slid beneath my rough hand, and I immediately let go. She stopped, turning her head so her eyes could tear through me like knives. Cuts I so totally deserved.

"Do you honestly think I could do something like that? Why would I?"

"I don't know, Kellan. Boredom? Or maybe you weren't ... I don't know ... sober?"

"You mean, maybe I was high."

Her eyebrow arched as I clearly found the word she was looking for. "Maybe."

I shook my head. There it was. I knew people thought I was rude, stubborn, and maybe borderline psychotic, but never full-blown evil.

"I have no idea who you are anymore," she said. "I thought I did, and sometimes I see glimmers of who you used to be, but that's it. It's actually really sad."

"Well, if it makes you feel better. I couldn't get high if I wanted to. I've tried once or twice before, but every time I did, the Shadow Keeper came. So I stopped. Don't drink, either."

She lowered her crossed arms and didn't look like she was going to bolt anymore. "But you were drinking Friday night."

"No, I ..." Bits and pieces of Friday settled to the surface of my consciousness. "Yeah, I did have one beer. Some girl gave it to me."

"Yeah, I saw that. Real classy."

I rubbed my hands over my face, already exhausted from defending myself. At least when this mess had been a secret, I'd only had to argue with my own conscience. "Hey, can you stick to judging me for one thing at a time, please? I really don't know what happened. One minute I was fine, then the next, everything got all screwed up. I couldn't see straight; my head was cloudy. Nothing made sense."

Her hard squint relaxed and she sat down on the bed beside me, the mattress barely shifting from her weight. "If you aren't an addict, then why would you let people think of you that way?"

I shrugged. "Easier than the truth. Now, what did you come over here to show me?"

She leaned forward and rummaged through her bag, giving me a chance to catch my breath. What was I doing? Was it even possible for me to carry on a conversation anymore without sounding like a total dick? Abby's elbow reared back and knocked my leg, bringing me out of my head. Her long hair fell in waves over her bare shoulders, exposing that little splat-shaped birthmark that had looked so much bigger when her shoulders had been smaller. I fought the urge to poke at it when she flipped back up, covering it again.

She laid a piece of paper on her lap and smoothed it with her hand.

"A Shadow Keeper is an offshoot of the supernatural species called a wraith, which means *ghost* or *apparition* in Scottish folklore. Wraiths are sometimes considered to be an omen and are usually only seen by people who are—"

"Near-death or dying."

Her eyes widened and fixed on me like I'd just spouted the secrets of the universe.

I continued. "Wraiths are also common in Irish and Welsh folklore but known under different names. Wraiths feed off the energy of human beings until finally collecting their souls and are deemed to be harbingers of imminent death. Some reports claim that individuals often see wraiths of their own likeness. Other versions of a wraith include the Irish Banshee and British Co-Walker. There are no known ways to destroy a wraith. Yep, already got the basics."

She scanned her page, probably making sure I hadn't missed some random fact, but she wasn't going to find any. I'd read that passage more times than I could count.

"Yep," I said, "that's not much further than I've found either."

"Okay. Then what do you suggest we do? You already said there's no known way to destroy a wraith, so what are we supposed to do?"

"If I knew, I wouldn't still be cursed right now, would I?"

She shook her head and swallowed the words it was so

obvious she wanted to spew. "Then why don't you try talking to your ex? You said she knew all about this stuff. Maybe she knows a way out."

"No way. Not doing it." I put the plate of pizza on the ground and started to pace. Just thinking about seeing Rhiann made the walls close in on me.

"Why not? It might be your only chance."

"I doubt it. If she knew another way out, I'm sure she would have taken it. Besides, I don't know where to find her, and even if I did, if she could have helped, she would have already." Or at least I hoped she would have.

"Are you sure? From what you've told me, she's not a really nice person."

"Hey, you don't know what happened between us. And besides, you won't find her."

"Why? Did she break your heart?" she mocked in a sing-songy voice.

"You know what? That's enough. I don't need this right now. You already said you have no idea who I am anymore and maybe you should keep it that way. I shouldn't have asked for your help. I should've just shut that window and kept you out of my life."

She crossed her arms and stared through me. This was the moment she was supposed to run out and tell her girlfriends that the world was right about me. I was mean and rude and a waste of skin. But she didn't. She just kept staring and making me uneasy.

"If you're waiting for an apology, you're wasting your time," I said, her stare still rattling me so that I started pacing again.

"Drop the tough act. You suck at it." It came out flat and direct and matter-of-fact. This wasn't a comeback; it was a command.

"Not an act, Abby."

"Really? Because right now, you have the same look as when you bailed on your skateboard outside my house and ripped open your entire leg. I tried to help, but you just got mad and then hid in your backyard and cried like a baby."

"I did not cry."

"Yeah, you did. And you've got that same pained look right now because you know you need help, but you're too stubborn to take it."

I put on my meanest face and stepped forward, using my few inches of extra height to maximum impact. "Stop trying to make me into some helpless loser. You don't know shit about what I need."

She closed the gap between us and glared up at me, refusing to back down as I'd planned. "You need help. Admit it. This thing has gotten too big for you and your lousy attitude to handle, and for some reason, the fates picked me to do you a favor. So, can you please get yourself in check before I walk out of here and let you die alone?"

"I don't want to die." The words came out in a rush before I could stop them. Angry. Harsh. Terrifyingly true. We stared at each other, both on edge and short of breath as red anger crept up her neck and her chest heaved without enough oxygen.

Then in a whisper I could barely hear, she breathed, "Then don't."

A knock rapped on the door, breaking the stalemate.

"Is everything okay in there? I thought I heard yelling."

I looked at Abby, and she shrugged.

"No, Mom, everything's fine," I called.

"Okay." It was an agreement but sounded uncertain. "Maybe Abby should come back tomorrow. It's getting kind of late."

"Sure thing, Mrs. Casey," Abby said to the closed door, a weird smile rippling across her lips.

"And, Kellan, next time, please leave the door open."

Abby slapped her hand across her mouth and choked on a chuckle, so only a sharp, snorting sound came out.

I couldn't help myself from laughing. "She probably thinks you're a bad influence."

"Uh-huh," she said, fighting back giggles. "I should probably go anyway."

She sat down and slid her piece of paper back into her bag, except now it was a wreck after having folded it and crushed it in her fist.

I sat down beside her and rubbed my palms across my flannel-covered thighs. "Did she talk about my dad much?"

Her face scrunched with confusion for a second, but she caught on without needing a prompt. "A few times, but not too much. She seems to be doing okay, all things considered."

"It's going to break her when I'm gone, isn't it?"

She didn't answer, only leaned over and pushed her shoulder into mine, then scooped up her bag and headed toward the door.

Something started to rise in my throat. I should say something to her. Anything. "Thanks for getting me home on Friday. I don't know what would've happened if you'd left me out there."

She nodded and kept walking. At the door, she stopped, her hand hovering over the doorknob, then she slowly turned around. "And by the way, you were roofied. Your buddy Chad slipped it in that girl's drink you stole. Probably saved her from a monster that night too."

Then she disappeared out the door, leaving me in the middle of my bloody mess.

CHAPTER SIXTEEN

Abby

The crimson red mark burned across the page. So bright, it almost glowed, as if to try to leap out and brand my skin. An 'F'? Really? The test was tough, but I didn't think I had done that terribly. But here was the truth in standard issue Bic red pen. I'd failed.

I tossed the test inside my locker, concealing it inside the cover of my calculus textbook. I didn't know whom I was hiding it from, maybe just myself, but either way, I couldn't stand to look at it anymore. I'd failed. I never failed.

"Hey." A deep, unsure voice rumbled from the other side of my locker door. I closed it to see Marcus leaning against the locker bank, his head down and clipping and unclipping the clasp on his oversized white watch.

"Hey." I crossed my arms at my waist as if I were trying to hold myself up or worse—hold myself together. I knew I wouldn't be able to hide from Marcus forever, but the thought didn't make this moment any easier.

"So, you're alive," he said, his gaze still locked on his wrist. "I've been calling and texting all weekend, but you haven't said more than two words to me since Friday."

"Sorry. I was busy." A wave of nausea started building in my stomach, its grip drifting toward my chest.

"I even stopped by your house last night so I could talk to you before school, but you weren't there. Your parents didn't even know where you were."

"Like I said, I was busy. I planned on calling you back, but the weekend went by too fast, I guess."

"Are you sure?" His brow went into a deep furrow as he dared to look up and stare at me, his brown eyes changing to a nearly full-on black. "I thought maybe you might want to talk about that hissy fit you threw at the bonfire? Or maybe why you made me drag your burnout neighbor up his own stairs and leave you to take care of his sorry ass? What's up with that?"

"Hissy fit? I didn't throw a hissy fit. You weren't listening to me."

"That's the part you pick up on? Not the fact that you picked up a stray so strung out that he couldn't even stand? My dad is the sheriff. What if it gets out that I helped him? And where did all that blood come from? It was all over me. It wrecked my favorite shirt."

"Then I'll buy you a new shirt."

"That's not the point." He wrapped his arms around me, linking his fingers and pressing them against my lower back. Part of me cringed and wanted to push him away, but the other part stared into his eyes as he pressed his forehead against mine and I just couldn't.

"You know I love you, Abby, but something's going on and I just want to know what it is. And you not talking to me—you not talking at all—isn't like you, and it makes me worry."

I let out a breath, the tension in my body going with it. The warmth of his chest near me was enough to give me some calm. For what I'd been through the past few days, I wanted to rest my head on his shoulder and stay there for the rest of the week. "I'm not trying to make you upset. I'm just dealing with a bunch of stuff right now."

"Tell me about it, then."

I bit my lip hard enough to make it hurt. "I can't."

His grip slackened. "What am I supposed to do with that? *I can't.* Are you even okay?" He stopped and took a sharp intake of breath. "Are *we* okay?"

I watched his face. The concern across his cheeks. The slight quiver of his lip. The problem was part of me was still mad at him. I hadn't had time to really think about our fight, but now that he'd brought it back up, the feelings came over me in a flood—and they weren't pleasant. But they were going to have to wait. Right now, I needed to not be failing calculus and finding a way to keep Kellan from an early grave. Arguing with Marcus wasn't a good use of my time or energy. I swallowed hard. "We're good."

The worry drained from his face, and he yanked me closer.

"Good," he whispered, then lightly kissed the top of my head, the heaviness around his eyes seeming to lift.

I placed a hand on his chest and did my best to turn my anxious lips into a smile. "Can I get you to do me a favor?"

"Sure."

He gave me a suspicious look, which I probably deserved. This was the worst time to be asking for this, but time wasn't something Kellan had much of anymore.

"Remember when you got your dad to look up that guy who did a hit-and-run on my dad's car?"

"Yeah, but I thought all that was settled?"

I reached over his arm into my locker and tore a strip of paper from my notebook and wrote down a name. "Can you get your dad to look into this girl?" I slipped the small scrap of paper into his hand and took my time pulling away, allowing our hands to remain together for a few moments longer than necessary. "I just need an address or a current job or something. I can take it from there."

"Why?"

"I need to talk to her. It's a surprise for a friend."

"You aren't going to do something stupid, are you? My dad isn't going to go along with this if something bad is going to happen."

"It'll be fine. I swear."

He raised an eyebrow at me.

"Is this about that guy who lives next door?

"No, of course not," I lied. A sharp pain jabbed my chest. Maybe after we got Kellan out of this mess, I could tell Marcus the truth, just not yet. It would be too dangerous of a secret if it got out now.

"Okay."

He took the slip of paper and put it into his back pocket. The look on his face didn't reassure me that he actually believed me, but at least he hadn't said *no*.

"And, Abby, I really don't like you being around that neighbor guy. He's obviously got problems and I don't want you getting caught up in all that. I don't think your parents would want you around him, either."

"I told you. I'm tutoring him. That's it."

"Well, he must be failing pretty badly to get that much attention from you this weekend."

"He is. He's basically dead if I don't help him."

"Whatever. Just promise me that you'll stay out of his business. Okay?" He put his hand on my cheek and I leaned into it, closing my eyes for a second and letting the warmth of his skin seep into mine.

"Sure. But you have nothing to worry about."

The bell rang and people started to shuffle out of the hallway.

I turned toward my locker to grab my books. "I'll talk to you later."

"Wait a second." His arm extended across my stomach, his hand clutching onto my side and pulling me back to him. "Is that it?"

I looked at him, confused. "We have to get to class, Marcus."

His lips grazed my ear and headed toward my mouth. "Besides, if that guy tries anything, I can make his life hell."

I yanked my head back, Marcus's head bobbing clumsily through the air as his lips missed their mark. "Did you just threaten him?"

"No. I'm just saying that if anything happened, I would look out for you, that's all."

"I don't need your protection. Kellan's not dangerous."

He sandwiched his hands on the sides of my face. "Relax." He lunged forward to kiss me again.

"Don't." I put my hands on his arms and tried to wriggle out of his grip.

He gripped me tighter. "What's going on, Abby? Why are you so upset?"

"I'm serious, Marcus. Let me go."

"Not until we work this out. I need to know what's going on with you. Whatever it is, it's been making you mad at me."

"*You're* making me mad at you."

He pulled me close again. "Then what is it? Tell me what happened Friday night."

"I can't. I have class. Just let me go."

"No. I don't care."

"I *said*, let go." I slammed the heels of my hands into his shoulders and pushed harder than either he or I was expecting because he flew back against the locker bank with a loud crash. The shocked look on his face matched the feeling in my stomach.

"I'm sorry, I—"

"What exactly is going on here?" a stern voice bellowed.

I twisted my head to see Mr. Joffrey standing inches from us.

"Nothing," I said, putting on my best good-girl voice and smile.

"That's not what it looks like to me, Miss Marino. We do not tolerate any form of violence between students here."

"But you don't understand. I—"

He raised an open palm and looked away. "I don't want to hear excuses. One day of detention should be enough to be the end of this."

"Mr. Joffrey, it really was nothing. I swear." Marcus jumped in, his hands moving through the air like he was conducting an orchestra.

"Don't try to talk me out of this. I know what I saw, Mr. Diaz. Would you care to tell me that my own eyes have deceived me?"

"No, sir." Marcus hung his head.

"Good, because I could have you join Miss Marino in detention if that's what you want."

"No, sir," he repeated.

"Then I suggest you get to class, Mr. Diaz."

Marcus looked over at me and held my gaze as he walked away, his eyes wide and apologetic. However, I had little use for his apologies right now.

"Four o'clock, Miss Marino. Now get to class and try to keep your hands to yourself in the future."

Mr. Joffrey straightened his tie and gave me one last whittling glance before he walked away. I sunk back against my locker. Detention. Really? I'd been in school for twelve years and never once had I ever been in detention. It was Marcus's fault. If he'd just let me go like I'd asked, I wouldn't have had to push him away. And clearly, Mr. Joffrey needed his eyes checked if he missed Marcus with his hands all over me. Or maybe he had seen and just chosen to ignore it. Either way, this was so not fair.

My veins bubbled with anger, but I wasn't sure if it was directed at Marcus—or myself for getting into this mess. I looked up. Across the hall hung a bright pink-and-green poster with a picture of me and Marcus smiling at the homecoming game, the words "King and Queen?" in regal script across the top. Good question. I looked down the empty hallway, ripped down the poster, and tossed the crumpled sheet into the trash can.

CHAPTER SEVENTEEN

KELLAN

My brain hammered against the inside of my skull in slow, constant pulses. Whatever sketchy pharmaceutical I'd been on Friday night was taking its time letting go of me—as if it hadn't already caused enough damage. The other things rolling around in my head were my own words: *I don't want to die.* It wasn't any sort of revelation—no one really ever wants to die—but for some reason, saying it out loud made it real. Like it was a choice instead of an inevitability.

As I pulled open the library door, I looked back to make sure no one had seen me. Not like anyone would care if they had, but I felt like I needed to keep my secrets truly secret all of a sudden. Too many people were getting involved in my life. Besides, if anyone saw Kellan Casey in a library, they would assume something was up. Something that probably involved dime bags or arson. I jutted out my chin at the librarian in a silent, *What's up?* She didn't respond, only followed me across the room with her laser-like eyes. Probably didn't know if I was even a student here, let alone who I was.

I snaked through the stacks toward a small table at the back of the library where Lasers couldn't watch me. Beside me, a large window looked out at the brick wall that ran around the back of the school. It kept out the nosy student bodies, but it was a really terrible view. Someone had sure been on their game when they'd designed this disaster of a building.

One last paranoid look around and my shoulders started to relax. Alone. I pulled a file folder out of my bag and set it on the table. The edges of the manila cardstock were frayed from being handled and a stack of papers and faded piss-colored Post-it notes stuck out past the edges. This thing had been jammed in my desk drawer for over six months, and I honestly thought I was never going to think about it again. But right now, it was all I had.

I flipped through the pages. Every ad I'd ever seen for every type of magic cure on the market. Scam after scam after scam. A complete waste of my time and money. There were pages and pages of notes. Every Shadow Keeper reference or sighting I could find, but not one word about how to get rid of one. Buried in there was likely a printed copy of the same sheet Abby had brought over last night. Maybe two. Then I found it. A sheet of paper with a jagged edge from where I'd ripped it out of the newspaper. There were plenty of psychics and mediums listed in there, but this one was different. Rhiann had mentioned this one before. She'd said she'd take me there one time if I wanted to try to talk to my dad because this lady was the real deal. I'd never gone.

The ad was hideous. A hokey crystal ball and what looked like smoke making up the phone number. Hopefully, she was a better medium than a graphic designer. Otherwise, I was screwed.

I dialed the number, my thumb hovering over the call button, when a sick sense of déjà vu clamped around my chest, making me wheeze like an old man. I'd been here before. Held this ad in one hand and my phone in the shaky fingers of the other. But last time, before I could dial, the phone had rung. The hospital. Mom had been in the emergency room. She'd passed out at work, and they didn't know what was wrong.

The hospital bills didn't help. I'd picked up every side job I could to help make that easier on her. She'd told me I didn't have to, but at least I could do something right by her. At least for once, I could be more than a total failure.

Eventually, she'd gotten better. And I had gotten worse. The visions had changed into inter-dimensional brawls. The discomfort was now searing, writhing pain. It was already too late, and I'd wasted so much time chasing after a solution that was never going to come. Wasted so much of the short life I had left. This ad had sat in this folder ever since. Until now.

I sucked in all the air my lungs could take and held it while I clicked the button and listened to the ringing. For all I knew, this place didn't even exist anymore. Maybe she'd packed up and left town. Joined the circus or something. This was stupid. I should just hang up. Then the ringing stopped.

"Madame Trumaine's House of Mystic." Her voice carried a deep drawl, almost too deep to be a real voice. I hadn't even talked to the woman and she already sounded like a complete fraud.

I considered hanging up, but instead, I sighed. "Can I speak with Madame Trumaine?"

"Madame speaking."

Great, so this hack was the all-powerful one. Fantastic.

"Do you have any openings this week?" I slapped my face in my hand while I said the words, knowing I'd probably regret this later.

"Hmm, let me see here. I'm free every night but Thursday. What were you thinking?"

A not-busy psychic? Red flag.

"So, you are free today then?"

"Of course. I'll pencil you in. Arrive ten minutes before your scheduled time. Services are three hundred dollars to start, cash preferred. Group reading and exorcisms extra."

"Three hundred dollars? That's ridiculous!"

"I'm good at what I do, young man. You want answers, I can provide. It's up to you. How badly you want to know?"

Three hundred. That was half the cash I had saved up for brake pads on the Nova. If I spent it, there was no way I was ever going to finish it. But if I didn't, I might not live long enough to finish it at all.

"Fine. What time?"

"Now, let's see ... Depends what you need to know. May I ask what your query is for the spirit guides?"

I glanced around the library. Still no one around, but I lowered my voice anyway and whispered into the phone. "Shadow Keepers."

"I'm sorry, what? Madame can hear the dead, but they sure as Hades speak louder than you, pet."

I leaned into the phone and spoke louder. "Shadow Keepers. I want to know about getting rid of a Shadow Keeper."

A heavy gasp came across the line and Madame's put-on accent fell away. "I'm sorry, but I don't know anything about that. Find someone else."

"Wait, wait, wait," I said, fully expecting her to hang up. "Are you sure you don't know anything? I really need your help. Please."

Silence. Then a sigh. "I feel for you, pet, I really do, but I know far better than to mess with those creatures."

"But you're the only lead I have. You have to help me."

"No. I. Don't." Then a click and a dial tone.

I slammed my phone down on the desk with a groan. Useless. I'd waited all this time to call just to find someone who knew something but still refused to help me. I grabbed the ad and shredded it into confetti.

The final bell rang. Great. Detention time, just when I wanted to wallow in my misery for a few more minutes. I jammed the folder back in my bag and walked out, Madame Trumaine and another hopeless lead still in pieces on the table.

❧❤☙

DETENTION WAS PACKED. Joffrey must have had a particularly large stick up his rectum today for this kind of crowd. Probably that time of the month.

My usual desk was taken, some newbie not knowing the laws of the jungle yet. I had no problem teaching them in my own unique and aggressive kind of way, but before I got the chance to put a divine fear into the pimply-faced sophomore, I spotted a ripple of blonde waves face down in a notebook next to an empty desk.

I walked across the room and smashed my bag down on the desktop, making Abby jump, but not enough to turn her attention away from her notes.

"You. In detention? I never thought I would see that."

"I don't want to talk about it," she said, still scribbling like a heretic writing her manifesto.

Mrs. Krull, the patron saint of detention, clapped her wrinkled hands until the noise of voices settled.

"Take your seats. You are all here for one hour. No talking, no sleeping, and no horseplay ..."

My mind drifted to the thought of horses playing football like it always did while Mrs. Krull finished her riot act and sat down behind her rickety wooden desk at the front of the room.

Okay. Sixty minutes to go. My gaze wandered around the room until it rested back on Abby. It was the first time I'd seen her today. The first time since she'd called me out to my face and lived to tell about it. Except Abby hadn't told. She'd promised she wouldn't and for some reason, I believed her.

I looked over to see her notes. Numbers and symbols were scrawled all over the page in smudgy charcoal.

I leaned over and whispered. "That one's not right."

She glared up at me. "What did you say?"

"Number three isn't right. It's minus one, not plus one."

She scanned the page and let out a *harumph* noise as she pulled a well-worn eraser from her fist and erased the equation so hard, she ripped right through to the cover, eraser bits flying through the air. "How is it that I can't get this and you can?"

"I'm good at calculus."

"Obviously." Her tone was sharp and pointed to match the look in her narrowed eyes.

"No talking!" shouted the Krull.

"Sorry, Mrs. Krull. Abby is just helping me with my homework."

She sighed. "That's fine. Just keep it down."

"Maybe it would be best if we moved to the library," I suggested. "It would be less disruptive."

She looked me over and then turned her attention to Abby, a smile starting to appear as her eyes shifted. "Do you think you can manage to stay out of trouble, Miss Marino?"

Her face started to burn a dishonest shade of red.

"We'll check back in an hour," I said, jumping out of my chair. A murmur started to rise in the room. Time to escape before the rest of the inmates got hostile.

I gathered up my books and nodded at Abby to do the same. She stared back at me with a blank, humiliated look. It wasn't like we were stealing a car or something. She really needed to lighten up.

"Let's go," I whispered.

She started moving with a jolt, like the thought had finally settled into her brain and sprung her to action.

My fingertips found the small of her back and nudged her forward through the crowd, other students already shooting their hands in the air to negotiate their own release. With one last sinister sneer at the sophomore desk thief, I pushed through the door and rescued us both out of purgatory.

"What did you just do?" Abby asked the second the door clicked shut behind me.

"Would you rather sit in there for the whole time? The warden's sick of me and everyone trusts you, so I saw an opportunity and I took it."

She gave me an uneasy smirk then sped through the empty corridors to the library, which was the last place I wanted to be.

She pulled open the door.

"Nope. This way." I kept walking and took a sharp left down a small, dead-end corridor.

"Where are you going? You told Mrs. Krull that we were going to the library. Aren't we both in enough trouble?"

"We're already in detention. Besides, Krull was reading one of her smutty romance novels again. She's not going to check up on us. As long as we come back before time's up, she'll never notice or care."

Abby glanced back down the hallway and slowly let go of the library door. "Are you sure?"

I didn't answer and kept on down the hall toward a bright yellow door. Abby followed behind, her hurried steps giving away her nervousness without me needing to turn around and check. But at least she came along.

Pulling my student card out of my back pocket, I slid it into the doorjamb, popping the lock open. I held open the door. "Right this way."

She rolled her eyes at me but didn't fight. Her disapproval

was obvious in her heavy stomps into the stairwell and up the dark staircase. I closed the door slowly, peeking out to take one last check that we weren't seen. Not that I really cared, but I didn't want to go back to the stuffy classroom under the eagle-eye surveillance of the Krull.

"I didn't think you could actually pick a lock with a credit card," she said as she plodded up the stairs. "I thought it was just something you saw in the movies."

"They had to get the idea from somewhere, and it doesn't work on most doors, but interior ones like schools and offices work pretty well. Less concern about security."

"I guess they weren't expecting *you*, then."

"Someone as awesome as me only comes around once in a while. You can't expect everyone to be ready."

She made a little snort noise from holding back her laugh, immediately slapping her hand over her mouth.

"Cute. Really."

"Oh, shut up." She stopped at the top of the stairs and waited for me, the only way out was either back down or through the closed door to her left.

"Go ahead." I waved her on like she was an eight-year-old forced to give her ancient grandmother a kiss.

She glared at me, her eyes wide, but she still pushed open the door, the warm breeze of freedom flooding in.

CHAPTER EIGHTEEN

Abby

I didn't know what I'd expected to find behind the door, but my shoulders sank when I realized it was the roof. At first, the black tar and concrete reflecting the scorching rays of the sun convinced me that maybe we had entered one of the lower circles of hell, but if it were hell, we would have gone down the stairs instead of up. However, from what I'd seen over the last few weeks, hell could find you wherever you were.

"Welcome to the prison yard," Kellan said as he brushed past me, his arms wide and drinking in the sunshine. In his black-on-black uniform and with the wicked smile that had broken across his lips, I could swear he was beckoning some sort of sun god for an evil plan. I shook my head. Clearly, I needed to get a better grip on reality. My brain was starting to jump to implausible conclusions. But he *had* said he'd dated a witch, hadn't he?

"And this sauna is better than the air-conditioned library?" I asked.

"Dumb question." He scowled and headed over to the edge of the building, leaning so far over, I no longer saw his head.

My stomach dropped into my shoes, and I reached out like I

could actually do anything from this far away. "Get away from there."

He pulled himself up and looked back at me, one eyebrow hiked higher than the other. Instead of backing away—the sensible thing to do—he grinned and hoisted his body on top of the ledge, standing like a statue over the courtyard.

I took a few steps forward. With every inch, I could see more and more of the ground sprawling out in front of me. The hard, unforgiving ground that would shatter every bone in his body if he made one wrong move.

"Are you trying to break your neck?" Dizziness clouded my head. I closed my eyes, but not seeing seemed to make things worse.

"What's your deal? There's a whole sidewalk up here before I'm even close to the edge. Or should I go closer?"

He took a step.

"No, no, no, don't." I braced myself with my hands, still several feet away from the edge, but far closer than I wanted to be. "I get the point. It's a great view. You're a huge rebel. Point taken. Now can you get down?"

He frowned. "Fine."

I exhaled and backed away.

He started walking toward me, but then stopped sharp and spun around on one foot, wavering toward the edge. "Whoa. Whoa."

"Kellan!"

I lunged forward. He laughed, straightening himself out then jumping with a thud beside me on the roof.

Crossing my arms, I turned away. "Not funny."

"Depends on what you find funny." He dropped to the ground and leaned his back against the waist-high wall beneath the ledge. He grabbed my elbow and yanked me down beside him. My heart beat too fast in my chest, but my skin reveled in the only rectangle of shade on the entire rooftop. I looked up, trying not to be obvious. Still a foot or so of the wall above my head. Good.

Kellan didn't say anything for a while, his eyes running over me as if I were suddenly a foreign object in his world. I straightened my skirt and adjusted the straps on my top, then clamped my arms tightly across my chest. "That was a really stupid thing to do."

His face twisted, the right side of his mouth jerking upward to match his crooked eyebrow. "Since when? I figured I'd have had to drag you down from that ledge at the end of the hour."

I laughed, the sound coming out unexpected and unnatural. "I don't really do heights."

"Said the girl who jumped off my tree house in third grade to see if she could fly. Besides, didn't you scale the side of my house and try to climb in my window just a few weeks ago?"

"Trust me. I didn't want to." I shifted in my spot, the gravelly rooftop digging into my butt. "But it was dark, and your roof is super wide, so I didn't have to see the ground."

"Weird," he said, then ran his hand over the back of his neck as if the thought that his memory didn't match the current reality was somewhat painful. "Did you want to go back down then?"

I looked around. No place to hide if we got caught—just us, the sun, and the sky. "No, I think I'm good."

Kellan settled back against the wall and closed his eyes. "I'm sorry, by the way."

"Don't worry about it. You didn't know I was afraid of heights."

"No, not that. I'm sorry for being a pain in the ass yesterday. That wasn't really fair."

"Oh," I said, happy that he still had his eyes closed, so he wouldn't see the confused look on my face. "Thanks?"

He didn't respond, instead sat completely still, letting the afternoon wash over him. I sat back too, suddenly being able to hear the birds chirping in the trees and the far-off rumble of cars driving down Scott Street past the front of the school. My skin prickled under the heat from the sun, but every now and then, a light breeze would blow by, giving me a chance to catch my breath and fill my nose with the clean smell of Kellan instead of the thick, greasy tar stench that hung in the air.

"What happened to us?" I asked after what felt like hours of silence. "We used to talk about everything. All the time."

"I think I found baseball, and you found friends that were way cooler than me."

"You mean my parents found them. Meet the right people, go to the right birthday parties, and all of a sudden, you're social elite."

"Sounds horrible." He shoved his shoulder into mine and nearly tipped me over. His lips twitched like he was purposefully trying not to smile. "That's why you're going to be prom queen and all that high school rah-rah crap."

"Yep. Maybe that's what they'll write on my tombstone—she was really popular."

"Please. As if you don't love being the center of attention."

"I'm about as much prom queen material as you are back-alley junkie material. And it's not as easy as it looks ... Oh, never mind. It's stupid."

He didn't push. Even though I think I kind of wanted him to. I had never heard these words come out of my mouth before, probably because if it were anyone else with me on this rooftop, they would laugh in my face. But he didn't, and for that, I was grateful.

"So, I guess we both voided the contract, then."

"The contract?" He looked at me, completely confused, but

I only smiled right back, wondering how long it would take before my words clicked somewhere in his memory.

Realization dawned on his face. "That stupid friend contract. You poked me so hard with that stupid needle, it kept opening up and bleeding for a week afterward. Who seals a contract in blood anyway?"

I laughed. "I always saw red seals on contracts in cartoons. How was I supposed to know that it was wax? Besides, it was just a sewing pin. Shouldn't you have gotten over that by now?"

"That wasn't a pin. It was a railway spike, and you had no idea what you were doing."

"You know, for a tough guy, you're a pretty big wuss."

He made a face.

"How did it go again?" I asked. "Something like I, Abigail Jane Marino, pledge my mind, heart, and soul to my bestest friend ever and for all eternity. Then something, something if I fail our friendship, then I promise for my eyes to be eaten out by garter snakes and then something about giving up all my My Little Ponies."

"It's better than mine. I had to give up my Hot Wheels. I had hundreds of those things."

"We were strange kids, weren't we?"

"Not strange, just a little messed up."

"I guess not much has changed then, has it?"

The humor disappeared from his face. "Now the stakes are just higher."

"We'll figure that out. I've already started following up on a few leads."

He nodded. "After we get out of here, I'm going to go see this woman. She's a medium. Madame Trumaine. Maybe she can help me out."

"Madame Trumaine? Are you serious?"

"I know. She sounds like the world's biggest hack." He

stared down at his hands. "But Rhiann knew her. She said she was the real deal."

"How come you never went to her before? Why only now?"

He shrugged. The ghost of something traveled through his gaze, but he shook it off and pulled out a put-on smile. "Some annoying chick keeps telling me that there's a way out and I need to prove her wrong."

I tried to look intimidating, but I knew it wasn't working. "It'll be fun. I've never seen a medium before."

"Oh." He stopped, his gaze dropping into his lap. "You want to come?"

"I thought you were asking ... but I guess you never ..." I shook my head and turned away, the weather suddenly hotter and ten times more stifling. "Never mind."

"I guess you can come if you really want to."

"No, it's okay. I should probably get home—"

"Abby." He put his hand on my shoulder and a shiver ran down my back at the unexpected gesture. "Would you please come with me?"

"Sure," I mumbled, still not ready to turn around, his hand still resting against my flesh.

"All right, then. Time to go." He pushed himself to his feet with an amazing amount of grace for being crouched so low to the ground and started walking toward the door to the stairwell. I jumped up and followed behind, trying to silence the alarm bells screaming in my head.

CHAPTER NINETEEN

KELLAN

"You knock."

Abby's glare burned through my skull, and I swore she might strike out and throttle me Mortal Kombat-style.

"It's a door," I said. "It's not going to bite you for knocking."

Except that maybe this one would. The grubby sign that told us we were at the right house could easily have been replaced with a demolition notice and it wouldn't have looked out of place. Patchy dead grass ran away from the crooked broken walkway that led to a front step with one railing hanging off into an overgrown shrub. Eavestroughs were missing. Paint was peeling. Someone was either prepping for Halloween early or just didn't care.

She let out a heavy sigh and rolled her eyes, but she rapped her fist against the door instead of around my neck.

No answer.

"Maybe she's not here."

"Someone's definitely here. The piece-of-junk Cavalier in the driveway was warm when we walked by. Try again."

"Fine."

The door creaked open, and a tall, frizzy-haired woman appeared. Long, lanky arms and legs flailed out from her thin body like bendy straws taped together to make a person under a shapeless green tunic.

"Welcome to Madame Trumaine's. Seer of spirits, mystic guide to the future." It came across so flat, I wondered how she had any customers at all. Maybe that was why the place looked like a dump.

"We have an appointment," Abby said cheerfully to the train wreck of a greeter, but she stared back at me.

"No appointments scheduled for today, miss."

Abby shrugged.

I stepped closer. "Not exactly an appointment, more like—"

"That voice." She pushed around Abby and waggled a finger in my face, her armful of bracelets jangling. "I know that voice. You're the one who called asking about Shadow Keepers."

I nodded. Not exactly psychic stuff, but at least her hearing wasn't going.

"Oh, no. I said I don't want to talk about those creatures. Good day." She backed up and tried to push the door shut, but I plunged my arm between the frame and the door and pushed back. She pressed harder, trying to crush my forearm. I shoved my shoulder against the door and as it flung open, I crowded in, an obviously irritated and confused Abby ahead of me.

I closed the door behind me, locking us all in the front room. "I know you said you don't want to talk about them, but I really need you to reconsider. This is kind of life-or-death."

"Yours?" Madame Trumaine said with a cheerful smirk. "Get bent. Besides, the world might be a better place without your Neanderthal attitude."

She turned and flicked her fingers over her shoulder, then vanished behind a curtain toward the back of the house.

"Nice, Kellan. Do you always charge into places uninvited?" Abby hissed, her raspy whisper sounding too much like a younger version of one of those troll-like teachers at school.

I shrugged. "We're in, aren't we?"

I charged toward the curtain, but Abby yanked on my arm before I could pull it back.

"Maybe you could tone down the hostility if you actually want her to help you."

I scoffed. She glared with her hands on her hips and standing in my way.

"Okay," I agreed.

She held the nasty look but stepped aside. Behind the curtain was a cramped, disorganized kitchen. Madame Trumaine stood at the counter dunking a tea bag in an empty cup, a kettle spewing steam beside her.

"Shouldn't you have left by now?" she said.

"Look, I know you said you didn't want to see me, but if there's anything you can do, you have to help me."

Abby's elbow slammed hard against my ribs.

"Please," I added.

Madame rested her hands on the edge of the counter and lowered her head toward the floor. Her nails clicked as she drummed them on the Arborite, and a frustrated sigh mixed with the bubble of the boiling water in the kettle.

"How dare you barge into my office—my home—and tell me that I have to do anything?"

"I'm sorry about that, but I don't have anywhere else to turn right now," I pleaded.

"Of course, you don't. There aren't many people who even know what a Shadow Keeper is, and if they do, they don't want to." She turned around. "Besides, you haven't told me what you are yet? Maybe I shouldn't help you."

"Huh?" The sound came out of both me and Abby in unison, like we shared a brain.

"Shadow Keepers don't terrorize just anyone. What kind of magic are you?"

"I'm not." I glanced down at my hands. Nothing out of the ordinary. Like every other day. "I'm just ... I don't know ... human."

"Well, that's unimpressive." Her face contorted into a wrinkly, disgusted state, hideous enough that I had to stop myself from defending my normalcy. "Then who or what did you anger, kid?"

"A witch." Abby stepped between us. "Rhiann Glenn."

Her jaw dropped open. "A fine mess that one is. No wonder you need help." She grabbed the kettle and filled her cup then sandwiched it in her hands. "She still owes me money from some herbs I imported for her last winter. You wouldn't know where I could find her, do you?"

I shook my head.

"Figures. Never give your enemies a forwarding address. And if she really did to you what you're saying, we're both on that list, cave boy."

Enemy? I'd never done anything to hurt Rhiann. I never would. If anything, I'd been the one to save her life. My jaw clenched, aching to argue, but at least my brain jumped in knowing there would be no point. I needed to stop defending her. "So, wouldn't you want to help me out then? Stick it to her for stiffing you?"

Her eyebrows scrunched together, the concept of revenge clearly the most appealing option I had to offer. I edged closer and fought every instinctual urge to scowl as I flashed her my best imitation of a pretty boy smile.

She let out an amused snort and sidestepped around me. "Good effort, but nope. Still not happening. This is your problem. If you play games with the devil, prepare to burn." She coughed on a still-too-hot sip of her tea and pulled back the curtain to the main room. "Now, blondie, take your dead boy walking and leave me alone."

"All right." Abby sighed as her shoulders dropped in defeat. "C'mon, Kellan. She obviously isn't powerful enough to help us anyway. We should just go."

Madame slammed her hand down on the counter. "It's not about power, it's about self-preservation. I'm not asking to get on the bad side of one of those things."

"He didn't, either." Abby pointed at me, and I felt like I was in the middle of someone else's private conversation. "He never used to be this way. He never used to be the rude, messed-up wreck of a human you see over there."

Messed-up? Wreck? What the hell was she playing at? I opened my mouth to defend myself, but Abby continued.

"He used to be so much better than this. He was caring and considerate and polite—"

Madame snickered. "Yeah, right."

"And he used to be my friend ... my best friend. The one person in the whole world I knew was looking out for me. Someone I could tell anything to, trust anything to, but now ..." She glanced back at me, her eyes hooded and suddenly very far away.

I coughed on the unfamiliar thickness spreading in my throat, some part of me still able to remember whom she was talking about. Part of me still remembered her that way too.

"But this thing changed all that," she said. "The only reason he ended up with this Shadow Keeper problem was because he was trying to help someone in need, but she betrayed him for risking his life for her."

Abby walked closer to Madame until she could look her directly in the eye.

"Haven't you ever had someone you care about betray you

in an unforgivable way? Disappointed you? Left you completely unfixable?"

Madame turned. She raised her hand and opened her mouth, then closed it again. There was a softness when she looked at me now. Abby had hit a nerve. Must have been some secret girl language I'd never understand.

"What you need is a binding spell. Something to keep that Shadow Keeper from being able to do you harm. Don't know how long it'd last, but it could buy you a few years. It'll cost you though, and I don't come cheap." She drifted into the main room, Abby following close behind. I shook my head, unsure how she'd managed to get that crazy woman to do me a solid, but she had. Maybe it hadn't been a mistake bringing her here.

I pulled back the curtain and stepped into the small room behind Abby, trying to keep myself as far away from Madame as possible. Not that she'd notice, as her eyes scanned over the words in a blue-covered book that spewed dust every time she turned the page.

"I can't do the spell for you. You'll need a witch for that," she said without looking up.

I shrugged. "I only know one witch, and I doubt she'll be willing to help."

"I can give you a few numbers of people who would love to get back at Rhiann. Now you'll need these." She walked to a low shelf and grabbed a handful of black candles, placing them on a small, circular table in the middle of the room. "Plus, a length of ribbon or rope, which I'll assume you can find yourself—cotton or organic fibers only—and then something from the spirit you want bound."

"Where am I going to get that?"

"Well, that is the one thing I *can* help you with." She smiled, baring her chipped front tooth. "For six hundred dollars."

"What? You said three hundred on the phone."

"I didn't know what I was dealing with then, and besides, that witch of yours owes me a debt. Consider it part of her payment plan."

"What if I don't have it?"

"Then have fun being the Devil's plaything for all eternity."

I slipped my wallet out of my back pocket, the grief from parting with my hard-earned cash fueling the death glare I was giving our psycho psychic, who seemed to be enjoying my misery a little too much. Thumbing through the bills, I remembered collecting each one. Every dirty car I crawled under, every seized motorcycle I tore apart, all to buy parts for a Nova I was never going to finish. Unless, of course, this actually worked.

"I've only got five hundred."

"That'll do." She snatched the bills from my hand and flicked her index finger across the ends. "Plus, I want whatever you've got stashed in the front pocket behind your license."

"What? I don't—"

"Can you please not argue with the psychic and just hand it over?"

I tugged on the worn twenty-dollar bill that had been in my wallet so long, it stuck and nearly ripped. I chucked it on the table next to the candles. "Can we get this done already?"

"Still just as volatile when you're poor. Maybe use whatever extra time I buy you to get a personality that others might actually like."

She grabbed a large, black bowl from the shelf behind her and placed it in the middle of the table. "Sit. Sit."

Abby shrugged and took a chair at the circular table. I did the same, a sudden feeling of dread running up my back.

Madame hovered around the room, grabbing unmarked jars

and pouring their contents into the bowl, each one smelling like a worse stage of decay.

I covered my nose and tried not to breathe. "What exactly are you doing? Making the Shadow Keeper so nauseous, he refuses to come near me?"

She placed two unlit candles in metal stands on the table instead of answering, then held her hand over the bowl of dead things. Two drops of blood fell from her fingertips into the bowl. I swallowed.

"Your turn, rookies," she said, holding up a needle the length of a pen. Probably used it on her last victim. Maybe for one of those dolls they use for voodoo in the movies.

"I'll use my own if that's okay," Abby said, pulling a safety pin out of her backpack as if this weren't the most screwed-up request she'd ever had.

She pricked out a few drops and added them to the bowl, then held out her pin toward me.

"Here." A twisted grin rippled across her face. "Unless you'd rather I did it for you—again."

I grabbed the pin and after a deep breath, I jabbed my flesh, red pooling immediately at the entry point.

Abby stifled a giggle as I made my contribution, but she quickly straightened out with a nasty glare from Madame.

Madame snapped a match and lit one of the candles, tossing the matchstick in the bowl. A putrid smell filled the air like last week's rotten garbage mixed with roadkill. Vomit built up in the back of my throat, but I swallowed it with great difficulty.

"Hold hands," Madame instructed as she clamped her bony fingers around mine.

Abby reached across and grabbed my hand, then burrowed her fingertips into my fist. Her skin was warm and soft, and I ran my thumb over her knuckles, the gesture more on instinct than anything else. Abby's perma-smile faded into a blank, her mouth opening like the sleeping kid in the back of the class who doesn't know the answer when called upon. I straightened in my chair and twisted my wrist so the least amount of her flesh pressed against mine.

"Okay, now take a deep breath," Madame said.

I squinted my eyes and took in a lungful of the dreadful smoke circulating the room. I coughed.

She tightened her skeleton grip on my hand. "Hold still."

"Sorry," I mumbled.

She glared at me. "Shh. Stop talking. I'm concentrating."

I rolled my eyes and Abby choked down a laugh, but Madame didn't notice. She started a deep, throaty-sounding hum as the smoke thickened and started rising through the air.

The temperature dropped. Cold seeped through my skin and turned my core to ice. Goosebumps burst down my arms and I fought the urge to shiver. I couldn't see any of the room beyond the table anymore. Whether it was the smoke or something else happening, I couldn't tell.

Suddenly, a flame erupted from the unlit candle. The tall, thin blast of light reached for the roof. I flinched and slammed back in my chair.

"Don't let go," Madame ordered as she dug her nails into my skin. "I have to ground you."

Ground me? What for?

The room started spinning. Or maybe we were spinning and the room was staying still. Either way, I wanted to yack into the bowl of nasty in the middle of a table. I tried to focus on a still point. Abby's face. Ghost white, as if all the flashes of red whirling around us had drained from her cheeks and were bouncing off the walls. It didn't help. I closed my eyes and the spinning stopped, my stomach finally settling back into my abdomen. But the relief was short. The smell had changed. Smoke. Sulfur.

I opened my eyes. A lone candle burned between Abby and me on the little table. My hand clutched tight to hers, both our knuckles straining against our skin.

"Where are we?" she asked so quietly, I wasn't sure if she was talking to me or the room itself.

I closed my eyes again and tried to steady my breath. "We're here. My own personal hell."

She ripped her hand away and stood up, walking around the cavernous room. "How big is this place?"

"I don't know. I usually try not to hang out too long in here." I rubbed my damp palms against my thighs and stood on shaking legs. I couldn't get my head straight. Every second of eerie silence sparked a fire in my veins. Coming here might have been a huge mistake.

"Is this where you go every time ... when ... you know?"

Her voice faded beneath the waves of my pulse pounding in my own head. Sweat beaded on my brow. "Yeah. The cage for vicious things that try to kill me."

She took a sharp inhale of breath and the sound bounced around the room, growing louder in the emptiness. "Sounds awful."

"You have no idea." I tried not to face her. If I looked how I felt, she'd freak out. Too risky. This nightmare couldn't just stay in my own head anymore; it kept bleeding into every part of my life. There seemed to be less and less of me and more and more of *it* all the time.

A weight landed on my shoulder. My uneasy stomach hollowed. I spun around and lunged forward.

"Kellan, wait!" Abby called as I pressed my forearm against her throat, her eyes wide and terrified. A breathless gasp escaped from her lips.

"Don't ever do that!" I pushed myself off of her and grabbed clumps of hair in my fists. This was so messed up. "You don't understand what it's like in here."

"Okay. Okay." Abby coughed and grabbed her neck. "Let's just find something for the spell and get back."

Every vile sensation in my body intensified. I'd almost hurt her. Badly. I needed to get myself under control. "Where Abby? Let's just go back. I don't see anything here but us?"

She rushed forward, her arms reaching out in front of her. "Maybe there's something behind these walls."

Walls? I'd never seen the walls. It was always just endless, but of course, there had to be walls. Walls that housed the beasts that tortured me. Walls that kept me trapped in here. Walls I had just pushed Abby against when I'd been seconds from choking the life out of her.

"There're holes in here. In between the stones." She reached her arm in so far, it disappeared around her shoulder.

"Be careful." I stepped forward as if to stop her, but I stayed too far back to be of any help. "You don't know what's in there."

She pulled out her hand, her palm full of dark-colored dust. "Looks like dirt. Do you think this would work? Something that belongs to the Shadow Keeper?"

"I don't know. Doubt it."

"Then help me keep looking so we can go already."

The rough wall scratched against my fingers. Every texture not helping take the edge off. I squeezed my arm into each of the small holes, stone ripping against my skin. Black dust billowed out around us in a cloud. Handfuls and handfuls of nothing but soot.

"I think I found something." Abby yanked her arm out, her hand dripping as she tightly clutched something the size of a baseball. She held it out toward me. "What is it? It's kind of squishy."

A sickening sweetness wafted off her hand. I gagged but

forced myself to look closer. Even in the dark, the thing took shape. A clump of smooth muscle-like something I'd seen once in science class. I swallowed hard. "I think it's a heart."

Abby threw her empty hand across her mouth as her extended arm began to tremble. "Do you think ... Do you think it's human?"

I stared, not wanting to tell her the truth. Not wanting to tell her that if it wasn't human, it was probably something worse.

Thump!

The heart in her jumped, beating against her palm. Abby screamed and dropped the heart to the floor.

"*Shh.*" I grabbed her by the shoulders and tried to keep her calm, but her entire body vibrated beneath my grip.

Bang!

The familiar thud of a staff on the floor. The shuffle of footsteps.

"We have to go," I said.

She nodded but didn't move. I pulled her arm and ran for the table. Damn psychic had never told us how to get back.

The footsteps grew louder. He was coming. In seconds he'd be here. Would he torture me in front of Abby for entertainment or would he hurt her as punishment?

"How are we supposed to get back?" I asked. "I don't know what to do."

Abby wasn't listening. She just stared at the sticky substance oozing down her fingers.

I grabbed her hand, feeling the blood squish between our palms, and tried to concentrate on being back in that cramped, smelly room with Madame.

"You need to help, Abby. We need to find a way out."

Abby shook her head. "Try the way we got here."

She stumbled to the table and leaned over Madame's candle,

her face illuminating like a twisted angel. Her lips puckered as she blew out the flame.

My body lurched like I'd hit a tree. I was falling. I couldn't see Abby, couldn't feel her anymore. I squeezed my hand tighter, expecting to touch her dainty fingers, but I only grazed my own rough skin.

"Abby," I called out.

No answer.

Then smack. My forehead smashed against the tabletop. A dead, disgusting smell still lingered in the air. I shook my head and looked around at Madame's living room, exactly how I'd last seen it.

"Did you get what you needed?" Madame's nasally voice called through my haze.

"No." I ripped my hands out of her and Abby's grips. "You need to send me back."

"I can't," Madame said. Dark purple circles had formed around her eyes while we'd been gone. "Only got enough juice for one round trip."

I slammed my fist into my leg. "I need you to try. I'll pay anything. I swear. Just send me back alone." I pulled my wallet out of my back pocket and flipped through, trying to find any money I might have stashed somewhere for safekeeping.

The candles on the table flickered and danced in front of me. A raspy voice cackled, echoing from everywhere and nowhere. It ricocheted off the rafters and the bookshelves, hitting right into my chest.

"Who dares challenge a Shadow Keeper?" the voice threatened.

An icy blast shot through my limbs. I jerked my head back, expecting his bony frame to be standing next to me.

"No one who faces me lives to try again." The flame of the candles burst into the air and light exploded out, blasting a surge that threw us away from the table. My back smashed into an antique desk. A picture frame stabbed my shoulder as it fell off the wall and shattered beside me on the floor.

Flames had erupted everywhere, eating at the walls and devouring the furniture like an army of bonfires. I scrambled to my feet. Madame stood upright, her hand pressing down on the back of her head but otherwise unscathed. Across the room, Abby twisted on the floor, pinned under a bookcase. I held my breath and ran to her, digging through the pile of hardcover books until I could push the shelf off her leg.

I slid my arm behind Abby's knees and her back, pulling her up, my arm twitching in pain.

"I'm fine. Let me down." She squirmed in my arms, trying to free herself.

"No time. Stop being so damn proud."

I didn't see the nasty look she gave me, but I felt it burning on my neck, or maybe that was the flames that had spread out across the floor, eating the nasty rugs beneath our feet and smelling like rotten patchouli.

Racing for the door, I glanced back at Madame, who was running around tossing her things through the busted-out windows.

Seriously? I pushed open the door and tossed Abby out. I didn't even have time to care about the terrified look in her eyes as she dropped to the dusty ground. It was just dirt. She'd get over it.

I pulled my T-shirt over my mouth and nose and ran back in, shaking my head for being such a dumbass.

Madame had hiked up her skirt and filled it with anything she could salvage. Her body swayed as the smoke and flames weighed down on her consciousness.

"You have to get out of here," I yelled over the noise of the burning house.

"Leave me alone. You've destroyed enough." She continued grabbing bottles and books.

I wrapped an arm around her waist as the contents of her skirt smashed across the fiery floor. Her arms flailed at my head. Hard fists pounded against my chest and arms. I should really just leave her here.

I charged through the flames for the door. Dizziness washed over me, but I forced my legs to keep moving. Only a few more feet.

Something creaked overhead. I charged forward, my hostage still fighting me with every step. A beam from the ceiling slammed down behind me, the flames singeing my back and eating through the bottom of my shirt.

I ran to where Abby stood just out of the path of the inferno and dropped to the ground. Madame shouted as she hit the patchy grass and crawled away from my aching arms. I sat back on my knees, panting and gulping in the muggy evening air, still warm but one thousand times cooler than in the middle of the blaze. My arms shook and my lungs ached like they'd been doused in turpentine. That deep voice still rang in my ears. *No one who faces me lives.*

Struggling back to my feet, I inched closer to Abby. "Are you okay?"

She turned, but before she could respond, Madame poked a blood-colored fingernail in my face, a matching ring of red glowing in her eyes. "Look what you've done. You're as evil as the one who cursed you. I'll see you rot in hell for this."

"I didn't mean for this to happen," I shouted. "How did I know he'd come for me here?"

Madame pushed right up in my face, the scarlet flames engulfing her home reflecting across her cheeks. "Because guys like you break everything they touch."

The words stung. Each one a carefully fired missile blowing

up what remained of my dignity. I tried to phrase a comeback. Anything. But she wasn't wrong. Even if I did come up with something clever or better yet, honest, she'd never listen to me now. My last hope, spitting on my soon-to-be fresh grave.

Sirens blared in the distance.

"Abby." I looked at her, but her eyes remained transfixed on her hand. There wasn't any more blood, but she could probably still see it there. Dripping off her knuckles. I grabbed her forearm. "Abby. We need to get out of here."

Her skin quivered under my fingers, but it was enough to break the spell.

"We can't leave," she said hoarsely, as she cowered in toward my chest.

"There isn't anything we can do." My arm trembled as I wrapped it around her back, and she let me. I'd shown her too many horrors for one lifetime, but I had no idea how I'd be able to make it right.

She glanced up at me, her welling eyes glistening in the firelight. "But the firefighters?"

"And what would we tell them?"

Her chin dropped to her chest. My point was too true to argue with, even for her.

CHAPTER TWENTY

Abby

He kept looking at me. Not in a weird way, just in an 'are you okay' kind of way that made me feel oddly guilty for the undue amount of attention he was paying me instead of the road. Fortunately, he didn't ask. He just looked, and I decided I didn't really feel like answering either way. My ankle throbbed. I wanted to reach down and rub it better, but that would mean I'd lied when I'd said I was fine. And even without the pain in my ankle, I was definitely not fine.

The car came to a halt in front of Kellan's closed garage door. The dingy, cream-colored panels stared me in the face as I looked blankly out the windshield. Kellan turned off the ignition and leaned back, his hands dropped to his thighs with a slap.

"Are you sure you're all right?" he said, his voice quiet and directed to the glass of his side window.

"Uh-huh."

I grabbed the door handle and pulled, letting a gust of early evening air into the car.

"Thank you for coming. I think it's better that I didn't go there alone."

I froze, halfway in and halfway out of the car, my sore ankle already shooting sparks up my leg as I balanced myself between the seat and the driveway.

"So, that's where you go all the time when you're ... well ... you know."

He nodded, his head hanging down to his chest longer than it needed to before he brought himself back up and locked eyes with mine so hard, I had to turn away, the gold rings circling the green still lingering in my head. Breathing came hard. Heavy. A challenge to be overcome if I wanted to feel normal again. That place. That emptiness was more terrifying than anything I'd seen with him yet. And that was his future. His eternity. My arms itched to reach across the car and touch him. I wanted to tell him that it would be okay. But unless we figured something out, it wouldn't be, and it finally sunk in that this was what he'd been trying to tell me all along.

Instead, I pushed onto my feet and got out of the car, the open air fighting down my sudden lapse into claustrophobia. Kellan's door thunked behind me and I turned, hoping to say something constructive, but my knotted tongue stuck firm to the bottom of my mouth.

He linked his fingers together and rested them on the roof of the car, leaning toward me. "Come by tomorrow and I'll help you with that calculus stuff you were working on. But only if you want."

"Maybe." I let out a hefty sigh and let my own door clunk closed. Tonight was still too fresh in my brain to even consider thinking about tomorrow.

He nodded, then backed away. There was no expression on his face, just eerie blankness painted in shadow and starlight. I shuddered and closed my eyes.

I waited until Kellan's storm door clicked shut before limping across the side yard and up my own front walk, stepping as carefully as I could. Feet from the door, I looked up and jumped with a pathetic yelp. A figure sat on the front steps, elbows to knees, still as a statue. Placing my hand over my heart to push it back into my chest, I looked closer. Marcus. Soundless and drenched in the orange glow of the front porch light, watching me.

"You scared me." I tried to put pressure on my foot and walk as normally as possible, but it was already too late.

"What happened to you?" He rushed to my side, positioning himself under my right arm and guiding me to the steps while keeping the weight off my foot.

"It's nothing. I just tripped and fell funny, that's all. I'll be fine."

He sat next to me and pulled my foot into his lap.

"Seriously, Marcus. Don't worry about it."

He rubbed the sensitive skin around the bone, and I winced. Noticing my nervous system betraying me, his fingertips lightened their touch and drew slow, tiny circles across my flesh. Heat rose near my collarbone, from pain or pleasure, I wasn't sure.

"Feels mighty puffy to be nothing, Abs, and why do you smell like an ashtray?"

I cringed but ignored the question. "What are you doing here?"

His head dropped so he could stare at the pavement. I heard him breathe deeply before he looked up at me again.

"What were you doing with him?" He snapped his head toward Kellan's house, doing his best to keep his eyes and hands still on me.

"He was in detention and offered to drive me home."

"But detention ended over three hours ago." He placed his

hand under my chin and made me look at him. The muscles along his jaw clenched so tightly, it made the muscles in my stomach do the same. "Are you really going to do this?"

"Don't get all worked up." I shook him off and focused on the small crack creeping at the edge of the concrete stair, my throat suddenly parched. "I helped him with his homework like I said I was going to do."

"Are you sure about that?"

Embarrassment prickled the tops of my ears. "Of course I'm sure. Why wouldn't I be?"

Marcus tipped his head back toward the starry night sky. "Because he has one of the highest GPAs in our class."

"What?" I jerked forward and my foot dropped out of Marcus's lap and slammed against the sidewalk. Pain spiked through my leg. I bit down on my lip and choked down a scream.

"I did some digging and found out that not only is he not failing his classes, he's top of almost all of them. So what subject exactly does he need help in?"

Think. Think. "Calculus," I squeaked.

Marcus squinted, probably seeing right through my lie. "I guess an A in calculus isn't enough for him. Needs that A+ to lord over everyone."

An 'A'? Seriously? He said he was good at it, but he never said he was a math genius.

"Are you sure? Besides, how did you get his grades?"

He glanced out into the empty yard. "Not important. But if he's doing so well, why is he so interested in having you help him, Abby? What's really going on?"

"I swear I didn't know about this." What else could he be hiding? "I'll talk to him."

"I told you that guy was shady."

I shifted on the stair, keeping my sore leg as far away from his hands as I could. "I said I'd talk to him, Marcus. Can you please just drop it?"

He sighed, clearly not wanting to listen to me, but smart enough to do so. "I didn't come here to argue with you. I came to apologize."

"Oh." My stomach made a painful twist, and I stretched out to try to ease the pain.

"When you told me to back off, I should've listened. I shouldn't have pushed you to talk to me if you didn't want to."

"Thanks. That's really ... decent of you."

"*Decent?*" He mumbled it more to himself than to me, then grabbed my hand and rested it in his lap, wrapping his long fingers around mine and making my whole body warm from the palm out. "You never used to be mad at me like this, Abby, but lately I feel like there isn't anything I do that makes you happy anymore."

"I don't know." I tried to slide my hand away, but he held firm. Not aggressive, just not willing to let me go so easily.

"And it's not just me. Rachel said you've been bailing on yearbook meetings for weeks, and you don't even ask me about prom stuff. Everybody else's girl won't shut up about it, but with you, it's like ... I don't know ... It's just not you."

The pain in my stomach grew stronger. "Why does all this prom stuff matter to you so much anyway?"

He lowered his forehead and stared up at me with wide eyes. "Why *doesn't* it matter to you?"

"It's a stupid popularity contest. You know everyone adores you. Do you really need some cheap plastic crown to prove it?"

He counted off on his fingers. "Athletics, academics, and popularity—it's the Grand Slam of high school, Abby. Everyone knows that."

"But why? In fifteen years, is it going to matter? Is anything we do now going to matter?"

"Where is all this coming from? We've all been talking about senior year since we were freshmen, but somewhere in the last month or so, you just checked out on me."

I rubbed my hands over my face. Good question. How was I supposed to explain something to him that I didn't even fully understand? All I knew was that maybe Abby Marino wasn't someone I wanted to be anymore. "I'm sorry. I'm not trying to make you angry."

"I'm not angry." He pulled my hands from my face, not letting me hide. "I'm worried."

His eyes smoldered deep and dark and full of something I couldn't quite read. It was like he was waiting for me to say something meaningful to put everything back together, but I didn't have the words. I leaned in closer and let my lips brush across his. He met me halfway, his lips twitching somewhere between kissing me harder and holding back. His uncertainty punched me straight in the gut. I'd done this. I'd made it weird.

I let my hand slide to the back of his neck and twined my fingers through his soft hair, the motion bringing back so many other kisses before this one. Kisses that didn't have any motive or agenda. Kisses that would have left me on a giddy high for hours afterward. Kisses I was never going to regret.

Marcus pulled back and held my face in his palm, his other hand brushing my hair behind my ear, his eyes still locked on me as if I might run away. What was with the boys in my life and their crazy stares?

"How about we do something tomorrow night? Just me and you. Alone." My lips curled into a smile as I said the words, mirroring the same effect they had on Marcus.

"Sounds perfect."

He gave me a soft kiss on the forehead, and I breathed him in as my nose buried into the crook of his neck. Coffee and cologne. For too brief a moment, I forgot everything else, resting my head against his thick shoulder and letting myself just be. Then as harsh as a water gun to the face, he pulled away, leaving me wanting more of him.

"I should go." He stood up and looked at me again. The raw confusion still crept in and mixed with his smile. "Oh. I forgot. I have a family thing tomorrow night. Wednesday?"

"Yeah. Wednesday's fine."

"I really am sorry for getting you in trouble today, Abby."

I recoiled a bit, making myself smaller on the step. "I know."

"And my dad is looking into that name for you. He said it will probably take a few days, but he should be able to come up with something."

"Thank you."

"No problem." He gave me a final nod, then disappeared across the shadowy lawn toward his car.

❧❦❤❦❧

MOM SAT in the living room, an open book spread across her lap and a glass of red wine within reach.

"Is that you, Abby?" She jerked her head toward the foyer. "What's that smell? Why do you smell like burning garbage?"

"Hi, Mom," I said, closing the front door and ignoring her nose perked up in the air and the twisted scowl of disgust on her face. "Where's Dad?"

"He has an overnight in Chicago for work."

"Okay. I'm going to grab something to eat." My stomach growled, accentuating the request. "Do you want anything?"

She grinned and shook her head. "That's sweet, but no, thank you."

I tucked my nose in my collar and headed for the kitchen. The smell wasn't *that* bad.

"Oh, Abby," Mom called after me. "Before you go, I have

some great news. Your father met an associate professor from Harvard, and he said he would be glad to take your application and hand deliver it to the admissions office."

"Great." I huffed, the venom in my tone a little too obvious.

"Excuse me? What's with the attitude? Do you understand how lucky you are to have this kind of break? It's far past the application time, but he's willing to do you a favor."

I dug my nails into my palms so hard that I thought I might bleed on the carpet. I was sure she would've loved that.

"There's a blank application and a business card for you on the island. He'll be expecting to hear from you before the end of the week."

I swallowed down the curse words I'd never utter but sounded so good in my head. "And what if I don't want to go to Harvard? I'm going to Cornell."

"You aren't really going there until you set foot on that campus, so until then, you'll do whatever you can to do better. Do you understand?"

I hung my head. "Yes."

She snapped her fingers. "I'm over here, Abigail."

I looked up and tried to hide the fury in my eyes. "I said *yes*."

"Very good. Now where have you been? You completely missed dinner."

I squared my feet and braced myself. "Detention."

She slammed her book shut and sat up straighter. "Abigail! You were in detention? What could you have possibly done to deserve that?"

"I pushed Marcus into a locker."

Her jaw opened wide enough for me to see her tonsils from across the room. "You pushed Marcus? The poor boy who has been sitting on our front steps twice in the last week waiting for you? That was extremely unladylike."

"He started it," I shouted back.

"You're not six years old, Abigail. Stop with the whining." She waggled a stern finger in my direction, then froze. The roaring anger drained as panic started to set in. "Wait. Are you saying Marcus hurt you? Because if he did ..." She pushed up from the couch and started for the outside door.

"No, he didn't hurt me, Mom."

She halted her charge, then pinched the bridge of her nose and inhaled deeply. "Well, then, what would ever make you do something like that?"

"He wasn't listening to me."

"And *that* is how you chose to make him listen? That's appalling. You need to learn to control yourself in social situations."

I looked away at the pictures on the wall. Happy pictures of everyone smiling. Disneyland. Grand Canyon. My tenth birthday. Anything to avoid looking at the disdain dripping off my mother's face.

"Harvard couldn't have come at a better time. It'll teach you a bit of the decorum you are so desperately lacking."

I bit down on the inside of my cheek. Pain shot through my jaw. "Are we done?"

"Yes. And if I ever hear about you in detention again, you will be spending the entire summer in your room, is that clear?"

My head nodded, even though my brain was willing it not to.

"If you want to continue to ruin your future, this is the way to do it. Do you hear me?"

"Yes," I said as I turned and hurried into the kitchen, listening to her mumble behind me.

"Detention. What's gotten into that girl."

On the island sat the paperwork. I grabbed the Harvard application, so familiar to me that I could recite the requirements without even reading it. In the corner, a business card glared at me, attached with a large paperclip. Across the creamy card stock was embossed the name, *Peter Crenshaw,* followed by a trail of degrees and titles longer than the alphabet. I could guarantee Peter Crenshaw did not want to hear from me. I tucked the application under my arm and grabbed a pear from the counter, even though my appetite had mysteriously vanished.

On the bottom step, I looked back into the living room, watching my mother read. The light from the lamp cast across her face showed the lines starting to burrow across her forehead. She held her pursed lips tight as if to whisper her disappointment without moving an unsatisfied muscle. My hands unconsciously balled into fists. I'd never please her, so why did I bother trying? I turned and headed to my room to dream of demons and hope that the real ones were easier to fight than the ones I'd created in my own head.

CHAPTER TWENTY-ONE

KELLAN

Waves of heat rose off the pavement. I watched them swirl and blur from my shady spot under the eaves beside the open garage door. Inside, the air burned enough to blister, and outside, it was hotter than a motorcycle engine. Even this one small sliver of shadow providing me the tiniest bit of solace was still stupidly uncomfortable. If I could just hold out a few more minutes, I'd be finished, and I could hole up in the house in front of the AC for the rest of the night. Assuming my face didn't melt off in the meantime.

I bent forward and reefed on my wrench one last time, locking the final bolt securely in place.

Thump. The sun disappeared, and a thick copy of *Calculus in the Modern World* clipped past my face and landed on the concrete.

"Jeez." I jerked back on my stool. "What were you trying to do, scare me to death with advanced math?"

"Is that a better or worse option for you?" said a sarcastic feminine voice.

I narrowed my eyes and glared up at Abby.

She shrugged, beaming back at me with a taunting smile. "What are you working on?"

"Really?" I pointed the wrench at the dirt bike. "Or does it need a BMW crest before you recognize it?"

"Funny." She rolled her eyes and whipped her head to the side. "I meant what are you doing to it?"

I scooped up my tools from the pavement, leaving the textbook baking in the sun, and kicked my wheeled stool back into the garage. "It had an engine problem, so I fixed it."

After dropping the tools on the workbench, I grabbed a rag and started shining up the exhaust. Abby followed me back and forth, silently watching every movement as if it fascinated her. The weight of her stare bashed against the back of my head and made me remember things I'd much rather forget. Things that had happened to her that were all my fault.

"Is it yours?" she asked finally after I'd rubbed down every part of the bike at least three times. "Looks like it could be fun."

"Nope. It's just a job." I wheeled the dirt bike into the garage and leaned it against the workbench. "Needed to earn back the money I spent on that crazy magic mojo lady. Finishing the Nova isn't going to be cheap."

Her nose scrunched, and her face twisted into a confused scowl. "What's a Nova?"

Seriously? Did this girl know anything that didn't come out of a textbook? I pointed to the oversized car-shaped tarp in the corner. "That."

She walked toward the tarp. "Can I see?"

"No." I leapt across the room and grabbed her wrist, her hand dangerously close to pulling back the vinyl. "She's not ready yet. It's still a wreck under there."

Abby snatched her arm away but kept an edge in her voice. "You know it's just a car, right? No offense."

"Yep. Just a bunch of hoses and spark plugs. A complete

waste of time." I marched across the garage, chucked the rag on the counter, and stared at the pegboard on the wall counting the holes. Anything to avoid looking at her and adding to the lump growing in my throat. Or worse, opening my mouth and coming off like an even bigger jerk. "It was my dad's car. He bought it for us to rebuild, but it's still not finished."

A soft 'oh' escaped her lips as her jaw probably hit the floor behind me.

"I'm sorry. I didn't know," she said, just a few decibels louder than a whisper. "I'm sure he'd be glad to know you're still working on it."

Doubtful. Dad was probably sitting in an afterlife somewhere wishing he'd never even had a son. Especially a useless waste of space like me.

"How's the foot?" My shoulders tensed as I said the words, but if I was going to be a dick today, I might as well go for it full out. No matter how many times I'd told myself that Abby didn't have to come yesterday, the guilt of getting her hurt still pumped through my bloodstream. Every time I tried to sleep, her pained face flashed through my mind. Looking up at me as she curled near my chest during the fire. Her body trembling under my arm. I ached to make the soft quiver in her bottom lip still. Shaking my head, I forced the image down. Technically, she'd put herself in danger, but I was stupid for telling her about the psychic in the first place. The tension in my shoulders spread across my chest, pushing hard against my ribs. Damn conscience.

"Stiff, but I think it'll be fine if I take it easy for the next few days." She dragged a stool from the corner of the garage and popped up onto it, just close enough so I had to see her in my periphery, but not enough to intrude. "So, if you have any more seances planned, you should probably move them to next week, if that's okay?"

She tilted closer and gave me a half-assed smile, the corners of her lips still edging down against her best efforts.

I wiped my arm across my brow, beads of sweat speckling on my skin. "What are you doing here anyway? Isn't there somewhere air-conditioned you'd rather be?"

"You said you'd help me with calculus, and I think you kind of owe me one."

She leapt off the stool, keeping her weight off her left foot, and bent over to rummage through her bag that she'd tossed on the one oil-stain-free spot on the floor. I grabbed the edge of the tool bench as her long, tanned legs stretched out in front of me. Miles of soft skin from the floor to the bottom edge of her perfectly too-short dress.

I shook my head, my face somehow managing to flame even hotter than the unbearable summer heat, as I continued shining up the already polished dirt bike, wishing she'd stand so I could stop checking to see if I needed to keep avoiding watching her.

Finally, she whipped out a purple coiled notebook in front of my face, so quick, it almost cut my nose. "So, are you still going to help me, or what?"

I flipped open the cover and looked over a few pages while Abby perched herself back up on the stool, her stare glued to me as I read. Not one to like an audience, I walked out of the garage and paced along the driveway.

Every equation was set up exactly like you'd see in a textbook. Perfect order, perfect lines, except for the awful frilly writing that gave a curl to even straight-looking numbers. There weren't any drawings in the margins, no stupid hearts or flowers or whatever girls drew when they stopped paying attention to the ancient corpses our school called a math department. The bland precision looked like she worried someone would go through to correct her personal notes. The oddest part, though, was her answers. She'd completely nailed the hard stuff, but the easy stuff, the things I'd learned over a year ago, were all wrong. She would start out on the right track, but then go off the rails and end up just left of where she needed to be.

"Are you failing on purpose?" I pulled the pages from my face and squinted through the sun at her standing just inside the frame of the garage door.

Her head tilted unnaturally to the left. "What?"

"You are so close, but you always get the easy stuff wrong."

"'Easy stuff'? Thanks for the confidence booster."

"What? You wanted my help. You need to be straight with me about the problem."

She stormed toward me and snatched the notebook from my hands, tucking it into her crossed arms. "Never mind. I shouldn't have bothered."

"Why? Because you knew I'd call you out? What are you so afraid of?"

Abby stepped closer, slow and stealth, her face looking like I had two seconds before her head exploded all over my driveway. "What did you just say?"

"Fine. Maybe I'm wrong." I backed away, hands up in surrender. "Maybe you're just overthinking it."

"Overthinking or whatever, I need to get this shit in check or I'm going to fail my exam next week, okay?"

She stomped her foot and let out a huffing noise, her cheeks beaming an irritated red. I looked at her, all attitude and curse words, and busted up laughing. Who did she think she was? Me? Besides, I did that act better than anyone, especially a high school princess, soon-to-be prom queen.

The longer I stared, the more pissed off she got, and I laughed even harder. "Why is this such a big deal anyway? I'm sure you're already into whatever school you want to go to. Why does one test matter?"

"Lots of reasons. One"—she started counting on her fingers

—"because I need to maintain my average to keep my spot at Cornell. Two, my parents will kill me. Three—"

Her reasons jumbled together in my brain as the sun beat down on my head and the skyline started to sway. I wiped my wrist against my forehead again and took a deep breath of hot stifling air.

"Get in the car," I said. "We're going for a drive."

◦◦◦ ❤ ◦◦◦

"WHERE ARE WE GOING EXACTLY?" Abby said as she stared out the open window. The AC blared on high, but it was just too hot out for it to make any difference.

I figured she would've asked this three turns and two highways ago, but she hadn't said much since we'd left my house, only quietly sung along to the occasional song on the radio. To be fair, I hadn't been good company, either. It was just too damn hot.

"You don't remember this place?" I asked as I turned the corner.

"*Pfshaw.* Of course, I do. It's just ... I don't know ... Why here?"

The temperature dropped fifty degrees under the thick cover of trees that edged the sides of the back road. Grass grew in a ridge down the center, with only two deep ruts for tires to follow, as if on the rails of a forgotten roller coaster.

A few miles in, the trees stepped back onto an empty field, where I pulled over and cut the engine. I tucked the keys into my pocket and got out of the car, then headed toward a small pathway that disappeared into the woods.

"Coming?" I asked Abby, who was still standing beside the car, her arms crossed tightly over her chest. Her sudden attempt at anger and intimidation had faded during the drive, but maybe she still had a few good blows left.

Without bothering to respond, she plodded the length of the field, following behind me as I continued up the path. Her strappy shoes and sore ankle probably didn't help the climb as the path wound higher up the side of a hill, but she never complained, letting out only a few frustrated huffs. I put out a hand to help her, thinking that I couldn't have any more injuries on my watch, but she shot me a disgusted look like I'd offered her poison, so I trudged on.

Finally, the dirt path changed into rock and spread out beneath our feet until it dropped off sharp about five yards away.

I walked right to the edge of the rocks, staring out across the calm, blue-green water. "Do you remember when we used to come here as kids?"

The sun melted the soles of my sneakers to the black rock, but just being closer to the water seemed cooler, even if it was still twelve feet below.

"Of course I do," Abby replied, still back by the path. "Your parents used to take us here. Your dad would take us swimming and your mom would pack the best picnic lunch, with chips."

"You remember the chips?"

"My mom never allowed me to have them back then. Said they were a waste of a vegetable."

I chuckled to myself, picturing Mrs. Marino saying those exact words with a stern look and a finger wagging in the air.

"All right," I said, drawing back from the water to where Abby sat on the ground. "It's hotter than balls up here. Let's go swimming."

She pulled her knees closer in and her back straightened. "I didn't bring a swimsuit."

"Go in your clothes, then. Unless you want to strip down to your underwear."

I winked without intending to and she rolled her eyes but followed it up with an easy laugh that seemed to forgive me for being a borderline creeper. Besides, this girl had a boyfriend, even though I'd bet she looked damn fine in the pink underwear she likely wore to match the pink bra strap slipping out from the top of her dress.

"Clothes it is," I said.

She slid her feet out of her fancy shoes and stood. Barefoot, she came in at least a head shorter than me, forcing her to shield her eyes from the sun as she stared up. "Okay, so how do we get down to the water?"

I shrugged. "The same way we always did. Jump."

"Oh, no. Not happening. That might've been fine when I was a dumb kid, but I know better now."

"What? You know how to *not* have fun now?"

She scowled, but it looked more funny than threatening with her eyes squinting at the sunlight. "No, I know better than to trust Kellan Casey."

"Really? Is that how this goes? Just remember *you* came to *me* for help this time." I bent over and scooped her up in my arms.

"Put me down," she squealed, her laughter echoing through the trees.

I pulled her tighter to my chest as she wriggled and struggled to get free. An elbow smashed against my jaw, sending a jolt up the side of my head. Feisty. Nice. But she'd pay for it. I bounded the last two big steps to the edge of the rock. Abby's body stiffened, but she stopped flailing.

"Don't think I won't drop you," I said, but she wasn't listening.

Her head had turned to the open water and her fingers knotted themselves in my T-shirt.

"Please don't," she pleaded, her voice broken, the sound still partly stuck in her throat.

The cadence of laughter from moments ago died in the distance as fear pulsed through her body, her limbs rigid in my grip. She wasn't just a little scared of heights—she was absolutely terrified. This wasn't the Abby I used to know. That girl was fearless. The girl who climbed the tallest trees. Who took any dare, from anyone, no matter how reckless. This Abby was different. Over the years, someone had wrecked her—and right now I wanted to punch that unknown someone in the face.

"Hey, hey. I was only kidding." I took a step back and let her down so she could stand on her own again. "But you've jumped off here hundreds of times. I didn't think it was a big deal."

"You're right. I've done this tons of times. It's fine ... I'm fine ... Everything's fine."

The words sounded unconvincing as her body began to tremble.

"You'll be okay, Abby. I'm right here." I placed my hands at her waist, the fabric so thin, I felt the goosebumps rippling across her skin. She twisted her fingers through mine and yanked me forward, wrapping my arms all the way around to her stomach, almost pulling us both over the edge. I steadied myself, suddenly regretting this stupid idea.

"Just forget it. I'll take you down to the bank."

I started to pull my hands away, but she gripped tighter.

"No. I can do this."

"You don't have to. Don't worry about it."

"I want to, Kellan. I need to." She glanced back over her shoulder, her head barely turning on her straining neck muscles. "It's not just jumping. It's everything. I'm so tired of being scared."

She took a huge breath and let it out slow, her breath wavering.

"You asked what I was afraid of, and I'm honestly afraid of everything. I'm afraid that I wasted all these years being someone that everyone else wanted me to be. My parents. My teachers. My friends. Marcus. And I'm afraid I'm not even doing *that* well. That I'm a huge disappointment. I'm not smart enough, or strong enough, or good enough. And I'm afraid that once all of this is over, once high school ends, I'm just going to keep doing what everyone expects of me and I'm going to be miserable and scared for the rest of my life."

Her fingernails bit into my palms as her skin flushed, patches of red growing up the back of her neck.

"And I don't know how to stop," she continued. "Because I can't just do what I want, because I don't know what I want because no one lets me think for myself. Ever. They just push, and push, and push, and one day, I'm just going to snap."

The words stopped flowing, but her breath kept coming hard and heavy, and for the briefest instant, her body relaxed in my hands before straightening back to perfect posture. The girl most likely to be everything, with a future brighter than the sun baking my skull right now, didn't have everything figured out. She was just as lonely and screwed up as the rest of us. Just like me. But at least she had a future to look forward to, even if it wasn't what she wanted.

"Then snap," I said as I freed my arms and took a small step back.

"What?" She gasped and turned to face me, her heels dangerously close to the edge.

"You have this whole long life ahead of you, Abby. If you aren't happy, change things. Tell them all to go to hell."

"It's not that simple."

I shrugged. "Why not?"

Her eyes narrowed and her jaw tightened, my logic clearly not computing in her brain. Maybe I didn't understand, or maybe she spent so much time in her own head, she didn't know how to get out. *Been there.*

She shifted to the left, trying to maneuver around me, but I stepped in front, forcing her right, then pivoted to cut her off again. She huffed and tried to stare me down.

"Answer me, Marino. Why not?"

Instead of answering, she whirled around to face the water and teetered on her sore ankle. Her eyes widened as her balance wavered. I reached forward to pull her back, but my fingertips grazed the skin of her shoulder as she fell forward, screaming my name the entire way down.

At the sound of the splash, a ten-year-old part of me felt vindicated in a nasty revenge kind of way, but the rest of me just felt like a jerk. Either way, she needed to get out of the blazing sun. She'd thank me later.

I stared over the side, waiting for her to surface and start laying into me, but she didn't come back up.

"Abby," I yelled down at the bubbling water.

No answer.

The surface of the lake flattened out.

"Abby!"

Nothing.

Oh, shit. I ripped off my shoes and dove into the water below. The cold-water bitch slapped me in the face and my brain felt like it might explode out of the top of my head. I pushed myself toward the lake bottom, the murky water clouding everything within a foot of my face. My arm banged against rocks, my ears ringing under the pressure. I was such an asshole. I shouldn't have cornered her. I should've minded my own damn business. And if I hurt her again, I'd never forgive myself.

My lungs ached and burned. I flailed one last time but found nothing and rushed to the surface.

"Abby!" I shouted with the last bit of oxygen in my lungs. "Abby! Answer me, damn it."

A high-pitched cackle sounded behind me and echoed out across the water. I spun around. Abby stood on the edge of the lake, drenched, and laughing at me.

"Seriously?" My heart stopped banging against my ribs. "I thought you were drowning."

She thrust her hands on her hips. "Just because I stopped stomaching heights doesn't mean I forgot how to swim."

In three quick strokes, I made it back to the shore and pulled myself out. Abby sat on a rock, her legs stretched out, drying off in the sun. I stood over her, blocking her light and dripping all over her already dry feet.

"Don't. Ever. Do. That," I threatened in the most menacing voice I could conjure from the depths of my gut.

"Um ..." She shuffled to the side and away from me. "You pushed me off a cliff."

"I didn't *push* you. And it's twelve feet. You weren't base jumping off the Empire State Building." I shook my hair like a dog spraying water all over Abby's face and dropped to the ground beside her.

"It was still a pretty shitty thing to do, Kellan."

"Maybe you jumped because you couldn't handle the truth I laid on you up there?" I raised my eyebrows in a smug smirk, and she shot me an angry glare back, her fat bottom lip sticking out at me. The spoiled princess look. I laughed, making her deepen the expression, which made it look even more phony.

I flopped down beside her and leaned back on my arms, the hot gray rock starting a slow burn in my palms. Closing my eyes, I stretched my face toward the sky, letting the sun cut the chill of the cool lake water running off my skin. Leaves rustled.

Waves lapped the shore. The heavy tension of the heat slipped from my bones and evaporated into the air. Just what I needed.

"So, you never did give me an answer. Why's the most perfect girl in Middleton letting everyone boss her around?"

She huffed a loud sigh, her breath shaking the small hairs on my arm. "Because sometimes it's easier than fighting it, and eventually, everything builds and builds until you're stuck. Trapped. Like you're sitting in a holding pattern waiting for something to give, but not sure what to do to get yourself out, either."

"Really? I have no idea what it's like to have a future you can't escape." I snorted. "Sounds awful."

"See? This is why I don't tell people things."

She shoved my shoulder, knocking me to the ground. I opened my eyes and sat back up, trying not to laugh too hard, but my amusement caught in my throat as I saw her sitting much closer than I'd expected. Her wet hair clung to the sides of her head, and she'd swiped it all to one side, so it dripped a puddle between us. The strap of her sundress hung just off her shoulder in a careless, lazy way, and the thin fabric plastered against her body, showing every single curve. Smeared makeup made dark rings around her wide eyes and gave her a sexy, wild night/early morning look that made you wonder what she'd been up to and wishing it'd been with you. A raw, stripped-down look polished girls like Abby never wore—unless some jackass knocked them into a lake.

I swallowed, all my words suddenly stuck behind my tonsils, and slowly slid a few inches backward.

She cast her eyes down and started playing with the hem of her dress. "Honestly, sometimes I wish I could be more like you."

I coughed, my voice forcing its way back into function. Be like me? I'd always wanted to be like her. Confident. Brave.

Everyone else would've given up on my sorry ass already, but she kept swimming along in my death pool of weird. "What?"

"You know what you want. You do what you want. You don't care what anybody else thinks," she whispered.

"Trust me. It's not all that great. So why don't you just tell your parents you've had enough?"

"Because I just ... I just can't."

Springing up from the ground, she stomped over to the edge of the lake. Picking up a rock, she chucked it across the water, where it skipped twice and sunk. She reached down for another, but before she could fling it, I rushed over and put my hands on her biceps. Refusing to look at me, she dropped her head down, watching herself turn the smooth gray stone over in her hands.

"Of course, you can. In the past few weeks, you've traveled dimensions, been to a screwed-up séance, escaped a burning building, and faced down a hell beast—twice. I'm sure your parents are less terrifying than that."

The start of a smile sparked on the left side of her lips. "Have you *met* my mother?"

"Good point." I laughed, and her smile spread. "Take it from someone who has barely any life left. You deserve to be happy."

She paused, as if letting the words sink in, then whispered, "And so do you."

She shook her head and looked out over the water, her smile setting like the evening sun. Her faraway gaze looked lost, lonely, and in that second, I saw my own feelings scarred across her face. If I didn't find a way out, I'd probably be miserable until the Shadow Keeper punched my ticket, but she could have a great life. She *should* have a great life. If I were her guy, I'd do everything I could to make her happy. But she was with someone else. Not like it would matter soon anyway.

"Thanks," she said, still watching the horizon, "I think I needed this today ... except maybe not being pushed off a cliff."

"You fell."

Abby chuckled.

Without thinking, I placed my hand on her cheek, her half-dry hair tickling against my knuckles, as she turned her head toward me. I leaned closer, the mouthwatering scent of her coconut shampoo clouding my head. Why did she have to be someone else's girl? I thought I heard her breath hitch, just a little, but maybe it was just my own struggle to breathe. My lips brushed against her ear.

"I promise," I whispered. "No matter what happens, I'll never let you fall again."

Abby

A faint puff from the inept air conditioning system wafted past my cheek and saved me from melting into the library table. I gathered my hair in the fist propping up my head, letting the barely cool air drift across my neck, and glanced across the table at Kellan. Sunlight from the massive window just behind the stacks beat down on his back, creating a soft glow around him as a few beads of sweat balanced on his forehead. But instead of losing himself to the swelter like me, he kept his scowling face buried deep in a book, his eyes flitting back and forth as they scanned the page.

I laid my arm on the tabletop and rested my head in the bend of my elbow, flipping my own book to the next chapter. The words shimmied in waves, and any that stayed still long enough to read didn't connect in my brain. I blinked and a hazy filter fell over my vision, like looking at the world from inside a dirty fishbowl.

Three days of scouring every book in the Middleton Library, and not one word about Shadow Keepers, or at least not anything we didn't know from the Internet already. Maybe, just for one day, we could take a break and head back down to the lake, except jumping in from the shore this time instead. I closed my eyes, feeling the cool, clear water rushing over my skin. The sun fragmented into glittering diamonds above me. The murky, mysterious bottom loomed below. And Kellan sitting by the water's edge in that tight, wet shirt clinging to the muscles in his arms, his dark hair hanging damp and dreamy across his brow .... I shook my head. Enough. I had to stop this. Stop picturing Kellan in my mind. Stop remembering the sensation of how his hand brushed across my cheek, and how the air rushed from my lungs as his lips grazed my ear. How in that moment I'd thought he was going to kiss me, and how I hadn't done anything to stop him. So close. Too close. Besides, I'd probably just dreamt the whole thing. And I had a boyfriend. A hot, fantastic boyfriend—who'd barely spoken to me in the last week except for canceling our Wednesday date, then ten minutes at the yearbook meeting in front of a dozen people yesterday.

Sinking deeper into the desk, I huffed, loud and sharp.

Kellan bolted upright in his seat, then peered over at me with a lazy, half-hearted smile. "Any luck?"

I flopped back in my chair, stretched my legs out beneath the table, and shook my head.

He pinched the bridge of his nose and blinked several times. "Maybe the Shadow Keeper's finally gotten the hint and screwed off."

"Maybe." I slammed the cover shut on the book I'd hardly read and watched flecks of dust billowing out from the pages. "Do you really think he'd let you go that easy?"

"Not likely. But it's been ten days since the last time he showed up. I think that might be a record."

"Then what do you suggest we do now? Just sit back and wait?"

"I don't know, Abby." He rubbed his hands over his face, red paths from his fingertips flaming then disappearing. "Could try that psycho psychic again?"

The temperature plummeted and I shivered, the biting stench of smoke suddenly hanging in the air. "We can't go back there. She'd kill you if she saw you again."

Besides, we'd never find her. I'd driven by once, late at night, when the guilt had built too thick in my throat to sleep. Nothing remained on the overgrown lot but a razed pile of ash on a concrete foundation. A whole life disintegrated into black charred spots on the ground. A message to Kellan. Or maybe a terrifying threat?

He leaned back, his head dropping behind him as he stared at the ceiling. "Then I'm out of ideas. At least for today."

Kellan sighed, his chest deflating as his outstretched calf brushed mine under the table. I jerked forward in my seat. He raised his head, one thick eyebrow arched in a questioning crook, studying my face. I flipped open my ancient book, studying the pages and hoping he'd stop staring. Instead, he slid his leg along mine, creeping slowly from ankle to kneecap, the rough denim teasing goosebumps across my bare skin.

I gasped and whipped my legs beneath my chair. "Cut it out."

"What? Something wrong, Marino?" He stooped over the table, his eyes narrowed to tight slits.

"No." I slid my chair back and crossed my arms over my chest. "Of course not."

He shook his head and laughed. Easy and light. So un-Kellan-like, I thought I'd imagined it.

"Be quiet," I hissed. "You'll get us kicked out of here."

Kellan snapped his mouth closed, still flashing a crooked smirk. "Why are you so on edge?"

"No reason. Just didn't want to be in your way." I forced a

chuckle through my fakest smile. "Everyone knows if you get in Kellan Casey's way, you'll regret it."

"Oh." His smirk collapsed along with his shoulders. "Are you being serious right now?"

"Why wouldn't I be? That's the reputation you've worked so hard for, right?"

His head recoiled to the left, my words smacking him hard. "What's with this all of a sudden?"

I bit down on the inside of my cheek, my fingers tying themselves in knots under the table. A snarky remark wasn't the best strategy here, but it had sort of slipped out. Better than my real thoughts spewing out of my mouth. All those thoughts I needed to bury deep in my brain and never think about again.

Kellan scanned the library slowly, left then right, finally leaning halfway across the table.

"Come here," he whispered, his fingers twitching in a beckoning wave.

I bit harder on my cheek but didn't move. We hadn't talked about what had happened, or thankfully what *hadn't* happened, by the water, but I knew I couldn't avoid it forever. If there was even anything to talk about. Maybe because I'd been upset that day, I'd just read too much into things. Plus, I was sure he'd absolutely *loved* me spilling my guts about my stupid problems.

"Please?"

The word fell off his tongue as if it burned, his eyes wide, almost vulnerable. I huffed, letting my breath flow out, and crumpled my chest onto the tabletop, dreading whatever he might say.

"How's it going? Are you ... like ... okay?" He shifted his gaze to my hair pooled next to me on the table and started twining a clump of strands around his finger, focusing on each loop as it twisted around and around his knuckles. "I mean, since that day at the lake. I want to know if you're all right."

"Yeah, I'm fine. Just had a bad day. Don't worry about it."

He cast me a side-eye. Clearly, my lying skills needed work.

"Besides, I'm here to help you figure out your problems, not burden you with mine."

He looked down at the tabletop. "You don't need to help me, you know?"

"Well, if you want me to stop, just say so." I started to pull back but stopped as my hair snagged in Kellan's hand.

"No. That's not what I meant." He leaned farther across the table. "I'd hate myself if I hurt you again."

His intense stare locked on mine, piercing deep into my brain as if he were searching for something he'd lost way at the back, or worse, trying to uncover thoughts I wasn't ready to or even capable of sharing. He was close. Too close. As close as he'd been when he'd whispered in my ear on the shore, but I shouldn't have been thinking about that. I should never think about that again. I held my breath as my hands clenched into fists underneath the table, trying to keep myself steady.

"Don't—"

A hollow buzz shook the table, and I flinched. My phone lit up, and a text message popped up on the screen. I grabbed the phone and slid back in my seat, my hair unraveling from Kellan's index finger.

"It might be important," I explained.

He nodded, but in a doubtful way that seemed to detect my lie before it had even managed to tumble out of my mouth.

I flipped to the text and a close-up photo of Rachel holding a bright yellow halter dress exploded across my screen.

Rachel: *Princess or banana?*

Followed by three bananas and a tiara emoji.

I chuckled at the photo, Rachel's face contorted to look like she was thinking hard, her thumb and forefinger in a "v" across her jaw. My fingers flitted over the screen.

> **Me:** *It definitely looks a-peeling.*
> **Rachel:** *Loser*
> **Me:** *Yep*
> **Rachel:** *Know you're busy, but you need to come shop-ping with me.*
> **Me:** *Thought you already had a dress?*
> **Rachel:** *Hate it. Clashes with the decorations. You would know if you came to a prom meeting this week.*
> **Me:** *Sorry*

I cringed, thinking of streamers and twinkling lights. I'd hid outside the art room door for almost twenty minutes before I'd bolted. What was wrong with me?

> **Rachel:** *Not gonna get any votes if no one sees you anymore.*
> **Me:** *I'll try harder.*
> **Rachel:** *Why do you need to try?*

Good question.

> **Me:** *Gotta go. Text later?*
> **Rachel:** *Sure.*

I put my phone face down on the table in case Rachel wasn't finished. A creepy-crawly ball of guilt burrowed a hole in my chest. Normally, I didn't go a day without seeing Rachel, but now I avoided her. Her and everyone else clambering toward the end of high school and off to the rest of their lives. I shuddered.

"Big emergency?" Kellan asked, a smirk across his lips as he flipped pages, pretending not to care.

"Nothing. Just a picture of Rachel."

He gasped and spread his hand across his chest. "Total crisis."

"Funny." I crumpled up a piece of paper and chucked it across the table, the ball bouncing off his ear and landing on top of a bookshelf.

He rolled his eyes up to glare at me without moving his head.

I grabbed my phone from the table and slid into the camera app. "Okay, grouchy, give us a smile."

He put his arm up, blocking his face. "What the hell are you doing?"

Avoiding reality and whatever it is you want to talk about. "Taking your picture so it shows up when you call."

"Why?"

"I have one for all my friends. You *are* one of my friends, aren't you?"

"If I say yes, do I have to take the picture?"

"If you say no, I'm still going to make you take the picture, so it doesn't really matter."

He scowled and turned his shoulders inward, trying to make his big torso as small as possible. "Great. This is exactly what I need right now."

"Oh, come on. You can't frown all the time."

His mouth drooped lower. "Try me."

"Okay." I shifted in my chair and held up my phone, trying to find the perfect angle. Even angry, he was very photogenic. His hazel eyes caught the sun in the best way, and his strong jaw gave a great profile. No matter which way I moved the shot, he looked good. Maybe I shouldn't have a picture of him on my phone. Marcus might freak out.

"Now give me your best model face."

"This is stupid." He turned so I could only see the back of his head.

"Please." I laid on the charm. If it were Marcus, I would simply bat my eyelashes and tease until he changed his mind. Kellan was a lot more difficult to manipulate. But a challenge made for a great distraction.

"All right." He looked as uncomfortable as possible, but I snapped the picture anyway.

"See? All done. No permanent injuries." I slid my fingers across the screen and opened the photo app.

"Except for my ego. If you sell that to some calendar, I better get a cut."

"Yeah. Somehow I doubt that's going to ... happen."

"What?" He looked at me oddly as I forced my jaw shut so he wouldn't see it hanging in an unnaturally wide-open state.

"It doesn't look right. We'll have to do it again."

He raised his arms and leaned back, covering his face. "Oh, no. Once was enough."

Without asking permission, I raised the phone and clicked it as fast as I could before he could dash out of the shot. I switched apps and looked at the second take, but it was the same as the first.

"I think there might be a problem." I turned the screen so Kellan could see the photo. The bookcase behind him looked great with brightly-colored volumes on each shelf stacked with precision. The shot had great light and composition, but no Kellan.

"Let me see that." He snatched the phone out of my hands and flipped between the two photos. His eyes widened as if he'd been pinched as he saw, or didn't see, the same thing I had: He didn't appear in the photos.

"That's really funny, Abby. Screw with the almost-dead guy. Is this some new app or something?"

"No." I shook my head as the words tumbled out. "I don't know what happened."

"Well, take it again." He thrust the phone back at me.

I clicked another photo. Same result. All scenery, no subject.

He started to shift back and forth in his chair.

"Why don't we try this?" I walked over to the other side of the table and crouched down beside him, pushing my head close to his. The burn of frustration radiated from his cheeks, or maybe it was just the heat of my own flushed skin bouncing back at me. Flipping the camera, I could see both of us clearly on the screen. This had to work.

"On three. One ... two ... three." The phone clicked, and I raced to look at the results. What should have been the two of us was the world's worst selfie. The agitated look on my face, floating next to nothing, a blank space where Kellan should have been.

"This can't be happening." Kellan grabbed the sides of his head and slammed his elbows onto the tabletop. "How is this possible?"

I sat back down and lowered my voice. "I don't know. Has this happened before, I mean, since you were cursed?"

His entire body shook as he tried to keep his head up, his fingers ripping at his hair.

"No. They took yearbook pictures last month and everything was fine. I mean, the proofs showed up at my house last week and I was definitely in them."

"So, something has changed, then."

"Really? What tipped you off?" He glared across the table, his go-to aggression not strong enough to cover the fear screaming out of his eye sockets.

"Hey. Relax, all right? I'm here to help, remember?"

"Sorry, but this is insane. What am I supposed to do now?"

My phone buzzed again, and I slid to the text message. Marcus. No greeting, just an address. I cringed, his unwritten words telling a louder story than the actual ones. Or maybe he was just busy? I hovered my finger over the screen and finally replied with a *thank you* and a winky face. I owed him a lot more than that, but he'd have to wait until later for my gratitude, especially if this address proved to be real.

"Maybe we need to do something a bit more drastic than combing through these books all day."

Kellan raised his head and stared at me, his eyes red and puffy. "Like what?"

"I know you aren't going to like this but remember I'm doing this to help you." I put my head down and slid my notebook and pens into my bag.

Kellan grabbed the strap and yanked the bag across the table, away from me. "Just spit it out, Abby."

"We need to go see Rhiann."

CHAPTER TWENTY-THREE

KELLAN

I tripped on a gaping hole in the well-worn carpet, and my hand smacked the cement wall to keep from falling. The dirty light fixture above me rattled, wavering the ominous orange glow that barely lit the hallway. Abby glared at me, her nose wrinkled, either from my clumsy approach or the rank smell that wafted in the air—a cocktail of piss, cheap beer, and smoke. Blindfolded, I would've thought we'd walked into a shady bar on the wrong side of town, not a place people actually paid to live. At least not people like Rhi.

Abby hadn't spoken since we'd left the library. It was almost eerie without her constant chatter, and it put me on edge. It wasn't like I had appropriate things to say for driving to visit my ex, though. I needed to hear her chirp on about something random, but instead, she decided to torture me by letting my thoughts pick and claw at my brain for the full hour's drive up here. And even after all that solitude, nothing made sense. Abby was right; something had changed. But what? Beasts jumping dimensions into my garage. My body disappearing like a ghost or whatever monster I was becoming. It didn't make sense. Why now?

I curled my fingers into a fist and stared at it. It didn't look any different. My bones showed white against the skin stretched over my knuckles. Blue veins striped the back of my hands. I looked human. I looked alive. Why wasn't I showing up in Abby's pictures?

"Maybe you shouldn't be standing there when she opens the door." Abby's voice cracked, her vocal cords likely shocked from lack of use.

"Why not?"

"She might not want to talk to you, considering that she condemned you to hell and all. Could still be some hard feelings."

"Why? *She's* the one who gets to walk away, free to do whatever she wants. Why would she have any hard feelings?" I punched my fist into the brick wall. Pain shot through my hand, but I fought back the wince.

She huffed and thrust her hands on her hips. "I wasn't talking about her."

"Fine. We'll have it your way." I let out a heavy sigh and backed up a few steps. This whole idea was stupid. Abby shouldn't have gone looking into my past. Or at least she should've told me first, so I could've forbidden her to try. As if she'd listen. My legs twitched, coaxing me to run, much smarter than my dumb brain shouting to stay still. Facing Rhiann wasn't something I wanted to do, especially not now with my world falling apart—more so than it already was.

Abby shot me an easy smile and knocked. The hollow sound of each strike echoed through my chest like she was hitting me instead of the pathetic piece of wood that passed for a door. I hoped no one would answer.

The door opened. So much for hope. I pressed myself against the wall and held my breath.

"Hi, are you Rhiann Glenn?" Abby asked with her bubbly

cheerleader attitude, one hand extended like she wasn't going to have a door slammed in her face in thirty seconds.

"Maybe. Who's asking?"

I knew that voice. A harder edge than I remembered, but definitely her. I closed my eyes and saw her as clearly as if I'd stepped the two feet to her door.

"I'm working on a project for school and someone gave me your name. I was wondering if I could ask you some questions."

"No one knows my name around here. Who put you up to this?"

Abby paused. Fatal mistake. "It's just a school project, really. Scottish mythology. Apparently, you're an expert."

"You're a terrible liar. Now get out of here before I make you regret looking for me."

She stepped into the hall to chase Abby away and froze. I peeled myself from the wall and stared back into her wide, green eyes. "Kellan Casey. I should've known."

An inferno ravaged through my blood as Rhiann flipped her scorching red hair to the side, revealing a few chunky strips of purple near the soft skin of her neck. Her tight green T-shirt clung around her breasts and fell loose where it cut off just above her belly button, my eyes trailing the miles of exposed skin to the band of her low-slung jeans. I used to love running my hands across that part of her stomach and feeling the goosebumps as she shivered under my touch. I shook my head.

"How did you find me?" She crossed her arms and planted her feet like a quarterback ready for a hike. We'd caught her off guard, but she was already preparing for attack. Rhiann could be a lot of things, but defenseless was never one of them.

"I didn't. Abby did."

"Great. I'm guessing you told her then?" She flailed her arms and glared at Abby, who stepped back to put some distance between them. Smart move.

"I had to. I had to tell someone. Do you know how much all this has been killing me?"

She scowled. "Of course, I know. It happened to me, too, remember?"

"But it's happening to me *now*. I'm running out of options." I paused, waiting for a reaction that never came. "Can we talk, please?"

"What could I possibly say to you right now? I can't believe you came looking for me." She gripped her head in her hands and began to pace in the small space. The orange hall light flickered. Hopefully, it was just shoddy electrical.

"Tell me there's a way out. A loophole. Something." I lowered my voice, trying to hide the pleading in my tone. I'd promised myself I wouldn't beg, but everything had flown out the window the second I'd lost myself in those eyes again.

"That's the catch. There is no do-over. This is your fate now, Kellan. I can't help you."

"Can't or won't?" Abby piped up, interrupting what had suddenly felt like our own private conversation.

Rhiann took a heavy step toward her, and Abby backed up. A wicked smile curled across Rhiann's lips as she jutted out her hip and posed, her arms across her chest. Fierce. Powerful. Gorgeous.

Abby glowered back, but with a lot less fire, as Rhiann's air of intimidation took hold of her. Two stubborn enemies locked in stalemate—Abby wanting answers and Rhiann unwilling to give them. It was pointless anyway. If Rhiann didn't want to talk to us, she wouldn't. No amount of mean girl posturing would change her mind. But maybe ...

"Can you leave us alone for a minute?" I glanced at Abby and raised my eyebrows, hoping she'd go quietly and doubting she would.

She looked at me, then Rhi, then me again, her mouth dropping open like an overheated dog. I nodded.

"Fine." She stomped halfway down the hall.

"New girlfriend?" Rhi jutted her chin after Abby.

"No, just a friend. She's trying to help me figure all this out."

"Clearly, she has no idea what she's up against, does she?"

I reached my hands out but pulled back and dropped them at my sides. "Can you please stop it? This isn't about her."

"Then why did you drag her into all this? Sounds pretty selfish to me."

"*Selfish*? You're really going to go there? It's not like I planned on getting anyone else involved." I started to explain but realized it wasn't necessary. She didn't have the right to know about my life now. "It's complicated."

"Well, at least she's your problem. Not mine." She shrugged. "But you shouldn't have hauled her up here. I've told you before. There's nothing I can do for you."

I grabbed the back of my head and popped my neck. "It's been getting worse. I've been seeing him more often—the Shadow Keeper. And other weird things have been happening. I don't know what to do."

"I don't know what to tell you. I've been there. I know what it feels like, but I can't make it go away. The only thing I know to lose a Shadow Keeper is to promise it a better pound of flesh. Maybe you can make it an offer?" She nudged her head down the hallway.

"What?" Her words punched me in the stomach and my lunch slid up the back of my throat. "I couldn't do that. I'd never do to anyone what you did to me."

"You might not think you would, but when the time comes, you might just be desperate enough to try. I was in pain for months. I didn't have any other choice. You saved me."

"Maybe if you would have told me what was happening, I could have done something else. Saved both of us." I looked down to avoid her eyes. "Maybe things could have been different with us."

"Maybe."

There was no tone. No tell. I couldn't read what she was thinking in that one word. "I haven't even seen you since that night. Are you okay?"

Her eyes widened as she stared at me, a softness creeping in at the corner of her gaze that might've made me think that she felt bad, except instead, she laughed, light and airy in a way I'd recognize from four blocks. She'd laughed that way when I would bite her earlobe when we'd made out. She'd laughed that way when I'd raced rich dickheads off the light and left them in the dust. She'd laughed that way the first time we'd had sex. I never realized how much I missed that laugh.

"You're the one who's going to spend the rest of time in some alternate dimension, and you're asking *me* if I'm all right? You really are the right sucker for the job, aren't you?"

"And it's your fault that my entire life is being wasted. No reason to be so heartless about it."

"What are you doing here then? Going to try to beg your way out of this? Well, there's nothing I can do to help you now. Take your groupie and have a nice afterlife."

Just like I thought. Nothing she could or would do to help. If we hadn't found an answer, she likely didn't have one. I sighed and started down the rank hallway, then cast one last look over my shoulder. Rhiann didn't move, her arms still crossed over her chest, posturing like a warrior queen. Except the fierceness in her eyes had drained away, leaving a faraway hollowness behind.

I turned on my heel and marched back to face her. "I have

to know. Did you ever give a crap about me or was I always just your mark?"

She opened her mouth to speak, but she changed her mind and stepped toward me instead. She ran her index finger down the side of my jaw along my chin. Her skin on mine felt better than the hundred times I'd imagined it over the past year. "I did care about you, Kellan. A lot. I still do. It's just that in the end, it was either me or you and I had to choose me. You would have done the same in my situation."

"But I didn't. I gave myself up for you."

The twisted snarkiness in her face faded. "And I am grateful. I really am."

Her hand slid around to the back of my neck, slowly weaving her fingers through the short strands of hair and coaxing my face up to meet her gaze. Somehow, without my noticing, she'd inched herself closer to me. Heat radiated from her skin and through the thin cotton of my shirt. My heart pounded out of time like the drummer in a punk band. I reached up and rubbed my hand along her forearm, feeling the small goosebumps rise along her flesh. She felt so good. So perfect. Like she'd never left.

"Now tell me why you're really here?" she whispered. Her hot breath fell on my face as she spoke. Her lips. Her deep red lips came closer to mine. Every part of me wanted to just let go.

I closed my eyes. "Don't."

CHAPTER TWENTY-FOUR

Abby

I hated that laugh. The way she threw her head back, proud and arrogant, a vicious lioness who'd captured her prey. Her knobby fingers ran over Kellan's neck like she owned him or something, and he just stood there and took it. As if she had him on an invisible leash. What had he ever seen in her?

She leaned closer, pressing her stunning half-naked body against him. It was pathetic, really. Clearly, this girl knew only one way to deal with a problem, and I was sure she had one hell of a reputation to go along with it. Her face moved closer, and I started to gag. Was she seriously going to molest him in the hallway of her nearly-condemned building with me watching? Or maybe she was going to bite him. Draw blood for some sort of evil spell with her venomous red lips. Enough. I didn't have to watch this.

"So, are you going to help him or not?" I yelled.

She glared at Kellan, then recoiled like a snake. "I already told you, there's nothing I can do."

"Well, you need to find something, then," I said. "This is your fault, and you need to fix it."

She stuck her hands on her hips and widened her stance. "I don't have to do anything. I'm free now."

"Only because you completely betrayed him. You nasty troll."

Rhiann splayed her hand across her chest and dropped her mouth open, feigning overdramatic shock. "Well, I'm not going to stand here and let you insult me. I have way better things to do than that."

She cupped her hand on Kellan's cheek and gave him two light taps. "Have fun with him while you have him. He's actually not a bad lay, either."

I stormed forward, my hands balled into fists. "You horrible, messed-up witch."

She rolled her eyes but didn't flinch a muscle. "What are you going to do? Annoy me to death with your high-pitch whining?"

My mind raced for my next move but halted at the crack of skin on skin. My head shot to the left as Rhiann's hand flew against my face. My cheek lit up, scalded by fury. I covered the spot with my hand, the skin pulsing beneath my fingers. "You shouldn't have done that."

I pulled back to crank the self-righteous smile off her face. I'd never hit someone before, but today felt like the right time to start. My arm thrust forward, but my fist whizzed by her nose, inches too short, as an arm around my stomach pulled me back and away from her. "Calm down, Abby. It won't do any good."

Rhiann laughed again. "You're right, it won't."

She twirled her finger in the air and muttered something in a language I couldn't understand. The veins in her body pulsed bright. Red webs of neon blood spidered across her flesh. The light fixture in the hallway exploded. Sparks flew. I stepped back and tried to run, but some unseen force wouldn't let my legs move. I struggled against the force, but it slammed me to the side and smashed me into the badly painted cement wall, head first. I crumpled to the floor, a shattered, broken doll.

"Good luck with your search." Rhiann reverted back to herself. The crimson lines disappeared, replaced by a satisfied smirk across her full lips. She sashayed back to her door and paused, her hand on the doorjamb like her palm held up the entire building. "And, Kellan, you really need to get some better taste. This vapid one isn't even a challenge."

Rhiann slammed the door, and it echoed down the hall, the vibration stabbing through my chest. She wasn't going to help. She wasn't even going to try. And there was nothing I could do about it.

Kellan looked at the door, then me, then back again, as if he were deciding which one of us he needed to handle. He crouched down beside me on the dirty floor. Probably for the best, as the wicked witch might've tossed him through a window or something.

Pain throbbed in the back of my head and the hallway faded in and out of focus. I reached back to rub my skull, but the pain surged worse as I hovered my hand over the spot. My body trembled, pain, fear, and anger ripping through my limbs.

"C'mon up." Kellan slid his arm underneath my shoulders and pulled me to my feet. "I should've mentioned her temper."

Wavering once, I tried to put one foot in front of the other, but Kellan held tight, not letting me fall. I gripped my hand on his upper arm, his bicep taut beneath my fingers, the citrusy clean smell of his skin a slight comfort from the ache in my head. Slowly, my coordination came back as he guided me down the stairs. All that remained was pain—a sharp, shooting pain burrowing between my eyes, straight through my skull, and down the back of my spine.

Kellan pushed open the door, and we burst into the sunlight, too bright and far too happy. Dizziness washed over me again and I sat down on the small fence that encircled the parking lot.

I hung my head in my hands and tried to concentrate on the small pile of gravel by my feet. Eventually, the rocks stopped swaying and I didn't want to throw up anymore.

Kellan stood in front of me, his eyes drooping. Tired or maybe just frustrated. He put out his hand and I took it, my own still trembling and cold against his skin.

He sighed. "Are you going to be okay? Should I take you to the hospital?"

I shook my head and regretted it immediately, as the vertigo rebounded in a tidal wave. He helped me into the car and settled into the driver's seat next to me. He turned over the engine but just sat staring out the windshield into the afternoon sun.

"What exactly were you going to do, hit her?" he asked, still not looking at me.

"I don't know. She *did* hit me first."

He sighed again, louder and deeper this time, and I leaned my head against the glass of the side window. "Did you actually kiss that smart mouth of hers?"

He turned, his face an angry shade of scarlet. "Don't judge me. You don't know anything about our relationship."

"I know she pretty much left you for dead. And then she just snaps her fingers and you come crawling back like an orphaned puppy. How's that for your relationship?"

"Maybe once the adrenaline wears off, you'll realize how totally over the line you are right now."

"Over the line? Me? I was the only one in that hallway standing up for you. *You* didn't even stand up for you." I pulled open the door and kicked my feet out onto the pavement. My legs shook and I doubted I could even stand, but I wasn't going to sit there and listen to him be delusional. I looked back.

"Rhiann doesn't care about you. She used you. Don't you get that?"

"Yes!" He yelled and slammed his hands on the steering wheel. "Of course I get it. I'm reminded of it every single day. And even if she never loved me, that doesn't mean that I never loved her because you know what? I did. I really think I did, and not only did she trade my soul to some supernatural collector, she ripped my heart out and spit on it. Not everyone in the entire universe is all hearts and friggin' flowers like you and that Marcus guy. Can you get over yourself for one second and realize that maybe this really sucks for me in more ways than you can ever imagine?"

I sat there silently. So, he did love her. He'd told me about a girl, but I'd never known he loved her.

"Look." He took a deep breath. "I'm sorry. Thank you for trying. Just get back in the car and I'll take you home."

I pulled my feet back in and closed the door. He didn't look at me as he shifted the car into drive and sped out of the parking lot with a squeal and likely a patch of rubber on the oil-soaked asphalt. Neither of us spoke for the entire drive home. I had no idea what to say to him anyway. What *could* I say? He'd never told me he loved her. But why would he? He didn't owe me anything. Still, it didn't make sense. How could he have been in love with someone as vile as her?

By the time we pulled into my driveway, the sun was fading behind my house into the deep violet sky. The dim light eased my headache instead of the harsh sun that burned my retinas all the way back. The bright yellow light screamed, even with my eyes closed.

I fidgeted with the door handle, but Kellan rushed out and opened my door, then grabbed my arm and helped me to my feet. The dizziness had faded, but my head still throbbed, and my eyes threatened to close any second. He started to walk me to my door, but I shook him off.

"Thanks for driving me home," I said as I tried not to stumble up the front walk.

"Abby," he called from behind me. I stopped but didn't turn around. "Don't ever go see her again."

Was that a threat or a warning? I couldn't tell. His tone was too flat, and my head was too cloudy. Didn't matter, though. I wouldn't be going back there. She didn't want to see me, and I definitely never wanted to see her. For the first time, I might've met someone I outright hated. I hated her for being nasty to me, for how she'd used Kellan, and for smashing my head into a wall. And knowing that he actually loved her only made me hate her more.

CHAPTER TWENTY-FIVE

KELLAN

The Civic engine revved as I pressed my foot harder on the gas pedal, climbing the one last twist in the steep, narrow road. The menacing shadows cast from the full tree branches thinned, giving way to infinite blue stretching out from the top of the hill. Scanning the horizon, I applied the brake and rolled to a stop. Alone. Just me and the cloudless sky.

No one ever came up here anyway. At least I'd never seen anyone since I'd rage-ridden my bike up this hill four years ago, but with my shit luck, today would be the day someone would stumble over it. I cut the engine and rested my forehead on the steering wheel, taking a deep, agonizing breath before getting out. The door creaked as it opened. I'd have to fix that later, but for right now, I didn't care. This day had already kicked the crap out of me and the simple act of breathing shredded my chest like I had inhaled razor blades.

A loud, rustling sound erupted behind me and I spun, my heart hammering and my fists clenched, ready to swing. Instead, a crow launched from a tall birch and flew overhead, cawing, as if to laugh at me in its evil bird way. I shook out my head, releasing the tension in my knuckles, and sighed. I was pathetic.

Grabbing the back of my neck, I followed the green patches of overgrown grass spotted on the broken dirt ground stopping just before they disappeared off a sharp drop into a bed of rocks and thick brush. Beyond the edge and the treacherous terrain below, the town spread out as far as I could see. A network of concrete zigzags created by tree-lined streets crissing and crossing into a maze.

Likely, no one could see me standing up here. Watching them from afar. Waiting for the day I'd vanish and everyone down there would continue on with their day like nothing had happened. Cars would stop and go. People would go to work and school, then come home to watch some horror movie on their stupid televisions that wouldn't come close to the hell I'd be experiencing for eternity. A hell that had chased me, and after today breathed vile and heavy on my neck. All of those people down there had no idea what was happening to me. They would live their mundane little lives and forget I'd ever existed until one day maybe I'd come to claim their souls just like the Shadow Keeper kept trying to claim mine. Maybe one of them would owe a debt like Rhi, or simply not want to live anymore and beg for mercy, but instead, they would get me. No mercy, just misery.

I walked back to the car and leaned against the hood, staring up into the sky as the last few rays of the sun beat down on my face. How had everything gone so wrong? I'd known seeing Rhi would be a huge mistake, but not how big of one. If anything, I'd thought she'd pull some sort of magic spell out on me and send me packing, but what she'd done felt worse.

She'd just laughed. Like I'd always just been the stupid idiot who'd fallen for her long con. A mark she'd used to save herself, then cast aside when she'd been done with me. Had she ever really cared about me? I'd thought I'd *loved* her. No. I *did* love her. Until recently, every thought of every day since we'd met had been all about her. How could she not care?

And Abby. I shouldn't have yelled at her. I smashed my toe into the ground, the dry dirt exploding into a dusty cloud, rocks bursting in all directions. Why did I have to keep screwing everything up? It'd been so long since anyone had bothered to stand in my corner that I didn't even recognize it when it happened. But it didn't mean I had to forgive her for dragging me out there to bring up all the stupid things I'd done.

In another reality, one that didn't involve Abby getting slammed into a wall, she probably would've really liked Rhi. Both of them were determined and strong, bold and impulsive. They were fearless. And, of course, both of them drove me absolutely insane.

But Rhi shouldn't have acted like a complete psycho. Abby's persistence worked my nerves too sometimes, but Rhiann shouldn't have punished her for our screwed-up history. Abby wouldn't even look at me on the way home. Kept staring out the window into the blinding sun. She'd rather see nothing than me. And why not? Only a few days ago, I'd wanted to kiss her until the sun fell away, but now who knew if she'd even speak to me? I was pathetic.

I pulled out my phone and swiped to the text screen.

Me: *Hey. What's up? Still pissed at me?*

I shook my head and deleted it. A text probably wasn't going to cut it. At least not that one. I owed her more than a text after the look she'd given me outside Rhi's apartment. I'd let her down. I didn't want to be that guy to her, but now I was, and it punched me hard in the gut. I dialed Abby's number and held my breath, not knowing what I'd say when, or if, she picked up, but hoping the right words would magically appear before she did.

One ring ... two rings ... three.

You've reached Abby Marino. Please leave a message.

Abby's voice filled my ears, but the sound seemed miles away. Invisible waves wafted through the air like heat rising off a highway. I gagged as the reek of sulfur burned in my nostrils. Uh-oh. Not now. I couldn't do this now.

I hung up the phone as pain shot through the back of my knees, forcing me down. The trees and the grass swirled in a cyclone of green, the sky becoming the ground and the ground becoming the sky. The sunlight burned brighter and brighter, then disappeared, and I fell into a void of deep, dark, black. I flailed, trying to grab a hold of anything, but the cold air breezed through my empty hands as acid from my stomach rose and burned my throat. Not now.

I slammed into the ground and shook my head. No matter how many times I'd come to The Meeting Room, I never managed to land on my feet. The Shadow Keeper probably wanted to see me on my knees. Watch me beg. *Asshole.*

Pressing my palms into the dusty floor, I pushed myself up and stood, then swiveled my neck to find the next trial before it found me. I scanned the black, searching for a door I'd never seen before, expecting a pair of red, green, purple, or yellow eyes to be staring back, stalking my every move and waiting to strike. Except nothing appeared. Just me and an obsidian pedestal stood in the always empty room. No noise, save for my own unsteady breaths.

The absence of everything made the room feel infinite. Wider, taller, as if a whole world of terror could be looming just beyond the shadows. I stepped forward and ran my hand across the cold, smooth surface of the pedestal, forcing myself to move, as standing still might make me an easy target. Where was he?

Heat surged through my body, and I swallowed against the thick, dry sensation spreading down my throat. Something was different. Wrong. And in a screwed-up place like this, different would never mean anything good. Different equaled danger.

I spun around and squeezed my fists so tight the knuckles might rip through my skin. The room whirled with me, cafeteria french fries and Gatorade churning in my stomach. Hot saliva built up on my tongue, but I gulped it back down.

"Face me, coward!" I screamed.

My words echoed back, over and over, until they fell away in the distant unknown, bringing back the eerie silence. Another wave of heat assaulted my body.

"You can't scare me. Not anymore. I'm not afraid of you."

The echoes continued and faded, then a low hiss like a deflating tire whispered back from the emptiness. I jerked my head toward the sound as it rolled into a dull laugh and finally erupted into a full-blown cackle.

"No longer afraid?" the voice called. "Then how come your fear beads thick and delicious on your skin?"

I glanced down at my arm trembling at my side and willed it to stay still.

"Your soul must taste exquisite," the voice hissed again.

Two red eyes pierced through the black. I held my breath, waiting for his question, but it never came. Instead, he appeared gliding—no, floating—up in my face, no feet visible beneath his robes. I stood my ground, chin high, refusing to back down. If he was today's fight, then I would take him head-on. He couldn't be any worse than his other pets.

Me and my devil. Face to face. For the first time, I could really see him. What he was, and what he wasn't. His head, just a skull. Weathered, white bone with those flaming cherry eyes smoldering in the center of each socket. This would be me. All my flesh worn away until only bones remained. My hand appeared beside my head and my fingers inched toward the skull. What would it be like to be him? To be nothing? My hand stretched closer. The Keeper never moved. Near his jaw, I hesitated, then swallowed hard and went for it. Blood against bone.

Ow! I snapped my hand away. Pain seared down my arm, like giving a handshake to a motorcycle muffler after an all-night ride. Jumping back, I shook my arm in the air and clenched onto my wrist as my hand vibrated in agony. Black circles of burnt and peeling flesh tipped my fingers. The Keeper hissed and if he could smile, I thought he would.

He floated past me to the pedestal.

"It's time," he said. "Time for you to join us."

I cradled my aching arm to my chest and did my best to stand straight, masking the pain.

The Keeper waved the end of his staff over the pedestal, the blue jewel on the end glowing brighter. Shielding my eyes with my good hand, I stared at the pedestal until the light faded and an hourglass appeared. All metal like a car part, but with sand that glowed bright white, even in this sinister space.

My heart raced, my pulse pumping hard in my ears. "What is this?"

"It's your life. Or what's left of it. When the sand runs out, your time is over."

"Over? What do you mean, *over*?"

"No more trials. No more chances. It's time to repay the debt that is owed."

I wrapped my fingers around the side of the hourglass, the cool metal soothing on my burnt fingers, and watched my life race, grain by grain, from top to bottom. "I'll never serve you."

"It's no longer your choice. Besides, you're the one who sped up the clock." He raised a bony finger and wagged it back and forth. "Sneaking into my world without my consent was not wise."

"How much time do I have?" I shouted, any fear left in me bubbling into a thick syrup of anger, my stare still fixed on the hypnotic glowing sand.

No response.

I slammed my open fist against the pedestal. "How much time do I have?"

"Six days." His voice pitched higher, joy ringing through his words as he lay down my death sentence.

"No." I shook my head. "No. No. No. I need more time."

"You've had more time than any other before you. Debts need to be paid and I will collect."

The air wrapped around my chest and squeezed like an invisible fist trying to crush my lungs. One week. Less than. That wasn't enough time. There would never be enough time.

I looked at the hourglass in my hand and threw it to the ground. It shattered, glowing sand and bits of glass scattering across the inky floor like fallen stars. "Now I have all the time in the world. Give me my test so I can get back to my life."

The Shadow Keeper swiped his staff again and another hourglass appeared on the pedestal, except this one had way less sand than the one I'd broken. "Five days left. Or would you like to smash this one and lose another day of your precious life?"

◈❤◈

I AWOKE on the floor of my room. My muscles ached, raw, every inch of skin that touched the carpet burning like battery acid. I stared at the blue-white moonlight carving lines in the carpet, trying to keep still and remember how I'd gotten here, but nothing since The Meeting Room flashed through my brain. Maybe I hadn't made it home on my own. Maybe the Shadow Keeper had just dumped me here when he'd finished tormenting me.

Thick scars cut across my fingertips where I'd touched the Keeper's face. The burn marks had disappeared, but I still had a reminder of what I'd done. As if I could ever forget. I pressed down on the jagged white lines of skin. They still hurt. Blistering pain still blazed from underneath my flesh.

He'd changed the game again, and I was losing. I'd lost too much already.

With small, slow movements, I pulled myself to sitting and fought the urge to collapse again as the hourglass and its ever-moving contents glowed from my nightstand. I reached for it, but my hand slid right through. Another trick. A hologram. Just a nasty reminder of how screwed I was.

Thanks a lot, Shadow Keeper.

CHAPTER TWENTY-SIX

Abby

I barely ate dinner. I pushed overcooked carrots and dry chicken around my plate while my parents made small talk until, finally, I excused myself and retreated to my room. Flopping down on the bed, I stared up at the ceiling. Fortunately, the dull pain in the front of my skull from my kiss with the cement wall had faded when I'd woken up this morning, but the sickening feeling in my stomach wouldn't give up and go away. And if I didn't already feel awful, Kellan had skipped out on school today, probably still mad at me for dragging him off to see his ex. When exactly had all this gotten so complicated?

When we'd been kids, everything had seemed so simple. The only problems we'd had were coming in late for dinner, which happened often. Back then, everything looked so hopeful. Bad things were never going to happen to us. We were invincible. A memory of me and Kellan twinged in my brain. Something from so long ago, I'd almost forgotten. Once upon a time when things had been less life-or-death.

I pushed myself up to sit and reached under my bed, yanking out a small box. Boy band stickers, marker drawings, and puffy paint all mixed together on the outside of a shoebox like some disturbed preteen vision board. I jumped up and rushed over to shut the bedroom door, then crept back to my bed and wiggled off the lid. On the top of the pile sat the letters, their boldface type staring up at me from their thick stationery stock. Yale blue, Harvard crimson, UPenn red. The colors and crests changed, but the words were the same as if they had all been printed at one giant dream-sucking factory, *We regret to inform you that your application ...* If my mother only knew.

I shoved the letters aside and kept digging through the pile. Underneath all the pictures, newspaper clippings of my vast history of achievements, and friendship bracelets, almost at the bottom, I finally found it. The colors had faded, everything looking a little more yellow than I'd remembered, but it was still us. My wide, tooth-deprived smile and two crooked braids, Kellan's wire-rimmed glasses on ears slightly too big for his head. We'd been seven. We'd just moved into this house, and Mom had decided to throw me the biggest fairy tea party that this town had ever seen. Except I hadn't wanted a fairy tea party, I'd wanted to move back to California. Mom invited every girl in the neighborhood, but I wasn't interested. I'd ripped off the pink tulle wings she'd strapped onto my back, kicked off my fancy party shoes, and ran away. I hadn't gotten far, especially in a strange new town, so I'd just trespassed into Kellan's yard and hid in his treehouse. Mom canceled the party, and the whole neighborhood spent the entire afternoon searching for me.

Kellan had found me hiding but promised not to turn me in, the crazy little fugitive he'd never even met. We'd played games, and he'd told me ghost stories while I'd pretended not to be afraid, and I'd told him all about my old life.

I remembered the sun fading because the sky had turned red when Mr. Casey had come to call Kellan for dinner. The surprised look on Mr. Casey's face when he'd realized that the missing girl had been tucked away in his own backyard.

He'd told me I needed to go home, but I cried, suddenly sad I'd missed my birthday party. He'd run back in the house and returned with a snack cake cupcake—the ones with the frosting in the middle and the white swirls on the top—a candle, and a camera. He and Kellan sang me happy birthday, and I'd made a wish. Then Mr. Casey snapped this picture and took me home.

Dad had scooped me up in his arms, given me ice cream, and kept kissing the top of my head. Mom lost it. She'd cried for two straight days. I'd never run away again. But that was the day I'd met Kellan Casey and we'd become best friends. That is until we weren't.

And now I didn't know what we were. That uncontrollable feeling, when I'd wanted to punch Rhiann, had nagged at me all day. It wasn't just the fact that she was such a relentless coward —because she totally was. It was something else. Something evil that started building and burning inside me from the second she'd touched Kellan. How she'd looked at him and how he'd looked at her. He didn't need to tell me he loved her. At that moment, I'd known it. It didn't make sense in my head, but I could feel it, thick-like fog filling the hallway. And from that second on, my entire body writhed uncomfortably. I'd wanted to hit her for so many of the reasons for which she deserved a good punch, but also for the one reason that she had no control over at all. He loved her.

I looked at the photo again in my hands, but it didn't seem quite right. I held it closer, but it was the same. Picture Kellan seemed to be fading. Couldn't be. Hitting my head must've broken something in my brain. I closed my eyes tightly and reopened them. But Kellan appeared even lighter than before. The wood beams holding up the treehouse started showing faintly behind him like someone had placed a translucent

Kellan-shaped sticker over top. Then as I stared harder, he disappeared. Just for a second and then he came back, like I'd blinked and missed something. Except I knew I hadn't. He flickered again, but this time, he never came back. One second ... two seconds ... thirty seconds ... still no Kellan.

I gulped and grabbed my phone from the nightstand, my eyes still fixed on the image. I didn't care if Kellan was mad at me or hated me or whatever.

Me: *We need to talk. Now.*

I waited for a response, staring at the screen, waiting for words to magically appear. Nothing.

Me: *I'm serious. SOS.*

I got up and looked out the window. His bedroom lights were off. I ran down and looked through the hall window. His car was still gone. I hadn't seen it in the driveway since he'd dropped me off yesterday. Did he go back to see her again? He'd be pretty stupid to do that, but it really wasn't my business what he did with his life. The sick feeling in my stomach worsened as I pictured the two of them together. I glanced at the phone again. Still nothing. Where was he?

CHAPTER TWENTY-SEVEN

KELLAN

Heat bled through the cardboard cup and made the thin scars on my fingertips throb. I hoped I'd gotten the right one. Ordering coffee should not be more complicated than disarming a bomb. But it smelled right. It smelled like her. And hopefully, it would make her happy. Once I told her we'd run out of time, she may never bother to speak to me again.

Or maybe I shouldn't tell her? Just let the next few days go by and pretend it wasn't really happening. I could still see her smile, and laugh, and maybe take me away from thinking about my inevitable end. Except that wasn't really fair. In fact, it was pathetically selfish, but who would deny a dying man his last wish?

Time had already moved too fast. The Shadow Keeper had promised me five days but then chucked me back into my life a day later, cutting the tally down to four. And to top it off, he'd screwed me again by leaving my car up on the hill. After I'd stopped staring at the hourglass, I'd had to run ten miles in the dark to go get it. *Bastard.*

I pushed the café door with my free arm, trying to make

sure I didn't upend the cup. I couldn't stand going through the process of ordering again, but as soon as I got outside, I almost threw the thing to the ground. Some jackass had parked right behind my car. A fancy BMW i8 Roadster sat directly behind my Civic, blocking me in. Only five other cars sat parked in this stupid lot, so either this guy had zero idea how to drive or someone had decided to send me a message. I walked past the car and tried to ignore the guy perched in the front seat. I tended to punch things, so confrontation never worked well for me, and besides, the illegal tint on the Beamer made it impossible to see through in the morning sun. Didn't matter. The dude hiding in the car was just a driver. The real asshole stood leaning against my trunk, his arms crossed over his cocky, puffed-up chest. Marcus. All shiny and arrogant and in my way.

"Caffeine's a little tame for you, don't you think? Or are you trying to slow the withdrawal?" He put a foot on my bumper and swiped the pair of aviators off his face. I bit the inside of my cheek until I tasted the sour tang of blood, determined not to rip off the leg propped up on my car and beat the hell out of him with it.

I jerked my head at him. "What do you want?"

He smirked and leaned back slightly. He looked like the biggest poser I'd ever seen, but he sure seemed to think he was important. "I just thought that since you've been spending so much time with Abby that maybe I needed to see what the appeal was."

"Well, I guess that's our problem. I don't really have the time to sit and chat about myself. Not that I would, even if I did."

He pushed his heel off the car and stood up straight. "Why? Is Abby waiting for you somewhere?"

"I don't know. Why don't you ask her? I'm not her keeper." I turned to get in my car. That BMW wouldn't sit there very long if I backed into the side of the overpriced piece of crap.

"I found that girl, Kellan. Your ex, Ryan, or whatever her name is." He gave me a crooked grin. "She's quite the catch. Way hotter than I expected. Good job, buddy."

I stopped. He'd talked to her and lived to tell about it. Surprising. I didn't think she'd even give the time of day to a douchebag like him. Seemed like there were a lot of things she wasn't telling me. "I'm glad you think so. Maybe she'd be more your type."

"She told me you're dangerous," he continued, ignoring my dig at him. "Told me I should avoid you."

"Well, she's a lying bitch."

"That's not a very nice thing to say. Is that what you call all your women? Bitches? Real classy." Marcus tutted and moved slowly toward me. Long careful steps. Either scared or trying to make a statement. Jerk.

"You don't know a thing about me."

"And to be honest, I really don't want to. I'm perfectly fine thinking about you as the scum that you are."

I put the coffee cup on the top of the car and reached for the car handle. "Do what you want, man. Just get out of my way."

Marcus rushed over and got up in my space. Big mistake.

"I'm not going to let you turn Abby into some trailer trash booty call—or worse. Ryan says you're just using her and are setting her up for some kind of fall."

"Get out of my face." What the hell had Rhiann told him? I lunged forward, planting both hands against his chest and pushing him back.

He stumbled and almost tripped back into the car but managed to regain his footing before he hit the concrete.

I doubted she'd told him the whole truth. He probably thought I was her dealer or something.

"Is there a problem out here?" Marcus's buddy stepped out and leaned against the top of the car. The zipper on his sweater clicked against the paint, probably leaving a huge scratch. At least a thousand-dollar fix on that car, and a patch job would never quite match right. But a guy like him probably didn't give a rat's ass about that. If it was dirty, Daddy probably bought him a new one.

I jerked forward at Marcus as the driver eyed me up from the other side of the car. He tried to look tough with that blond buzzcut and cracking his knuckles like some clichéd gang-banger, but he was probably shit scared that I'd come over and beat the crap out of him. I'd seen him lurking around the office before, all black eyes and bloody lips. Probably some football idiot who had a problem with his fists, but I could tell by the way he stayed back that even he wasn't willing to take me on. Looked like that reputation of mine was still intact.

"No." Marcus waved off his sidekick. "I think we're pretty much done here anyway."

The goon gave me a sneer and retreated into the car.

"I won't let you mess her up," Marcus said, trying to get his tough guy act back.

"Abby's smart. She can make her own decisions. However, I am questioning her judgment when it comes to dating you."

"See? That's the trouble. I don't think she's been making her own decisions. She's been acting all weird lately and I'm sure you've been the one influencing her."

"Do you even hear yourself? I'm not some puppet master. If you have a problem with your love life, take it up with your girlfriend and get the hell away from my car."

He poked himself in his chest. "You're right. She's *my* girlfriend."

"That's what I just said, so you and your driver can screw right off."

"She'll never pick you, you know. She might consider it for a while, what with your I-don't-care attitude, but soon enough, she'll figure out what a waste of skin you are. A girl like her will never go for a loser with no future like you."

I closed my eyes and took in a deep breath as I fought the urge to dropkick this mouthpiece into the McDonald's lot next door. "You really are a dickhead, you know that?"

"I just don't like to share things that belong to me. Or worse, see a great girl like that slum it with a nothing like you."

"If she only heard the crap you're saying right now, she'd—"

"She'd what? Realize that I'm right and never speak to your sorry ass again?"

I looked over at the coffee and resisted chucking it at his smug face.

"That's what I thought." Marcus nodded. "You know it too. You don't stand a chance, so don't waste your time."

He flipped back on his sunglasses and jumped in the passenger side of the car. His idiot friend stood on the clutch and the car peeled out of the parking lot, laying a patch of melted rubber that singed my nose hairs.

Screw it. I drew back and hurled the coffee cup at the back of the Beamer, hitting it square in the back window. The brake lights pulsed as the driver stuck his arm out the window and flashed his middle finger over the top of the car. *That the best you got, jerk face?*

Coffee dripped down my hand and burned like acid on my skin. I shook it off and made a fist as I watched them drive away.

A loser like me. As if I needed a reminder of how much I hated myself, now I had the friggin' prep school mafia on my ass. What the hell did she see in him? Did she like the fact that he thought he was all-powerful? Was that some sort of turn-on?

I got in the car and faced the roof, letting out a sigh. My hands were still shaking as I visualized the physical pain I wanted to cause Marcus and his witless accomplice. But I couldn't. Besides, now I needed to know what Rhiann had told him. All this time hiding my secret just for it to come out and kick me in the face now.

And besides, what was that guy's problem with me? If Abby didn't want to be with him, which was probably the smartest decision she'd ever make, how was that my fault? I was just her charity case. A problem to be solved before she sailed out of this town and never looked back. There was no way that she saw me like that. People didn't see me at all, and if they did, it was as something to be pitied or disliked, not coveted. Especially girls like Abby. Pretty girls who smelled like coconut and raspberries and wore sparkly things and pink nail polish were definitely not into guys like me. But would it be different if I weren't dying? Of course, I'd thought about it. Way more lately than I should have. Especially since I knew I'd let her down.

That was it. If I was just a distraction for her to avoid her boyfriend, then I needed to tell her about the hourglass. She couldn't hide out with me forever and avoid her problems, and I sure didn't want to get stuck in the middle of them. I should tell her that all hope was dead, and she should start forgetting about me, just like everyone else soon would.

Okay. I popped my neck and stretched my fingers like a fighter before a brawl. *Drive straight over to her house and tell her it's all over.*

I turned the key in the ignition and listened to it roar a couple of times. As much as a Civic could roar.

You need to tell her.

I pulled out of the parking lot, signaled left, and stared down the road toward her house.

Turning right, I hit the gas and sped off.

CHAPTER TWENTY-EIGHT

Abby

I ran my left hand through the cool blades of grass on the front lawn of the school, my right hand clenched tightly to the magazine article in my lap. I should have been studying, or at least that was what the open textbook on the ground kept yelling at me, but the words kept swimming in circles before my eyes. The sun beat down on my head, adding to my lack of concentration, but moving would mean losing my view of the main entrance and I couldn't miss Kellan's arrival, if he decided to show up at all. He'd never responded to my SOS text message, and this couldn't wait any longer. We were running out of time.

Parker's car sped past and into the parking lot, then screeched to a stop on the far end. Parker flung open the driver's door and stomped out, slamming it closed with a thunk that echoed loudly through the courtyard. He rushed to the back of the car and started rubbing down the trunk and bumper with a rag. I laughed. A bird had probably looked at his paint job and made him nervous enough to buff the entire back end before the bell.

A few seconds later, the passenger door opened, and

Marcus stepped out. He slipped his sunglasses on top of his head, the sun reflecting off his mirrored lenses. The ethereal glow blended with his own natural luminosity and made him look like an ancient god in designer shoes or at the very least Middleton's beacon of popularity. He flipped an effortlessly cool wave at Parker, then headed toward the school doors, languid and detailed movements as if he moved in slow motion for the world to bask in his perfection. I stood up and walked toward him like the moon being pulled by the sun. Sometimes I forgot how much Marcus could affect me. How his smile, or his laugh, or even the way he swaggered through life drew me in. An empty aching in my chest to be near him and his light. But the ache had faded over time and now my limbs reacted on reflex more than need.

He'd called last night, making final arrangements for prom, and graduation, and all those things I should have cared about. Any other girl in my place would be annoying with excitement. Rachel was. Rachel. I'd been an awful friend to her. Her giddy anticipation for these "rites of passage," as she called them. I couldn't do it. Her calls went to voicemail and her texts were answered with canned phrases or emojis. This was senior year. Less than a week away from getting out of high school and being anyone I wanted. Less than a week away from everyone finding out I was a complete fraud. I wasn't the girl who had it all together. I wasn't the golden child my parents thought they'd raised. I was a nobody. If high school ended, how long could I keep faking my way through life before someone figured me out?

My foot barely hit concrete as Kellan's Civic sped past. I shook my head, snapping free from Marcus's draw and pushing down the thoughts plaguing my brain, then changed course, racing toward the empty parking space near the back of the lot.

Before the car came to a complete stop, I ripped open the door and jumped into the passenger seat.

"Are you ignoring everyone or just my texts?" I said, forcing a half-hearted smile.

"Morning?" Kellan looked me over with sleepy eyes, then huffed as he pushed his foot harder on the brake. "Can you let me park first?"

"Sorry, but you need to see this."

I reached into my bookbag and pulled out the birthday picture from his treehouse, then deposited it into his lap while he maneuvered the stick shift and turned off the ignition.

He picked up the photo. "What's this?"

He stared at it for a few seconds, his brow furrowed tight until it hit where he'd seen it before. His face relaxed as the realization burst across his face and erupted in laughter. "Hey, it's that birthday party you went MIA from back when we were kids."

"Right. But do you see anything weird with this picture?"

His face scrunched up again as he studied the photo, but he didn't answer.

"Until the other night, you were in that picture with me and now you're gone. Just like the pictures on my phone. Vanished. Disappeared."

"What? Just gone?" He held the picture closer to his face as if a better look would make my words untrue. "Wait. What do you mean, the other night? The other night when?"

"Two nights ago. After you dropped me off from seeing Rhiann."

Kellan slammed his palm against the steering wheel, then grabbed a fistful of hair at the front of his head. "Are you shitting me? Why can't he just leave me the hell alone already? I already got the message."

"The message?"

"Forget it. Stupid Shadow Keeper being his asshole self again."

"But maybe *he* can help." I took the magazine article still clamped in my fist and gave it to Kellan, pointing my finger at the glossy headshot on the left of the page. "This guy is a professor at the University of Kansas, and Lawrence is only a couple of hours away, so we can get there and back in no time. I've already called ahead and made an appointment. We'd already be halfway there if you'd decided not to be late for first period."

His eyes skimmed down the article and then glanced out the window to somewhere farther away than the parking lot. "Not sure this is a good idea. I mean, shouldn't you be going to school and stuff? You probably shouldn't be skipping."

"Ha. Since when did Kellan Casey have an issue with skipping school? Not like you've never done it before. Besides, life-or-death is more important than English class."

Kellan swung his head down toward his lap and gripped the gearshift so hard, the knuckles in his right hand bulged. "I need to tell you something."

Uh-oh. From his melancholy tone, this couldn't have been anything good. Had something else happened yesterday? Had he had another episode? Or something worse? Maybe he had gone back to see Rhiann without me. The memory of her pressing her sultry self against him appeared in my brain and started to drift into what could've happened between them over the last twenty-four hours. Bile built in the back of my throat, but I pushed down the image before I threw up all over his floor mats. Sure, maybe Rhiann was pretty in an obnoxious kind of way, but beyond the body, her personality definitely needed a makeover.

I reached back and pulled the seatbelt across my lap,

clicking it into its buckle. "I guess you can tell me on the way, then."

"Seriously, Abby, I really don't think this is a good idea."

I reached my hand across the car and grabbed his from the gear shift, wrapping my palm around his long fingers. He flinched for a moment, then relaxed under my touch. "Look, I know you're super mad at me, but I'm really trying to make this up to you."

His head jerked back. "Make it up to me? Why would I be mad?"

"How I acted the other day. Taking you out to see her when you didn't want to. And you're right. Rhiann is your problem ... I mean ... *past* to deal with. It's not my place."

Kellan looked up, his eyes wide and serious. Distant. "It's fine, Abby. I don't care about that."

"Whatever." I dropped his hand and crossed my arms over my chest. Of course, he wouldn't care. I'd found the girl who'd dusted him all those months ago. He was probably grateful. "Why don't we just get this saving your life thing over with, then if you want, I'll leave you alone and you won't have to deal with me anymore?"

"Hey." He placed his hand on my chin and turned my head to look at him. His eyes darkened, deeper brownish-green than greenish-gold like normal, and formed a shadow of sincerity over his face. I dug my fingernails into my arm. Too close. Way too close. "Do you really think I want you to leave me alone?"

I cast my eyes toward the floor, unable to hold his unwavering stare. Scared of what I might see next. Scared of what I might show. "I don't know. But I guess that's your choice. All I know is I don't want to wake up knowing that you aren't safe, ten feet away in the house next door. That's not a reality I'm ready to deal with. Not yet."

Kellan released my chin and brushed his knuckles against

my flaming cheek. My stomach hollowed, and I turned toward the window. Kellan sighed, his breath moving the strands of hair on my neck, then turned to clutch the steering wheel. "I guess we're going on a road trip, then."

I settled back in my seat. Kellan shifted the car into drive and tore out of his parking space. As we neared the other side of the lot, he veered closer to Parker, still buffing out his bumper, even though the bell had already gone.

Honk!

Dropping his cloth onto the pavement, Parker jumped as Kellan laid on the horn and sped off toward the exit.

"What was that for?" I looked back and watched Parker glare after us. He flipped Kellan off and shouted something I couldn't hear and likely didn't want to.

"Hate that guy. He's a real dick."

I narrowed my eyes and stared as if it could bore a hole into his head. "Some people say you're a real dick too, you know?"

"I am. But not as big of a dick as that guy."

"Sure." I slipped off my sandals and curled my knees up to my chest, resting my elbow against the window. "One last thing. Before we go, do you think we could stop by a Starbucks? I'm craving a macchiato so bad, I think I can actually smell caramel."

CHAPTER TWENTY-NINE

KELLAN

Dr. Colin Walsh looked like the perfect person to discuss Shadow Keepers with, as the decrepit old man resembled a bag of bones closer than any other human possibly could. He walked with a cane that appeared to be carved out of the wood from some ancient tree, but the way he paraded around his office, it was probably just for show. Hopefully, this guy wouldn't be one of those self-indulgent 'I'm more important than I really am' types. I didn't have time to humor some old guy's oversized ego.

"One moment, please. Feel free to take a look around," the doctor said in a rough foreign brogue as he shuffled through a pile of books and papers on his desk.

I turned away from him, his hectic demeanor frustrating to watch, and wandered around the office. No, not an office. More like a storage closet.

Statues, artifacts, primitive scrolls, and things in jars that I kept my fingers far away from littered every available surface. This guy must have had a shit ton of frequent flier miles. Or maybe the relics were just part of his act.

"Who is he again?" I asked Abby as she moved around the room taking in all the weird, her hands clasped tightly in front of her.

"Anthropologist and historian. Specializes in ancient folklore and the occult."

"They teach classes on that stuff?"

"Beats me, but he's our only shot right now."

"Great." I'd talked to an occult expert once, but he hadn't been much help. I'd actually paid him for information because I'd had no other options, and all I'd gotten was a sales pitch for some magical protection device that looked like a discount store humidifier tagged with black spray paint. No, thanks. Months later, at the depths of my desperation, I'd called him up again, but the number was out of service. Shocker.

Abby knotted her fingers near her chest, pulling her arms close to her ribcage, clearly avoiding contact with anything and everything in this den of macabre. The ghosts and ghouls in paintings behind her seemed to watch as she paced slow laps, her stare cast down on the same four feet of tile for the past three minutes. Seeing her cautious version of fear made me glad I hadn't told her about the hourglass on the drive up here. I didn't need to upset her. She didn't need that. Eventually, she took a chance and peeked up at the wall at a particularly gruesome portrait of a monster with bloodthirsty eyes and a face made of more oozing scar tissue than skin. She shuddered then backed away, the small hairs on her arms standing on end. Except she banged right into an antique table, knocking a pile of dusty books to the floor.

"I'm so sorry," she apologized, flapping her hands and dropping to her knees to pick them up.

I crouched down to help, laughing at her sharp, frenzied movements.

"Calm down. He's not going to carve out your eyeballs or anything." I took the book from her trembling fingers and piled it with the rest as she thrust her hands behind her back.

"Are you sure?" she breathed, the lowered volume of her voice more polite than mine, although I doubted the old man could hear a freight train running through his bedroom.

"I'll make sure of it."

She forced a grin as she straightened the books into a sturdy pile and placed them back on the table.

"What can I do for you?" Dr. Walsh had stopped puttering and taken a seat in the pretentious oversized armchair behind his desk. He fanned a wrinkled hand in front of him. "Come sit. Talk. I promise not to use you as sacrifices."

He chuckled at his own joke, drowning out the sound of Abby swallowing so hard, she'd likely ingested her own tonsils.

She shook her head, then marched over and took a seat in the hard metal chair across from the doctor. "Thank you for seeing us on short notice. The reputation for your work in the occult is very impressive."

A proud smile split across the old man's face and Abby leaned slightly forward, beaming back at him. As terrified as she'd been five seconds ago, this girl sure knew how to lay on the charm, even if it was completely fake. When the world challenged me, I spit fire in its face, but she shone—beams of blistering sunshine flowed from her smile to decimate the shadows. If only she could see what I saw, she'd never have any reason to be afraid. Hopefully, she'd always stay that way, even after I checked out later this week.

I flung myself in the chair next to Abby, the reminder of my dwindling humanity sparking all my nerve endings, my limbs jumpy and struggling to stay still. "So, you're Scottish then?"

"No. Irish, but I've spent time studying all the folklore in the Isles. I have some fascinating research on the Fae people, if you're interested."

Abby politely shook her head, then glanced over each shoulder and lowered her voice to just above a whisper. "We want to know about your research on wraiths, specifically Shadow Keepers."

"Strange choice." Dr. Walsh reclined in his chair and bent his index finger into a hook, resting it against his lips. "Why would normal-looking kids like you want to talk about nasty creatures like them?"

Abby's stare wandered in my direction and fixed on my face, requesting permission to tell him.

I nodded.

"Kellan's been cursed by one, and we need to find a way out of the deal."

The old man's eyes widened to the size of soccer balls, then he slammed his hands against his desk and pushed his chair back. "What are you? What do you want from me?"

"Him?" Abby pointed toward me. "He's not a Shadow Keeper; he's still human."

Still human. Barely.

"I didn't think he was a Shadow Keeper, love. But what is he?" Dr. Walsh sprung to his feet like a boxer looking for a fight —a boxer less than half his age. "Only the souls of the magical are condemned to service; normal souls are just collected. So, tell me what you are before I start every incantation I've learned in sixty years and send you back to wherever you came from!"

I raised my hands in surrender. "I'm human, I swear. It was all because of a girl."

The old man's eyes drifted to Abby.

"Not her. Another girl, Rhiann. She tricked me into taking her place as its victim."

"Must be some girl." His shoulders dropped and he closed his eyes as a hard breath pushed out from his lungs. "I'm assuming she's a witch, then."

I nodded. "But I'm not a witch or whatever. Why is the Shadow Keeper coming after me?"

"Doesn't matter. That girl was, and you took her place. How long ago was this?"

"About eight months," Abby interjected before I could do the math. "And things have been getting weirder. He's having more episodes than normal, he doesn't appear in pictures anymore, and sometimes creatures are coming into this world. Chasing him."

"Okay, Abby, relax." I took her hand and felt her pulse hammering through her skin. I squeezed tighter and the blood started to slow.

"Dreadful creatures to deal with, Shadow Keepers. They have their job to do and they don't quit until they have their pound of flesh. They're created from betrayal, so vengeance comes easy for them."

"So, doctor, is there anything he can do to get rid of it? Make the Shadow Keeper go away?" Abby asked.

"Shadow Keepers are the spirits of the occult. Practitioners of magic. They thrive on control, through deals and acquisitions. No one breaks a deal with a Shadow Keeper. Your *friend* cheated by exchanging her soul for yours, but in the end, the Keeper still got what they came for, so she went free."

I stood up and paced in front of the desk. No one breaks a deal with a Shadow Keeper. Well, someone had. Someone who'd thought I'd make really good bait.

"There must be others, then. People cheating their contracts?" Abby said, voicing my frantic thoughts.

"Only once have I heard of someone managing to cheat the

Keeper's game—until now, I guess—but I wouldn't recommend it." He tightened his lips into a thin line and shook his gray head.

"Why? What happened?" Abby asked, sitting entranced at the edge of her chair.

"Years ago, there was a miller. He was young, resourceful, and proficient in the black arts. He had made a small fortune utilizing magic for profit, which, as most fairy tales will tell you, is usually not a wise choice. Anyway, the miller began to flaunt his wealth and was brutally attacked by some hooligans outside of a pub one night. A Shadow Keeper came to the miller and tried to claim his soul, but instead, the miller offered him the soul of his firstborn child in exchange for his, even though the miller knew that his wife was barren. The Shadow Keeper accepted, and the miller continued on. Several years later, the miller was again visited by the Shadow Keeper, who insisted that he redeem the soul of the miller, as he was still without a child. The miller insisted that a deal was a deal, and the Shadow Keeper should have done his research before agreeing."

Abby nodded as she took in the words, each one tightening her knitted eyebrows. "If the Shadow Keeper was bound by the deal he'd made with the miller, why didn't he just take him anyway?"

"All magic has rules, love. Wraiths are dealmakers, businessmen who deal in lost souls. They uphold their ends of bargains, but if anyone deceives them, it doesn't mean they don't always get their reward."

"What happened with the miller? Did he have to give up his soul?" I asked.

"No. The miller survived, his soul untouched as agreed, but the Shadow Keeper collected the souls of every single person in his village, leaving his wife for last. He watched as the Keeper destroyed every single person, every woman, every child. The miller went mad and roamed the countryside for years telling everyone his story until eventually they found him at an inn having slit his own throat."

Abby shuddered hard enough that the air between us vibrated.

"And that's it?" she asked.

The doctor's face scrunched up, and he turned his ear toward her. "Pardon me?"

"That's it?" She tugged her hand away from mine and gripped the bottom of her seat until her knuckles went bloodless. "It was just over? No fight? No revenge? He just gave up?"

"Gave up? Do you understand the weight of the torture done to this man?"

"Yes, but you said you knew of someone who cheated a Shadow Keeper. He didn't cheat. In the end, he still died, freeing his soul for the Keeper to take. He didn't win. He just ..."

Abby glanced in my direction, pools gathering in the corners of her eyes. She blinked them down, but the lost hopelessness that remained sliced hot and sharp through my chest, as if she'd ripped one of the doctor's knives from his collection of artifacts off the wall and flayed me open like an ancient sacrifice.

A kind smile twisted on the doctor's lips. "I'm sorry, but not all stories have a happy ending."

The world seemed to stop turning as the room plummeted into silence. Abby grimaced, and I saw her change. The light inside her, the one that I'd held on to, the one I envied, dimmed just a bit. The tiniest crack zigzagged across Abby's worldview bubble. A dark mark that I had inked on her and she'd never be able to erase. Not even after I was no longer here.

"Well, thank you for your help. If you think of anything else that might be useful, please give me a call." Abby shook her head, regaining her laser focus, then launched from her seat, making long strides to the exit.

"Of course. It was wonderful to meet you both. But I recommend staying far away from the supernatural in the future."

I nodded at the old man and followed behind, aching for the chance to make things right in her world again. Make things better.

As we reached the door, the old man stood behind his desk and cleared his throat, watching me hightail it out of there. His creepy, old guy stare locked on the back of my head and a shiver rippled through my body.

"Mind if I chat with the young fella for a spell?" he asked, much politer than his unnerving glare.

Abby looked at the doctor, then at me. I shrugged but still hoped she'd argue.

"Sure, I guess. I'll be right outside." She gave me a wary look and slipped out the door, clicking it closed behind her.

"You've been marked, haven't ya?" Dr. Walsh asked as he settled himself back down at his desk, his fingers laced together in front of him.

"Excuse me?"

"Marked. The Keeper's put a date on you now. I can see it in the way you can't look at me straight. You know when he's coming for you."

I nodded, my head dropping low onto my chest. "I have until this Friday."

"Aye. And your lass doesn't know, does she?"

"My what?"

"Your bird, son. Your girl." He raised a shaky, wrinkled finger toward the door.

"Abby? She doesn't know that a date's been set. And she's not ... We're not a thing." *I'm not that lucky.*

A high-pitched whistle escaped his motionless lips. "You've really made a bags of this one. She will find out, you know?"

"I know. I just hoped I'd figure something out before it happened."

"It's a sin for such a travesty to befall a young man, but I'd recommend getting your affairs in order." He clicked his tongue against his teeth and sighed. "Two days isn't typically long enough for miracles."

CHAPTER THIRTY

Abby

It could've been the fast food burgers we grabbed on the way out to the highway swirling around in the bottom of my stomach, or maybe it was just the lingering creeps from being in that freak show of an office, but something just didn't feel right. It had started with a slight twinge the second Kellan had walked out of Dr. Walsh's door, stone-faced and ashen, then had grown with every turnoff and crossroad we'd passed as it seemed stranger and stranger that Kellan hadn't told me what the doctor said. When I'd tried to steer the conversation in that direction, or even once flat out asked, he'd simply shrugged and given a dismissive grunt.

Except I wasn't sure I could handle more bad news. I'd been so hopeful that Dr. Walsh would give us the answers we'd searched for, but the visit had actually made Kellan's future seem bleaker if that were even possible. Now a gloom seemed to have descended over me. Until now, I'd always thought Kellan would be there, and the reality that he wouldn't stung more than I'd thought it would. Like someone had injected me with a dose of the truth and as it flowed through my bloodstream, spreading through my body, the pain of potentially losing him became very, very real. Once the poison flowed back to my heart, who knew what I'd do.

The early evening sun drew long shadows of trees on the side of the highway, casting ominous shapes over the faded Middleton sign as we blew by it. Almost home. Another day wasted in a life that would be cut short too soon.

I yawned and tried to stretch my arms, without elbowing Kellan in the head, then stared at the familiar landscape as we neared town.

"Tomorrow I'll call Oklahoma State and University of Arkansas, or do you think I should try getting a hold of someone in Scotland or maybe even Cambridge or something?" I tried to remember my European geography.

No answer.

"Hey, Kellan." I quickly waved a hand in front of his face. "You awake?"

He swatted my hand away, then glanced over his shoulder and put on the turn signal, slowing the car and pulling over to the side of the road.

I swiveled my head and peered out all the windows. Nothing around. "What's wrong?"

He unclipped his seatbelt and shifted in his seat to face me. The unsettled feeling in my stomach flared and I held my breath, hoping my intuition was off, but somehow knowing it wasn't. He covered his hand over mine, his palm warm and a bit clammy from gripping the steering wheel. He ran his thumb over the back of my hand, tracing the bones under my skin. Then he looked up. A somber sense of defeat smoldered in his eyes, muddying his hazel color. "There's something I need to tell you."

A siren wailed in the distance. I tried to push it out, my eyes still locked on his, waiting for his words.

The wailing grew louder. Red and blue lights strobed in the

rearview mirror. I blinked and looked back between the head-rests to see a police car pulling over behind us.

"What now?" Kellan grumbled.

He turned off the engine and rolled down the window as a tall, lanky officer approached. The officer leaned into the window, his pair of mirrored sunglasses covering the majority of his face. As if I weren't nervous enough, the inability to see his eyes shook my core and I froze in my seat.

"Can I help you, officer?" Kellan said politely, although I could sense the hint of irritation in his voice.

"License and registration, please."

Kellan pulled out his wallet and looked over at me, the blank look on his face frightened and eerie. What was going on here?

The officer looked over the documents closely, looked at Kellan, then back at the papers again. "The registration is to an Evelyn Casey."

"My mom," Kellan added, although the officer glared at him like he should've just kept his mouth shut.

The officer pushed his head farther into the car and looked me over, *Officer English* in bold, black letters now visible on his badge. He scanned the interior and breathed heavily as if looking for something. But what had we done wrong? Kellan hadn't been speeding, for once, and he hadn't blown through a stop sign or anything. Maybe he had a dead taillight or some-thing? The officer circled the outside of the car, glaring in the passenger window as he walked by me and came back to see Kellan.

"Can you please get out of the vehicle, sir?"

Kellan stepped out the door and I threw open mine as well.

"Whoa." Officer English tossed an open palm in the air, the other hand dropping to his holster. "I'm going to have to ask you to stay inside the car, miss."

I wanted to argue, but instead bit my tongue and closed the door with a *thunk*. Rolling the window down, I crawled up on my knees to listen.

The officer tapped his hand on the back of the car. I could see his partner in the squad car nodding his approval. "Can you open the trunk, please?"

"Why?" Kellan asked.

"I asked you to open the trunk."

"You don't have to do it, Kellan," I called as I shot my head out the window. "They need a warrant to search anything."

Officer English glared at me, and I pulled myself back inside.

Kellan shrugged. "I have nothing to hide."

The trunk popped open and Kellan stood to the side, his hands in front of him.

The officer scanned the trunk, then glared at Kellan. He smiled back, and I exhaled. Nothing. Good. But instead of leaving, Officer English leaned deeper into the trunk.

He pulled out a baggie of green leaves and swung them in the air. "What's this?"

Kellan's face drained of color, and he flicked his stare from me to the officer and back again. "That's not mine."

"Are you saying it's your mother's then, as it is her vehicle?"

"No, she never drives this thing." He stepped forward to inspect the baggie, but the officer pulled it away from him. "But I didn't put that there. I don't do drugs, officer."

"Sure. This just magically appeared in your trunk. You're going to have to come with me."

The officer placed a hand on Kellan's arm and pulled it behind his back. The clink of metal on metal echoed along the highway as the handcuffs closed around his wrists.

"You have the right to remain silent ..."

Kellan's head dropped to his chest, as Officer English

continued his speech and guided him toward the squad car. He didn't fight. He was smart enough to know it wouldn't do any good, but the panic in his eyes made it look like he could explode at any minute.

Leaning across the driver's seat, I yelled through the still-open door. "This is ridiculous. He said he didn't do it."

"Well, it looks pretty bad from where I'm standing," the officer said as he opened the rear door of the squad car.

"Go get my mom. She'll be at the diner." Kellan nodded toward the steering wheel, his keys still dangling from the ignition. Before I could climb over the stick shift, Officer English snapped his hand through the door and plucked them from my reach.

He placed his hand on the hood of the car and leaned in toward me. "That won't be possible. You need to come with us as well, miss. This vehicle needs to be impounded."

I never thought I'd ever experience being wedged into the back of a squad car, but as the officer lowered my head under the roof, it became all too real. Fortunately, he didn't put me in handcuffs, but he still treated me like a petty criminal who'd just knocked off a liquor store with a sawed-off shotgun. A kaleidoscope of nightmares cycled through my brain. My parents. My friends. My permanent record. How did this turn so bad so quickly?

Kellan sat on the cracked leather seat, his head dropped low to his chest as his cuffed hands kept him from leaning back. "It isn't mine, Abby. You might not believe me, but I'm not into that stuff. I swear it."

I propped my elbow against the window and watched the green trees blur outside as we passed. His words sounded honest. No attitude or pretense. "I want to believe you."

"Then do it." He shuffled closer and swung his arms to the

side, catching my hand as it rested on the seat. His fingers shook against mine as his thumb rubbed up and down my palm.

"If I get high ... if I lose control ... it calls him. No matter how miserable I might be, I'd be stupid to do that to myself." His voice cracked. Broken. "I wouldn't do that to you."

I squeezed my hand tight around his and dared to look over. His dark hair matted across his forehead and the gold flecks in his eyes tarnished against the pain flowing out of his devastated stare.

"It wasn't someone else's?" I asked, still not sure where I stood. He'd told me before he couldn't get intoxicated. The hellish night at the bonfire proved it. He did need the cash for his car project, though.

He shook his head. "No one has even been near my car in months, other than you. And I'm not dealing if that's what you're thinking. I wouldn't do that."

"So then, how did it end up in your trunk?"

"I have no idea." He smacked his head back against the seat and closed his eyes. His jaw clenched tight. "Except there was one person."

I jerked upright and turned toward him. "Who?"

"I didn't want to tell you, but Marcus ambushed me this morning. He was in the parking lot with his buddy, leaning on my trunk, and I thought he was just being an asshole, but him lurking around my car and now this happening. I don't think it's a coincidence."

Marcus? Seriously? "Do you honestly think he would do that?"

"He is the sheriff's son. It makes sense. Why would they just ask me to open my trunk unless they were looking for something?" He smashed his head against the seat cushions again. A second time. Then a third. "And you didn't hear the things he said. About me. About you. I don't think this is a fluke, Abby. I think he's out to get me."

My blood bubbled hot in my veins. The back of the squad car suddenly very stuffy and claustrophobic. Marcus said he could make Kellan's life hell, but I thought he'd been acting tough. Could he really be responsible for this? Was he really capable of it? "Why didn't you tell me?"

"What was I supposed to say, your boyfriend cornered me in a parking lot to tell me to stay away from you?"

"He actually said that?" I slid my hand away and tucked both of them under my legs, trying to hold myself together as everything fell apart. My last doubt about Kellan's innocence evaporated as I seethed in my seat.

"Yeah. I didn't want you to hear it from me. I've messed up your life enough already. The last thing I needed to do was get in the middle of you and your boy. Even if he is a total bastard."

I rocked forward, trying to slow the burn of anger coursing through my limbs. "Why did he tell you to stay away?"

Kellan sat in silence for a moment, his mouth closed as if weighing his options. Finally, he shook his head and spoke. "It's not important. But do you think Marcus would be capable of setting me up?"

Of course, he'd be capable. His father, in his position, owned this town. Marcus probably knew more about police procedure than half the precinct. But would he really go that far?

"Or maybe it was Rhiann?" I asked, desperate to cast the blame elsewhere.

"Maybe, but she's already screwed me over as much as anyone can, so why would she bother? Besides, if Rhiann wanted to get to me, she has a lot more firepower than planting drugs."

He had a point. She could probably turn him into a toad or

something. But Marcus? Sure, he'd been mad at me lately, especially with all the time I'd been spending with Kellan, but would he really do something this terrible to get him out of his way? If so, I'd kill him.

They rushed us into the police station and immediately took Kellan into another room. The look on his face as they pulled us apart. The blank, hopeless look. I couldn't let this happen to him. I believed him. He wouldn't lie to me about this. This wasn't right.

"Sit here." Officer English ushered me to a line of chairs near the wall. "We'll call your parents to come pick you up."

"What is going to happen to him?"

"That is none of your concern, miss. Now please sit until your parents arrive to claim you."

Claim me? As if I were their property. I swallowed down the spiteful comeback burning on my tongue and recited my father's cell phone number to the officer. Maybe I'd be lucky and he'd come alone.

Officer English seemed satisfied and disappeared to call my dad, unknowingly condemning me to a life of grounding and shame.

I collapsed in the hard, wooden chair, extending my feet in front of me and scanning the collage of wanted signs and alerts on the far wall. Kellan wasn't one of those people. He shouldn't be here. How could this day have actually gotten worse? I rubbed my hands over my face and exhaled but with little relief. What if they locked Kellan up and one of those beasts showed up? There wasn't anything anyone here would be able to do to save him. And it wasn't fair. Kellan didn't do drugs. If only someone would believe him.

Across the station, the door to Marcus's dad's office sat open, his tall frame bent over the desk filling out paperwork. I'd seen him in the station a ton of times before, but never as an arrestee.

Maybe he might be rational in this situation, or maybe he'd at least listen to me. I glanced around and slowly stood up. No one seemed to notice. Holding my breath, I sped toward the office and knocked on the door.

"Can I help you?" he said, still staring down at his desktop, the gold star on his chest glinting in the light from his desk lamp.

I stepped carefully into the room, my hands clutched at my waist as I watched him scratch away at his paperwork. "Sheriff Diaz?"

He glanced up and smiled, a warm, charming smile, just like his son. "Oh, hi, Abby. What are you doing here?" He stood up from his desk and looked past me out the door. "Is Marcus with you?"

"Um ... no, sir." I dared to step closer into the room until I stood across from him. He towered over me and in his uniform seemed way more intimidating than when he sat holed up in the Diaz family den watching Sunday football. "I need to talk to you about Kellan Casey."

He let out a deep breath, the disappointment in his tone impossible to miss. "I wasn't aware that you were wrapped up in all this. What would you like to say?"

"You need to let him go. This whole thing has been a huge misunderstanding."

His face softened as he tossed his arms open in the air. "He broke the law, Abby. It's out of my hands."

"Sheriff Diaz, please. I know the drugs aren't his."

"I'm sorry, but there isn't much I can do. Someone sent in a tip that he was selling at the high school this afternoon and he had drugs on him. The evidence is pretty clear. There is no reasonable doubt here."

"You can't prove that he was selling anything. He wasn't even in town today."

He tucked his index fingers through his front belt loops and glared down at me, his eyebrows raised. "How do you know that?"

"Because we were up at the University of Kansas all day. We'd just got back when we got pulled over."

"That still doesn't change the marijuana we found in the car." His face fell to a frown. He probably didn't like me calling him on the fact that Kellan had an alibi, maybe more so that I was it. "That's something you can't talk your way out of."

True, but maybe I could. "The pot is mine."

"What?" He jerked his head forward and slammed his hands down on the desk, leaning closer to me. "Please don't tell me you just said that."

"It's not his. It's mine." I didn't plan it. I didn't even realize I'd made a confession until the words had flown out of my mouth. My chest tightened, heavy from lying and terrified for what the consequences may be, but they couldn't lock Kellan up. I knew in my bones he didn't do it. Marcus's involvement was still to be determined, but if he had planted the drugs, then Kellan getting arrested was partially my fault. I couldn't out Marcus to his father without proof, but if I could buy some time, maybe I could get him to confess. "I left my backpack in his trunk and it must've fallen out."

He rubbed his left hand over his forehead and let out a frustrated sigh. "This doesn't sound like you. Please, don't go making a huge mistake for no reason."

I laced my fingers together, gripping them tightly as fear pulsed through my body, my limbs trembling. "I'm just telling the truth, Sheriff Diaz. You wouldn't want to catch the wrong person, would you? Can you imagine the lawsuit?"

KELLAN

The room was small and gray. The kind you saw on primetime cop shows. But on TV being arrested never ended well, especially for guys like me.

I paced the dirty linoleum floor concentrating on each individual tile trying to keep myself calm, except trying to force it just had the opposite effect. For every controlled breath I took, I saw Marcus's stupid face and imagined ways to break it. I'd known he was a jackass, but I'd never thought he'd be low enough to try something like this. Most guys with a pompous attitude like that just postured but never really hit back, but I underestimated him. Big mistake. And he definitely had the connections to make the rest of my short life a disaster.

If I ever got a chance at him ... I balled up my fist and slammed it into the concrete wall. Pain surged up my arm, and sadly, gave me a bit of relief. I shook out my hand as the door creaked open and a uniformed Officer English entered, closing us both in the room and making the walls seem closer.

He walked slowly and silently toward the small table in the center of the room, dragging out his entrance, or maybe trying to get me to crack. Interrogation mind games, maybe?

"I didn't do this," I said in a low rumble, trying to sound as serious and stable as I could. "Don't I get to talk to a lawyer or something?"

"No need. The charges have been dropped. You are free to go."

"What?" I shook my head before I realized that questioning might make the tables turn again. "I told you that stuff wasn't mine."

"We know. Your friend made a full confession."

"My friend?" I wouldn't call Marcus my friend. I wouldn't even call him to save me if I started on fire and he had the only water in town. But at least he'd grown a pair and fessed up.

"Yeah." The officer scanned the pages of the file in his hand. Likely my file. My permanent record. "Miss Marino admitted that the drugs were hers, so we have nothing to hold you on."

"Abby?" She hadn't done this. I knew she hadn't. Why risk herself like this? "Can I talk to her?"

"I'm afraid not. Now, because you've just turned eighteen" —he scanned my file again—"on February 8th, we don't need to call your parents, but if you want them contacted, you can let them know at the front."

Officer English strode across the room in his too-tight pants and opened the door wide for me to exit. I bit my tongue, still wanting to ask more questions, but knowing that being released made me more useful than being detained.

"I can let myself out." I stopped in front of him and held out my hand. "Can I have my keys?"

He shook his head. "Your car is in impound for the night, but you can come pick it up in the morning. Luckily for you, we didn't find any other substances in it."

Luckily for me? *It wasn't luck, buddy. I just don't do drugs, or did you not hear me the last ten thousand times I said it?* "Thanks."

I scanned the bullpen looking for Abby, hoping I could see her at least once and know that she was okay. Unfortunately, only a few officers milled around their desks, but no Abby. I dropped into a chair along the wall, trying to make myself comfortable. I had nowhere else to be, so camping out for the girl who'd sacrificed herself for me seemed like a great time.

Officer English marched to my seat and loomed over me, his perceived air of authority wafting off him like bad body spray. "Do you need some assistance?"

I sat up straighter, fighting against my basic urge to push his buttons. "No, just waiting."

"Then I suggest you wait outside the precinct. Unless there is something you still need to get off your chest?"

He refused to move, clearly meaning every word he'd said.

"Fine."

The officer took a step back to let me stand, his hands crossed military style behind his back, watching me walk away. *Dick*.

I chucked open the first set of glass doors to the lobby, just as Abby's parents pushed in from outside. I nodded in greeting and held open the inner door for them to enter.

"You!" Mrs. Marino said, pointing a finger at me. "I should have known that you'd be responsible for this."

"Meredith." Mr. Marino put his arm around his wife and clutched her shoulder.

She shrugged him off and closed the distance between us, her finger still pointed at me like a loaded gun. "No, David, this needs to be said. What have you done to our daughter? Don't think we don't know about your reputation in this town, young man. Our Abigail is a good girl—"

"I know, Mrs. Marino. But I swear I'm not responsible for this."

I held up my open hands in surrender, but the gesture only seemed to fuel her anger.

"Well, things like this don't just happen. Since she's been talking to you again, I think it's safe to assume that this downturn in her behavior is from your sway."

"That's not true. She's the best person I have in my life right now. I would never do anything to hurt her."

"Then maybe you need to find someone else to drag down. Abigail has a future, a wonderful boyfriend, and a great life that you do not belong in. I think it would be best if you walked out of here and never darken our door again."

My body shook—vibrated—as it rejected Mrs. Marino's punishment. "You can't do that."

"You bet I can," she continued. "The last thing she needs is a bad influence in her life."

"Bad influence? If you're looking for bad influences, you're looking in the wrong place. Maybe you should take a look at that wonderful boyfriend of hers." I dropped my voice to a low mumble. "Or you know, a mirror."

"What did you just say?" Mr. Marino piped in, his normally kind eyes morphing into solid stone.

"Nothing." I hung my head. I took it too far. "I just said that there are people in her life hurting her a hell of a lot worse than I ever could."

Mrs. Marino retreated and crossed her arms. Her scowl still dug deep across her brow, but her watery glare seemed to have lost its fight.

"But we don't have to worry about you anymore." She turned her head toward the community bulletin board on the wall and blinked before facing me again. "Do we?"

I opened my mouth to argue. So many thoughts ran around my brain, kicking the insides of my mouth, fighting to get out.

But I'd never win this argument. They'd already made up their minds about me. Like everyone else. Maybe they were right. Maybe I wasn't worth it.

"Forget this." I pushed open the door and walked out of the station. *Well played, Marcus. Well played.*

CHAPTER THIRTY-TWO

Abby

They didn't yell, or at least not yet.

My mother wouldn't even look at me, her pursed lips and sour stare directed angrily at the floor of the tiny interview room that Sheriff Diaz had sequestered us to. But my dad, his stern grimace ripped deep into my flesh, as his pupils became laser beams searing the word 'disappointment' across my heart. And I just sat there, hooking and unhooking my fingers on the rickety table in front of me, begging in my head that all of this would soon be over and that hopefully, it hadn't been for nothing.

Finally, after what seemed like forever, the door opened and ushered in a waft of fresh air that soothed the burn of my flaming cheeks. Marcus's father entered the room, his hat in his left fist and his hair slightly a mess from running his hands through it.

He nodded at each of my parents. "Meredith. David."

Dad peeled himself from the wall he'd been holding up and slid a hand out from his pocket, extending it toward the sheriff. "Thanks for calling us before moving forward."

Sheriff Diaz nodded and shook my father's hand without a word, just a matching look of displeasure across his face. He grabbed the chair across the table and sat down, his dark brown eyes, Marcus's eyes, hooded and weary from what had probably been a rough night for Middleton standards. "There is barely enough marijuana for a possession charge, and since Abigail is a minor with no prior record, I talked to the captain, and I can let her go into your custody without charges being filed."

Mom's hand shot across the tabletop and cupped Sheriff Diaz's fingers, giving them a firm squeeze. "Thank you, Andre. We really appreciate your help with this."

He gave her a soft smile. "No problem. I would hate for something like this to affect her future. She's a bright kid and I hope that she's not getting mixed up with the wrong crowd."

Yeah. Like your son. And 'she' is sitting right here.

"However," he continued, his voice low. "I do want her to understand that these are serious allegations and next time, there might not be a way out. I've talked to Marcus—"

"Great," I blurted out as I rolled my eyes. My mother stared me down.

Sheriff Diaz glanced from me to my mother and back, his measured calm on the verge of breaking as he sat back in his chair. "And he said that this guy might be involved in some other criminal and dangerous activity."

"That's not true," I said, trying to keep collected. He wouldn't listen if I sounded like a petulant brat. I'd already pushed my luck too far with him. Besides, he wasn't the Diaz I had a problem with right now.

"Look." Sheriff Diaz lowered his forehead and tried to meet my gaze. "I don't have anything on him right now, but he will be part of an ongoing investigation. There have been some very strong allegations against him."

"Like what?" I asked.

He didn't answer, just looked over at my father and shrugged.

"You're wrong, you know. Kellan is being set up."

Sheriff Diaz sighed. "I know it's hard to believe that someone you care about isn't who they seem. I've seen it before, far too many times, but the honest truth is that it happens and if you aren't careful, you can get pulled into things you weren't prepared for. I would really hate to see something bad happen to you because of a few misguided choices."

Mom stood and straightened her purse over her shoulder. "Don't worry, Andre. We'll make sure there aren't any more issues."

I looked at her and she looked back, the mean glare in her eyes telling me to just shut up already.

"Well, I'm glad. Honestly, Abigail, I think of you as part of our family and this situation upsets me as much as I'm sure your parents are upset right now."

I crossed my arms. I was *sure* he was upset. He might even have been part of the conspiracy that had landed me here in the first place. Mom discreetly nudged my leg under the table with her pointed-toe shoe.

"It won't happen again," I said on cue.

"Okay, now I'll let you get on with your evening. I'm sure you have a lot to discuss."

Sheriff Diaz headed for the door, holding it open for Mom to parade out with Dad close behind.

"I'm telling the truth, you know?" I whispered as I passed.

He nodded. "We'll see."

Dad swung open the police station door, and I immediately saw Kellan. He stood draped against the railing of the front steps, his arms crossed and drenched in the glow from the streetlight. A ghost of a smile haunted his lips as his eyes locked with mine.

Without thinking, I broke rank and ran down the steps toward him. He pulled me to his chest, his arms wrapped tightly around my back and my feet almost leaving the ground. I breathed deeply, inhaling the scent of him as my face pressed against his T-shirt.

"Are you okay?" he mumbled into my shoulder as he hung on to me.

I nodded.

He let me go and rested his palm against my cheek, then lowered his head to meet my gaze. "Why did you take the fall? This wasn't your fault."

"I know. But if I'd let you take the blame, you'd still be locked up in the station waiting for a lawyer."

The hardness of panic in his eyes melted as he shook his head at me.

"Abby Marino, you are—"

A tight grip on my arm wrenched me away from him and I tripped back down over one of the wide stone steps.

"Get in the car, Abigail," Dad said, never taking his eyes off Kellan, as if Kellan might reach out and carry me away, or maybe just steal his wallet.

"Mr. Marino," said Kellan, "I want you to know that this is a big misunderstanding."

Dad dismissed him with a wave. "I've heard enough for one night, young man. I suggest you get yourself home."

The hollow *thunk* of the door closing sounded like a guillotine. My head was going to roll. I just wasn't sure who would chop first, Mom or Dad. Instead, I received a stay of execution as they chose to fume for a few extra minutes. The engine sputtered to life in chorus with the huffs and scoffs both my parents tossed from the front seat. As we pulled out of the parking lot, I slid closer to the window and slouched down, trying to keep out of the reflection of the rearview mirror.

"Drugs, Abigail?" Dad started as he turned onto the street. I wasn't sure if he was asking a question or recounting my charges to himself, so I stayed silent. "I never thought we would have this problem with you. I thought we'd raised you better than that."

"Don't you even care about your future?" Mom added. "You are extremely lucky that Sheriff Diaz dropped the charges. A criminal record is not something that looks good on your college applications." She turned around in the passenger seat and glowered at me, the look so intense, my hands itched to grab the handle and roll out into traffic to avoid her. "How are we supposed to trust you if you're going to be involved in this kind of trouble?"

I dug my nails into my palms. "I'm not doing drugs, Mom. I'm not stupid."

"Are you sure about that? If you were being smart, we wouldn't be called out of dinner to go to the police station to pick up our delinquent daughter, now would we?"

She turned back around and stared out the front window. I watched the streaks of streetlights pass along the upholstery of the seats in front of me. Blips and dots like Morse code. Maybe the universe was trying to send an S.O.S. I definitely needed any help I could get right now.

"And you are not to see that boy again," Mom continued. "I don't want to see you anywhere near him."

"What?" I shouted. "That's not fair. He didn't do anything wrong."

My phone buzzed in my pocket, but I couldn't look. If it was Kellan, I couldn't answer. If it was Marcus, I would throw a perfectly good phone out the window.

"Well, before he reappeared, you weren't getting arrested.

Whether they were his drugs or not, he's not someone you need in your life."

"How do you know what I need?"

"You don't seem to know what's good for you, so as your parents, we're stepping in." Mom pulled out her wagging finger and looked back over her shoulder. "No more contact with Kellan. Straight to school in the morning and straight home after school."

I cringed. "How long?"

"Until I'm not angry with you anymore, and right now I'm not sure that that is ever going to happen, so I would toe the line very carefully."

This was ridiculous. They weren't going to listen. It wouldn't matter what I'd said. "When are you ever *not* angry with me?"

Dad slammed on the brakes, and I lurched forward, the seat-belt cutting against my throat.

He pulled over and shouted at me in his mirror. "Don't you dare say that to your mother."

"What? It's the truth, isn't it? Don't you even see how disappointed you are in me all the time? Or are you just so used to it you don't notice anymore?"

Mom's face exploded into every known shade of red. "That's not fair and you know it. You're just trying to be hurtful now."

"*I'm* trying to be hurtful? How about you?" Tears streamed down my cheeks. I wiped them away, hoping Mom wouldn't see them. No showing weakness. That was never the way to win an argument. But they just kept coming. "'Good girls don't do that, Abby.' 'What would people think, Abby?' 'We don't care what you want, Abby.' 'Sit up straighter. Be better. Be perfect.' No matter what I do, it's never good enough."

I flung open the car door and jumped out onto the pavement, determined to walk—even if it was only four houses to home. Unaffected by my exit, Dad started the car again, speeding the rest of the way down the street, and turning into our driveway. I could keep walking. Clear my head before diving headfirst into what would be a long night of arguing, eventually leading to nowhere. Or ... The brake lights on the car flashed, illuminating the street. Kellan stood at the end of his drive, buckled over and hands on his knees.

"Did you run the whole way?" I asked as I rushed over to him.

He let out a few more labored breaths. "Yeah ... cut through the park ... had to see you."

"Abigail, get in the house this minute," Mom barked as she stepped out of the car and slammed the passenger door.

I didn't move. Instead, I let Kellan take my hand and pull me closer to him, his racing pulse surging against my skin as he wrapped his arms around my back.

"Maybe you should go," he whispered against my hair.

Dad walked down the driveway and stood inches from us, his disapproving gaze sliding from Kellan to me and back again. "*Now*, Abby."

Kellan's chest heaved against mine as he sighed and released his arms. I looked up and he nodded, his eyes dark and endless like the night sky. I knew I needed to go. I knew I needed to deal with my parents, but I wanted to stay. I wanted the entire world to fall away so I could just stay in Kellan's arms, listening to him breathe. To block out the world, at least until the dust settled. When we could explain everything and make it better. He ran his fingertips along my arm, and I melted into his touch.

He nodded. "It'll be okay. I'll be right next door if you need me."

Slowly, I peeled myself away and turned back toward the house. Mom stood at the front door, holding it open and likely making sure I didn't bolt. I took a deep breath. The fear coursing through my veins fought against whatever I'd felt in Kellan's grasp and my stomach hollowed.

This would be a long night.

CHAPTER THIRTY-THREE

KELLAN

Abby's front door closed, and I exhaled, my breath the only sound on the night air. Then a sharp beep sounded as Abby's father clicked his remote, locking the doors of his Cadillac.

He tossed his head back for a second, then let out a heavy sigh. My fingers twitched, watching him drink in a moment of peace before entering into what would likely become one of the worst nights of his life. And it had all been because of me.

"Mr. Marino," I started.

He stopped and slowly turned his head in my direction.

"You have to know. The drugs weren't mine and they weren't your daughter's. This is just a big mistake."

He rubbed his hands over his face, then settled them back in his pockets. "You both keep saying that, but I still find it very hard to believe."

"I know. But it's the truth. I would never intentionally do anything bad to Abby."

"Now, see, that's your problem. No one *intends* to get arrested, Kellan. No one intends to get into trouble, but for some people, it just finds them."

I cast my eyes down to the pavement searching for words, but there weren't any to find. Trouble seemed to go out of its way to screw with me.

"And I get it," Mr. Marino continued. "I did things when I was young that I'd rather forget. It happens. But"— he pulled his hand out of his pocket and pointed the car key fob in my direction—"even if what you're saying is true, you must've made some pretty bad choices for someone to go through that much effort to set you up."

"Maybe." Or maybe Marcus was just that focused on destroying me?

"I know things have been rough for you the last few years, but that doesn't mean you have an excuse to screw up your life. Let me give you some advice: Be someone you can be proud of. There's a lot of shit that can happen in your life, but if at the end of the day, you can look in the mirror and know you've done right by yourself and the people around you, then you'll be just fine. And hopefully, no one will need to be picking you up in the middle of the night at the police station, or worse."

"Thanks, Mr. Marino."

"Now go home, Kellan, and leave us alone to figure this out."

He turned to go, striding slowly up the driveway toward the front of his house, either making a statement or trying to delay walking into the battle royal happening in his living room. As he reached the front walk, he looked back. "But remember what I said. Be someone you can be proud of. I can tell by the way she looks at you that Abby sees something good that, right now, I just can't. The best thing you can do is to become that guy. Make yourself worthy."

I watched him disappear into the house, then jogged up the drive and threw open my garage door. The welcoming gritty smell of oil rushed out into the night, and I breathed deeply to help calm my trembling fists.

Be someone you can be proud of. Right. Like that was going to happen.

The moment Abby had walked out of that precinct and into my arms, I'd known. I'd been selfish. I hadn't told her about my death sentence to protect her. I'd hid it because I knew once she found out, she'd be free. She could write me off like everyone else and move on with her life, and I couldn't let that happen. I didn't want her to let me go.

And now I definitely couldn't tell her. After taking the fall for me, it would be a huge kick in the face to know I would've been gone before they could even file the paperwork for the charges.

I plunked down on the floor and stared at the ceiling until the overhead sensor light went out. In the dark, nothing seemed any clearer, and without being able to see, all my other senses strengthened. The heady smell of her on my T-shirt, the feel of her skin against my hands, the tightness in my chest at knowing I didn't deserve her. Everything mixed together into a dangerous virtual reality experience designed to rip me to shreds.

Everyone knew I was no good for her. Hell, even I knew it. And besides, she had a boyfriend. A boyfriend I wanted to pound into the earth right now, but even if I hated him, I wouldn't be around much longer for it to matter anyway. Besides, if I laid a hand on him, the cops would be all over me. The sheriff's son wasn't someone you wanted to teach a lesson when, clearly, he was the one doing the schooling. Stupid prick.

I slid my phone out of my back pocket and started typing.

Me: *I'm so sorry, Abby. You are the best thing that has ever happened to me. I will do whatever I can to make this up to you. I owe you so much.*

Delete.

Me: *I'm sorry, Abby. Forgive me?*

Send. I typed again.

Me: *Please?*

I stared at the screen for a few seconds, then tucked the phone back in my jeans.

How had things gotten so screwed up? I'd never expected to be spending my last few days in a police station, or worse, sitting on the ground in my garage wishing I could walk the ten feet to her house and kiss her. I ran out into the backyard. No lights. Either she was still downstairs getting the riot act from her folks or she'd already gone to bed. I clenched my fists, fighting the instinct to scale the side of her house and crawl in her window, if only just to apologize. But who knew if after tonight she wouldn't completely hate me?

That was it. I had to stop. I had less than three days left and holding on to Abby wasn't fair to either of us. I needed to cut myself off before I hurt her since it was already too late for me. Losing her would break whatever I had left of a heart, but maybe cutting myself off now would do us both a favor. Abby needed a safe guy. Someone who could treat her better than I could. Someone who had a future that extended past this weekend.

I grabbed the back of my neck and groaned. All this pain and regret for a girl who'd never be mine anyway. But if I couldn't keep any promises to her, there was still one promise I could keep. At least one person could be proud of me for something. I returned to the garage and closed the door, then checked my phone one last time before switching it off. No messages. Not like I should expect one anyway. I rubbed my hands over my face and pulled a brown paper wrapped box out onto the workbench. The last few pieces I'd been waiting for.

This would be a long night.

CHAPTER THIRTY-FOUR

Abby

I chucked my books to the back of my locker and the thunderous rumble of paper bricks and cardboard crashing on the metal floor echoed through the hallway and vibrated in my brain. Stupid move. I rubbed my hands over my face and massaged my temples, trying to make the ache subside, but it didn't help. The slow, dull throb behind my eyes appeared to be the only thing I'd gained as a result of my night of yelling and crying and more yelling—oh, and the fact that I was now grounded until I turned forty—but it wasn't like I'd actually expected my stint in the slammer to change my parents' minds about me. Now they'd moved into damage control mode, hoping no one in town found out about my 'incident.'

Resting my head against the cool metal door, I slid my phone out of my back pocket. 2:34 pm. I so wanted to ditch class and go home, but being on house arrest meant being on my best behavior or at least trying not to cause a ruckus. Besides, Mom worked from home today, so any chance of relaxing would be shot.

My thumb flipped in and out of my social apps, skimming posts and updates, searching for any sign of Kellan. His last message: *I'm sorry.* What did that even mean? Nothing that had happened was his fault, but he hadn't returned any of my messages this morning and hadn't picked up when I'd tried to call during lunch. Since yesterday, everything had gone from complicated to almost impossible, but I kept trying to find a way out of the Shadow Keeper's deal. When Rhiann had screwed over Kellan, it wasn't like the Shadow Keeper had slaughtered half of the Midwest. I needed to talk to him. At least he could text to let me know he was still alive.

A dark silhouette fell across my phone screen and two arms wrapped around my waist, pulling me backward. My body tensed.

"There you are," Marcus said in my ear as he kissed my shoulder. "I've been looking for you all day."

And I'd been hiding all day. I hadn't wanted to see him. Or Rachel. Or anyone I'd need to explain things to. Head down. Keep quiet. Get out.

I twisted in his grip until we faced each other, his smile collapsing the second he noticed my less-than-impressed expression.

"What?" I snapped. "You expected me to be in jail or something?"

He let me loosen his hands laced across my lower back and take a step of much-needed space.

"No ..." He leaned forward, his hands posed like they might try to touch me again, but then they suddenly fell to his sides, likely realizing how stupid that move would be. "It's not your fault your neighbor is a drug dealer. I know you didn't do anything wrong. But you could've at least answered your phone or messaged that you were okay."

"After what you did, do you really think I want to talk to you right now?"

"What *I* did?" His eyes rolled left, glancing up at the ceiling. "Did that loser tell you that he yelled at me in a parking lot and threw a coffee at Parker's new car?"

My hands squeezed into fists, my nails digging into the fleshy part of my palms. I'd forgotten all about the chat between Marcus and Kellan. "No, he told me you confronted him. What the hell do you think you were doing?"

"I was trying to protect you." He ran the back of his index finger down my arm, following it with his stare, his warm, charismatic smile coming out to try to ... I don't know ... defuse me or something. *Not gonna happen.*

"Protect me? From what? Making my own decisions? You're a regular superhero."

He retracted his hand and held his palms up wide in defense. "Hey. Don't get mad at me. I thought you'd appreciate someone looking out for you."

"I do, but only if I need looking out for, and I don't. Besides, did looking out for me have anything to do with why you planted the weed in Kellan's car? Real nice, by the way."

He scoffed and backed away. Smart move. "Wasn't me. Kellan's the stoner. Don't you think he might have some stuff on him?"

"He's not a stoner, Marcus. He doesn't do drugs. He can't."

"He can't?" Marcus's face screwed up into an odd twist.

"No. He can't." I scanned my brain for the most logical explanation that wasn't the truth. "He has a medical condition where he can't do any of that stuff, so I doubt he's going to be carting around a baggie full of illegal substances when he can't even use them."

"Is that why you told my dad it was yours?"

"Of course." I tossed my hands in the air. "I knew he didn't do it."

Marcus's face flushed the color of a candied apple, a shade too telling to be innocent. He'd never admit it to me, but he knew more about my trip to the police station than he was saying.

"Doesn't change anything, though. He's still not someone you should be hanging around with."

"That's for me to decide. Not you."

I slammed my locker closed, the clang of the door in its frame silencing the argument Marcus seemed to be concocting behind his startled stare. Instead of digging himself in deeper, he simply stuffed his hands in his pockets and stared at the floor.

"So ..." he started, then he glanced down the hallway, the confidence in his voice completely stripped, his voice naked and raw. "What does this mean? Between us?"

The pain in my head throbbed, and I rubbed the back of my neck, rolling my skull in a circle. "I don't know what it means. But I do know I'm pretty pissed at you right now."

Marcus gasped and locked his wide-eyed stare on mine. He lowered his voice and dared to step closer. "Please, Abby. You've had a rough night, and everything seems really bad right now, but you just need to sit back and see that this really isn't a big deal."

I crossed my arms and stood up straighter. "Are you saying you set Kellan up?"

"No." His eyes narrowed and flitted toward the floor. I'm saying that maybe you need to take a look at what you've been doing lately. Maybe you got in this mess yourself."

"Me? Drugs or not, you went behind my back and trash-talked me to Kellan. That was a pretty dick move, Marcus."

"I know. And if I'd known you'd be this upset, I never would've done it, but you've just been so different since he's been around. You even skipped out on school with him yester-day. Don't think I haven't noticed how much time you've been spending with him. You haven't exactly been telling me what you've been doing lately either." He took my hand and sandwiched it in his palms, his skin damp and his fingers shaking. "Why don't we just forget about everything that happened and try to fix this?"

I yanked my hand away.

"What if I don't think we can?" I grabbed my aching forehead as the truth rippled through my body. One I'd been hiding from myself for far too long now. "I think we're done, Marcus."

"What?" He tried to come closer, but I held my hand out for him to stop his advance. His eyes widened and I swore tears welled up for a second. "You can't be serious, Abby. We've been together since sophomore year. You're going to let a misunderstanding come between us. I'm sorry for what I've done. If you're sorry too, this doesn't have to happen."

"I think you know it does."

He locked his gaze with mine and gave a weak half-smile. Always trying to fix things. Always managing to stir up guilt, like it was my fault, not his. I studied the floor, examining the dingy tiles. Anything to keep him from gaining control of the conversation.

"Abby, talk to me," he pleaded. "Maybe you just need some time. Take as much as you need. Go home, get some rest, and then call me later and we'll talk. Really talk. Okay?"

"I don't think—"

"Please?" He raced backward down the hall, running away from my response. When he'd reached the end of the corridor, he stopped.

"And, Abby. No matter what happens. If the last three years still mean anything to you. If I ever meant anything to you. Please, just stay away from Kellan Casey."

CHAPTER THIRTY-FIVE

KELLAN

Daytona Blue Metallic for the body, white pearl for the stripes across the hood. I'd wanted silver stripes, but Dad had insisted on the pearl. Said it reminded him of a car he'd had when he'd been young. I'd tried to argue, but the nostalgic look on his face as he'd held up the paint swatch in the body shop told me I'd never win that fight. Didn't matter anyway. Pearl or silver, this car was cherry. Only two things would make her absolutely perfect: getting rid of the small hairline mark of clear coat on the bumper that I couldn't buff out and having someone here, so I wasn't staring at her all by myself.

I ran my hand over the guard, close enough to feel the cool of the metal on my palm but not enough to actually touch the finish. So many hours I'd spent in this garage learning about this car. Her every angle, every bolt, every weld—I knew them all. Four years of building her from a junkyard castoff into the most impressive machine I'd ever seen. A 1963 Chevy Nova back from the dead. Finally complete.

My foot twitched, aching to push down that gas pedal and open up the engine. On a night like tonight, with the air slightly cooler than it had been lately, she'd probably roar like a lion. I couldn't wait. I slid my phone out of my back pocket.

Abby'd been texting. The messages had started in the morning and then a new one had popped up every couple of hours for the rest of the day. After 5:00, it looked like she'd given up, but then one last one from only fifteen minutes ago striped across the screen.

Abby: *This isn't funny. Are you okay?*

I swallowed hard, my throat tight and making it hard to breathe. No. I wasn't okay. Not even twenty-four hours had passed since I'd promised myself I'd stay away from her, and already I couldn't fight the temptation to call her. Maybe because I hadn't slept all night. Maybe because I still felt like a complete jerk for us both getting arrested yesterday. Most likely because thinking about her undid every stupid thing I'd built up to protect myself and burned like fire in my veins.

Me: *Want to go for a ride?*

I typed into the screen. Stupid move. Stupid and selfish. But maybe she wouldn't bother to answer?

My phone chimed immediately.

Abby: *What exactly are you asking?*
Me: *Look outside.*

No response. I waited. Thirty seconds. A minute. A door creaked in the distance. Footsteps raced down the side of the house from the backyard.

"So, what do you think?" I crossed my arms and stood next

to the car, prouder than I'd ever been in my life. She'd be the first one to see it. The first one to know I'd actually done something. I just hoped she cared.

"You finished it." She lunged forward and wrapped her arms around my neck, the sweet smell of her blasting what remained of my defenses, then turned to look at the Nova. "Is this what you've been doing all day?"

I nodded. "I was almost done. I wanted to take it out for at least one drive in case anything happened."

"It's so pretty, Kellan." She stopped. "Do you call a car 'pretty'?"

"Not really, but you can do whatever you want, I guess." I laughed, my shoulders relaxing as I watched her bounce around with excitement.

"I really like the stripes. How the purply color blends in with the white like that. It's awesome."

"You don't think they would be better silver?"

She scrunched up her nose and looked closer, hovering just over the hood. "No. This is perfect."

I glanced up at the sky. *Maybe you did know a few things about cars, Dad.*

"So how does it run? Is it exactly how you'd planned it?" Abby asked.

"Actually ..." I rubbed my hand across the back of my neck and looked down at the oil-stained concrete. "I haven't taken her out yet. Want to take the first ride with me?"

"Of course," she squealed. "But we should probably get out of here before my parents catch me. They're probably figuring out that I'm not in my room right about now."

"So you're grounded, huh?"

"Something like that."

The front door of her house slammed shut as her mother

appeared on the front step, her blazing cheeks visible from the driveway. *Oh, shit.*

"Abigail, you get back in this house right this minute!"

Abby glanced at me as she bit down on her lower lip and yanked open the passenger door. "Get in."

"Maybe we shouldn't."

"Do you want to take this beauty of a car for a spin or not? I'll deal with my mother when I get home. Right now, I just want to get the hell out of here."

I looked back over my shoulder at Mrs. Marino tearing down the front walkway at an impressive pace. A nasty feeling built up in my stomach, but it faded away seeing Abby in my car with her eyes wild and open for excitement. She looked good in my car. Her dark blonde hair blended with the tan leather seat and her long legs seemed to fill the space perfectly. I swung open the door and jumped in.

The leather-wrapped steering wheel melted like soft butter in my hands. The pedals became an extension of my legs, the perfect distance for my feet, and the racing seat cradled my hips as if it had been molded for my ass alone.

The engine rumbled as I turned the key and we sped out of the driveway, Mrs. Marino still cursing near the garage door. The powerful feeling ripped through my limbs like car and driver were one entity. One giant engine.

We cruised down Main Street, alone, except for the occasional random car rushing to get home. The dark shop windows spread out beside us and the glow of the streetlights created a runway for us to follow, stretching into the mysterious night that headed down the highway. Abby sat quietly, staring out the car window and idly twisting her hair tight around her fingers.

"You okay?" I asked.

She peeled her face away from the window, her lips still

smiling, but her eyes dark and distant, screaming the opposite. "Yeah. Of course."

Words collected in the back of my throat, stabbing at my tonsils, but I stayed silent. If she didn't want to tell me, she didn't have to, and I could respect that. Or maybe I didn't want her to tell me the broken look that had eked into her normally sunny expression was because of me? That I'd been the one to hurt her above everyone else.

Up ahead, a car turned into my lane from Carlton Street. The sequence of numbers and letters on the license plate tugged at my memory, and the impeccably clean exterior of the BMW reminded me of someone behind the wheel who didn't deserve to drive it. At least not that Parker asshole. If I'd been in the Civic, I probably would've rammed the back of it and kept on driving, but I wouldn't taint my baby, even if it meant giving him the 'screw you' he deserved.

A red light.

I pulled up beside the i8 Roadster and glanced at the driver. Sure enough, the football punk I expected sat behind the wheel, practically jonesing for a run, his loser co-captain in the passenger seat. Seeing his smug face after what he'd put me through, I considered tossing open the door and choking him on the hood of his friend's car. But there were other ways to fight.

Parker stomped the gas, and his engine whined. I knew what that meant. I'd made that noise plenty of times before. I craved it like oxygen.

I revved my engine back. Something in my chest popped awake. Adrenaline.

The Beamer responded. Angrier. Ready to go.

My lips curled into a smile as I pressed the gas pedal to the floor. The Nova rumbled beneath me, the sheer power tunneling up through my feet and coursing through my veins.

"What do you think you're doing?" Abby said, reminding me she was still there.

I shrugged, never moving my eyes from the light. "They started it."

She leaned forward and looked past me to the other car.

"Damn it. It's Marcus." She slid down in her seat, almost crouching on the floor. "I don't want him to see me."

"Why not?" Wow, this had to be the world's longest red light.

"I can't explain right now. You need to get me out of here."

The red light disappeared and clicked to green. "Remember, you asked for it."

Tires squealed across the concrete. Mine? The other guy's? Maybe both? I didn't care. Nothing mattered but putting this guy behind me.

His front bumper nudged ahead off the line. He might have more torque, but I doubted he could handle it. The needle hit the red zone, and I slammed the stick shift into gear. The Nova's nose pulled out in front of the Beamer. My hand gripped the wheel tighter, my fingers tingling.

Streetlights flew by in neon streaks, the air buzzing electric around me. Parker's car jerked forward, putting us neck and neck. This guy could actually drive, but I wouldn't let a lousy import beat a legend of American muscle. No way in hell.

The engines thundered, roaring closer to the turn at the end of the strip, closer to victory. At least for one of us. The needle surged again.

"Slow down, Kellan! You're going to get us killed," Abby shouted.

"Can't yet." The Beamer lagged a second. He'd shifted too slow. Maybe missed a gear. A fatal mistake. I slammed the gas pedal to the floor and applied pressure on the shifter. Clutch almost down. Shift. Click. Engaged. The Nova lurched forward and pulled ahead.

"Woohoooo!" I yelled, drumming my hands against the steering wheel as I sailed the last few feet to the finish.

The other car hit its brakes at the corner, Parker tossing his hands up in my rearview mirror. Instead of stopping to bask in my win, I downshifted and drifted down the highway. I didn't need to gloat. He knew he'd been beaten, and that was gonna hurt more than anything I could say to his ugly face.

The gleam of town faded as trees started filling in the sides of the road. My blood still pumped fast and fiery through my limbs, the stars suddenly seeming bigger and brighter than I'd ever seen. I glanced up at the silver cross hanging from the mirror and tapped my hand on the dash. Not only had I finished building this stunner today, but she'd also leveled that BMW like a champ. If only there were more time left to drive her.

I glanced over at Abby, her heavy puffs of breath finally catching my attention as the rush of the race faded. Her left hand gripped the seat cushion, the other gripped the door. Her knuckles glowed ghost white.

"You're going to live. You can relax now."

She stared forward, not moving, not even bothering to blink. The endorphin rush flooded out of me as I waited for her response. Maybe I'd gone too far?

"Say something," I said. "You're creeping me out."

"That was the most terrifying thing I have ever done in my entire life." Her body eased and started to fill out her seat again, then she leaned her head back and laughed. "And it was awesome."

Without thinking, I grabbed her hand. Her skin was like a sheet of ice against mine and she trembled. Her face beamed Arizona cardinal, and the hint of a smile breaking across her lips evaporated into uncertain shock as our eyes locked. I let go and put my hand back on the shifter. Shouldn't have done that. Shouldn't have touched her.

I pushed my foot heavier on the gas pedal. The last of the streetlights blurred and disappeared as we headed farther down the highway into the night, the dark making the inches between us into miles.

CHAPTER THIRTY-SIX

Abby

I rolled down the window just enough to let the cool night air brush against my face. I breathed deep. The damp smell of dew-covered leaves and grass wafted in and mixed with the heavy odor of the leather seats. Wisps of hair whipped against my cheeks, and I slid them behind my ear, only for them to blow back out again.

My body still surged with the thrill of the race, muscles charged and ready to explode, like I could throw open the car door and run for hours into the darkness. But I kept the door shut, letting Kellan take me wherever he wanted to go. I didn't really care where we went, as long as he didn't take me home. At least not right now. The second I chose to jump in the passenger seat, instead of conceding to my mother's very loud demands, a knotted feeling had appeared in the depths of my stomach, a visceral acknowledgment that I would pay for what I'd done. When I got back, my mother would probably unleash a huge bag of fury on me for taking off—and right in front of her too. I'd never defied her to her face before.

The car slowed as we approached a rundown chain-link gate. Kellan shifted into park, then jumped out.

In the radiance of the headlights, he jerked back the gate and slid it open. No locks. No chains. Just a lonely 'Keep Out' sign that hung on by only one corner.

He jumped back in the driver's seat and raised his eyebrows with a smile, a lightness enveloping his expression since he'd left Parker in his dust.

"What's this place?" I asked as he drove slowly through the gate onto an overgrown dirt road.

"You'll see. I found it a few years ago. You don't mind a little trespassing, do you?"

"Well, considering I was in jail yesterday and we've already broken every speed law in the state tonight, trespassing seems like no big deal."

He laughed. Not loudly, more like a chuckle. But it sounded honest.

We pulled up on the side of a cliff and he cut the engine, the sudden silence almost overwhelming—just the song of crickets and the tinkling sound of the engine cooling down up here. Kellan got out of the car and ran around to open my door as I unclipped my seatbelt.

I exhaled, letting the frenzy of the evening flow out and bring the calm back in. Ahead of us, tiny houses spread out below like fireflies in a field. Each one a speck of light in the glow that rose above the town and settled in the air between us and them.

"Pretty cool, isn't it?" Kellan said, stepping to the side and letting me see the whole view at once.

I moved toward the edge and sat down on the ground, close enough to see but far enough away that I wouldn't hyperventilate and pass out, then pulled my thighs to my chest and rested my head on my knees. In the daylight, you might be able to see to the state line from here, but in the dark, I could just stare out into nothingness. Kellan sat down beside me, leaning back on his arms with his legs extended in front of him.

"You told your boyfriend you weren't going to see me anymore, huh?" He didn't look over, just kept staring up at the sky.

I hung my head. I didn't need to answer. It wasn't really a question.

"Sounds healthy."

"Hey, don't judge me, Mr. My-Ex-Turned-Me-Into-A-Mythical-Demon-Creature." I scowled at him, but I doubted he noticed with his stare so far away and laser-focused that he could likely see the surface of Venus. "Besides, Marcus isn't my boyfriend. Not anymore."

"I'm sorry. I hope it's not—" His chest deflated as he sighed, the uninhibited delight of his victory dissipating into the infinite black. "Have you told Marcus about what's been going on? About me?"

"Of course not. It's just that ... I don't know ... things with him have been kind of confusing lately. And it's not your fault." My stomach churned, and I shifted in place, the taste of reality not going down as easily as I would've liked. Or maybe I hadn't really let myself process it yet? "There's been a lot of stuff going on with him that has absolutely nothing to do with you."

"Does that mean I can come back and haunt him forever when I'm a 'mythical demon creature' for getting us arrested?"

"Kellan."

I shoved his shoulder, and he wobbled on his elbows, nearly falling over. He raised his left eyebrow and tilted his head toward me, the hint of a smirk breaking across his lips.

He smiled wider. "So ..."

I shook my head and laughed. "We don't know for sure that he called in the tip. He didn't deny it, though."

"But I could still make him pay for pissing you off. Besides, I want you to be happy."

"Oh, really? Since when did you become my fairy godmother?"

He shrugged. "Just thinking, I guess. How it's all going to end." He glanced up at me, his stare locking on mine then darting down to the ground. "What I might leave behind."

I inched closer and reached out to put my hand on his arm, then pulled away just as awkwardly. When had this suddenly become so strange? "Don't think that way. We're going to figure this out. I promise."

"But maybe there isn't a way out. Maybe these are the cards I've got, and I have to play what's dealt."

"All right. How's this supposed to go then?"

"I don't know. I just wonder about it all sometimes. Will I keep flipping through dimensions forever or will I stay in one for a long time? Will I know who I am anymore, or will I just be this thing? Will I remember my old life?" He breathed in deep and then exhaled hard, his shoulders dropping and his entire body collapsing into itself. "And will it hurt? When I die."

His words stung the corners of my eyes and burned in my throat, making it hard to swallow or breathe, choking on his last shred of confidence that he could be saved. When exactly had he given up completely, and how come I'd never noticed?

"And the part that kills me is that I'll never see my dad again. As a human, I'm fifty-fifty for seeing him when I'm gone. Heaven or hell. Up or down. But now I won't get that chance. I'll float around forever watching everyone I love die and disappear."

I cleared my throat, a tightness growing in my chest. "I'm not going to let that happen."

Kellan sat up straight and wound back to toss a rock over the cliff, the momentum of his arm whipping his entire body forward. He watched it sail over the edge in silence. Then he tossed another. And another. Until his breath hung heavily in the air and his chest heaved in and out as if he'd just run a mile.

"Why do you keep trying to help me?" he asked. "Don't you have your own life to worry about?"

"Because I know you're always looking out for everyone else. Doesn't matter how big of a jerk you think you are to the rest of the world, I know you're the one who digs out the neighborhood's cars in the winter. You do so much to take care of your mom. And I know back in tenth grade when Scott Perkins told everyone that he'd slept with me that you were the one who made him publicly apologize or you would tell his father he was skipping football practice to smoke up behind the metal arts building."

He laughed, pressing the heels of his hands in his eye sockets and falling back onto the grass. "You weren't supposed to find out about that. Did he actually tell you?"

"No. But I have my sources." I followed his lead and lay back. The stars hung dull and far away as if they didn't dare to interrupt, or maybe they'd just turned their lights down for us. I twisted my fingers in the soft blades of grass beneath me and wondered how many nights we might have left here—in this town, in this life, just the two of us. "Besides, you may not have noticed, but I actually care about you."

I turned my head, watching Kellan's chest rise and fall as he breathed in the night air, the grim, heavy frown finally fading. He looked calm—peaceful—for the first time since he'd told me about his curse. Maybe laying out all his worries had given him solace, while they'd ripped my insides apart. Or maybe he really had no idea that he wasn't actually alone in this. As if sensing my stare, he dropped his head toward me. In the dark, even this close, his face became a study of contrasts. His stark lashes against his pale eyelids, the glittering gold irises of his eyes against the white, his deep red lips against his skin.

He laid his warm palm against my cheek, his thumb tracing small circles in the flesh behind my ear.

"Thanks," he said, so quiet, I felt the word breeze against my skin instead of hearing it. "I'm going to miss you so much."

And then my lips pressed against his. I didn't know if I'd kissed him, or if he'd kissed me, or if we'd both breathed too deeply and then simply fallen together by force of gravity, but one second, I was lost inside his sad eyes and the next, nothing existed but lips and tongues and teeth and the night sky and the stars.

Kellan's heart beat faster under my palm, as the smell of his skin surrounded me. Clean and real. Like soap and honesty. Spotless truth. I'd tried hard to deny how much I wanted this. How many times I'd imagined how his lips might taste and then forced myself to forget. But there wouldn't be a way to scrub this from my memory now.

His hand gripped tightly on my hip just beneath the hem of my tank top, and he rolled me onto my back, our kiss never breaking as we moved. I slid my hands onto his biceps, his muscles straining under my fingers as he tried to hold himself up without crushing me. Holding back. Keeping us together, even as both of us threatened to fall apart.

He traveled down my neck, placing small burning kisses all the way to my ear, the tip of his nose brushing against my earlobe. I shivered and let out an embarrassing moan as I laced my fingers through his hair.

"You won't miss me," I said, "because I'm not going to let you go."

Turning my head, I took the lead and found his lips again, suddenly unable to stop. Wanting more. Wanting the sun to stay asleep so this night could go on forever. No one's opinions in my head, no realities in the way. Just me and Kellan and the moon.

His warm hand cupped my cheek as his mouth stiffened against mine.

"I can't do this."

Kellan fell back on the grass next to me, the raspy sounds of our heavy breaths echoing in the air.

I didn't move. I simply lay there, letting his words swirl around in my head, deciding that they didn't make any sense. "What?"

"Everyone knows someone like you should never be with someone like me."

I propped myself up on my elbows. "Since when do you care what other people think?"

Kellan stood and brushed the dust off his jeans, then looked out over our little town. I watched his head tip back toward the sky, silent, as if considering my words or just ignoring them completely.

"I should take you home."

CHAPTER THIRTY-SEVEN

KELLAN

Abby didn't say anything on the way home. Instead, she stared out the open window into the dark, while I clutched the steering wheel to the point of nearly crushing it in my hands, mentally ripping myself a new one over being so stupid. I'd decided to stay away from her. How the hell had that turned into making out on the side of a cliff? I considered explaining, telling her it wasn't her fault, but my brain couldn't find the words. Probably because explaining would mean telling her the truth, telling her goodbye.

As soon as the Nova slowed close enough to a stop, she jumped out and sprinted toward her house. She stopped for a second in the middle of her front lawn and looked back at me.

"I'm sorry," I said as I slunk out of the car and shut the door behind me with a *thunk*. The hollow sound echoed through the night, dire and final, like shoveling dirt on a coffin. "I'm not ... I mean, trust me, you'll be better off without me screwing up your life. Stop trying to save me. I'm the last person you need to waste time on."

She walked toward me and stared, the disappointment in her sapphire eyes reflecting in the hazy motion lights on the garage. "And you're the last person I thought would tell me what to do."

I reached out to touch her, an unconscious need to make her feel better pulsing in my limbs, but she backed up a step and then turned away, her jaw clenched like I might bite her instead. A rabid dog that should be put down.

My stomach hollowed as I let her walk away, biting my tongue instead of saying the things I desperately wanted to. But it would be better this way. A pissed-off Abby would forget me faster than a sad one. And that was what she needed to do—forget about me.

I stood for a long time, focusing on the blobby shadows of oil stains on the concrete until the shards of moonlight moved from one side of the driveway to the other and the damp chill of the night cut into my skin. Giving her up was the right thing to do, wasn't it? She sure as hell deserved better than me. So why did it feel like the wrong decision?

As I slipped through the front door, the eerie, bluish glow of the TV washed over the living room, a dull rumble of voices coming from the speakers. A half-eaten plate of chicken and rice sat on the coffee table and Mom lay curled up on the couch, sound asleep. I clicked off the television and grabbed a blanket from the armchair in the corner. She looked so small on this big couch, in this big room, in the big house that would soon be nearly empty. The Abby-shaped lump in my throat crashed down into my stomach, banging around, making the nauseous feeling in my gut a thousand times worse. Leaving Abby hurt enough; leaving Mom would be unbearable.

I unfolded the blanket and draped it over top of her. She groaned and rustled around, catching my hand at the hem of the fabric near her face.

"You're home," she said in a drowsy whisper.

"Yeah, Mom, I'm home. Now go back to sleep."

She let go of my hand and rubbed her face. "No. Sleeping down here will kill my back."

Mom pushed herself up and stretched, then staggered toward the stairs, still half-asleep. "Were you out with Abby again?"

I dropped my head toward the floor. "Yeah."

"Good." She gave me a sleepy smile. "I like her."

"I like her too, Mom."

She stopped on the bottom stair and turned around. With the extra step, she could finally look me in the eyes without having to stand on her tiptoes. She placed her palms on the sides of my face and held my stare for what seemed like forever. She still had the greasy diner smell leaching off her, but I didn't care.

"I love you, Kell. You know that, right?" The look in her eyes wasn't sleepiness anymore. It was something else. Something that during the day she might've hidden better.

I tried to nod but couldn't, still locked in her grip.

"Sometimes I think that I don't tell you that enough and that one day you're going to leave for college, and I won't get the chance."

"I love you too, Mom." I scooped her up in my arms and buried my face in her shoulder, the air thick and hard to breathe. "I love you so much."

She hugged me back and rubbed her hand gently down my spine like she used to do when I'd been sick. "Just remember that no matter where you go, this will always be your home. Okay?"

"Okay," I mumbled, trying so hard not to cry. The last time I'd cried had been at Dad's funeral. I'd cried so much I'd sworn I wouldn't let that happen again. But right now, it seemed like the stupidest pact in the world.

"Now go get some sleep. School tomorrow." She gave my

shoulder a quick pat to signal for me to let go. Except I didn't want to.

Eventually, my arms started to seize from holding on so tightly and I relaxed them. She shook her head and gave me a gentle grin, then turned and staggered up the rest of the stairs.

I let out a breath so painful and dark, it ripped from the bottom of my lungs all the way out my mouth. I blinked. Once. Twice. Still, the haze of pending tears clouded my view of the staircase.

Steadying myself against the wall, I pounded up the rest of the stairs and closed the door to my room, falling back against it and knocking my head against the wood. I'd played out the end of my life so many times in my head that it shouldn't have been able to affect me anymore. It shouldn't have been able to shred me like this. I'd had a plan. A good plan. One that didn't involve all this hurt and regret. It was a lot easier when no one cared.

From the nightstand, it stared at me. The cold metal hourglass with its handful of sand left. The reminder that everything I cared about in this life was floating by and I'd never catch it.

My mom. I'd miss her so much. More than I'd let myself accept until now. But having her arms around me jabbed the knife deeper into my heart, turning and twisting through the layers of muscle, leaving a raw, bloody massacre.

And Abby. It had taken everything I'd had to push her away, but I hadn't wanted to. I hadn't wanted to stop. To have her there, wanting me. The screwed-up, half-dead idiot who couldn't figure out what he'd wanted until it was too late. Being around me put her in enough danger. I didn't need to make things worse. But I wanted to. Everything in me wanted to kiss her until neither of us could breathe. Let her wash over me like water on stone. Etch me.

Maybe I should've told her about my death sentence. Let her make her choice if she still wanted to kiss me. If she still wanted anything from me. But I couldn't. I'd punked out. I was such a coward.

That stupid dickhead Marcus knew it. Even her own father knew it. I wasn't worth the trouble. And once that sand disappeared, I would be gone. I grabbed the edge of the nightstand and flipped it over with a growl. The pressboard splintered as it hit the floor. Books and magazines flew across the room. And the hourglass, it vanished. I stepped over the shambles and squeezed my head in my hands, grabbing at my hair. I was a waste. A nothing.

Something flickered on my desk. I looked up. The hourglass reappeared, still ticking away the rest of my life. Only one day left.

Abby

Bright morning sun attacked my vision as I opened the front door to head off to school. I covered my eyes with my hand and groaned. Was the universe actively trying to make me feel worse than I already did?

I'd barely slept last night. After the inevitable blow-up with my parents when I got home, I'd been wired. But even as the anger faded, I still couldn't rest. Tossing and turning for hours with a bunch of crazy thoughts swirling through my head. About me, my future, Marcus ... Kellan. I shouldn't have been thinking about Kellan. Kissing him was probably a huge mistake. Clearly, he thought so. So why did I still burn up when I pictured the rush of his lips on my neck and his hands on my skin? And then he'd just backed off, citing some lame excuse. I ran my fingertips across my lips and swore I could still feel him there. Like he'd kissed me so hard, he'd left a brand underneath the skin. Because I felt guilty, or because kissing him was exactly what I'd wanted? But what did it even matter now? I shouldn't have been thinking about Kellan.

I dragged my feet the rest of the way down the walk. My head hung toward the ground, trying to block the cheery light mocking my misery. A pair of navy-blue Nikes appeared where the sidewalk met the driveway. Marcus. I looked up to see him leaning against his car, his arms crossed against his chest and a frown across his face. The last person I'd expected to see first thing in the morning, especially this morning.

"So, you got home late last night?" he said.

"What's that supposed to mean?" I said, taking a step back. Light filtered around Marcus's head, blurring his face, but the burning anger seething off his skin screamed his feelings better than the scowl I couldn't see.

"I mean, I sat on your front steps for hours last night waiting for you to come home so we could talk, but you never showed. Should I just assume you were still out with him, or did you think I didn't see you ducking in the passenger seat of his car?"

His words sliced through my flesh, hundreds of tiny incisions stinging and burning my entire body—and every single one of them I deserved.

"I'm sorry, Marcus, but what I do shouldn't be of your concern anymore."

"Sorry? I didn't ask you to stay away from him for me, I did it for you. Why don't you see how much trouble he is? I don't get it."

I stuck my hands on my hips. Sure, I hadn't wanted Marcus to see me with him, but it didn't make it his business. "You can't tell me whom I can be friends with."

"I'm not worried about your friends, Abby, I'm worried about how that scumbag looks at you. Like some toy that he has to have."

"I'm just someone's toy, then?"

Marcus let out a growl, threw his arms in the air, then started to pace up and down the driveway. "That's not what I meant. You know that's not what I meant. I just don't get you anymore. Why won't you just tell me what's going on?"

I stood silently, the throbbing in my head fighting with the ache in my chest over which could kill me first. I didn't need to bait him into a fight, but being angry seemed easier than being honest.

He took my hands in his, rubbing his thumbs over the skin on my knuckles. Classic Marcus. Trying to smooth things over and make them all right. But he couldn't this time. I'd already moved on, even if I hadn't realized it until now. Who knew how far I would've gone if Kellan hadn't pushed me away? Not like it mattered. Not wanting to stop him was equally as telling.

I gazed up into Marcus's endless eyes, warm and comforting like cinnamon and hot chocolate, drawing me closer and trying to wrap me up in him. His brow furrowed, but he still forced a half-smile that twisted the pain in my chest, wrenching it deeper down into my gut.

"I think things have been over for a long time and I just haven't been able to admit it. We should've broken up a long time ago before we could hurt each other like this," I said.

"What?" He dropped my hands and recoiled as if I'd slapped him across the face. "I came here to try and work things out. I don't want this to be over, I just want to know why you're lying to me."

I studied the cracks in the concrete, unable to meet his confused glare. "It's done, Marcus."

"Please don't tell me you're with him. Seriously?" He rubbed his hands over his face and looked back at Kellan's house as if he might walk out the door on some unseen cue, but his front door remained shut. "I saw this coming. I *knew* it. I mean, all that time you were spending with him. I tried to tell myself it was nothing, but it was right there."

"Kellan and I aren't together," I said. Kellan didn't want me. He'd made that clear last night, but I couldn't be with Marcus, either. Things had changed. I'd changed. It was just one kiss, but to me, it felt like so much more.

"Then why?" he pleaded.

"Lots of reasons. I think you know it too."

He stuffed his hands in his pockets and fell back against the car, his head tilting up toward the sun. My arm twitched, reflexively wanting to touch him, to try to make him understand, but I shouldn't. Tears flooded my eyes and ran down my face, dropping in dark splashes on the pavement as all the good memories of Marcus bombarded my brain. The late nights we talked for hours and I never wanted him to leave. The trip to his cabin last summer with all our friends. His arms wrapped tight around me as if he'd never let me go. How easily I'd forgotten the positives when things had gotten rough?

He looked up, his frown crumpling as he placed his warm palm on my cheek and wiped a tear away with his thumb. "You're the first girl to ever break my heart, Abby Marino. I hope you know what you're doing."

He tore his hand away and pulled his car keys from his pocket, spinning them around on his forefinger. His body turned toward the driver's door, but his sad eyes stayed locked on mine. After a few seconds, he shook his head and huffed a huge sigh then climbed into his car and turned over the engine.

Backing slowly into the street, he rolled down the window.

"I'll see you later," he yelled as he hit the gas and the tires screeched away.

I dropped to sit cross-legged on the crisp grass, my head cradled in my hands, allowing the reality of finally letting Marcus go crash through me. The tears came fast and hard at first, but slowly they dried, replaced by a lighter sensation. Relief.

Marcus and I hadn't been working for a long time. I knew it. Somewhere deep down, he knew it. But for some reason, we'd kept hanging on, neither of us brave enough to walk away. Now it was just over.

And I wanted to tell Kellan. Tell him I didn't care what anyone else thought, and he shouldn't, either. He'd stirred something inside me that had been asleep for a long time, and I couldn't go back now. I didn't want to.

I rubbed the back of my arm across my face, wiping away the last few tears I would ever cry over Marcus. I tapped my phone screen. 9:20 am. Already late for first period, and besides, going to school would bring up too many questions that I didn't want to answer. Not yet, anyway. I needed to get my head straight before I saw anyone else. I picked myself off the ground and scooped up my bookbag, charging right for the Caseys' front door. Closing my eyes, I took a deep breath and knocked.

KELLAN

Light reflected off the hood of the Nova as I raced out of town, the sun rising at the end of the highway. Bands of yellow, orange, and the deepest scarlet slid into the sky, swirling together like a painting I could drive right into. Like if I kept going, I would eventually just fall into the sun. But the brighter the horizon, the darker the shadows weighed on my shoulders, knowing that each second would be one more wasted of my last sunrise. At least my last sunrise as a human. Except when I was no longer human, would I even care?

I cranked the stereo, trying to drown out my own thoughts with the whine of electric guitars. Right now, I didn't want to think. I didn't want to replay how I'd peeked into my mother's room and given her a silent goodbye and then slipped out the front door in the dark. How I sat behind the steering wheel staring up at Abby's house hating myself for hurting her. Hating myself for being such a coward. But that was what I was. I might as well own it.

On the passenger seat sat a half-filled backpack, and I dug through the front pocket, making sure I hadn't forgotten anything. Not that I had any idea what to pack for an afterlife of hell, but loose ends needed to be tied up before I died. I owed Mom that. Richie down at King's Garage would pick up the Nova on the weekend and then sell her, putting the money in Mom's bank account. Emails would start coming to Mom tonight, tomorrow, and for the next couple of days, telling her I'd gone to check out the campus at USC. By the time she'd start to worry, I'd have every trace of my existence wiped clean. Hopefully, over time, she'd think I just didn't care instead of the truth. It might not work, but I had to believe it would. At least for a little while.

My head bobbed along to the music, my brain still prisoner to my thoughts with the memory police having a hell of a time working me over. The bright blue Oakville town sign streaked through the passenger window. *Damn it.* I slammed on the brakes and gripped the wheel, nearly swerving into a cornfield but recovering enough to make the one lane turnoff. *Stupid.* I slapped my hand against the steering wheel once I'd gained control again. I needed to get it together, or I'd end up killing myself before my scheduled appointment with death. No way would that bastard get me one second sooner than he should.

I shook off the sudden detour and drove down the narrow highway past the lines of Dutch Colonial houses with their perfect little yards. Past the grocery store and the elementary school with its flag flying high. Past the old stone church at the edge of town, the one with the wobbly front pew I'd sat in to hear my father's eulogy. And then I hit the brake, coasted to a stop, and stared out the windshield.

The sun shone high in the sky now, bouncing off the hood of the Nova and highlighting the blue and purple tones in the pearl striping. She'd looked amazing last night, but out here in the blazing sunlight, she radiated like an American muscle angel sent straight from Heaven. The last good thing I'd managed to do, and no one here to admire it.

I unhooked the silver cross from behind the rearview mirror and slid it into my back pocket before stepping out the car door into the blistering hot day. The rusted gate squealed as I yanked it aside and I cringed as if someone might hear or even care. But any souls in this cemetery probably wanted the company, and besides, what better place to wait for death than with a bunch of people who'd already met him?

My feet started moving, carrying me deeper through the maze of grave markers and monuments to lives lived and lives lost. I knew the pathways so well, I didn't need to think anymore. I just let my muscle memory guide me, freeing my brain for other things. Today, I wished it wouldn't. Five generations of Caseys had been laid to rest in this cemetery, and now there would never be a sixth. I hadn't just screwed up my own life; I'd messed with a legacy. The only son of an only son, defying nature and becoming a monster.

Two left turns followed by a right, then the familiar crushing weight pressed against my ribs, halting my steps and trapping my breath in my lungs. The granite slab stood tall out of the ground. Strong. Sturdy. Permanent.

Robert Casey
Husband, Father, Friend

I crouched down and put my hand on the overgrown ground. The lush, green grass grew thick here as if decades had passed instead of only a few years. Some days it felt like eons ago, but today the wounds ached fresh like I'd lost him yesterday. The sun at my back cast a dark, looming shadow over the gravestone, the etched words seeming to cut deeper like my unnatural presence had carved them a half-inch thicker this morning. More ominous somehow. Like my father voicing his disappointment over me wasting my life from wherever he'd ended up.

Flopping down beside the grave, I rested my head against the marker, the stone cool against my neck. I pulled the cross out of my back pocket and rubbed it over in my hands. Dad said he'd hung it from the mirror for protection, but what good had it done? It hadn't protected him, and it sure hadn't protected me, but I'd stolen it from Dad's things after he'd died, so it had never belonged to me anyway. At least now I could make things right and bring it back to its owner. Someone who deserved to be saved.

I placed the cross on the small stone ledge surrounding the tombstone and closed my eyes, whispering a prayer to who knew for no good reason, other than a humbling feeling like I should. A peace offering, maybe? Or just preparing for the unavoidable?

Burying my head in my hands, I breathed deeply, my arms pebbling with goosebumps as a light breeze wound through the monuments. How had I even gotten here? Eighteen, sitting in a cemetery saying my last shameful goodbye because of one stupid choice. One I'd give anything to take back. Especially because Rhiann didn't deserve my mercy. I knew that now.

"I'm sorry," I said, the words ripping and tearing my insides before falling out of my mouth, weak and broken. A million pieces of regret fell into my hands. "I'm so sorry."

Tears stung my eyes, but I raised my head and clenched my jaw, refusing to let them fall. The grave markers blurred, creating watery auras around the stone as if the ghosts had risen to witness my weakness. A coward in their yard. I wiped my face and the world solidified, the ghosts vanishing into the sunlight. The souls returning to rest in peace as they should. If only I could do the same—die with at least a shred of honor, instead of an eternity of disgrace.

I pushed off the ground and bolted back to the Nova, ripping open the backpack and dumping it on the seat. My fingers shook as I pulled my wallet from the mess and dug through the pockets until I found a ratty piece of paper with well-worn edges and curly handwriting scrawled across the front. The sight of Abby's pen strokes sucker-punched me in the gut, but I didn't have time for guilt. I exhaled and dialed the number. One ring. Two rings. Three.

"Hello?" said an irritated voice at the end of the line.

"Rhiann. It's Kellan. I need you."

CHAPTER FORTY

Abby

I closed my laptop lid and rubbed my knuckles over my eyes, my retinas burning from reading all day long. Still nothing new. No magic bullets to kill a Shadow Keeper—at least not on the Internet. I pushed my shoulders back and stretched, then slid my computer into my bag and checked my phone again. No texts. Not a huge surprise, as Marcus wouldn't bother texting me after this morning, Rachel had given up on me about a week ago, and Kellan, he hadn't answered my message at nine, so I doubted he'd answer it now. Mom's name appeared on my call log several times, but I'd let it go to voicemail, which I hadn't checked. I needed to get my head straight before I could summon the energy to argue with her again. Besides, if she realized I'd been sitting less than twenty feet away on the Caseys' front steps, she'd probably charge over and start back on her "how big of a disappointment I was" speech she'd started when I'd tried miserably to sneak in last night. And maybe she was right, but telling me for the millionth time wouldn't fix that problem.

The ferocious roar of an engine in the distance penetrated my brain fog, and I stopped flipping through social media, my thumb hovering over the like button. A column of light, beams of the late afternoon sun reflecting off a car's hood, turned the corner and slowed near the end of the driveway. Finally. I stood up and rubbed my palms against my skirt, the prospect of Kellan being only feet away jumbling the well-rehearsed speech I'd had hours to plan. Most of the words seemed stupid now, and the ones I needed to say mimicked Kellan's snarling hell beasts—ripping up my insides and threatening to take down my entire world if set free.

The car took the turn slowly and halted near the garage door, the rumble of the engine dying on the early evening breeze. I marched out into the yard, the sound of my pounding pulse drowning out the chirping of sparrows and hiss of the neighbor's sprinkler. The entire world was muted and muffled compared to the thump of my heart and the clunk of the driver-side door closing.

"Hey." Kellan's head jerked back, and his eyes widened as he walked around the car and charged toward the front door. "I didn't expect to see you."

"Didn't expect to see me here, or at all?"

He stood still, his head dropping to stare at the keys he kept turning over in his hands. The jingling sound of metal against metal not giving me the answer I wanted.

"Where were you today? I've been waiting to talk to you," I said.

"What? I—" He looked up. The skin on his face hung red and puffy, heavy thoughts weighing on his eyebrows and slanting them downward. Maybe he'd had an awful day already. Maybe he didn't need to hear this right now. But too bad. I needed to say it.

"Never mind. It doesn't matter. I just don't understand what happened last night."

He nodded.

The keys jingled.

I waited.

He looked away.

"What did I do wrong?" I crossed my arms, my hands clamped tightly into fists, digging into my ribs, holding myself together. "You regret kissing me, I get it. But now you won't even talk to me. Just tell me what I did."

"No. No, Abby." He crossed the patch of grass between us in two long strides until he stood less than inches away, the panic setting into his eyes and twisting his expression from steady to stumbling. "You didn't do anything wrong."

"Then what's going on? I thought ... I don't know ... I just ..."

He clenched his jaw, the muscles making tight ridges in his cheeks as he pressed his forehead against mine. "I've never regretted a second with you. I never will."

His left arm wrapped tightly around my waist, and I let my arms fall, knotting my fingers in his T-shirt, the heat of his skin bleeding from his chest to my palms. He smoothed a few stray strands of my hair back over my ear with his index finger, tracing slowly from the top of my ear to the bottom, goosebumps teasing their way across my shoulders until his hand rested warm on the side of my neck.

I closed my eyes. His uneven breath fell on my skin, and I shivered, our bodies drawing closer. Magnets. Forces too strong to fight, even if we'd wanted to.

"You are one of the only good things left about me." His words whispered across my ear and tangled in my hair.

Easing up onto my tiptoes, I tugged his shirt, pulling myself toward his lips. My brain exploded with memories of our last kiss. The desperate feel of his hands on my skin. His mouth on mine, erasing every other kiss I'd ever had and replacing it with that one perfect moment. I looked up into his beautiful, pained face and my knees quivered, threatening to give out and drop me to the ground. In his eyes, I saw myself. The person I wanted to be. Free. Loved. For who I was, not something I'd never be.

My stomach hollowed. Kellan stopped breathing.

"Don't," he whispered.

He stepped back, his arms slipping away.

"If I kiss you," he continued. "I'm not going to want to stop. And I have to. You need to forget about all this. Forget about me. I don't want to hurt you."

"And what about what *I* want?" The soft cotton of his T-shirt slipped through my fingers as he turned to face the ground, unable or unwilling to meet my eyes. "You were the only person who didn't treat me like some sort of breakable doll who can't think for herself, but I guess that's what I am, aren't I? Everyone's doll. Why do you get to decide what I need, Kellan?"

"Because this won't work. Everyone else knows it. I can't be that guy for you."

I crossed my arms, digging my nails into my arms, hoping the exterior physical pain would overshadow the ache in my chest. "What guy?"

"That guy. The one who can make you promises he can actually keep. The one you can make plans with and know he'll be alive to do them."

I leaned forward, dipping my head to the side, trying to get him to look at me, not let him shut me out. "We're going to figure that out. It's all going to be okay."

"And what if it's not?"

"It will be."

"Besides, even if I wasn't leaving, you wouldn't want to be with me anyway. I'm not the kind of guy who ends up with someone like you."

"You keep talking about some fictional guy. Who is this person?"

"The kind of guy who would put on a stupid suit and show up to take you to prom."

"What?"

He pointed to something behind my shoulder, his stare following the direction of his finger. I turned as Marcus closed the driver's side door of his car in front of my house, donning a bowtie and holding a plastic corsage box.

I dug my fingertips deeper into my skin. Prom. I'd completely forgotten. It still felt like it should be weeks away.

"Don't you understand?" I said. "I don't want to be with a guy like that. I want to be with you. I'm in love with you."

Kellan opened his mouth to argue, but nothing came out, his eyes wide and glassy. My face burned. I'd said it. I couldn't take it back. I didn't want to because it was true. I'd been falling in love with Kellan Casey for a lot longer than I'd realized, and now I'd gone and blurted it out.

To the right, another car door slammed behind me.

"What's *she* doing here?"

That voice. High-pitched and irritating, with a heavy shot of arrogance. I whirled around. Rhiann in all her fierce witchtastic glory stepped out of a cab onto the curb.

"Oh," I said. "I get it now. It's not that you need to protect me, it's just that I'm not her. How could I be so stupid about so many things?"

Kellan lunged forward, his arm extended, but I jerked my shoulder away. "I can—"

"Don't." My body froze. Ice filled my veins as the world spun around me.

"Abby," Marcus boomed from my yard.

I glared back at him. "Don't come any closer."

"Were you even planning on tell—" I turned around again, but it didn't matter. Kellan's black sneakers disappeared through his front screen door, while Rhiann smirked at me as she dangled the Nova's keys around her claw-like middle finger, Kellan's Chevrolet keychain sparkling in the sun.

She spun them in the air and clasped them tightly in her fist. "Looks like you did a number on him. Told you it wouldn't last."

The world burned a thousand times hotter as I stood across from the devil and realized she was right. As if Kellan had actually changed. He'd probably been nice to me so I'd help him, but now that he had his witch queen back, he didn't need me anymore. I choked down the dictionary of insults I ached to spew at Rhiann, none of them worth the effort nor fully capable of describing her vileness. Instead, I breathed deeply, pushing down the tears threatening to fall, and retreated.

"You aren't ready yet?" Marcus said, rushing to meet me halfway and staring at the front of the neighbor's house with a snarl on his lips. "Wait, are you okay? What happened?"

"Nothing. It's fine." I wiped my hand across my left eyelid and blinked until everything stopped resembling the inside of a fishbowl. "What are you doing here?"

He jerked his head back. "I'm here to pick you up for prom. I told you I'd be back when I left this morning."

"But we broke up, Marcus." I rubbed my forehead. I figured 'see you later' was a general comment, not a directed statement. "What makes you think I'm still going to go anywhere with you?"

"We don't have to be a couple to go to prom, but I already have the tickets and you have the dress. Why waste it all? Besides, no one at school knows we broke up. I haven't told anyone, and you went M.I.A. today, so I doubt you told anyone, either. At least no one mentioned it when we decorated today, which you completely skipped out on. We still have a chance at king and queen. If you still want to go? Where were you today anyway? I figured you were getting your hair or makeup done, or something, but clearly not."

"Not quite. I wasn't thinking about any of this today. I was a lot more concerned with other things."

"Big surprise. You aren't going to tell me." He stood in front of me as I stared at the still screen door, pathetically hoping Kellan would come charging back outside to tell me I was wrong about Rhiann, but he never came.

Marcus put his hand on my waist, and I pulled away, his touch not the one I wanted. "Look. Something is going on with you. I get that. And I know I probably said a bunch of stuff I shouldn't have this morning, but it doesn't mean I stopped caring about you. I was just angry, but it's just because I don't know what to do to get you to tell me what's happening. Maybe it's just nerves about school ending, or maybe you're worried about college, or your grades, or whatever, but when you're finished dealing with all that, I'll still be here for you."

I looked into his eyes. They were the same warm brown they'd always been. The ones I used to be able to lose myself in for days and not want to come up for air. But even though they looked the same, they didn't feel that way. And I needed to say something. Anything. Explain that even though he was willing to wait for me, I didn't want him to. Not anymore. With or without Kellan. I was over us. Plus, part of me just wanted to kick him in the shins, but before the words formed cohesive sentences in my brain, my mother appeared in my doorway.

"There you are." She marched across the lawn and grabbed my hand, leading me back into the house. "No time for chitchat. We need to get you ready. Marcus, why don't you join David in the living room and leave us girls to our magic?"

She winked at him and stormed straight into the house and up the stairs in one fluid motion. No stopping. No pausing. No breathing, unless you counted the huffing noises she made every few seconds to remind me how mad she was.

"Where have you been?" She snapped her fingers at the

chair in front of my mirror and I obliged. She lined up bobby pins into a perfect row, then started brushing out my hair with the tact of a drunk dog groomer. "The school called. They said you skipped all of your classes today."

"So?"

"*So!*" She yanked the brush through my hair and it snagged, making my neck snap back. "This is not like you. I told them you were sick and that I forgot to call, but maybe next time I'll let you suffer the consequences of your actions."

"Which would be what? Detention. Maybe it wouldn't be the worst thing in the world if I had detention once or twice in the thirteen years that I've been in school."

She stopped brushing and placed her hands on her hips. "Is that what all this is about? Some sort of adolescent rebellion nonsense? I expected better than that from you."

"You always do." In the mirror, my face changed. Harder. Angrier. Broken. "Maybe I'm not the little angel you think I am."

"Don't be petulant. It's getting exhausting."

She gripped my hair and finished brushing it out while she glared at me through her reflection.

"And poor Marcus. He shows up here, all dressed up, and you didn't even bother to get home in time to change your clothes. Where has your head been?"

"I thought I was grounded for the next forty years, why would I be allowed to go to prom? Besides, Marcus shouldn't be here. We broke up."

"You broke up!" She slammed the brush down on the dressing table, the row of pins scattering, half falling to the floor. "What has gotten into you, Abigail? Please don't tell me this is all about that train wreck of a boy you have been spending far too much time with."

"You used to like Kellan."

"I did until he almost had you tossed in jail. Besides, you don't need to be associated with someone with his kind of reputation."

"You know that's just lies and gossip, right?"

"I doubt that, but even still, he's not an upstanding guy like Marcus."

I choked. "He's not as innocent as you think. Even if he was, what if I don't want to be with Marcus?"

"I'm really getting tired of you and your second-rate choices. Are you trying to hurt me? Because frankly, I'm a little sick of it."

"*You?* You honestly think any of this is about you?" I ran to the bed and pulled out the memory box, dumping the entire contents on the duvet. I snatched the first letter from the stack. "This one's from Yale. '*Dear Ms. Marino, we regret to inform you that we will be unable to accept your application.*'" I grabbed another from the pile. "Here's Harvard. Dartmouth. UPenn. Princeton. Do you want to see more? I'm damn lucky I got into Cornell. It's not a second-rate choice. It's my only choice unless you want me to try to get into law school from the community college downtown."

She gasped, her jaw dropping open. "This is ridiculous. How come I'm just hearing about this now?"

"I'm not as smart as you think I am. I'm not perfect. I'm just who I am and no one seems to care about that. You all want me to be what *you* want, not what *I* want. Hell, I don't even know what I want. The only person in my life right now who actually listens to me is K—"

"*Do not* even say his name right now, or so help me ..." Lines etched across her forehead so deep that years of expensive face creams couldn't hide them. "I don't know what kind of idealistic garbage he's put in your head, but right now you are going to finish your makeup, get dressed, put on the best smile you have, and get downstairs for that boy who actually had the decency to show up for you tonight."

"But, Mom—"

She raised her hand in the air and turned her face away from me. "I don't want to hear it. I'm not about to let you create another scandal for this family. You'll go. You'll smile. And then you will get back home where we are going to have a serious talk about this, with serious consequences. You have ten minutes."

Mom marched out and slammed the door, rattling all the picture frames on my desk.

Dropping down in front of my mirror, I fought the tears threatening to fall. Instead, I pulled out my make-up bag and laid out my tools across the dressing table. Going to prom with Marcus wasn't exactly my favorite plan, but it would get me out of this house and some time to figure things out without my parents hovering over me. Besides, after tonight, I was sure they'd lock me away like a fairy-tale princess in a tower until I left for college. I should at least take advantage of even a small mercy.

I swept my hair up and fought the raging shake in my hands as I pushed a handful of pins in the twist to keep it secure. I should have been excited about tonight. My prom. Most girls waited years for this night. Dreamed about it. But for some reason, it didn't feel like the magical experience television and movies tried to tell me it should be. Maybe it was because I wasn't going with the one I wanted to be with. Why didn't Kellan get that? I didn't care about all of those things that he had rambled on about. I just wanted to be with him, and I'd thought he wanted that too. I couldn't get his kiss out of my head. His lips pressed hard against mine. Hungry. As if he'd always wanted this. But had I imagined it? Couldn't be. You couldn't fake that.

After wriggling into my dress and pulling on my heels, I

sighed at the mess of souvenirs scattered across my bed. My entire life in a box. I picked up each of the letters and placed them back on the cardboard bottom. Pictures of friends and smiling faces tossed in one after the other like memory confetti. There was one of me and Marcus at Homecoming last year. We both looked so much younger than we did now. Happier. But for some reason, I didn't really recognize the girl in the photo. She wasn't me anymore. She was someone else's version of Abby.

I leaned over and picked up the last few pieces off the floor. One final piece of yellowed paper lay in the middle of my carpet. I snatched it up and took a deep breath as I turned it over in my hands. The friendship contract. Maybe the universe was trying to tell me not to give up on saving Kellan just yet.

The edges of the paper had already worn to a soft fuzz, threatening to rip as I carefully unfolded it. On the bottom of the page, in blue magic marker, were the words *Kellan Matthew Casey* and a brown faded spot of blood at the end to make it binding—or at least that was how we'd thought contracts worked back then. I didn't even need to read it. I still knew the words by heart. After all, I'd signed the exact same one in green pencil crayon.

The thought of him tore up my insides. Maybe after I escaped this house, I could try talking to him again. I bit my lip. Even if I wasn't her. But even if he truly didn't want me, he didn't deserve to die. I looked over Kellan's primitive signature and slipped the paper into my purse.

I put on a sweep of makeup and braced myself as I walked into the living room. Marcus's and Dad's laughter echoed up the stairway as I approached, but honestly, I really didn't care to hear the joke. I wanted to get this night over with. Right now, I felt betrayed by pretty much everyone. Marcus. My mother. My father. And Kellan. Most of all, by Kellan.

"You look beautiful," Marcus said as he stood from the couch and rushed to my side, sliding his arm around my waist. I clenched my stomach muscles, hoping to put even a quarter inch of distance between us without tripping alarms with my parents. He handed me the plastic box in his hand, an exquisite orchid he'd probably paid a fortune for.

"This is for you," he said.

A flash snapped in my periphery as my dad took pictures and I plastered on my trained plastic smile.

Here we go.

CHAPTER FORTY-ONE

KELLAN

There wasn't enough stupid sand left in the stupid hourglass to fill my fist. Every grain fell like a jagged piece of glass tearing down my esophagus—ripping me apart from the inside out. I shouldn't have come back inside. I should've ducked around the side of the house and waited for Abby to leave for her magical night with her dickhead ex-boyfriend, then got in my car and made tracks for the highway. I should have, but I didn't, and that only left regret.

The smell started it. Clouding my head. Dulling my urge to run. Slapping me in the face as soon as the front door creaked open. That distinctive aroma that encompassed a little bit of everything that made up my life. Food, cleaning supplies, stuffy furniture, a hit of Mom's favorite perfume, and something else—something that wasn't really anything, except that to me it was home.

I stumbled up the stairs, drunk on the scent, and ping-ponged between the walls, trying to keep it together. My breath came short and shallow, my eyes stinging with the threat of tears I'd never let myself cry. I leaned my arm against the doorjamb and surveyed my room as if I'd forgotten something, knowing I hadn't. Everything I needed sat in the trunk of the Nova.

My throat closed tight like hands were gripped on and squeezing. If the Shadow Keeper didn't kill me, being in this room would. My covers lay neat and flat on my bed, the first time I'd made it in years. The lines of my books and magazines sat on their shelves holding stories of worlds I would never get a chance to visit again. My clothes hung in neat black lines behind the open closet door. Every last thing in its place, exactly as it should have been, but how long would it stay like this when I never came back?

I walked over to the desk and ran my hand over the lacquered top. Mom had insisted that I needed a desk in my room. She and Dad had spent hours putting it together, the pieces not fitting together like the instructions had said they should. I'd sat in the corner, nine or ten years old, playing with a deck of cards, watching them argue until he'd taken her hand and pulled her into his lap. He'd whispered in her ear, and she'd laughed. She'd called him ridiculous and laughed again, then we'd all gone for ice cream. It had taken a full week before the desk had been finally finished, but they hadn't argued about it again. Dad had been like that. He'd had a way of making things better. I swallowed hard against the steel grip on my neck. I wished he were here. If not for me, for Mom. To tell her it would be okay and make her laugh. I needed to know she would still laugh.

I glanced out the window at the treehouse looming in the fading light, trying to stop my vision from getting all wet and hazy. Nothing left of it now but rickety boards and a broken ladder that should have been torn down years ago. Now it just stared at me, looking pathetic. Reminding me how much I'd screwed up. Reminding me of Abby.

She'd said she loved me.

I slammed my fist against the window frame. She'd actually said it. Out loud. All this time, I'd tried to keep everyone away so they couldn't hurt me, but all I'd done was hurt her. The one person who really got me. When Rhiann had ditched me, I'd fallen apart. Swore not to let myself get attached to someone else like that again—never hurt anyone like she'd hurt me and leave them to pick up the pieces. But it was already too late. She'd said she loved me, and I had to leave her.

Rubbing my face with the back of my arm, I pounded down the stairs, trying my best not to look at anything else. I didn't want any more memories showing up. I needed to put some distance between me and this house. Between me and this life. Who knew if I'd even remember it later anyway?

I slammed the front door and turned the key in the lock for the last time. The tightness in my throat came back, making breathing impossible. I swallowed. The house keys rattled in my trembling hand.

Voices echoed from across the lawn as Abby's front door opened and she stepped out. She'd twisted her hair up behind her head and slipped into a killer blue dress that cut short on her thighs and tight at her waist. It fit perfectly in all the wrong places. I'd be the luckiest guy to have a girl like that with me, even if only for a night. But she wasn't. If I hadn't been such a jerk, she might have been standing over here in that gorgeous, ridiculous dress while I imagined how she would feel in my hands. But that wasn't going to happen. I'd blown it. But it didn't matter anyway. This time tomorrow I would be gone. And she'd be better off without me.

I'd fought everything not to kiss her, not to let myself get carried away as she'd held tightly on my T-shirt, the heat of her body so close, my skin had burned beneath the thin cotton. It had seemed like the right thing to do—the chivalrous thing—and the stupidest thing I'd ever done.

Behind her, Marcus walked out. So she was giving him another chance. The hands around my throat moved to my chest and started punching. Hard. The two of them walked together slowly across her front lawn, her parents standing in the doorway as if this was how it was supposed to be. Didn't they know? She'd said she loved me. Me. Not him. She turned and looked back. Watching me watching her. Too soon, she turned away. Couldn't really blame her. And Marcus, that jack-ass, just smiled at me like he'd won the stupid lottery. *Prick.* He even made a point of running his hand down her back so I could see him touch her. It looked like she might have tried to shrug him off as he led her into the car, but maybe I was just being hopeful.

The car's taillights flashed once and disappeared around the corner. Letting her go was supposed to be the right thing to do, so why did it feel so absolutely wrong? A blood-red line streaked across the sky as the sun set behind the houses across the street. I only had a few hours left of my life and I stood like a loser on my front step, regretting everything I'd done. I banged my head against the closed door and dug the house key into my palm until the metal bit into my flesh. She'd said she loved me. Out loud. No matter how many beasts I'd faced in the last year, it turned out *I* would be the one who did me the most damage.

Rhiann blasted the Nova's horn in the driveway. What was I doing? Maybe I could still do one thing right. She'd said she loved me, and the only certain thing in my brain was that I loved her too. My blood pumped faster in my veins as a new plan formed in my head. Only a coward would sit and wait for their life to end without spending it with the girl he loved. Screw this.

CHAPTER FORTY-TWO

Abby

Music poured out of the front door of the school like water breaking through a dam. A flood, pummeling you in the face as you tried to enter, almost to the point of pushing you back out again.

Marcus's hand fell to the small of my back, urging me forward through the door, which worked better than he'd anticipated as I quickened my steps to add some distance. He'd spent the fortunately short drive here explaining all the reasons why he'd been pleased that I'd changed my mind and come with him when the only real reason had been to avoid any more fights with my parents and to get out of that house.

As we entered the gym, a sharp pang jabbed at my stomach.

No tacky crepe paper streamers or silly banners, just simple and elegant decorations transforming our school into another world. Clouds of balloons and white lights covered the entire ceiling. Dark navy curtains draped every wall, and even coordinating mats lay across the floor to hide the basketball court. Each table had fresh flowers, the scent of freesia and gardenias wafting around the room. Even the royal blue tablecloths didn't look like castoffs from some low-end cafeteria.

"Wow, they really did a great job," I said despite myself.

"No thanks to you." Rachel appeared beside me with Parker on her arm. Her flowing, red halter dress gave her the illusion of being ten feet tall. Or maybe I just seemed smaller after being called out. Her vicious death stare locked on my head, not matching her glamorous outfit.

"Hey, Parker, man, looking tight." Marcus high-fived Parker and continued in some bro code handshake I couldn't follow.

I hooked my arm with Rachel's and leaned into her ear. "Can we talk for a second?"

She nodded, slipping out of Parker's grasp and sliding back into the crowd. She threw her hands on her hips, the burgundy rose around her wrist bobbing as her hands shook.

I forced myself to meet her glare. "I'm really sorry I wasn't here."

"Yeah, well, I'm kinda getting used to it. You totally ghosted me for the last few weeks. You don't answer my texts. You're never around. Even Marcus keeps calling me, telling me that he never sees you. I thought we were supposed to be friends?"

The pain in my stomach gnawed at me again, and I crunched forward a little. "I know. And I have been a really awful friend to you. There's just been a lot going on. A lot of stuff I've been dealing with."

"So why don't you just talk to me about it?"

Good question. But I wasn't ready to unload all the crazy thoughts churning through my head on her. "I didn't want to upset you. Plus, I didn't know if you'd understand."

"Well, if you don't tell me, I guess you'll never know." She turned her head away, her expression hard but, in her silence, it softened and she let her arms fall to her sides. "Are you okay?"

"I'm getting there." I clasped my hands together. "But I promise I will make this up to you. I'll do better."

"I don't need you to be better. I just need my friend back."

She wrapped her arms around me, pulling me into a hug. I squeezed her tightly, a strange balance between feeling better and feeling even worse.

"I think I can do that," I said.

"Good. Maybe after all this prom stuff is over, we can ditch our phones, ditch the guys, and just hang out, the two of us."

"Yeah." Ditching guys sounded like a really good idea right now. "You are so much better to me than I deserve."

She smiled and cocked her head to the side, the soft curls surrounding her face bobbing around her shoulders. "I know. But I know you'll have my back someday when I need it. Just remember when you need it I have yours."

"Deal." The darkness lifted from her face, replaced with a light, easy, reassuring smile.

I forced out a deep breath and let my lips curl up to match hers. I'd missed her.

"That's a smile I haven't seen in weeks." Marcus's voice drifted across my ear. He settled in beside me as Parker took his rightful place beside Rachel. Parker did actually clean up pretty well, and the awed look he gave Rachel when she wasn't looking made me sort of jealous. She totally deserved it, the way the top hugged her curves and with the sexy open back, but I realized he always looked at her that way, not just tonight. Marcus never looked at me like that, but Kellan did, or maybe I'd just imagined it.

"I have to go check on the king and queen ballots." She winked at Marcus and me, then turned to Parker. "Come with me?"

He rolled his eyes, but a smile burned on his lips as she tugged his hand across the room.

"Did you want a drink or something?" Marcus rested his hand on my shoulder, and I shirked it away. He sighed.

"Look, I get it. You obviously don't want to be here, or

maybe you just don't want to be here with me. But here we are." He shoved his hands in his pockets and moved in closer, the smell of his cologne stirring up memories I forced myself to push down. "I'll make you a deal. Give me an hour. Take some pictures for the yearbook, make our parents happy, maybe even try to have a little fun, and if after an hour, you still want to leave, I'll take you anywhere you want to go. To anyone you might want to see."

"Seriously?" I crossed my arms, fully expecting some sort of trick. But his eyes lacked their mischievous twinkle. Besides, other than stomping home in my heels to confront a guy who clearly didn't want to be with me or my fuming parents, what else did I have going on?

"Yes, seriously. I've tried to make this work, but clearly, this wasn't the way to do it because you seem even more mad at me than this morning. But I think if you left now, you'll regret it. You only get this night once and I have spent so long wishing for it to be with you. I had just hoped you wanted to be with me too."

I stared out to the middle of the floor. Everyone else was laughing and dancing and just excited to be there. I should have been excited too. I wanted to be, but I just couldn't.

"Fine. I'll try." I pointed my finger at him. "But this doesn't mean it changes anything between us. We're still broken up and I'm still pissed at you."

"Got it. Absolutely." He held his hands up in surrender, a small hint of accomplishment teasing its way into his smirk. "But would you at least let me dance with you? One last time."

I shuddered but nodded. "Just one. That's it."

"Fine by me." Marcus took my hand and led me out into the middle of the dance floor. His hands found their way to my waist, and I tried not to cringe. Amazing how much things had changed in such a short time. A month ago, I wouldn't have been able to wait to sneak Marcus off somewhere and now I could barely force myself to dance with him. How had everything gone so wrong, so fast? Kellan's curse seemed to have brought out the monster in Marcus, and me as well.

I tried to get into the music. I closed my eyes and let him lead me, forcing my brain to stop thinking about being elsewhere. But I couldn't. No matter how hard I tried, I really wasn't feeling it.

"So, can you at least tell me what went wrong? Why you suddenly dropped off the face of the Earth?" His eyes looked like they might well up, big and wide, and he held me just that little bit tighter, a little bit more desperate. "Why you'd give up everything we had going for that guy?"

I let his words sink in for a moment, swaying back and forth to the melody. Hurting Marcus had never been a plan, or Rachel, or my parents, or anyone. And it wasn't new. Helping Kellan had let me hide out from my real life, but I hadn't known it wouldn't be temporary, that I'd actually change.

"You don't get it. There's more going on here than you think, Marcus. I've been spending all my time trying to be this thing, this person that everyone wants me to be—my parents, my teachers, you. But it's not me. I'm not even sure who that is anymore. And Kellan ... This thing with him has nothing to do with any of it. Besides, he doesn't want to be with me, so don't worry about that."

"Really?" His hand gripped tighter around my waist, not the quiet desperation like before, but his fingers digging deep into my lower back. "You never used to lie to me before. Or maybe you were just better at it."

"What are you talking about?"

People sidestepped in awkward movements. Lines of satin and sequins separated, clearing a path across the dance floor. The music played on, but we stopped moving and stared out through the crowd. Toward us walked a figure in a white-collared dress shirt that pulled in all the best places, pressed to a crisp and rolled up to the elbows.

Kellan.

He gave me a bashful smile as he fidgeted with his left sleeve, the jaws of half the senior class dropping at his feet as he swaggered across the floor. But he didn't seem to notice any of them, his hazel eyes locked on mine leading him straight to me.

"Can I talk to you?" he said as he approached.

"Maybe you should've asked her here yourself then?" Marcus scoffed, trying to put as much distance between him and Kellan and as little distance between him and me as possible.

"You're right, I should've. But I didn't and now I'm asking to talk to her, so can you please let her go?" He stepped right up to Marcus, using the slight height advantage he had over him. Instead of backing down, Marcus stood up straighter.

"There isn't someone else you should be with right now?" I snapped to Kellan. Ripping Marcus's hand from my hip, I crossed my arms.

"No, Abby," said Kellan, ignoring Marcus. "The only one I need to see right now is you."

"What about Rhiann?"

"She's here to help with"—he eyed Marcus and scrunched up his nose—"my problem. That's it. I swear."

He moved toward me, but Marcus sidestepped in the middle.

Kellan tapped him on the shoulder. "Can you screw off for a bit, buddy?"

"I'm not your buddy."

"Yeah, I know. But can you still go away?"

"Abby." Marcus's jaw tightened, deep lines cutting across his red face. "You promised me an hour."

"I said I'd stay for an hour. I didn't say it had to be with you."

He opened his mouth to argue, the red changing to nearly purple, but instead, he stormed off the dance floor, nearly taking out three couples in his wake.

"Nice guy," Kellan said.

"He used to be." I placed my hand on Kellan's arm and the shadow of a smile formed across his lips as he wrapped his arms around my back. "What are you doing here? And all dressed up. I'm impressed."

"I know I probably look stupid, but I needed to see you."

"You look good. Take a compliment, would you?"

I ran the tips of my fingers through his styled hair. Still floppy, still messy, but from intent instead of gravity. A casual kind of handsome.

He leaned into my touch, his eyes hovering almost closed. "I don't like you being mad at me."

"I don't want to be mad at you, but you were being such a jerk. And then Rhiann showed up, and I just thought ..."

He pulled me tighter, his voice dropping to a whisper. "I know. And because of that, I didn't get to tell you how beautiful you look."

"Is that why you came all the way down here? To tell me you like my dress?"

"Maybe. Would it be okay if I did?"

I nodded. "Is that the only reason you're here? School dances don't seem like your thing."

"They're not. But I realized I didn't want you to think I didn't care about you. That the kiss the other night meant nothing. Because it did. It meant everything to me."

My pulse quickened. It was all I'd wanted to hear. To know I hadn't imagined everything. To know he felt the same way.

"Then why did you stop?" I asked.

"Because I didn't want to hurt you. I'm so used to just pushing everyone out, to keep them from getting too close to me, but you kept coming back. You didn't give up when you should have, and I didn't know what to do about it. Before you, I was just angry and miserable, but you managed to give me hope when I needed it. I know you don't think you're perfect, but I think you are amazing exactly the way you are. I'm just a coward for not telling you sooner. I should've kissed you today. I should've been the one to bring you here tonight. I may not be that guy for you, but I should've tried, at least until I'm gone."

His body quivered beneath my hands as all the breath in his lungs flowed out on his words.

I pulled him closer. "Enough of you feeling sorry for yourself. I've had enough of you going on about how everything is going to end. Nothing is going to end. We are going to figure everything out and you're going to live a long, happy life."

His hands gripped tighter on my waist. "Can we talk about all that stuff after this song? Right now, I just want to be the luckiest guy in the room, dancing with the most gorgeous girl he's ever seen."

A hundred other things that I wanted to say flooded my mouth, but I bit my tongue and held them back. Marcus was right. Senior Prom only came around once. Everything else could wait.

"I'm glad you're here." I swayed into him, settling my head against his chest. People stared, but I didn't care. Nothing else mattered except his arms around me and his heart pounding through his thin dress shirt against my ear in the same quick rhythm as my own.

He rested his chin on the top of my head, bringing us closer. "I think I've fallen in love with you too."

The last few chords of the song faded away, my hand still

locked tightly in his, his hand gripping my waist, as if it would stay there forever.

"Song's over." Marcus appeared beside us, the scowl on his face still cutting deep across his jaw. "I think it would be best if you left, Casey."

"Back off, Marcus." My voice must've been louder than I'd expected, as a crowd started to gather around while Marcus and Kellan sized each other up.

"I don't get it. I just don't get what you see in him." Marcus grabbed the back of his neck and stared at the floor, pacing quickly between us.

"And because you don't is probably the reason why it happened," I hurled back at him.

A collective 'ooh' went through the crowd as a few people snickered and chuckled behind us.

Marcus stared them all down and leaned closer to me. "Abby, I'm serious. This guy is trouble and you keep going back. Even if you don't want to be with me, that's fine, but please, please don't end up with a guy like him."

"A guy like what, Marcus?" Kellan stepped in front of me, his arms crossed. "Say it? An addict? A criminal? What exactly is your problem with me?"

"Everything. You come in here, steal my girl, mess with my school, and you just don't even care. You had Abby arrested because of the drugs in your trunk and she still hasn't gotten rid of you. What is it about you?"

The music stopped, Marcus's yelling hitting a new level of loud.

"You mean the drugs *you* planted in my car?" Kellan asked, his voice calm.

Marcus looked around, searching for support, but no one came forward. "You're a liar too. Nice look."

"Maybe, but if I were evil enough to frame someone, I

wouldn't do it at a Starbucks that has a parking lot camera," Kellan said.

Marcus's face blanched, his entire body vibrating in his expensive suit. He glanced over at Parker, and he shrugged, his eyebrows raising. Rachel glared at her boyfriend and stormed off the dance floor. Marcus pulled back his fist and swung. Kellan dodged the assault.

"Come at me, Kellan." Marcus waved his hands, beckoning Kellan forward. "I can take it."

"No, Marcus. If you think I'd fight you, you have no idea who I am."

"What is this nonsense?" Mr. Joffrey rushed into the crowd and stood between the two boys. His stare scanned from Kellan to Marcus and back to Kellan again.

Marcus stood up straight and jabbed a finger toward Kellan. "He took a swing at me, sir."

Ugh. Another lie. Didn't he know when to quit?

"Is that true?" Mr. Joffrey searched the crowd, but no one made eye contact. "Kellan, I'll have to ask you to leave."

"Whatever." Kellan tossed up his arms and turned toward the door.

I rushed over and slipped my hand in his as everyone cleared the way for us to leave.

"Don't go, Abby," Marcus called after us.

I squeezed Kellan's hand and looked over my shoulder. "There was no point in picking a fight, Marcus. Kellan's already won."

CHAPTER FORTY-THREE

KELLAN

The Nova jerked to a halt as Rhiann ground the gears and my heart crash landed into my stomach.

I gripped my forehead in my hand and begged for the noise to stop. "You know, if you took it easy with the shifter, it wouldn't make that sound."

She glared at me through the rearview mirror, her eyes burning hot enough to start an inferno. "Well, then, I guess you're lucky it's not your car anymore. And besides, I never signed on to be your chauffeur."

Rhiann jumped out of the driver's seat and slammed the door, then popped the trunk behind Abby and me.

Abby tugged on my sleeve. "What is she talking about, not your car?"

I ignored the question. Instead, I ran my index finger down the soft skin of her cheek and rested my palm on her chin. Her eyes fluttered as she leaned into my touch.

My chest tightened as I scanned every feature of her face. The gentle curl of her eyelashes. The delicate slope of her nose. The tiny splash of barely-there freckles that dotted her cheeks. I committed each minute detail to memory, just in case I got the privilege to remember, wherever I ended up. "Are you sure you don't want to go back to the prom? Or home? Or anywhere but here? I don't want you getting into any more trouble because of me."

"And I don't want to spend one more second not knowing what's going on with you." She placed her hand over mine and twined our fingers together, bringing them both down into her lap.

I forced a smile and swung open the back door. Tugging Abby along behind me, I stepped out onto the patchy grass cliff-side and breathed in the fresh air. In the distance, the sun dipped lower over our little town, nearly gone except for a dark crimson glow on the horizon, a navy-blue sheet of stars falling into place over top. My last sunset in my favorite place. At least I had that.

On the other side of the car, Rhiann had already started preparing. She'd moved rocks and sticks into a perfect circle formation and sat just outside, her hands resting on her crossed legs, her eyes shut tight. A stench of smoke bit in the air as it billowed from the random junk pile amassed in the center of the circle. But if this plan worked, the entire world could smell like rotten eggs mixed with month-old sewage for the rest of eternity, for all I cared.

Abby slid out from beside the car and stood across from me with her hands on her hips, her face contorted into confusion. "So, what did Rhiann mean it's not your car anymore?"

"I gave it to her." I hung my head, watching her heeled foot tap on the ground. "I knew she wouldn't help me for free, so I offered her the car and the last of the cash I had left over from the side jobs I've been doing to pay for the repairs. Fortunately, it was enough."

"Oh." Her voice dripped with pity. I didn't want pity. Especially not from her.

I focused on the horizon, trying not to let her sympathy weaken my resolve. Not like I had many options left anyway. "It was the only way."

"What exactly is the plan? You haven't told me what you're planning to do?" Her foot tapped faster, lightning fast, the movement making my head swim.

The plan clicked into place as I sat alone in the cemetery. I'd run everything over in my head. Every hopeless effort to save my soul. Then I remembered Madame Trumaine. Her twisted lips condemning me to hell. Reminding me how much I made a mess of everything I touched. But she'd made one thing clear. A witch had gotten me into this, and one might be able to get me out. "It's a binding spell. Except instead of binding the Shadow Keeper to me, Rhiann will bind my soul to my body. He won't be able to take it."

"That's awesome, Kellan." Abby launched up on her tiptoes, wrapping her arms tight around my neck. I closed my eyes, letting myself breathe her in. Coconut and raspberries. Then I unhooked her arms and clamped my hands around hers.

Her beaming smile deflated into a wary frown. "What's wrong?"

My stomach churned as I choked on the words I knew I needed to say. "The spell is complicated. It requires a lot of magic and Rhiann won't be able to hold it very long."

"What does that mean? A few years? A few months?" She tugged her hands out of my grip as tears welled in her eyes. Each drop burned through me like acid.

"More like a few hours. If it works." I took a deep breath and continued, "Just before the Shadow Keeper comes for me, she'll start the spell. Hopefully, it will hold long enough."

"But if he comes to take your soul and can't have it, he'll ..."

I nodded, unable to look at her, all the right words sticking in my throat like a piece of dry bread.

"Rhiann isn't going to save your life, is she?"

I coughed. "No. She's going to stop me before I become something hideous."

"What?" Abby grabbed her forehead and paced. The tears in her eyes overflowed and cascaded down her cheeks. "No. She can't. You can't let her."

"It's not her fault. I've thought this through. If I can't outrun death, I can at least choose how I die, and I sure as hell am not going to be a Shadow Keeper's bitch for the rest of time. Dying with my soul intact sets me free from that devil's curse. I don't know what comes next, but dying human gives me a way better shot. Besides, I can't let you remember me like that. As a monster."

She stopped and stomped her foot in the dirt, her hands in trembling fists at her sides. "I don't believe you. You've thought this through? We've been trying to find a way out of this, and all of a sudden, you've thought this through?"

I tipped my head back to stare at the star-dotted sky, hoping the right thing to say might drop down from space.

"This isn't new, is it? You knew your end was coming?" she asked. "How long have you known?"

The last of the red sky disappeared on the horizon.

"Kellan. Answer me. How long have you known?"

I closed my eyes and sighed. "A week."

"You've known for an entire week?"

She flew at me, the tears coming harder. "You didn't tell me. You were just going to go off and die somewhere and never tell me, were you? You didn't plan on coming to prom, or any of it? You were just going to die. Without even saying goodbye." She pushed at my chest with her fists. Black makeup streamed down her cheeks and clumps of her hair shook loose and fell to her shoulders. She hated me right now. She hated me so much for the same reason I'd gone to that dance tonight. For the same reason, I couldn't get her voice out of my stupid head. For the same reason that I didn't want to die today. Because she didn't really hate me at all.

"Kiss me, Abby," I whispered as she scraped her heeled foot in the dust and dirt of the cliff.

"And did you ever think about what that was going to do to me? Just leaving like that? You can be so thick sometimes, Kellan Casey. Such a complete idiot."

She wound up to pummel me again, but I took her wrists and twisted them against me. She started to gasp, her breathing all wrong, and then she slammed her forehead into my chest. She cried, her hot tears soaking through my shirt and falling warm against my skin. Her body twitched against mine as she sucked in air against her sobs and then sunk deeper into my embrace, her head on my shoulder.

I couldn't hold back any longer. My eyes prickled, hot and wet as my whole world shattered like a windshield after a crash. Shards of her reflected in my watery gaze, refracting her image over and over, then slicing deep into my flesh. Her hair tickled against my chin, her scent flooding my senses as I traced my fingers along her smooth skin. I pulled her tighter. I might lose my soul tonight, but the girl in my arms had stolen my heart already.

"Kiss me, Abby," I said again.

"What?" She pulled her face back and stared at me, her beautiful sad eyes glistening.

"I said, kiss me. Because I don't want to spend the last few minutes of my life listening to you yell at me, or wishing I had the right words to make it better 'cause I don't. Kissing you is the only thing in the world I want to do right now." I pressed my forehead against hers. "Because I'm in love with you, Abby Marino."

She glanced up, questioning, and I wiped away the tears

forming on her lashes with my thumb. She tried to force a smile as she pushed up on her toes and crushed her lips against mine. Her sweet lip gloss mixed with her salty tears, and I craved her even more. A thirst I'd never quench.

I kissed her harder, deeper, every inch of me wanting to tell her so many things in that kiss. So many things I'd never have the nerve to say. I wrapped an arm around her waist and spun her between me and the door of the Nova. She placed her warm hands on my neck, holding me to her like I might consider letting her go. But I couldn't. Not now. Not ever. Anyone who'd thought I was an addict had the wrong drug. I'd give everything for a steady supply of her.

Dizziness started in my head, clouding my thoughts. It came in waves, but my lips still found hers over and over again. The lightheaded feeling rushed over me, but I pushed it down. I didn't have much time left, and I wanted to let myself go. I wanted to feel Abby trembling in my hands. I wanted to hear her say my name in a breathless gasp. I wanted to look down and drown in her bottomless cool blue eyes. I wanted to lose myself.

She broke away and buried her face into my neck. Her lips seared hot on my skin as she kissed along my collarbone. A weightless feeling rumbled through my stomach. Anticipation. Want. Desire. I wasn't sure. I pulled her face away from my body and kissed her lips again. Harder. Faster. The feeling in my gut turned sour and pain shot through my limbs. Electric. Lethal. I froze and dropped her chin, prying myself away from her.

"What's wrong?" she gasped, her breaths strained and labored.

"I don't know," I yelled as I collapsed to my knees. My arms shook. I was barely able to hold myself up as the knife in my gut twisted again, dropping me closer to the dirt.

Abby pulled at my arm and tried to yank me back to my feet, but I couldn't move. The pain rippled through me like poison in my blood. It burned and tore from the inside out. Then another sense took over. Something heavier. Sinister. I glanced up as a cloud of purple smoke erupted in front of us. The Shadow Keeper.

CHAPTER FORTY-FOUR

Abby

The air changed. The late spring swelter thickened, heavy like it had gained a thousand pounds. Like I could break off a piece and hang it on my wall.

"Get up, Kellan." I yanked on his bicep, but I couldn't lift him against the dead weight of his body. The muscles in his limbs quivered as his arm shook in my hands. Maybe if he could stand, we could run? I doubted we could outrun it, but at least we could try. We had to do something other than cower here and let it take him.

Smoke and the sour smell of sulfur clouded around us. I coughed and peered through the billowing haze. A figure appeared in the middle of the fog, towering tall in a swath of deepest purple robes, a hood shielding its face. Two red orbs burned from beneath the hood in the darkness.

I shivered in the heat, the sensation running from the top of my head to the tips of my toes as I stared at the motionless presence. At least with its pet beasts, I'd known what to expect—brute force and fangs—but the Shadow Keeper maintained an eerie calm that made my knees quake wondering what he might do.

I pried my stare away and kicked off my heels, then placed Kellan's arm over my shoulders. "Get up. We need to get out of here."

"Run," Kellan whispered. His voice broke into barely a hiss. "I need you to leave me and run."

"You've brought an audience, boy. How absolutely delicious." The Shadow Keeper slammed his long, crooked staff on the ground. The blue light glowing from the gem at the top cast over the Keeper's face, or a lack of face, reflecting off the white bone of its skull.

I pulled Kellan forward, his body limp against my grip. "No. I'm not going anywhere."

"I'll never stop loving you, Abby." Kellan pushed my arm off his shoulders and his T-shirt slipped through my fingertips. He stumbled forward as his knees threatened to drop him back down, sheer terror blanching across his expression.

"Your time has come to an end," said the Keeper. "It's been fun playing with you. I haven't had a cursed one fight as hard and as long in a while. But even the strongest eventually fall to my wrath."

Rhiann's voice hissed behind us, lilting over foreign syllables as clean and clear as English. I glanced back behind the car. She stood frozen, her left hand extended toward Kellan, her ginger hair splayed out around her as if blowing in the nonexistent breeze.

"I bind thee by the sun, I bind thee by the moon, I bind thee by midnight, I bind thee by noon," Rhiann repeated, flipping between languages as the spiderweb of blood-red veins blazed against her pale skin.

Kellan glanced back at me and nodded, his hazel eyes disappearing into the blackness of his stare. A green glow started at his ankles and spread up each leg towards his torso.

"No," I mouthed, reaching for him, but my hand shot back from the strange energy.

"I bind thee by the sun, I bind thee by the moon, I bind thee by midnight, I bind thee by noon." The words came again and again as Kellan bucked in the beam of Rhiann's magic.

I closed my eyes. "Please, please, let this be working."

A scream ripped through the evening air. High-pitched. Feminine. I ripped my eyes open as Rhiann fell, landing on her hands and knees. The Shadow Keeper cackled, his sinister laugh echoing all around me. The green glow around Kellan vanished. He gripped his arms over his stomach, moaning in pain. Rhiann attempted to stand but was knocked back down again, her face in the dirt.

The Shadow Keeper turned its head toward Kellan. "How dare you try to foil me again? Stupid human."

He swiped the staff through the air, blowing Kellan around like an empty plastic bag, then whipped it forward, knocking him onto his chest. "If I weren't already here to claim you, you'd serve lifetimes in Hell for this."

The Shadow Keeper held out its hand. No flesh, just bright white bone. He waved his staff over his palm. A black ball appeared and levitated, spinning and twisting. Purple smoke rose from the ball and streamed out toward Kellan. I ran in front to stop it, putting myself in front of its target, but the smoke changed course and slithered around me like a python. Kellan's scream echoed on the night as the purple death started to set away the skin from his arms. I threw my hands over my ears, my lungs aching as I held my breath.

"Stop!" I shouted. "You'll kill him."

I rushed to Kellan's side, brushing my arms against the smoke. Tears poured down my face and dripped on his thin dress shirt while he writhed under my grip.

"That's what I'm *trying* to do." The Shadow Keeper raised his staff in the air again and cast it to the side. My body rose off the ground and flung backward ten feet, my elbows slamming into the ground.

"You can't do this." I cried. "You can't have him."

The Shadow Keeper hissed back, "Yes, I can. We have a deal."

I pushed myself up to my feet, worried he might strike me down, but determined not to let him win without a fight. "He didn't understand what he was doing. That's not fair."

Kellan screamed again, the agony ripping his vocal cords as the sound came out his mouth.

"I don't deal in fair," the Keeper said. "I deal in souls. He offered his for the witch girl and now I'm here to take it."

His soul. He couldn't take his soul. He ...

I ran back to the car. Throwing open the door, I grabbed my purse and dumped it over the backseat. Between the lipstick and a pack of gum sat the aged piece of paper still folded in eighths.

"Stop," I yelled again, waving the paper in the air. "You can't have Kellan's soul. It's mine."

The Shadow Keeper raised a boned hand above his head and the smoke dissipated, stopping its assault. Kellan dropped back down to the ground, grabbing at his chest and gasping for air.

"You said Kellan offered up his soul for Rhiann's. But he couldn't because he didn't have the right to give it away. He's already given it away once—to me."

The thing slammed his staff on the ground. "Don't play games with me, girl. You will pay if you lie."

I wiped the tears away from my eyes, doing my best to hold the Keeper's penetrating stare. "I have the contract right here.

He signed himself over to me when he was eight years old. His soul is mine."

"Bring the contract to me." The Shadow Keeper hissed like a cross between a snake and a boiling teakettle. He held out his arm and twisted his bony hand toward the sky, beckoning with his index finger. An invisible force pulsed through my bones and yanked me forward. My body skidded toward him on my bare heels, skin ripping and tearing as I slid, then flopped me down at its feet—if feet actually existed beneath its cloak. I unfolded the contract, my trembling fists gripped tight onto the page as I held it up.

"See?" I croaked, fear wrapped tight around my throat. "He can't give you a soul that isn't his. It's mine."

"Enough. This proves nothing. Anyone could have signed this." He raised the staff again as the purple smoke started to rise.

"But the blood. His blood. It's on the contract. You can't deny that."

The Shadow Keeper dropped his bony skull toward the contract. The paper rattled as my hands trembled and threatened to give out. A scarlet forked tongue slithered between its exposed teeth and licked the sheet.

"It's true," the Shadow Keeper shouted as he pointed his skeletal finger at Kellan.

I folded up the contract and crept backward. The Shadow Keeper slammed his staff on the ground three times, the earth shaking beneath my legs.

Rhiann's blistering screams shattered the night again. Her body levitated behind us, drawing closer until she dropped from the sky on the far side of Kellan. Her face erupted as a kaleidoscope as emotions cycled through her wide eyes, resting somewhere between anger and blinding fear to be facing the demon she thought she'd already escaped.

"What's going on?" she squawked, her voice breaking as she took turns staring each of us down. "Your problem is with him. Not me."

The Shadow Keeper flicked his finger, and she dropped to her knees. "Deal's off. But I'm still short a soul."

KELLAN

"What did you do?" Rhiann stared at me lying on the ground, her shoulders sunk down and her hands limp at her sides.

I pushed up on my raw hands, the nerves in my body tripping like live wires, sparking over and over, ripping me apart as I stood.

Abby brushed the dirt off her legs and glared at Rhiann. "His soul wasn't yours to trade."

Stupid move. Never tease a tiger. Especially a tiger witch.

"*You* did this?" Rhiann charged across the open space toward Abby, veins already aflame and eyes glowing red to match. "This isn't how it's supposed to work. I'm not going to let you take me down like this."

I struggled to run, every piece of muscle hanging limp on my bones, but I grabbed Rhiann by the forearms before she could get to Abby. "Rhiann, don't do this."

She looked up at me, her eyes flicking back to their deep emerald green. Big sad eyes with tears pooling in the corner and streaming down her cheeks. This side of Rhiann didn't come out often. Vulnerable. Afraid. Deadly.

"I can't do this, Kellan. Not again. You know what it's like. You know what he'll do to me," Rhiann cried.

The night I'd given up my soul flashed in my brain. The same look on her face. The same desperation. But this time, I wouldn't be so stupid. "I'm sorry."

She cast her stare down toward the ground with a quiver across her lips.

"But *sorry* won't help me now that you little prom queen's gone and messed everything up." Her tears flowed harder, dripping off her face and splashing onto my shirt. "Or maybe she can help, Kellan. Maybe ... Maybe she can take my place."

"What?" I shook my head as the nonsense request processed through my brain. "No, Rhiann. It's over."

She pivoted to the left, trying to escape my grip, but I held tight and moved with her, determined not to let her pass.

"Think about it. Maybe she can go, and we can be together like we used to be before all this happened. I never wanted to hurt you, Kellan. Believe me. I didn't, I swear. I just had to save myself. I know you get that, and I know you understand. The world will never miss a cookie-cutter do-gooder like her. We're special. We could be amazing together."

Her voice pleaded, begging, her options completely run out. Maybe she had loved me once. Maybe she still did. My ribs tightened around my chest, making it harder to breathe. I'd never want anything bad to happen to her, but she wasn't my concern anymore.

"I can't. I love her," I said.

She put her hand on my cheek and forced my face close to hers. "But you still love me too. I know you do."

"I did." I ripped my head out of her hand. "Just not anymore."

Rhiann stiffened in my arms. Her demeanor flipped from

fear to fury, quick as a drag race and as serious as a car crash, her glare searing vermillion over my shoulder.

"Kellan!" Abby shrieked behind me.

I whipped my head around, still keeping Rhiann firmly in my grasp. Abby hovered just beyond the cliff, her feet flailing in the open air, her eyes staring down at the bed of rocks below.

"Stop it," I screamed. "You need to stop this."

"No, *you* stop it. Trade her for me. We're strong, Kellan, you and me. Survivors. She's weak. Just let her go."

"You're sick."

I released Rhiann and ran to the edge.

Abby's loud gasps echoed, each breath hard and short, hyperventilating as she stared into the dark below. Her arms crossed tightly over her chest, holding herself together. *This is all my fault.*

"Don't look down, Abby. Just look at me. Look here." I waved one hand in front of my face and extended my other aching arm out as far as I could, questioning if I'd have the strength to hold her if she grabbed on. My fingers swiped just inches short of her skin. "It'll be okay. Just look at me, Abby. Take my hand."

She tore her stare from the rocks and locked on mine. *Good. Stay with me, Abby.* I extended my arm again, and this time, she reached forward as far as she could, her arm trembling so fast, it barely moved at all. Just as the tips of her fingers brushed mine, she whirled back through the air another foot. Just a little bit too far away. Just out of reach.

"Damn it, Rhiann," I shouted. "This isn't going to solve anything."

"Maybe not. But if you think that I'm going to go down without a fight, then you don't know me very well."

"I never thought you were a murderer."

"She dies or I do. It's self-preservation."

I crept closer to the edge, my feet halfway on and halfway off, my toes dangling in the air. I reached for her again, her arms out toward me but no way to come any closer. Her sobs came louder, the realization that she would never be able to reach me casting over her face. A flimsy layer from her dress flapped as she hovered above the earth, strangely like a goddess with her blonde hair wild in the wind except for the fear in her eyes that showed her mortality.

"Enough games," the Shadow Keeper bellowed.

The stench of smoke and sulfur blended behind me, but I wouldn't break my connection with Abby. She needed me. She'd risked everything. Stood up to a monster that I could never face. For me. I wouldn't let her down.

The Shadow Keeper clucked.

Rhiann shrieked.

Abby cried, "Kellan!"

Then she fell.

I leapt forward into the open air and wrapped my arms around her body, both of us plummeting down into the dark below. My face buried in her hair, the smell of her overwhelming my brain, and forcing my arms to grip tighter against the pain. She held onto me, her face in my chest, her heart pounding against my ribs.

My left arm hit the ground, pain shooting through my elbow to my shoulder, but I held tight to Abby, keeping her close to me as we rolled farther down the side of the cliff. Rocks pierced into my sides and back, tearing at my skin. Dirt caked my nose and mouth. Abby fell limp like a doll in my arms. My head smacked the ground as we finally stopped.

"Abby." I pulled my arms away and screamed, every motion shooting pain through my limbs. She tumbled off of me, and I managed to pull myself up to my knees.

"Abby."

She didn't move. I rolled her onto her back and leaned across her chest, my head on her heart. It pounded slow, deep in her chest, as her shallow, shaky breaths streamed onto my forehead. *This is all my fault.*

I ripped at my hair and curled closer to her body. "Abby, please. Just wake up."

Overhead, Rhiann's final cry repeated in the night as purple sparks lit up the sky.

My hands shook as I pulled my phone from my pocket and dialed 911 on the cracked screen. I twisted my hand into hers, feeling her pulse fading while the line rang. One. Twice. Three.

"Hello. Emergency."

This is all my fault.

CHAPTER FORTY-SIX

Abby

The door creaked somewhere in the distance. I rolled over and groaned, smashing the pillow against my face. My body ached, a dull, throbbing pain pulsing through my limbs and aching in my joints as if I'd been asleep for decades.

"Are you awake?" Mom whispered, barely loud enough to hear.

I groaned again and forced my eyes open, blinking against the harsh light of wakefulness. Across the room, Mom placed a vase of Casablanca lilies on my dresser. The pristine, white petals exploded in all directions, delicate and exquisite.

"Thanks. They're beautiful." I tried to sit up straight, but it hurt to move, so I decided against it, lying back against the headboard.

"They're from that boy ... er ... I mean Kellan." She arranged the stems in the vase and sat down in my desk chair, her legs crossed impeccably, but her face a mess. No makeup graced her skin—not even a hint of mascara—the lines of worry blinking as bright as neon.

"We've run out of room for them in the kitchen. He comes

to the house at least a few times a day and always brings flowers. If I didn't know better, I'd think they had a greenhouse in that backyard."

"How is he?" I'd thought about Kellan in the haze of blinding hospital light and sterile sheets to the long car ride home and the fitful bouts of half-sleep over the past ... how long had it been? Hours, or days, or, my chest squeezed hard around my lungs and forcing a gasp, maybe weeks?

"He's all right, except he's very worried about you." She tapped her fingernails on the top of my textbook, then lifted the cover and thumbed through a few pages of physics. "How are you feeling?"

"Better. I think." I forced myself to sit up even against the sudden wave of vertigo, but fortunately, it subsided quickly. "Everything still hurts, but I think it's starting to let up."

She nodded, words jumbling themselves inside her mouth as her lips twitched, holding them back. Finally, she sighed. "Are you ready to tell me what happened?"

My brain fought against the ache. Fuming Rhiann. The Shadow Keeper. The weightless feeling as I'd suspended over the rocks. Kellan's arms tight around me as we'd tumbled down, his voice whispering in my ear. *I love you, Abby.*

I blinked a few times, wiping the memories away. "I fell."

Her lips pulled into a tight line. "You just fell? That sounds ludicrous. What were you even doing up there?"

The rest of the flashes of last night whirled through my mind. "We'd gone for a drive. Marcus tried to fight Kellan at the prom, so we left. I wanted to look at the stars and I guess I got too close to the edge and fell."

Her eyebrows crumpled in toward her nose. "Why would Marcus try to fight him? This isn't making much sense"

"Marcus planted the drugs in Kellan's car. He's the one who got us both in trouble. He admitted to it and then took a swing at

Kellan. I didn't think it would be a good idea to stay with someone like that."

Mom's eyes widened, her posture straightening to an unnatural stiffness. I expected a tongue lashing, but instead when she opened her mouth the only sound was, "Oh."

"I told you it wasn't Kellan's fault."

She paused, tearing her stare from me and flipping it toward the sunlit window on the far side of my room. "And Kellan just jumped off the edge after you?"

"Yeah ... pretty much. I know you don't like him, but Kellan really isn't anything like what people think."

Silence hung thick between us as she stared at her palms, processing all the information or maybe just unsure of what to ask next. As I watched, her reflective gaze shifted, morphing into something darker as her breath hitched. "I thought ... I thought after the fight we had that maybe you had tried to ..." Glassy tears spilled down her face hard and fast. "I don't know what I'd do if I lost you."

"Mom." I slid across the bed and tapped her leg with my hands until she looked up at me through her flood of tears. "No. I told you. It was an accident."

"Are you sure?" She wiped her arm across her eyes, the tiny hairs on her skin standing tall. "If you need help, we can get you help. I'll do anything to make sure you're safe."

"I'm sure. You can ask anyone. Ask Kellan. He knows what happened."

"Okay," she said, between gasps. "I just couldn't help thinking that maybe ... maybe it was my fault."

"Then don't go looking for things that aren't there. I wouldn't hurt myself. But that doesn't mean those things you said to me were right. I haven't forgotten that."

Mom jerked forward but stopped before she unleashed whatever response had sent her flying forward. Instead, she closed her eyes and breathed in deeply through her nose. Then she stood and straightened her blouse as a frown crested across her lips.

"Soon you'll be off to college. A fresh start. A new beginning." She rubbed my feet through the comforter and gave me a forced smile, my words tripping her up for now. But this conversation was far from over. My body stiffened between the sheets, her comfort coming at me like a threat.

"I don't think I'm going to college." The words came out slowly as they rolled over my tongue sharp and foreign, but true to my heart. "Actually, I know I'm not, at least not right now."

Mom's eyes bulged out, the blotchy redness from her tears transforming into a crimson rage. "What?"

"I mean. I'm going to take a year off. All this time, I've been doing whatever everyone tells me to do. But being everybody else's version of me hasn't let me figure out who I really am."

"I don't think you know what you're saying. You've been in the hospital with a concussion. It's probably still affecting your thinking. Why don't you wait until you're better before you make any rash decisions?" She pulled her hand from my feet and crossed her arms. "Decisions that could impact your entire life."

"No, Mom. This isn't just a snap decision. I've been thinking about this for a long, long time. I'm going to defer my acceptance for a year. When you're faced with the prospect of dying, you finally realize that most stuff isn't important."

"Not important?" His lip quivered. "This is your future we're talking about."

"No. It's a year we're talking about. A year so that when I do go to college, I can do it on my own terms. I can be myself, whoever that might be. And"—I pulled my knees up to my chest and wrapped my arms around them—"I'll do this with or without your support. I just hope that you can be there for me.

If not, that's your choice. I've made mine. The pressure I've been under isn't healthy. I know that now. I don't want to be a disappointment, but I don't want to live your life anymore."

She opened her mouth to argue, but nothing came out, her pointed finger suspended in the air as if the world had stopped and she'd frozen in time. I bit down on the side of my cheek, wanting to say so much more but smart enough to quit.

Eventually, she dropped her fist to her side, knuckles still white but appearing slightly calmer. "Well, I guess you don't leave me much room here. I just wish you would've said something earlier. This could have saved all of us a lot of trouble."

I exhaled, letting years of anxiety start to finally ooze out. "Yeah, I wish I would have too."

She lingered in the doorway, fussing with the makeup and hairbrushes on my dresser, straightening and tidying but never looking at me.

"I hope you understand. I'm not doing this to hurt you. I've never wanted to hurt you, but I have to do what makes sense for me," I said.

"Get some rest. Less than twenty-four hours until graduation, if you're up to it." She sighed and rolled her eyes toward the ceiling, a few last tears threatening to fall. "And I'll talk to your father and then we can discuss this again."

She nodded, then slipped out the door, closing it behind her. All my breath flowed out of my body as my pulse raced under my skin and I collapsed into my pillow. I reached for my phone to text Kellan, but it wasn't there. Pulling my arm back under the blanket, I curled into a ball as my heavy eyes closed. Only one small step, but at least in a forward direction.

CHAPTER FORTY-SEVEN

KELLAN

"And I challenge you to not only look forward and see the future but to stand up and be the future. Thank you."

Marcus ended his speech with a solid fist pump. Idiot. Probably bit his lip for impact too. And "be the future"? This could possibly have been the lamest graduation speech in history. At least if I would've died, I would've been spared from sitting through his pointless dramatic rambling.

I shifted in my hard, plastic chair as Mr. Joffrey approached the podium, my arm sweating in my cast.

"We are pleased that you all could join us today to recognize the achievements of this terrific bunch of students. Remember that graduation may be the end of your high school days, but it is the beginning of a new life for each of you." Joffrey's eyes scanned the crowd and seemed to rest on me for a few seconds longer than comfortable. Right until the end, huh?

"Jessica Abalon."

A tall, leggy redhead stood up as Joffrey called her name and sashayed to the stage, more like a beauty pageant contestant than a graduate. I shifted in my spot, the uncomfortable chair making my back sweat beneath the afternoon sun and the thick layer of my graduation gown. I glanced back over my shoulder at the lines of happy, smiling faces behind me. As much as I couldn't wait to get out of there, something inside me calmed at the thought of making it to this day. Graduation had seemed like something that was never going to happen for me. A far-off dream for people who weren't damned. But here I was, baking in the sun, waiting for my name to be called.

My eyes followed the alphabet back until I could see her face among the 'M's. Abby watched the show with a light, happy smile. Would she still be smiling if she saw me watching her? Maybe she didn't want to see me anymore? She didn't answer my texts or my calls. Her parents hadn't let me see her. She hadn't even answered when I'd scaled her house and knocked on her window. The last time I'd been this close to her, I'd held her head in my hands and begged her not to die. Losing her seemed to be the price I needed to pay for her life. Besides, she'd done as she'd said. She'd saved me. She'd saved me, and I'd told her I loved her. Maybe she'd changed her mind about me when she'd realized I wouldn't really be leaving?

I tapped my foot, nerves in my body crackling and sparking like micro electric shocks, while I watched the senior class parade one by one onto the stage. My mind wandered. I imagined jumping over the line of 'C'-named students and bulldozing my way to her. Pulling her into my arms and pleading for her to forgive me. I glanced back again, but she didn't seem to notice.

"I repeat. Kellan Casey." Mr. Joffrey bent closer to the microphone, and I shot to my feet, racing toward the side of the stage.

"Congratulations." Mr. Joffrey maneuvered my diploma between the fingers of my broken arm, a strange twinkle of joy in his stare, or maybe simply relief at knowing I wouldn't be around to darken the office door next year. He gripped my good hand tightly in a handshake and leaned into me. "I knew you could do it."

Sure, buddy. Keep telling yourself that.

I bit my tongue and nodded, pumping his hand and smiling for the photographer.

Holy hell. I'd actually graduated.

❧ ♥ ☙

THE PROCESSION FINALLY ENDED, and Joffrey said his final words to send us out into the world as functioning human beings. Something I was sure he'd take full credit for if one of us actually made something of ourselves. The recessional march started, and the graduates filed off, starting from the back.

I stretched up on my toes to try to find Abby in the crowd. A sea of blue mortarboards made it impossible to tell people apart from above. I pushed past the students in my row and broke for the center aisle.

"Abby!" I called, but the music blared too loudly and the swarm of parents and guests already swooped in to steal their respective graduates.

An elbow nudged me in the chest, and I glared down at some guy trying to cut in front of me. High school may have ended, but I could still intimidate the hell out of people when I needed to. He twitched and turned away, letting me pass and sidestepping as far from me as he could get. Perfect.

Abby appeared on the edge of the field. Her mother rushed over and fussed with her hair, while her father placed his arm around her shoulders and pulled her close. I swallowed hard, half-wishing my own dad could be here and half-wishing her dad had waited in the car so I could talk to her alone.

"There you are, Kell." Mom cut off my lane to Abby and wrapped her arms around me. "I'm so proud of you."

"Thanks, Mom," I said, squeezing her back. She deserved so much more than just a hug, and at least I had my whole life to make it up to her. But in that moment, my attention turned back to the edge of the field, but the Marinos had disappeared.

"Mom, I'm really sorry." I thrust my diploma into her hands. "Can I just have five minutes? I just really need to see someone. Right. Now."

She laughed. "Of course, Kell. Just hurry back."

I scrambled past her, my head swiveling between all the bodies still lounging in the field, but not one of the Marinos appeared. Running out into the parking lot, I spotted Mr. Marino's Cadillac pulling into the street, the taillights blinking red as he negotiated the turn. I pushed harder, bolting over the asphalt after the vehicle, but it was too late.

Damn it. I stomped my foot against the ground, gravel spitting into the air as I buckled over and held on to my knees, waiting for my breath to slow again.

The sun beat down on my skull and a few beads of sweat built on my forehead. I unzipped the front of my gown and trudged back toward the ceremony, grabbing my mortarboard from the ground where it had flown off during my futile sprint. I stopped outside the crowd of people and sighed, then turned back around and sat on the stone railing in front of the school and pulled out my phone.

Me: *I'm out front.*

I texted Mom as I breathed in deep and let the summer air fill my lungs. I didn't need to go back with those people. None of them gave a damn about me, so best to cut myself off and start over. Because starting over was a luxury I finally had.

Eventually, Mom appeared around the corner.

"Can't wait to get out of high school, huh?" She joked as she slipped her arm over my shoulder and leaned into me.

I tipped my head to the side and closed my eyes as the sun beat down on my face and made weird light formations under my eyelids. "You have no idea."

Mom handed back my diploma and rested her hand on my knee. "What was all that running about?"

"Nothing. Doesn't matter anyway."

She rolled her eyes up, not believing a word, but kind enough not to question. She glanced at her watch. "Are you ready to get going? Reservations aren't until six, but maybe they can seat us early?"

"Sure, but maybe we could go home first?" I asked. "Change into something less sweaty?"

She nodded, and her lips curled up in the corner of her mouth. "And so you can check on Abby, again?"

"Maybe." I jumped down off the railing, the polyester gown catching on the uneven, rocky surface.

"Or maybe you don't need to go there. Maybe she'll come to you." Mom's smile spread across her face as she jerked her chin forward. My head shot back. Abby approached with slow, careful steps, her gown unzipped and her muted pink sundress showing through.

"Congratulations, Abigail." Mom sped past me and gave her a hug, then turned and tapped her palm across my cheek. "I'll wait for you by the car."

"Hey," I said, as my mom disappeared across the schoolyard. All the swords I thought I'd say when I finally saw her had gotten lost on the way out my mouth, or maybe they'd stopped to stare at her like I couldn't stop doing.

"Hey," she replied.

She leaned against the stone railing and slid off her heels, digging her toes in the grass and letting out a soft groan. The hem of her skirt brushed the top of her knees but scrapes and faded bruises dotted down her calves. My lungs ached in my chest, knowing I'd been responsible for every single one.

"I got the flowers—all of them. They're beautiful," she said. "Thank you."

I nodded as my heart raced. Finally, the moment I'd dreamed about since the paramedics dragged her limp body from my arms. Since I held her hand that last time at the hospital while she lay unconscious, her pulse slowing at her wrist, until the doctors escorted me from the room. My fingers twisted in my graduation gown as I gathered my courage to ask the question I feared the answer to. "How are you feeling?"

"I'm okay." She brushed her golden hair over her shoulder, today's curls slipping through her fingers, as she cast her stare off into the distance. Pain etched across her cheeks. "Still weak, but getting stronger. The medication I've been on has kept me pretty knocked out."

I looked at the ground, studying the blades of grass and her painted toenails that matched her dress threading through them. "I'm sorry. If it weren't for me, you wouldn't have been up there. And besides ..." The image of her suspended above the ground flashed in my mind. The dark dread that bottomed out my stomach as she slipped out of my hands oozed under my skin. "I promised I'd never let you fall."

Her feet shuffled in the grass, as she straightened her stance and moved toward me. Her hand rested under my chin and pulled my face up to look at her, her blue eyes wide and bright. "You didn't exactly let me. I'd say jumping off a cliff to break my fall doesn't count as a fail."

"I thought you hated me for what happened. You didn't answer any of my calls or texts."

"Well ..." She tapped her hand on my cast. "Your arm wasn't

the only thing that broke when we landed, so I haven't had a phone to answer. When I was in the hospital, I didn't hear from you, so I just thought you'd moved on. You'd got your life back and I ..."

I placed my hand over hers and clenched tight. "Of course, not. Your parents and the doctors asked me to stay away to let you rest. I don't think they believed the story I gave them about what happened that night, but I waited in the lobby every single day to find out if they would let me through. I swear it. I would never do anything like that to you, Abby. I owe you so much for what you did. I could never."

"Shh," she whispered and placed her index finger across my lips. "I know that now. After I came home, I saw the flowers and my dad told me that you'd been waiting for me."

"They weren't just keeping me away from you?"

"Maybe." She laughed. "But it took me a while to recover, and we had a lot of stuff to deal with. I think things are going to be better in the future, though."

She dug her hand inside her gown and pulled something out of the pocket of her dress.

"I went by your house this morning, but you must've already left. Here." Abby thrust a small silver box at me, a red ribbon tied in a perfect bow across the top. "Happy Graduation. I also heard that you registered for community college. That's great."

I cringed. I'd just missed her. All those times waiting and the one time I left. "I'm so sorry, I didn't know. My mom took me for a late breakfast at the diner before the ceremony. And community college is just for now. I missed registration everywhere else since I didn't think I'd be around to get in, but I'll apply again for next spring."

"Still a reason to celebrate."

She shook the box, urging me to take it, but nothing in there would be the answer I wanted to hear. I yanked off the ribbon.

Inside the box sat a faded piece of lined paper. I took it out and carefully unfolded it, staring at the primitive scrawl that belonged to eight-year-old me. The memory hit me like a line drive to the gut.

"I figured now that you had your life back," she said, "you might want your soul too. But just promise to take better care of it this time, okay?"

My hands shook as I read over the words from so long ago. When things were simpler. I read my name across the bottom and shuddered. "How come you don't want it anymore?"

"It never should've been mine. Everyone should be free to make their own decisions."

I nodded and tucked the box in my pocket. "I didn't know this was going to happen. I didn't get you anything. I'm sorry."

"It's okay." She twisted her dark blonde hair around her finger, a mischievous smirk curling across her deep cherry lips. "But you could do me a favor. Your pretty car. Would you let me borrow it?"

"The Nova? What for?"

"I think I need to see what's out there in the world. For myself, not for anyone else." Her eyes sparkled as she spoke like sunlight hitting the water on a perfect summer day. A lightness I hadn't seen from her in years.

"But what about college?" I asked.

"I'm still going. I think I still want to go—just not yet. I deferred my acceptance for a year, so I'll be hanging around Middleton for a while yet too."

Really? She was staying. My pulse quickened for totally selfish reasons, but I didn't care. "That's a pretty big change. Are you sure?"

She nodded, a contented smile brightening her already beautiful face. "My mom almost had an aneurysm, but she'll get over it. Or at least she promised me she would try."

"I don't think I'd mind having you around more." We stepped closer, both moving in time, drawn together and, finally, with nothing to drag us apart. I slipped my free arm around her waist, the heat of her skin bleeding through her thin cotton dress as a hint of coconuts and raspberries swirled in the faint summer breeze.

"But I only have one problem left," she said. "I don't know how to drive a stick. Know anyone who might be interested in a road trip?"

I laughed. This girl might kill me yet, but I'd let her. "I've got nothing but time."

She clasped her hands behind my neck.

"I love you, Kellan Casey."

I slid my hand onto her cheek and kept her gaze, savoring this one perfect moment I never thought I'd get, until she started to giggle, breaking my concentration.

"I love you too, Abby."

I pressed my lips against hers and she raised up on her toes to challenge me. The world started to spin, but this time, nothing happened, just Abby's mouth against mine until I couldn't breathe. No more obstacles, no more complications, just her and me. Who would've thought almost dying would help me get a life?

Some secrets should stay buried — especially when the truth might kill you.

I hate Shady Creek. It's the middle-of-nowhere small town my mom dragged me to when my grandmother died. The same one she ran away from seventeen years ago, where vicious rumors about our family descending from witches run wild. And it's the last place anyone saw my father before he disappeared.

After all these years, everyone at Shady Creek High still believes the lies and trying to fit in while everyone whispers behind your back isn't easy. I'd do anything to get back to Detroit and my old life.

Then I met Drew.

Wicked Descent is the perfect read for those who love magic, a bit of mystery, and swoon-worthy romance.

When night falls, all hell breaks loose...

Senior year was supposed to be the best year of Berkley's life—until it turned into a nightmare. Parental problems, boyfriend issues, scholarship competitions, and volleyball playoffs have her so stressed she can't sleep. But when an insomnia driven excursion leads her to cross paths with some amateur witches, she'll wish she stayed in bed.

Now she can finally sleep, but doesn't seem to get any rest. Each day blurs into the next as strange things start happening around her. Dark, sinister things that lead back to Berkley, except she can't remember any of them.

Desperate to regain control of her own life, she searches for an explanation to her nighttime amnesia. The answer will drag Berkley and her friends into a dangerous world of magic and mayhem—one where she may never wake up.

ABOUT THE AUTHOR

Born and raised in Northern Manitoba, Scarlett Kol grew up reading books and writing stories about creatures that make you want to sleep with the lights on. She believed that the treasures in her mother's jewelry box were magic amulets that would give her immeasurable power and old books could transport her to secret worlds. As an adult, not much has changed. Connect with Scarlett on social media or on her website www.scarlettkol.com.

facebook.com/scarlettkolauthor

instagram.com/scarlettkol

bookbub.com/profile/scarlett-kol

amazon.com/stores/Scarlett-Kol/author/B078RZ4PWF

ALSO BY SCARLETT KOL

Dystopian

Mercury Rises

Paranormal

Wicked Descent

Sleepless

Faraway High Fairytales

Falling

Dreamer

Fierce - Coming Soon!

Never miss a new release from Scarlett Kol by signing up for her
newsletter at scarlettkol.com.